VIKTOR

IMMORTALS OF NEW ORLEANS

KYM GROSSO

MT CARVIN PUBLISHING

MT Carvin Publishing, LLC

Carlsbad, California

Editor: Julie Roberts

Proofreading: Rose Holub, Read by Rose

Cover Design: Clarise Tan, CT Cover Creations

Photographer: Wander Pedro Aguiar, WANDER AGUIAR:PHOTOGRAPHY

DISCLAIMER

This book is a work of fiction. The names, characters, locations and events portrayed in this book are a work of fiction or are used fictitiously. Any similarity to actual events, locales, or real persons, living or dead, is coincidental and not intended by the author.

❀ Created with Vellum

DEDICATION

"The purpose of art is washing the dust of daily life off our souls."
~Pablo Picasso

This book is dedicated to my mom, Lorraine Teti Grosso, who shared her love for art with me. My mom was an artist, she'd studied at The Philadelphia Academy of the Fine Arts, and for as long as I can remember, she painted beautiful paintings and worked in all kinds of mediums. Our home was filled with artwork, from portraits of people to animals to landscapes. She displayed her artwork at exhibits, sold paintings and often shared them with friends and family. During the holidays, she'd often create Christmas cards by drawing a picture onto a piece of wood, carving it and then using ink and paper to make the cards.

My entire childhood, I was surrounded by art, and creativity was celebrated. I went to art exhibits with my mom, and because we once lived in Chester County, Pennsylvania, we often went to the Brandywine Museum in Chadds Ford. My mom was a huge fan of Andrew Wyeth, who was a realist artist, and she'd also studied under another well-known Chester County artist, Tom Bostelle.

One of her favorite Impressionists was Edgar Degas…she loved his series of dancers. After my mom died, on one of my many trips to New Orleans, I visited the Degas house and spent the afternoon on a tour of his home given by his great grand-niece. The experience was incredible and made me feel closer to my mother even though she'd passed away.

Vincent Van Gogh is one of my favorite Impressionists, and my favorite painting of his is *Sunflowers*, closely followed by *Starry Night*. My mom and I went to one of his exhibits at the Philadelphia Art Museum for her birthday one year and it was amazing. Claude Monet is another Impressionist that I love, and my favorite painting of his is *Woman with a Parasol - Madame Monet and Her Son*. My all-time favorite art museum is the Louvre Museum in Paris, but I love going to just about any art museum.

My mom was an amazing person, loving, fun, creative and smart….a wonderful mother and grandmother, my best friend. Every day I miss her, am heartbroken without her. But her spirit lives within my mind and heart, and I see her every day within my own daughter, who is also an incredible artist.

While Viktor is a fictional novel, my mother's love for art is alive within my words and in his story. So this book is dedicated to her, and I hope that if you've never had the chance to visit an art museum, that one day you immerse yourself inside the world of the art and discover the beauty of whatever artist brings you joy.

ACKNOWLEDGMENTS

~My readers, for waiting patiently while I wrote Viktor! I'm so thankful to have each and every one of you, supporting me and my books. I hope you love my ancient vampire as much as I do, and I look forward to writing more adventures in the Immortals of New Orleans series!

~Aunt Debbie, who I love so much. Thank you for always being there for me, for supporting me in everything I do. I don't know what I would do without you in my life. You are an amazing person and I love you so much! You have become like a second mother to me and Kevyn and we are blessed to have you in our lives.

~Julie Roberts, my friend and editor, who spent hours reading, editing and proofreading Viktor. As always, there are not enough words to thank you for all you do to help me! I appreciate your patience and humor, willingness to help me no matter what is going on. I can't wait to come visit you in Scotland next year! You seriously are the best ever...love you!!!

~Wander, Andrey & Verlene...you guys have been

amazing and our group chats and fun adventures make me smile. I'm so lucky to have you guys in my life.

~My dedicated beta readers Carolyn, Christine, Denise, Jara, Karen, Kelley, Kim, Rose, and Vicki for beta reading. I really appreciate all the valuable feedback you provided. You guys rock!!!

~Shannon Hunt, publicist and all-round assistant who gives me support! Thank you so much for everything you do to help me, your patience and friendship! Love you, Shan!

~Lacy Almon, thank you for helping me admin my group. You are wonderful & I want you to know how much I appreciate you!

~ CT Cover Creations, for designing Viktor's sexy cover. Thank you for the wonderful covers & bookmarks! You are so talented.

~ Wander Aguiar Photography for the gorgeous cover image! As always, you shoot the perfect picture!

~Rose Holub, Read by Rose, for proofreading. You are awesome! I really appreciate your eye for detail and helping me make my books the best they can be.

~My reader group, for helping spread the word about the Immortals of New Orleans series. I appreciate your support more than you could know!

CHAPTER ONE

$\mathcal{V}$iktor sank his teeth deep into the sweet, fleshy thigh. A cry of ecstasy brought pleasure to his ears as her life essence flowed down his throat. Ah, so difficult to stop, the urge to drink every last drop always present, but he never gave in to the temptation.

As his tongue brushed over the bite, her fingernails dug deeper into his shoulder, delivering a sweet balance of pain to his pleasure. It was at this point in the feeding he'd normally slam his cock into his donor, bringing them to a new level of heaven, but as he licked his lips a cold chill ran through him.

"Master, please," the naked blonde pleaded, writhing on her back.

"Off with you," he growled, adjusting his erection.

"I can't—" she moaned.

"Sorry, pet, but I've got business to attend to," he lied.

"But I don't want to stop," she whined, her legs splayed wide open on the sofa.

"Most delicious, but as I've said, got to run." Without hesitation, he shoved away and buttoned his dress shirt, readying to leave.

A desperate moan escaped her lips as she reluctantly gathered her clothes. With a sexy smile, Viktor waved a dismissive hand and disappeared through a crimson, beaded curtain. He brushed away the glass baubles and stepped into the smoke-laden club.

Through the din of the music and rumble of conversation, the tremors of fear from a female drew his attention. He homed in on a darkened corner where a petite blonde violently tugged her arm away from a tall, pale vampire.

"I'm not a donor. I just told you why I'm here. I'm looking for a friend." Her eyes flashed in defiance. She stood firm, not backing away.

"Came here for what?" the male growled, releasing his fangs.

"A friend. The bartender said you knew her." She glanced to the burly man behind the bar who shot her a creepy smile.

"Women," the vampire sniffed. "You don't know what you want or why you're here. Come to me, little princess. I will show you the pleasure of the darkness."

Viktor rolled his eyes. *Cliché.* The dude went full out vamp on her, but she made no move to run. As he watched her stand strong, staring the vampire down, he couldn't decide if she was brave or simply had a death wish.

Ah, humans. They're such interesting creatures, he mused.

Viktor studied her defiance. With determination in her eyes, she lifted her chin, her fingernails digging into her leather purse. Courage laced with a healthy dose of humility was always the sign of a warrior. The beast could shred her within seconds, and something told him she knew full well what the monster in front of her could do. Whatever or *whoever* she was here for must be seriously important to her, for her to risk her own life.

Viktor contemplated whether or not to get involved. Perhaps she deserved the consequences of her actions. Humans who came to a seedy blood club should know the score. It wasn't his responsibility. Stopping in for a nip of blood had been an impulse, a reprieve from his pain-in-the-ass chore of playing daddy to the wolfman.

He didn't even know the human. It was none of his business. *Don't do it, Vik. Not your problem.*

But as he caught the flicker of rage in the vampire's eyes, the decision was made. *Time to save the world again.*

Viktor flashed in between the blonde and the thug, glancing at a speck of dirt embedded into his thousand-dollar Dolce & Gabbana derby shoes. *Oh, for fuck's sake. This is exactly why I don't slum it.*

"This doesn't concern you," the vampire snarled, spit flying. His enunciated speech, spoken in a rhythmic staccato, reminded Viktor of a vampire he'd met once in Saint-Tropez. Viktor's lips drew tight into an icy smile, his eyes cold and dark.

"As much as I'm enjoying this little tête-à-tête, this darling little sprite belongs to me. Now, lovey. You mustn't run off on me." Viktor looked to the woman, whose anger radiated off her like wildfire. Detecting the slightest air of arousal, he shot her a sexy smile and winked at her, then quickly focused back on the vampire.

"She didn't mention you. Claimed she's looking for a friend. Now which is it?" The vampire bared his teeth with a low growl.

"She's mine. So it doesn't quite really matter, does it?" As he spoke, the voice in the back of his head warned his words would haunt him.

"I'll have a quick taste, and you can have seconds."

Viktor glanced to the woman. "He's small dick energy. I promise you won't have that problem with me, pet."

"I saw her first." His face reddened as he pumped his fingers, readying to fight.

"She. Is. Mine," Viktor repeated, his voice calm. He briefly touched her shoulder. "Off you go, pet."

"But I—" she began but Viktor promptly interrupted.

"No need for you to be here for this unpleasantry."

"But I...." Her words failed her as Viktor dropped his fangs.

"I said, out!" Viktor growled and whipped his attention to the vampire, wrapping his fingers around his neck.

"Who do you think you are?" He gasped for breath, struggling to break free.

"Master Christianson." Viktor gave a cool smile. He always enjoyed this part.

Silence engulfed the room, the jazz band in the corner easing down their instruments. Every single creature in the club froze. "The human belongs to me."

"But she's nothing. A blood bag, you piece of shit. This is her fau—"

Without warning, Viktor crushed the vampire's throat with his bare hands. The head dangled from its neck as blood sprayed onto the crowd, eliciting screams of shock from the humans.

"I do believe it's been a while since I've been to this dump. I regret you've all forgotten who I am. It appears you need a reminder. Tell your friends." Viktor threw the body to the floor and stepped over a puddle of blood. "The girl. No one is to ever touch her again, am I clear?"

Viktor didn't bother waiting for a response as he strode toward the door, stopping at the maître d'.

"Who's the human?" A waitress dressed in black latex appeared and handed him a bar towel, quickly scurrying away into the smoky room.

"Um, sir. She's new. Let me just check the register of new donors." He nervously ruffled through stacks of paper on his podium. "I'm sorry sir. We don't use computers here. Just a minute, I know I have it somewhere."

Viktor's jaw ticked in annoyance as he impatiently waited. Papers spilled onto the floor, drawing his attention to his own blood-splattered shoes. *Fucking hell.*

"What's a girl like her doing in a place like this, anyway?" She'd been wearing Vans and a pair of faded jeans, her hair in a messy bun. She wasn't a typical Miami club scene girl, let alone the typical blood donor. *Surfer maybe? Yogi, he'd guess. Something about her didn't quite fit the Miami vibe. No, California. Definitely California. Now what was she doing in a Miami blood club?*

"We get all kinds, sir. The vampires prefer different donors. All ages, races, genders. We generally cater to the more economical price point, shall we say but..."

"She didn't belong here."

"Ah well, here we go. Waverly."

"Last name?"

"Sorry sir, but I can't seem to...it must be here somewhere." He sorted through several pieces of scrap paper scattered all over his desk. "But you must know that I'm very busy...sometimes someone slips off my list. We try to get last names, but we do not require ID. If a donor chooses to withhold their last name, and they have tested and passed, demonstrating quality, there's no questions asked. No drugs, no disease, that's our trusted rule. Although we don't always cater to the most distinguished palates, we run a clean place. You might not know it from the way it looks, but we've got some very important guests. Celebrities, even. We've got a reputation to uphold."

"Yeah, sure you do," Viktor said, his voice dripping with

sarcasm. Although he was the first one to enjoy a pretentious party in South Beach, hot nights with knockout models and the upper echelon of Miami, he hadn't been in the mood for such festivities. And this clearly was not that kind of club.

Earlier, he'd craved blood. Fresh blood. Planned to get in and out quickly. No complications. No expectations. However, surfer girl had been an unexpected ripple in his evening.

"Ah, here it is," the maître d declared, holding up a torn piece of paper. "Her name is Waverly. Waverly Pisoff."

Viktor laughed, the right corner of his mouth ticking upward. "Piss off, you say?"

"That's right, sir. Waverly Pisoff."

"Do you hear what you're saying? Come on, man." Viktor blew out a breath, shaking his head. "Piss off?"

"Well, I suppose her last name could be…" He shrugged in confusion. "Sorry sir."

"Last name is fake." Viktor smiled. *Clever human.*

"Perhaps it was but—"

"Fake." Viktor pinned him with a challenging stare.

"Yes, well we are very busy here. Hundreds of donors."

"Address?"

"Sorry, no. We don't keep records on everyone who—"

"What do you know about her?"

"I have no recollection of her being here before. That right there," he pointed to a V next to her first name, "V. As in V for Virgin. As in first time. Not all donors are forthcoming with their donations. As you know sir, donors can request anonymity for a variety of reasons. It's difficult to tell with certainty if they've donated."

"Was she alone?" Viktor asked.

"She was alone. Persistent little bird. Kept asking about another girl. Looking for a friend and such. But of course, I told her that I couldn't provide her with the answers she was seeking. Confidentiality and all."

"Of course." Viktor rolled his eyes. *Jesus fucking Christ. Don't kill him, Vik. Patience.*

"But she was welcome to become a donor, to mingle with the other guests. I mean who am I to stop her from seeing who's already here? That's none of my business."

"Who's the friend?" Viktor tapped a finger on the cold marble stand.

"Teagan Rockwell. She's a regular. She's in at least once a week, sometimes more. She used to own a botanical shop in South Beach. I've heard it recently closed."

"Witch?" Viktor guessed.

"I don't believe so, sir. I have her categorized as human, but that doesn't mean she doesn't dabble."

"This Teagan Rockwell. Does she have a home address?"

"Of course, sir, but I'm afraid that's confidential."

"Just give me the damn address," Viktor demanded, baring his fangs.

"No need for alarm," the host assured, his voice wavering. His hands trembled as he reached for a pen, scrawling down the information.

Viktor snatched the paper and turned toward the door.

"Sir, please." The maître d' held up a finger. "You cannot tell them where you got this information. We have a reputation to uphold."

Viktor stopped cold and smiled. "I was never here."

Within seconds, he'd released his power and dematerialized, assured that no one in the entire club would ever recall his presence.

Viktor materialized in the bright pink hallway. A devilish grin bloomed on his face as he confirmed the apartment number. Lucky *777.* As he lifted his hand to knock, he noticed the lock had been forced open, splintered wood edging the doorjamb. A slice of light speared through the slightly ajar door onto the hallway floor.

Viktor's smile faded as he nudged the door open with the tip of his bloodstained shoe. Though he'd immediately sensed other humans in the building, the silent, ransacked apartment appeared empty. Books and knick-knacks littered the floor. The upturned sofa had been shredded, a knife tossed amidst the mounds of cushion stuffing. Viktor glanced to the small efficiency kitchen. The cabinet and refrigerator doors hung open; empty food containers had been strewn about the counters.

He stepped over a toppled bookcase and headed toward the bathroom. As he caught sight of the dingy sink littered with hypodermic needles, a growl rolled through his throat. "What the hell were you into, Miss Rockwell?"

Viktor shook his head and entered into the otherwise quaint bedroom with its key lime green painted walls and white rattan furniture. The drawers had been emptied, the mattress flipped, and the sheets stripped and bunched onto the floor. Aside from torn mounds of batting, the room was completely empty. No clothes. No shoes. No humans.

He peeked into the empty closet and spied a crumpled piece of paper wedged into the back corner. He reached for it, unfolding what appeared to be an envelope addressed to Teagan Rockwell. On the upper left corner, he recognized the first name. *Waverly.* But now, he had a last name and an address to go with it.

Waverly LaFleur. San Diego, California.

"Found you, surfer girl." Viktor's lips formed a satisfied

smile, entertained by his own sleuthing skills. "Ah, I do believe happy hour in La Jolla is overdue."

As he turned to leave, a pink plastic hairbrush lodged into the mattress caught his attention. Long gray hair was twisted through its pins. As he drew closer to the object, the familiar putrid scent of sulphur registered. *Demons.*

Viktor's lips tightened in consternation. Something had gone terribly wrong in this apartment, possibly with Teagan Rockwell, and while the witch wasn't his concern, his curiosity about his blonde sprite had been piqued. Had she become intertwined in this nefarious situation? If so, what was the extent of her involvement?

The sound of shuffling feet in the hallway broke his contemplation. A black figure appeared in the hallway but as he rushed toward it, the smoky aberration quickly dissipated. *Ghost? Shadow figure?*

As Viktor readied to dematerialize, an elderly woman, dragging a creaking rolling cart, exited the elevator. The wheels ground to a halt and she stumbled toward her apartment door.

Viktor rushed to her side and reached for her elbow. "I've got you."

"Oh goodness. Thank you." She lifted her gaze to meet his and gave a broad smile. "My knight in shining armor."

"Ah yes, I've been rescuing damsels in distress this evening." He gently released her, careful to make sure she steadied her feet before stepping back. "Are you okay now, lovey?"

"Yes, yes. Thank you." She blushed.

"Let me get this for you." Viktor took the keys from her hand and opened her door. With ease, he lifted her cart full of groceries and set it into the foyer of her apartment. "There we go. Right as rain."

"If I say no, will you carry me across the threshold and be mine forever?"

"Forever is a long time, beautiful. Be careful what you wish for."

As she waddled inside and closed the door, Viktor smiled, his thoughts drifting to his California girl. *Waverly, Waverly. I do think it's time we had a proper introduction.*

CHAPTER TWO

*W*averly paddled and ducked under a wave, the icy water rolling over her body. She sucked a breath as she rose to the surface. Her thoughts churned, replaying what had happened in Miami. She'd gone to find her friend, Teagan, who'd gone missing.

Months earlier Teagan had called Waverly and told her she'd begun dating someone. She'd met him in a gothic-themed coffee shop while sitting on a coffin bench and sipping a Drac-chai latte, and had instantly connected with the darkness he offered. He'd been involved with a 'brother-hood', a group who professed the virtues of drinking human blood. He'd not only promised her eternal life, but the excitement Teagan craved.

Waverly had warned her to stay away from vampires, real or otherwise, so when she'd received the cryptic text, she'd immediately booked a flight. *I've found eternal life. Don't look for me.*

When Waverly arrived in Miami, she'd found her friend's apartment ransacked. With no clues to Teagan's where-abouts, she'd decided to look for her in the one place she swore she'd never go, the blood club that Teagan mentioned in her texts. But not only had Waverly not found Teagan, she'd managed to get in an altercation with a monster who wouldn't take no for an answer. Though she'd been acutely aware of the dangers that lingered within seedy blood clubs, she hadn't anticipated the valiant stranger who'd intervened, saving her from her attacker.

Otherworldly and strikingly handsome, he'd commanded her attention. Fascinated with the beautiful predator, she'd struggled to remain calm, but soon lost herself within his piercing blue eyes. Terrifying yet intoxicating, the hum of his infinite power danced through her palms. She'd kept silent as the vision struck, shocked that the stranger could break her reign over her visions. For ten years she'd successfully controlled her affliction, but at his touch, they'd come rushing back.

When he'd screamed at her to leave, for a split second the sense of impending doom washed over her like a wave. Her hands stung with the magick she had fought so many years to suppress. As she slid into the cheap rental car, the chilling vision swallowed her, a tunnel of blood closing in on her.

Although shaken by the violence she'd witnessed, she managed to make her way to her hotel, safely fleeing danger. Fearing the worst, she'd contacted the police and filed a missing person's report with the Miami PD. With no leads and pressing work projects waiting for her on the West Coast, she'd reluctantly hopped the next flight to San Diego.

The strong pull of the undertow shook her contemplation, a huge swell rolling toward her. She paddled hard as the wave drove forward. Heart pounding, she jumped up onto her feet, adjusting her stance until she stood solid on her board. Exhilaration rushed through her as the wave curled around her. She shot through its perfect tunnel, her mind focused solely on the moment.

"Hell, yeah." She smiled, her slick ride slowly easing through the surf. She gave a few last pumps to the board, edging it forward.

Screaming from the beach caught her attention. Two young girls laughed as they jumped back from the icy water. But it was a shadow near the bungalow that caused her stomach to drop. A beam of sunlight shone upon the vaguely familiar silhouette, illuminating the hard lines of his jaw.

What is he doing here? Waverley lost her balance as panic struck, sending her tumbling into the churning sea. As she broke the surface, air rushed from her lungs. She frantically treaded water, panting for breath. Waverly scanned the beach for the vampire. *Where is he?*

"Oh my God. What is he doing in California? This cannot be happening." Waverly reached for her board and slid on top of it. "Shit."

Waverly took off, paddling hard toward the shore. As she reached the edge of the surf, she slid off the board, her feet touching the sand, and slung it under her arm. Saltwater burned her eyes, her legs shaking as she left the ocean and reached the shoreline. With intense determination, she trekked toward the cliff. Aside from a few groups of teenagers, the sandy stretch was empty.

Oh my God. Is he stalking me? Where did he go? He can't be here. No, no, no. Waverly spun around, confused. Fear and excitement churned in her gut.

There was no way he could have climbed up the cliffs without her seeing him. She turned to the ocean, scanning the horizon. To her right two college girls stood ankle deep in the surf. Engaged in a conversation, they paused and looked over their shoulder at her. Her friends, Barry and Kyle, waiting on a wave, bobbed in the water to her left.

Waverly took a deep breath, her heart pounding in her

chest. She released her board onto the sand and sat, her arms leaning on her knees as her head lolled forward.

"What the hell just happened?" Waverly wiped her eyes dry and looked to the horizon.

Get it together. You're just seeing things. It's impossible. There's no way he knows where you live. "It's just the stress. It's going to be okay."

She took a deep breath. Her pulse slowed as the bright orange sun descended. It was as if all the world paused to give a nod to the sunset. Surfers floated in the water on their boards. Runners stopped running. Cars pulled over to the side of the highway. Conversations fell to whispers. As the sun touched the horizon, the ocean enveloped the bright ball of light, signaling the end of another day. Waverly sighed, a chill running through her, a cool breeze blowing in from the ocean.

"There's no way he is in California," she said out loud. Waverly shoved to her feet and brushed the sand off her hands.

Logic told her he was in Miami. There was no way he could find her. She hadn't told him her name, and on the off chance he'd asked the maître d', she hadn't left her last name. *You're just being paranoid. Calm the fuck down, Waverly.*

Convinced her mind was playing tricks on her, she picked up her surfboard and headed toward the stairs on the cliff. "He doesn't know who I am. I'm just seeing things."

Waverly smiled as she looked down into the museum's atrium from the top of the wide marble staircase. A sea of benefactors milled about the lower level, mingling among San Diego's most prominent citizens. Later in the evening, supporters of the museum would outbid each other in an attempt to win donated prizes. More donors meant more bids. More bids meant more money for the prestigious art museum which would produce unique, celebrated exhibits and provide more funding for community outreach, bringing art directly to the world.

"Dr. LaFleur. Dr. LaFleur," a voice called out to her. The sound of heels tapping on the floor grew louder.

"Please, Sheila, call me Lee," Waverly insisted as Sheila Hertz, the museum's new event planner, hurried toward her.

"But you are the head curator and—"

"Can you believe this crowd? Has everyone checked in?" Waverly interrupted, hoping to curb her need for formality.

"Just a few more are expected." Sheila swiped her finger over her tablet and fiddled with her headset. "David? David? Yes…David. Please tell Dr. Williams that Dr. LaFleur is on the second-floor balcony by the staircase." She smiled at Waverly, looking her up and down. "Killer black dress," she whispered. "Yes. Yes. Security? Everyone here in the lobby? Can we do a roll call?" Sheila covered her mic. "Sorry. I'm triple checking. I don't want guests wandering into places they aren't supposed to be yet."

"No worries." Waverly focused her attention back on the guests as Sheila gave her a wave, leaving to attend to her duties. An orchestra played Bach while waiters passed hors d'oeuvres and glasses of champagne. A ding sounded and she turned to see her boss heading toward her, elevator doors closing behind him.

"Ah, my dear Waverly," he called to her in his familiar British accent.

"Hello, sir." She returned his smile, noting his formal attire. The sixty-four-year-old museum director appeared young for his age. Handsome and fit, he didn't look a day over forty. He ran a tight ship and was well respected by the staff. Under his direction over the past ten years, she'd watched the museum grow, acquiring diverse and rare art as a result of targeted fundraising.

"Quite a crowd tonight. Sheila's outdone herself," she commented.

"Ah yes, well, nothing but the best for the one percent. They expect a luxurious experience and that is what we aim to give. When you auction off a loan of one of the rarest Monets, that's going to draw quite a crowd."

"So, are you going to let me see it or do I have to wait?" Waverly asked with an excited smile. He'd been teasing her all day, promising the appearance of a last-minute donation, but unwilling to reveal its owner.

He laughed and clapped his hands together. "As promised, you will have access to it before the others see it. It is your exhibit, after all. Can't wait to get your thoughts. I know you're going to love it. Let's go check it out."

"I'd be lying if I said I wasn't tempted to go sneak a peek, but I didn't want to ruin your surprise," Waverly confessed.

"Indeed, I'm sure you were. But wait until you see how it fits with your exhibit. I took your suggestion as to its placement. I know how hard you've worked."

"If it's a Monet, I'm sure it will be perfect." For over a year, Waverly had worked on the project, bringing together the most eclectic exhibit of rare Impressionist paintings the West Coast had ever seen. The design of the space had been renovated to reflect the mood of an era. Rebellion. Creation. Innovation of art.

"It's not every day we get such a generous offer," he told her.

"Yes, about that," Waverly commented, pausing to lift her gown as they ascended a staircase. "In all my years, I've never experienced such great luck. It's unusual that a donor would offer an item from their private collection last minute like this. Just transporting it must have been a feat. Security and whatnot."

"Agreed. It is quite unusual. He contacted me last night, and well, given the resources in attendance tonight, how could I possibly say no?"

"He?" she asked, her curiosity piqued.

"Yes, well, I didn't actually meet him yet. You see, he sent his associate. All very cloak and dagger. From his behavior so far...strikes me as an eccentric fellow. Of course, I can't wait to meet him."

"The mystery is quite intriguing."

"Your average billionaire, I suppose." He laughed as they rounded a corner to the exhibit. "Bienvenue en France! C'est magnifique."

"Merci beaucoup." Waverly beamed with pride, admiring its entrance, a replica of the Arc de Triomphe. She smiled as she stepped inside the archway. "I love this. It really does look cool."

Waverly had worked tirelessly to create an immersive experience. Visitors would not just see the exhibit but would indulge all their senses as they experienced Impressionism. Monet. Cezanne. Renoir. Pissarro. Sisley. Degas. As patrons first entered the exhibit, it was as if they had stepped into the birthplace of Impressionism itself. Its entrance had been painted with wall murals depicting Normandy, France. From its white cliffs to its beaches and gardens, the inspirational scenes mimicked the environment that had surrounded the original Impressionists as they'd created their masterpieces.

As the exhibit progressed, the experience morphed to the streets of Paris. Murals depicted the cultured city's scenery including the Eiffel Tower and the river of the Goddess, the Seine. One could rest on the varied vintage park benches that she'd had flown in directly from Paris, while listening to the babbling water of an authentic Parisian park fountain.

Periodically the scent of fresh-baked croissants and pastries was piped into the area. When visitors looked upward, they were greeted with a cloud-painted dome, the daytime sky above them.

Waverly teemed with excitement. "I've been to Normandy. Paris. And well, this may not be those places, but it *feels* like Normandy. It *feels* like Paris. I want visitors to *feel* the art. To imagine the painters who collaborated and shared ideas about their new style."

"It's brilliant. It's going to draw many people to the museum. Although I'm afraid I'm going to be ten pounds heavier with the new pastry chef you hired for the café downstairs."

Waverly scanned the space and spotted the display in the corner. "Is that it?"

"Yes, do you want to see—"

Before he could finish his sentence, Waverly made a beeline for the painting. Her heart pounded in her chest, her eyes widening at the sight of the spectacular piece. "What is this? This can't be—"

"Real? Why yes, I assure you it is. Just as real as me," Viktor said, wearing a cool smile.

The blood drained from Waverly's face as she heard the smooth voice. *What is he doing here?* She spun around, her knees weak as her gaze caught his. Dressed in a well-fitted, blue velvet tux and bow tie, the six-foot-four vampire towered over her. Her jaw dropped open, words failing her as she attempted to maintain her composure.

"Ah, Mr. Christianson, so good to finally meet you. I'm David Williams. We spoke on the phone."

"Please, call me Viktor." He kept his eyes locked on Waverly.

"I'd love to introduce you to our brilliant curator, Doctor—"

"Dr. Waverly LaFleur, I presume?" Viktor extended his hand to her.

Waverly's pulse raced as she glanced to his fingers, recalling the night he'd touched her in the blood club. *How did he find me? What is he doing here?*

Carefully, she reached for him, not wanting to appear rude. Never taking her eyes off the vampire, she shook his hand. As if she'd touched fire, she quickly released her grip. Her cheeks flushed pink, her pulse racing in response.

"Please tell us more about this piece. It's outstanding," the museum director enthused.

"I've had it for a very long time," he replied.

"It almost looks like a sister to Sunrise." Waverly attempted to shake off her nerves as she studied the painting, astonished at the authentic details in the brush strokes. "But I'm afraid that doesn't exist. There's no way this can be real."

"Indeed, I assure you it is very much real. It appears it's part of the series. It's possible there're others. As I said, it's been in my possession for a very long time. Would you believe me if I told you Monet lost a bet with me?" Viktor chuckled.

"Very funny, Mr. Christianson. You do realize peddling stolen or fake art pieces will land you in jail," she warned.

"Jail?" Dr. Williams laughed. "She's joking, of course."

"It's authentic I assure you. And yes, it did involve a bet." Viktor gave a sly smile, his attention set firmly on Waverly. "As you know, new paintings have been discovered throughout the years. It's not unheard of."

"We're honored to be included in your decision to announce the existence of the new painting. It's very generous. We certainly appreciate you donating the piece for our exhibit and for a private exhibit to raise money. Don't we, Waverly?" Dr. Williams urged, raising his eyebrows with a nod.

"Of course, we do," Waverly said, her mouth drawn tight with anger. "I look forward to inspecting it further."

"I expect the bidding for time with your item to raise quite a bit of money." Dr. Williams glanced at his watch. "I apologize, but I need to get back downstairs to speak with a few key donors. I cannot wait to spread the word of this truly exquisite painting. I'm going to leave you here with Waverly. There isn't a single person besides myself who knows the museum better than she does. She'll be happy to give you a private tour. You're in good hands."

"I believe I am," Viktor agreed, still smiling.

"But Dr. Williams, we don't really have time to do it justice. I need to check on—" Waverly protested.

"I promised Mr. Christianson we'd give him a private tour. Given his generous donation, I knew you'd be happy to do it." He turned to Viktor. "She can take you throughout the museum. Show you all the exhibits. I'm giving my permission for you to show him behind the scenes as well."

"Of course," Waverly gritted out with a sardonic smile.

"There. It's settled. I'll see you both downstairs before the auction?"

"Of course. Wouldn't miss it for the world," the vampire told him.

"Yes sir." Waverly took a deep breath, steeling her nerves.

"Thank you for such a warm welcome. I can't tell you how much I'm looking forward to my private tour with your curator." Viktor looked to Waverly, his eyes locked on hers.

"See you soon." Dr. Williams gave a wave and promptly exited the exhibit.

Waverly glared at Viktor, waiting several seconds after her boss left before speaking. "What are you doing here?"

"I thought we established why I'm here. This is my painting." Viktor glanced at a bench. "Nice touch with the original seating. I do love Paris."

"But why did you come here? How did you find me? This is where I work." Panic laced her voice.

"Indeed, you do." He scanned the exhibit hall. "I do believe you owe me a tour. As the director pointed out, I am a generous donor."

"Do you think this is funny?" she asked. "That night in Miami..." Her voice dropped to a whisper. "I never thought I'd see you again."

"I promise you, Waverly, there is nothing more I'd like to discuss, but let's enjoy the night, shall we? There will be plenty of time to talk about Miami."

"You can't be here." She shook her head in disbelief.

"Ah, but I am here. And so are you. So much more civilized than Miami, wouldn't you agree?" Viktor closed the distance between them.

Waverly stood perfectly still, refusing to show fear as he approached. Terror lingered in her memories. Yet with a refined confidence, the debonair vampire concealed his lethal nature.

She studied the face of the clean-shaven, handsome as sin, well-dressed gentleman standing before her. A hint of his woodsy cologne teased her senses, but the flicker of danger in his eyes reminded her of the moment she'd met him in Miami. She took a deep breath as she recalled the sight of his fangs and the blood in her vision. He could kill her in an instant, but reasoning told her she'd be safe within the confines of the museum.

"Doctor?" His smooth voice broke her contemplation.

"What would you like to see first?" she asked, changing the subject as she turned toward his painting. "We don't have a lot of time. Where did this artwork really come from? Why did you wait to let the world know of its existence?"

"I'd be happy to meet with you privately to discuss this specific piece," he offered.

"I don't know if…" Her words trailed away as her internal voice of reason overruled her racing thoughts. *I need to know where he got the painting and look at it closer.* "I actually would very much appreciate it. I would love the opportunity to study it if you'd allow me."

"Of course. I suspect we shall be spending quite a bit of time together," he mused as he sidled up next to her.

Waverly's heart pounded in her chest as the soft fabric of his jacket briefly brushed her bare arm. "I didn't mean to imply we'd do it together."

"I anticipate we'll be doing many things together."

Waverly opened her mouth but quickly reined in her pithy response. *No, this can't be happening*, she thought to herself. She'd watched him murder another vampire. All the blood she'd seen in her vision. This was who he was.

"I will tell you one thing today that should not be a surprise to you," Viktor continued.

"And what would that be, Mr. Christianson?"

"I've been around a very long time. I've always been an avid art collector. Play your cards right, I may have another rare painting to show you as well."

"I'm afraid I'm not very good at cards," she lied.

"I suspect you'd do quite well at poker."

"We all have our secrets, don't we?" she replied, her eyes on his.

"That we do. And I'm looking forward to learning more of yours." He winked at her. "I do think I will enjoy it."

"I…I…" she stuttered, her face flushed. Waverly struggled to think clearly as her body reacted in a way that didn't mesh with the fear in her mind. Reverting to what she knew best, she put distance between them and relaxed into her profession. "As curator, I've hosted several exhibits over the years. With active fundraising, we've been able to participate in larger collections and do structural improvements to the showing space. The domed ceiling was an addition that will enhance future events. It has retracting panels that reveal the sky should we need to."

"Nice. Very impressive." Viktor nodded.

"I'm afraid I don't have time to go through all the individual paintings, but I'll do my best. I have to get downstairs before the auction begins." Waverly began to walk away from him, attempting to appear unfazed. But as they made their way through the exhibit, he kept close. She attempted to tamp down her nerves, sensing his energy. *Please God, no more visions.* "We have a self-guided audio tour as well. I'd be happy to get you a headset if you'd prefer to peruse by yourself."

"No need for audio. I much prefer this tour. You are an excellent guide."

"As you may know, as a private owner of a Monet, Impressionism was born in the mid-eighteen hundreds. While the public often believes the origin was Paris, the birthplace was actually—"

"Normandy," he interjected.

"Yes, very good, Mr. Christianson. Monet was one of the first painters to embrace the free-thinking style of Impressionism. He had a home there. You can still tour it to this very day. He was inspired by his surroundings. The shore. The cliffs. The sea. The flowers in his own yard. All inspiration. You can see it in his paintings." Waverly smiled. "Of course, he spent time in Paris as well. Had shown there. One of his very first critically acclaimed pieces, the model—"

"Camille. The Woman in a Green Dress."

"Yes." She glanced to Viktor, who studied the artwork, finding it interesting he knew the name of the painting. But of course, he owned an original so most likely had studied the artist. "She modeled in many of his paintings. I'm afraid she had quite a rough go of things. As did he. Although he did become more prosperous later in life. So many of his pieces were an expression of what he saw, the sea, his gardens. If I'm boring you, please, I can stop. It just occurred to me you know about the artist who created your painting."

"I knew him well," Viktor mused, "but please continue. I enjoy hearing you speak about art. Tell me, do you keep art around you when you sleep?"

"Um, excuse me, what?" She stifled her laughter.

"I just imagine your home is filled with art. I can hear the love in your voice as you speak." He gave a closed smile that didn't offer a hint of impropriety.

"Well, yes, I keep art in my home. Of course, most of the pieces are from local artists. It's unusual to be the owner of a rare piece of artwork, such as a Monet." Waverly glanced at him, attempting not to stare too long. *Who was this cheeky vampire? Asking about her bedroom. He was dangerous. Cultured. Peculiar. Sexy. No, Waverly. No vampires.*

She grew more determined to keep the conversation focused on art, on the tour. Afterward, she'd offer a sincere but short thank you for saving her, explain that she was simply looking for her friend, and that would be the end of it. Her boss and Sheila would handle the details with the painting and auction. After the tour, there was simply no way she'd entertain him any further or spend time discussing anything else. Whatever Viktor Christianson had in mind with the donation, this game, it wasn't going further than tonight.

"I'd be happy to give you a few minutes to take a stroll through the exhibit, but we really should get going. While I'm afraid we don't have time to see all the exhibition rooms, I'd like to take you over to the Renaissance."

"Perhaps you have some pieces from the Romantic period?" A playful smile tugged at his lips.

"You enjoy clouds and doom?" she asked.

"You can't have flowers without rain," he countered. "I find beauty in every period of art."

"True." Waverly smiled, genuinely impressed. So many patrons were all or nothing. "The Romantic exhibit it is. It's on the same floor as Academic and Realism. Follow me."

WAVERLY LEANED into her retinal scan for mere seconds before the light turned green. As the lock opened, she placed her hand onto the fingerprint reader, releasing another set of locks.

"Please, come inside." She opened the door and gestured for him to enter.

Aside from the director, she rarely allowed any other staff members into her private office. A large desk sat in the corner, allowing the morning sunlight to shine on her as she worked. Automatic shades could be activated to seal out light when she worked on different pieces. Two easels placed in the center of the huge space held different paintings, a work-bench between them housed her tools.

Viktor scanned the room, making a beeline for the paintings. "Nice studio."

"Thanks. I'm lucky to have an amazing space to work. Plenty of room for larger pieces."

"So you're the sole curator?"

"There are others that work under me, but I'm the head curator. I inspect the pieces when they arrive, document everything. Some require extensive work. Take this one, for example." She pointed to a small painting that depicted angels.

"Renaissance art?"

"It appeared so at first anyway. I was told to expect a painting from Plautilla Nelli. I could hardly believe it and

25

was very excited to be able to show it. But the size is an issue. She was well known for large artwork, but the style itself is nearly identical. I'm still verifying its authenticity."

"The nun?"

"Yes." Her eyes widened in surprise that he'd recognize the name. "I was told it had been passed down by its original owners through the generations. Apparently, they'd kept it a secret. It's possible they had connections within the Roman Catholic Church. There are private estates that still have churches on them and some hold secret collections… artwork, religious relics."

"Churches hold many secrets."

"At first, when it arrived, it seemed lovely. But upon inspecting it I noticed irregularities on its surface. Something about it isn't quite right."

"There." Viktor pointed to a raised rough patch in the right-hand corner of the painting. "That looks like more than over-restoration."

"Yes, I agree. So you understand why I question the authenticity. The paint must be removed and restored before it's presentable for exhibition. I'll have others in the community look at it as well."

"I'd love to hear how you came by the painting," Viktor began.

"I'm sorry. Unfortunately, that's confidential." Waverly declined to offer any other details.

"Tell me about this piece," he said, appearing willing to leave the conversation without further question.

"This." She smiled. "This is mine."

"She's beautiful," Viktor noted, coming up behind Waverly. "Who is she?"

Heat rushed to her cheeks, sensing the warmth of his body behind her. She hesitated to answer. *What is this man doing to me?*

"I didn't expect to show this to anyone. I don't usually—"

"She must mean a lot to you."

"Well…" She turned to meet his gaze, her heart pounding, so close to the dangerous vampire who had saved her.

"You have her eyes," he said, his voice low.

"She's my grandmother. Mary. We were close."

"You create *and* curate art. You're very talented. I'm honored to have been able to meet you."

"I…I've always loved art." Warmth bloomed inside her chest as he smiled at her. Drawn to the powerful vampire, she struggled not to let the seeds of attraction take root. Instinct warned her to remember what he'd done and who he was. She lost time, gazing into his mesmerizing blue eyes.

Waverly dug her fingernails into her palms, allowing a sting of pain to snap her out of the trance. "I suppose what I'm saying is that art history is fascinating. It's not just the artwork itself, but the artists, the painters, the masters. The actual creation process ranges from painstaking labor that takes years to complete to easy, simple creation. The result is often perfection."

"Perfect, indeed," Viktor replied, his eyes locked on hers.

A pregnant pause hung in the air, energy sizzling between them. Unable to take another second of the silence, Waverly broke the gaze, her focus returning to the painting.

"I was looking for a friend that night in Miami," she blurted out, confessing out of the blue. "I swear I've never been to that club before. I don't go to those sorts of places. I promise I won't tell anyone what happened."

"What exactly do you think happened?" Viktor inquired.

"That guy…he was going to…well, you know…he was attacking me and then you saved me." Her voice fell to a whisper. *Did that satisfy for a thank you?* She couldn't be sure it would. She had to be certain. Her hands trembled as she continued. "So I just wanted to make sure you know how grateful I am. Thank you for what you did. So, um, you can go now. I mean, you don't have to do all this. The painting, the tour."

A broad smile broke across Viktor's face. "Ah, pet. That's very sweet, but I don't plan on going anywhere. You see, I visited your friend's apartment, and I have many, many questions. Perhaps even more now."

"Pet?" Waverly gave an audible sigh and rolled her eyes. "Okay, look. I'm not sure how you found me. I don't even think I want to know. But it doesn't matter. So, let me try this one more time. Thank you for saving me from that monster, but I'm fine now. It won't happen again. Like I said, I don't go to those kinds of places."

"And yet you did," Viktor challenged.

"But I won't again." Her watch buzzed, interrupting her. She glanced at its face. "I'm sorry but I have to get back to the auction. Like I said, thank you very much. If you're ever in San Diego again, well, the museum is always open. I suggest you take a whole day, so you have time to see all the exhibits. It's a beautiful city."

Viktor casually walked to the door, reached for the handle and held it open for her. "You know. I think you're right. I'm going to spend a few days in La Jolla. We'll have plenty of time to discuss Miami."

WAVERLY SMILED AT BRENTLY KIRKPATRICK, attempting to appear interested. The trust fund baby joked about his missing balls and bragged about the new yacht he'd bought, inviting her to a private sunset cruise on the bay. She nodded and took another sip of her champagne. Her mind wandered as he spoke. She'd tried her best to say thank you and goodbye to the stubborn vampire. But instead of leaving, he'd acted as if she'd asked him to stay for vacation.

What could he possibly want from her? She'd promised not to speak about what she saw that night. While it was true that Teagan was involved with vampires, he didn't know her. Or did he?

From across the room, Waverly glared at Viktor as he flirted with a well-to-do socialite. Casually laughing, the debonair vampire oozed sexuality. Both men and women appeared drawn to him, captivated as he made his way through the crowd, introducing himself.

Quick-witted and cultured, he blended into the sea of one percenters, discussing his latest win at the stock market and his European escapades. He spoke with a slight accent that she couldn't quite place. She heard hints of Italian and French phrases from him as he worked the room.

As her boss took the microphone, she thanked God the auction was almost over, hoping that as soon as it ended, she could prepare to go home. The wealthy benefactors would enjoy a night of dancing and art that would extend into the wee hours. She'd already contacted her list of regular donors, and she wasn't required by her boss to stay any longer than needed.

"Is this thing on?" Dr. Williams joked, signaling to the orchestra to close out their piece. "Thank you, everyone. This has been a very successful evening. Not only have we come together for a celebration of the arts, but you are now part of history. The money we raised here tonight will go to expand exhibitions, bring in new and rare items. And most importantly, provide outreach programs to future genera-tions, future artists, future art lovers like yourselves."

Waverly clapped her hands in appreciation. As she caught Viktor's gaze, he shot her a sexy smile and winked. *What is he doing? Is he out of his mind flirting with me in front of all these people?*

She nervously tapped her fingers against her thigh and focused back onto her boss. He waved an envelope in the air and the room erupted in applause.

"That's right. One lucky winner is going to have a private showing of this rare unseen Monet. I'd like to thank our generous donor, Mr. Viktor Christianson, for this outstanding donation. Please, come up and help me announce the winner."

Viktor waved at the crowd and quickly took his place next to the director, who handed him the envelope.

"Please. Tell us who the winner is."

"Before I open it," Viktor began, "I'd like to thank everyone for their support of the museum. And I'd like to give a special thank you to the curator, Dr. LaFleur."

Waverly's face flamed red as the applause grew louder. From the stage, Viktor smiled in amusement. Uncomfortable as an ant caught under a magnifying glass, she squirmed, and returned his smile, her eyes lit with anger.

"And the winner is…" Viktor tore the envelope open, casually nodding at Waverly. "Mr. and Mrs. Benedict Rollings."

The well-known philanthropists, who'd made millions in the oil business, had supported the museum for nearly three decades. They smiled politely, acknowledging their prize, almost as if they'd known they could outbid anyone in the room.

Viktor handed off the microphone to Dr. Williams who addressed the crowd. "And so ladies and gentlemen, dinner will be served soon. Please feel free to mingle about the open areas of the museum, enjoy dancing and drinks. Thank you once again for opening your hearts and wallets. Well done."

The orchestra commenced playing a Viennese waltz.

Waverly breathed a sigh of relief, and tapped at her cell phone, answering a list of text messages.

No, I don't want to go shopping.

No, I don't want to go clubbing.

Drinks? With Jen? Absolutely.

Whale watching on Ryan's boat? Hell yes.

Yoga tomorrow morning? I'm down.

As she lifted her gaze to look for her boss, she caught sight of Viktor, staring at her. His expression, dark and intense, caused her heart to skip a beat. Her mouth gaped open as a corner of his lips ticked upward into a sexy smile and he pointed at her.

Waverly looked around at the many people watching their interaction, her cheeks once again heated in embarrassment. As he strode across the room toward her it was as if he was a magnet, drawing her to him. Laser-beam focused on his target, he approached, ignoring all else but Waverly.

"Shall we dance?" He extended his hand to her.

Six-foot-four of pure lethal seduction towered over her. Waverly trembled, as she considered his offer. Without him laying a finger on her, she sensed his energy. She took a deep breath, aware of the consequences. The visions would consume her.

"I...um...I can't. I mean..." She shook her head, her mind spinning. "But I need to go soon, Mr.—"

"Viktor. Call me Viktor."

Waverly flinched, bracing for a vision as he gently reached for her hand and took it in his. Her eyes widened in relief, and she allowed him to put his arm around her waist, his fingers gently touching the small of her back.

"I can't dance," she fibbed.

"Everyone can dance. You just need to stop and feel the music." Viktor smiled, and took the first steps, leading her into a waltz.

Waverly acquiesced as she relaxed into his arms. As a child, her mother and father had taught her to dance, insisting that it brought culture into an otherwise uncivilized world. She couldn't recall how many times she'd catch them in an embrace, swaying to Motown. But this wasn't home. And Viktor wasn't family. He was a dangerous, albeit charismatic, vampire.

"See there, you're doing quite well," he encouraged her.

"I'm sorry. It's just—" She attempted to concentrate, still shocked she was dancing with the vampire who'd saved her.

"Is this about Miami?" Viktor laughed.

"Of course it's about Miami. I'm sorry to disappoint you but I really am not into that scene. I'm just an art nerd who loves to surf and eat burritos. Watch sunsets. Whatever Teagan was into, that's not me."

"No, I don't imagine it is."

"Did you know Teagan?"

"No, I'm afraid I don't know her. I rarely frequent that establishment. I was looking more for what you'd call fast food. An in and out sort of thing."

"But you live in Miami, right?"

"Sometimes. There are at least another half dozen or so locations around the world that I also call home. The world is a big, beautiful place. Why just stay in one home?"

"You don't need to stay in San Diego."

"Let's just say I'm concerned about your safety given what happened in Miami. Just because you've decided you're done playing in the occult playground, doesn't mean that paranormals are done playing with you. That was a very dangerous place to be. That vampire. He seemed quite attached to you for someone who has only been there once."

"I didn't even know him. I swear it. It was just a mistake."

"But your friend is still missing?"

"Yes, she is," Waverly told him, her body close against his.

"And do you plan to stop looking for her?" Viktor pressed.

"Well, I don't know. It's not like I can take off from my job all the time, but I can't help but keep looking."

"Then perhaps you do need protection."

"I'm going to be fine. There's nothing else you can do for me." Waverly struggled not to stare at his mouth, recalling his fangs. She gasped as he gave her a knowing smile.

"They're not there now, pet. They tend to scare people. Wouldn't want that, now, would we?" He laughed.

"I'm sorry. I didn't mean to…" Embarrassed, Waverly exhaled a deep breath, reconsidering her words. "It's just I'm not used to seeing—"

"Fangs?" Viktor smiled broadly, amused with the human.

"Yes. Well, I suppose it's just a word." She refused to say anything more about his 'fangs' lest he show them to her.

"I'm not uncivilized." Viktor spun her around as the tempo of the song increased. "I will help you find your friend. And keep you safe. You're in my charge after all."

"But this has nothing to do with you. You aren't responsible." A nervous laugh escaped her. "This is crazy. You can't stay here."

"I'll admit it's been years since I've been to San Diego. Do you fancy sailing tomorrow? I'll charter a boat."

"Sailing?" Waverly loved a day on the Pacific Ocean nearly as much as she enjoyed surfing. *What is happening? Don't say yes. Don't say yes.* "You've found my weakness."

"I aim to please, Dr. LaFleur."

"I'm sorry, Mr. Christianson. I appreciate everything you did for me but I'm not like Teagan. I don't date vampires. I'm not food."

"On the contrary, I believe you're quite delicious." He winked. "And I haven't even tasted you yet."

Arousal and fear threaded through her at the thought of his lips on her neck. "I don't want to be bitten."

"Maybe you haven't been bitten by the right vampire," he mused.

"Indeed, but I don't ever plan on letting anyone bite me," she countered.

Time suspended as she gazed into his eyes. His magnetism enveloped her, and she struggled to break free.

"You all right, pet?" Viktor asked, his voice soft.

"Yes, yes. Everything is fine." She blinked, focusing on Viktor, attempting to shake off the spell.

Viktor slowed to a standstill, holding her hand, his arm still around her waist. "I've got you."

"I can't do this." Her eyes fell to his lips, her voice wavered. "I really should go. I have some work to do."

Waverly's heart pounded in her chest as he leaned toward her, his warm breath upon her ear.

"I assure you when I bite you, you will be begging me to do it," he whispered.

"Viktor, I…" Words failed her, her chest touching his. Her traitorous body responded, flooding with arousal. She imagined his lips on her skin, his tongue slipping between her legs.

Gunshots rang out, shattering the moment. Patrons ran for cover, scurrying about the lobby, ducking behind tables and exhibits. Screams echoed throughout the room as the hail of bullets shot up into the ceiling, raining chunks of glass onto the event.

"Get down," Waverly cried out, clutching to Viktor as they ducked behind a large stone column.

"I'll be back," he whispered and in a blink of the eye, he'd disappeared, leaving her safely behind a thick column.

Waverly sucked back tears as a hot stabbing pain tore

down her leg. With her dress torn, she could only see a red pool of blood on the floor. *What's happening?*

She searched for Viktor in the pandemonium. From across the room, she saw her vampire, fangs bared, pinning the gunman to the floor. *How did he get there so quickly?* Although the gunfire was silenced, the chaos continued, people pouring out of the front doors.

Sirens sounded from outside the building, and she breathed a sigh of relief. A gentle hand touched her shoulder and she looked up to Viktor.

"I...I think I've been shot." Tears streamed down her face as she held up her hand to him, blood dripping from her fingers. Strong arms surrounded her, and the room began to spin.

"Hang in there, love," he told her. "It's going to be okay. I promise I won't let anything happen to you.

"Help me," she begged as another stabbing pain sliced through her entire body. A black tunnel swirled in her line of vision, a pin of light fading fast. As if suffocated under a wave, she succumbed to the darkness. "Viktor..."

CHAPTER THREE

*V*iktor sat in the velvet chair, staring at the beautiful woman in his bed. He shook his head, inwardly cursing. He should have just taken her to the emergency room. Instead, he dematerialized her to his home in Miami Beach. Her injury revealed itself to be a flesh wound, which he easily healed. Sealing it over with his tongue had been the easy part. As he suspected, the taste of her would haunt him, her exceptional blood both potent and flavorful.

"Dude."

Viktor looked up to see the shifter standing in the hallway, wearing a smug smile. Rafe Beaumont. Five months ago, Viktor had rescued the wolf after a demon attack. In a last-ditch effort to save him, the vampire had done the unthinkable, and fed the wolf his blood and that of a high priestess.

Foolish decision. He'd created a hybrid. Both beast and vampire, the wolf could shift and run free, but he'd need blood to survive. Rafe had remained in his care ever since.

"I'm busy," Viktor grumbled.

"Whatcha doin'? Is this all part of the vampire 101 super-secret bat-flying handbook?" Rafe joked.

"Curiosity killed the cat," Viktor replied flatly.

"Good thing I'm a wolf."

"I don't have time for your shit right now."

"Yeah, yeah." Rafe glanced to the bed and back to Viktor. "I see that."

"Whatever it is, now is not the time," he warned.

"Say, Vik. Is that a girl in your bed?" Rafe entered and sniffed, looking down to a bloodied heap of fabric lying on the floor. "Oh no, man. What did you do?"

"Nothing." Viktor exhaled an audible breath.

Rafe studied the woman. "Is she naked?"

"None of your business. Get out."

"Whatever's going on, looks like it could have been worse." Rafe shrugged.

"How exactly is that?"

"You've got a beautiful woman in your house. Obviously, something happened. Did you bite her? Hey, did you turn her? Then you'd have two kids. I'd have a sister."

"Jesus, don't even say that." Viktor could barely handle the hybrid but was determined not to fail him. He refused to be like his sire.

"So, is she staying? Can we keep her?"

"No. No, we can't keep her." *I'd like to, though.* "I'll return her tomorrow."

"From where? Is she from a blood club?"

Viktor shrugged and rolled his eyes. "Yeah, no."

"What did you do, Vik?" Rafe pinned him with a stare. "She's from Miami?"

"Not exactly," he hedged.

"She's not a donor?"

"Nope."

Rafe exhaled loudly, plowing his fingers through his

unruly hair. "I thought you said you were going out. Like here. In Miami. The way you're all dressed up...Jesus, I thought you were going to the opera or some shit."

"I said I had an event. I did not say where," Viktor hedged.

"Where did you get her?"

"San Diego."

"California? What the...are you crazy? What were you doing?"

"It was an art exhibition. Impressionism."

"Sorry, what?" Rafe shot him a look of astonishment. "You did not just say you skipped off to San Diego for an art show."

"She was a person of interest," Viktor commented blithely.

"A person of interest? Who the hell says that? No, don't answer. I'll tell you who says that. The FBI. PCAP. Last time I checked you weren't either."

"It's nothing really. You're making a mountain out of a molehill. I met her once at a blood club. Here in Miami. She had a bit of a tussle with a vampire. I took care of it."

"You're just a regular hero, you know that? Better watch out, people might actually discover you're not the asshole you pretend you are."

"I'm not sure what overcame me." Viktor sighed. "When I went to her friend's home—"

"Wait up...you didn't know her?"

"No, but I wanted to make sure she got home all right. She was looking for her friend. After I saved her at the club, I popped over to the address I was given by the maître d'. The apartment was empty. Ransacked. But there were needles in the bathroom. I scented a demon. So yeah, not cool. But while I was there, I stumbled upon her address, and voilà, I nipped off to San Diego."

"You said you were meeting a friend at an event." Rafe shook his head in disbelief.

"I was at an event. Long story short, I discovered she was a curator at an art museum. So, I donated a Monet for a fundraiser they were having. It's a loaner of sorts."

"Of course you have a Monet; because everyone does."

"There's something about her," Viktor replied, ignoring Rafe. "I can't put my finger on it just yet."

"What about the blood? What happened?" He glanced to the clothes crumpled on the floor.

"There was a shooting last night during the event."

"Trouble follows you everywhere."

Viktor shot him a look of annoyance. "I prefer to think of myself as someone who can offer assistance."

"Like a superhero? Does your cape have a big V on the back of it?"

"I just got off the phone with her boss," Viktor continued, ignoring him. "Spoke to the SDPD too. It appears she was the only one who was injured."

"And the perp?"

"He's dead. He was human. Semiautomatic weapon. No one else was injured. Just our lovely curator there."

"You shouldn't get involved," Rafe warned. "If her human friend went missing at a blood club, the police aren't going to take it seriously. You know some of those places are sketch."

"All true. But what the police don't know is that I scented demons at her friend's apartment."

"Again, not your problem. Tell PCAP," Rafe insisted. "They handle all the paranormal problems the police don't."

"But there is a problem now of my own doing. I healed her." Viktor sighed, his gaze settling on Waverly, who gave a soft moan. "I tasted her."

"And? So what? You've bitten men, women…anyone who

39

wanted it. And a few who didn't." Rafe laughed and contin- ued. "I'm not saying they didn't deserve it."

Viktor shook his head and shrugged.

"Why get involved with trouble?" Rafe asked. "It's one thing to help a girl out in a bar. It's another to go across the country to do it. I mean, come on, Vik. She's just another human with human problems."

"Perhaps." Viktor recalled the taste of her blood, the energy that flowed between them as he held her in his arms, dancing. "She may be human, but there's something else about her. I'm not sure what it is."

"Dude. Don't take this the wrong way, but you aren't the kind of guy who loves to babysit. Call PCAP. Jake probably already knows if something is going on in San Diego. He's an Alpha. He can help her."

"I'm not handing the human over to a wolf. I found her. She's my responsibility," Viktor whispered, noting a slight change in her breathing pattern.

"Don't say I didn't warn you."

"You don't need to worry about her. She's my problem not yours. I have this."

"Are you hungry?" Rafe changed the subject. "I ordered a donor. Do you want me to call one in for you?"

"Yes." Viktor gave a hint of a smile as she stirred, rolling onto her side. "Please leave us."

"You got it. But I'm hoping the next time I walk in here you've already flashed her back to Cali." Rafe closed the door as he left.

Viktor rose and slowly approached, careful not to startle her. While he usually was a 'fuck your feelings' sort of guy, something about this frail human in his bed gave him pause. But the wolf was right. Bringing her to Miami was a mistake. He'd have to return her and consider contacting the Alpha like Rafe suggested.

"Hmm..." Waverly moaned and shifted in bed, tugging at the covers, her tanned skin exposed. A hint of her nipple peeked through the sheets.

Although tempted to reach for her, he resisted the urge. Long before he tasted her blood, the attraction to the quick-witted curator had been sparked.

While his interest in her had been piqued in Miami, the sight of her in the ocean had captivated him. She navigated the waves like a pro. Her lithe, muscular body, one with the board, appeared as if it could tame the sea itself.

When he'd discovered the serendipitous fundraising event, he'd decided to meet her at the museum. Having collected art throughout the centuries, he'd been delighted at the opportunity to lend a piece from his private collection.

The sight of Waverly in the ebony, floor-length gown had taken his breath away. Her wavy blonde hair had been swept up, revealing the creamy skin of her neck. Her eyes shone with the same fire and defiance as the first time he'd met her, yet she was a far cry from the shaken girl he'd rescued in a blood bar. The brilliant, eloquent curator captured his attention throughout the tour, demonstrating her vast knowledge of art. When they'd danced, he'd been tempted to taste her lips, but desire had quickly been thwarted by the shooter.

Enraged amid the melee, Viktor had acted without thought, killing the attacker. Within seconds, he demateterialized them both to his home. While he reasoned Rafe was correct, that he should have allowed humans to care for her, he didn't regret keeping her safe, still not convinced the shooting was random.

Viktor's thoughts focused back onto Waverly as he knelt beside the bed. He studied the contours of her face, her full, pink lips pursed as her eyes slowly blinked open. He braced for the firestorm he expected to come from his spirited human.

"Hmm," she moaned, clutching at the comforter. "Lights."

Viktor reached for the night table, dimming the brightness.

"Dr. LaFleur," he whispered.

"Just one more," she said, her eyes closed.

"Well, of course I'd love to indulge you in whatever fantasy you're having," Viktor said, his voice soft.

Waverly fluttered open her eyes. Several seconds passed as she took in her surroundings.

"Where am I?" she asked, panic in her voice.

"It's all right now. You're safe. You're in my home."

"Oh my God." Still curled in a ball, she quickly pulled the covers over her head.

"It's okay, Waverly," Viktor said, keeping his tone calm. "How are you feeling?"

"I...I was shot." She lowered the covers, revealing just her eyes. "My leg. Wait...my leg."

Viktor smiled, watching as she shuffled underneath the sheets, ducking her head back under.

"There's no wound." Waverly popped her head halfway out of the covers. "But...I'm naked! Why am I naked? Where are my clothes?"

"I'm afraid the dress didn't fare as well as you did. It's drenched in blood. It's black but I'm not sure your dry cleaner will be amicable to removing that big of a spot." Viktor glanced to his bloodstained shoes and inwardly cursed that yet another pair were damaged. "No worries. I'll have my personal shopper replace it for you. I've already sent her a text."

"You have a personal shopper?" Waverly asked, her mouth still covered by the sheets. "Of course you do. Why am I even asking that?"

"It's a time saver."

"You saw me naked," she gritted out.

"Well, yes but I promise you I didn't look. I swear to you on the graves of my ancestors."

"Seriously? What are you saying?"

Viktor gave a small smile. "I promise I was not looking."

"Did you bite me?" Her eyes lit with anger.

"Of course not, but I could later, if you'd like." Viktor shot her a devious smile. She simply had no idea how much he would have loved to sink his fangs into her skin.

"Please tell me you took me to an emergency room." Her leg shot out of the sheets, and she continued to inspect it.

"It was unnecessary. I healed you. Was just a bit of a scratch." Viktor's expression fell flat as he recalled killing her attacker. He'd easily wrestled the gun out of his hands and crushed his trachea.

"But...I was shot. Oh God...the pain. It was horrible." Her face was awash in confusion. "This doesn't make sense. Are you sure you didn't bite me?"

"I've already told you that when I bite you, you'll beg me to do it. And believe me, you will most certainly remember it."

"In your dreams," she huffed, regaining her defiance. "I don't date vampires."

"So you've told me." Viktor gave a small laugh, slightly amused.

"I'm pretty sure I got shot. What really happened?"

"You did. I took care of your leg."

"I'm sorry. Are you a doctor? Did you go to med school?"

"I'm a vampire, Waverly. I can heal most wounds. Contrary to popular opinion, not all vampires go around biting people without their consent. Well, usually anyway."

"This doesn't make sense." Waverly slowly lay back, rolled onto her side and curled into a ball.

"You're going to have to trust me." Viktor watched the

stress seize her, her eyes closed tight as she attempted to rationalize the unthinkable.

"I don't know what happened last night. That man. He was shooting all those people," she whispered.

"They don't know what happened yet or what his motives were. But I can tell you that the gunman…he was human." Viktor didn't think she was ready to hear that she was the only one who'd been shot. He rose from the floor where he'd been kneeling and gently sat on the side of the bed, careful not to get too close to her. "I don't know if this is related to Miami. But I think it's safe to say that your friend may have been involved with some bad people."

"I'm so tired," she responded, defeat in her voice.

Viktor struggled to reconcile the seed of concern threading through him. Humans certainly sated his hunger, but he didn't form attachments. This one, however, piqued his interest. Much more than amusement or curiosity, he found her fighting spirit admirable. This intelligent, brave, beautifully imperfect human attracted him like a moth to a flame. He'd saved her twice, and now that he had, he'd commit to doing it again.

"I won't let them get to you," Viktor offered, his palm gently brushing her shoulder. Several seconds of silence passed, before she relaxed under his touch. "I promise it's going to be all right."

"Thank you for saving me," she whispered. "Twice."

"It's late. Get some rest. We'll talk when you're feeling better."

Viktor reached for a folded blanket at the end of the bed and pulled it up over her shoulders. As she began to drift off to sleep, Viktor closed his eyes, sensing her energy. A vision of her smiling formed in his mind, her hand reached for him, her fingers touching his lips.

Viktor's eyes snapped open, surprised. Interesting, he

44

mused. Could this human communicate with him in her dreams, her energy forming an actual picture? Did she intentionally show it to him or was this simply a more active form of dreaming? Like the art she dearly loved to study, he suspected Dr. LaFleur also held many secrets.

"WE MAY BE TAKING A TRIP," Viktor commented nonchalantly. He lounged on a chaise and stared at the twinkling lights reflecting onto the water that filled his large rectangular penthouse pool. "The weather's exceptional this evening, don't you think?"

"Why, might I ask, are we leaving? No, don't tell me, it has to do with the chick upstairs." Rafe scooped a spoonful of ice cream and slid it in his mouth.

"I'm afraid I'm not going to be able to let Dr. LaFleur go back alone," he confessed.

"Big mistake, man."

"I can't quite explain it myself. There was a demon in that apartment. I'm sure of it. Tonight, there was a shooting by a human. Her friend is missing. Apparently, she was involved with a vampire wannabe group."

"Let PCAP deal with the missing friend. You know that donors take a risk going to places like that. As for the shooting? Humans love their guns. They do sketchy shit all day long."

Viktor sighed. "I don't know. My immediate concern is getting her back to San Diego. The police have questions. I have questions too. I want to know more about the shooter."

"You killed him, right?"

"Well, yes, but he deserved it."

"What is there to know, then?"

"I want to know his background. His motive." Viktor

shrugged. "We'll go to San Diego. A day or two tops, and then we can move on to Jackson Hole so you can get back to Hunter."

"Come again?" Rafe asked, setting his spoon into the bowl.

"I thought you'd be happy to go home. Back to Hunter. Back to the pack." Viktor set his gaze on Rafe. His prodigy appeared more confident than he was.

"I don't know." He hesitated. "I like Miami."

"You're going to join a pack here?"

"I dunno. Maybe I'll go rogue," Rafe casually suggested, looking into his bowl.

"I don't think we should talk about this right now," Viktor replied without emotion, concealing his concern. How was he going to explain to the Alpha that Rafe was thinking of going rogue? It wasn't going to be pleasant. "You'll come with us then. We'll deal with this rogue business later."

"It's not a big deal." Rafe shook his head. "Wolves go rogue. I'm just thinking maybe the big pack isn't for me right now. You know, considering all the changes."

"We'll talk about it later. Nothing's set in stone. Right now, I need your assistance with the human."

"Seriously dude? She's your woman, not mine. Just do what you usually do when you have a girl over."

"I don't have women to my house. Not humans anyway. And there's a reason for it."

"How's that? She's alive. You've got that going for ya. She'll wake up eventually and then we'll split and hit the West Coast. No worries."

"Humans," Viktor mused. "While I enjoy a bite and a cuddle, I'm not typically in the business of taking care of them."

"It's easy enough. Just get her dressed. Feed her. Help her get back home. What's the problem?"

"Feed her," Viktor repeated. He didn't eat human food, let alone cook.

"Yeah. You know. Like I do. I've got some food. You could make her something."

"Yeah, I don't know about that."

"Then order out. Call the deli down the street. Mazilli's. Get her a cheesesteak."

"A cheesesteak? It's two in the morning."

"Or a salad. Or a pizza. I'll take a slice."

"You're a bottomless pit."

"My appetite for food and blood are healthy. I'm good."

"Yeah, sure you are. You'd better get some rest, wolf. We're leaving tomorrow."

"Do I need to pack or are we flying VikAir?" Rafe asked.

"No flashing anywhere. She's already freaked out enough." Viktor reached for his cell phone and pecked at the screen. "We're taking the jet."

"The PJ, huh?" Rafe smirked knowingly. "Nice."

"What is it now?" Viktor rolled his eyes and continued to text the pilot.

"Nothing. Nothing at all." Rafe chuckled.

"Spit it out, already. What's so funny?" Viktor set his phone down on the table and sighed.

"The royal treatment." Rafe smiled wide like the Cheshire cat. "You're sweet on her."

"Wrong." The ancient vampire gave a sly smile. "I'm intrigued. Yes, yes, I'm definitely intrigued."

"You mean horny."

"No. Intrigued." He sniffed. "Her blood is as sweet as honey. I suspect there's something…" Viktor stopped short of airing his suspicions. "Someone shot at her last night. And succeeded in spilling her blood. I was hasty in killing the human. I will return the good curator and do a bit of investigating."

"That's why they have police."

"I'm very aware of the human police. But I am also very old. And this means I have instincts. And my instinct tells me that a demon is involved with humans. But for what purpose?"

"I don't get why you'd get involved when you don't have to."

"Duty. Glory. Honor."

"Sex?" Rafe laughed.

"Wrong. Sex is easy to find. I've had as much as I've wanted. But in thousands of years...I don't have time to explain, except to say there's more to it. Life can be..." He sighed, considering how he'd repudiated his humanity. "It can be many things. The years pass and many of us, we choose to forget, perhaps, what was important to us when we first entered this realm. And so, when there is a spark, a human who intrigues you, you make time to explore the magick. When you are intrigued, when you find an opportunity, you must seize it."

"We all come by the magick one way or another."

"Wolves are born with the magick."

"Yeah, well. I'm no longer a wolf. Not a pure one anyway. I'm something else. I was made too." Rafe paused reflectively and quickly changed the subject. "So, you're not just trying to impress her with the jet? You know...so you can get laid?"

"I'm a gentleman." Viktor stood. "She's not accustomed to our ways. Not wolves. Not vampires. But I do believe she's what I'd consider curious. I don't want to scare her."

Rafe raised a questioning eyebrow at him.

"I have held her in my arms. I've looked into her eyes. And do you know what I see?"

"Do enlighten me, oh ancient one."

"I see passion. Passion for friends. Passion for art. Her

work. The sea. Passion for life. And I'm certain she's intrigued with me as well."

"I guess we'll find out, lover boy."

"You best respect your elders. Trust me, when I say, I know what I know."

"Goddammit." Smoke billowed up into the air, the high-pitched scream of the fire alarm piercing his ears. He reached up to the ceiling, switching it off. "Jesus, that thing is loud."

Viktor grasped the burnt toast with a pair of tongs and tossed it in the sink. He stared at the eggs he'd seen Rafe cook many times yet had never paid attention to his recipe. He should have arranged to have food delivered but for some ungodly reason he'd grown determined to make it himself. Big mistake.

As Viktor reached for his cell phone, he smiled, hearing soft footsteps behind him. *Waverly.* He turned slowly, his eyes set on hers as she drew closer.

"So…um…" Waverly glanced at the charred bread, then to the eggs still in their carton. "What are you doing?"

"Ah, well, you see I was trying to…" For the first time in a thousand years, he suffered from an unfamiliar loss of words. Dressed in nothing but a white t-shirt, she brushed a lock of her golden hair away from her eyes. A beam of sunlight teased across her throat.

"Are you cooking?" A corner of her lips tugged upward as she sniffed the smoky air.

"You must be starving. The Ritz Carlton delivers…I can order you something from there."

"Why?" Her eyebrows furrowed in confusion.

"So I can order breakfast. You're human. You need to eat

food." Viktor began his text. But as she boldly brushed by him and peered into the bowl, his attention fell to Waverly.

"I can make the eggs." She opened the egg carton and shrugged.

"No. I'll order you something. I should have done it to begin with."

"Don't waste your money. It only takes a few minutes." She reached for a frying pan hanging overhead.

"No, you really don't have to—"

"I said I'd make breakfast." She pointed the pan at him. "Sit."

"Bossy thing, aren't you?" Viktor gave a small chuckle, amused that this feisty beauty challenged him.

"So I've been told." Waverly switched on the gas.

"Are you okay? How do you feel?" Viktor asked and leaned against the counter.

"I feel like I'm living in another dimension. Like I just got shot at." She glanced back at him. "Why are you looking at me like that?"

"I was worried about you," he confessed, inwardly shocked that he meant it.

"You just met me." She knifed off a pad of butter and tapped it into the pan.

"This is the third time we've met. Fourth if you consider last night. We better be careful. People will talk." He smiled, enjoying the sight of her in his home.

"You like your eggs over easy? Over medium?"

"I don't eat eggs."

"You're vegan? I could make something else."

"I drink blood, my clever doctor."

"So…you want scrambled eggs?" she asked, toying with the egg in her fingers.

"I eat humans. Not human food," he replied flatly.

"Okay." She blew out a breath. "But you used to eat eggs?"

"Yes, I suppose at one time I did."

"So did you eat them over easy or over medium?" she pressed.

"I don't know. It was many years ago."

"You strike me as sharp. You must remember. Come on now."

"I ate them however they were made. Food was food," he recalled, not wishing to remember details.

"All right then. You get what you get." She cracked an egg. It sizzled as it dropped into the frying pan. "Why don't you eat? Is it a vampire thing? Are you broken inside? Pipes clogged?"

"Pipes clogged?" He laughed. "No."

"What is it then?"

"It's simple. I eat people." Viktor watched as she continued cracking eggs.

"Food tastes good. Why would you ever give it up? Is there some kind of vampire rule that doesn't let you have it?"

Viktor sighed, feeling woefully unprepared for this discussion with the human. Hours had passed since she'd fallen asleep in tears. Yet this morning her air of confidence had returned to her like a pair of comfortable slippers.

"No super-secret vampire rules, it's just that, well…I was human a long time ago. And I felt like a human. Heard the birds sing like a human. Smelled, tasted food. All human." Viktor's expression fell flat as the somber memories weighed down his soul. "But then one day you die. You see the light of the Goddess. In those seconds of dying, there's this most beautiful warm light. It's more than acceptance, it's almost as if it's a conscious decision to let go. And in a snap of a whip, you're sucked back to the earth." Viktor cocked his head, his voice brightened. "That's it really. But you're no longer human. You wake with the most intense hunger you've ever had. For blood. Not food."

Viktor detected her heart beat faster at the mention of blood. But as Waverly casually reached for the spatula and swiftly placed the eggs onto the plates, she turned to him, her face devoid of fear. He moved to the side as she set them on the table, noting how effectively she concealed her emotions.

"Sometimes when I wake up, I make a protein smoothie. It's very nutritious," she replied, facing him. "But I still eat eggs."

"But you see, pet. There is nothing more I need. Blood is my only sustenance."

"Blood? Your only need?" she challenged, taking a step toward him. "That's not living. It's existing. Why would you ever want to live life like that?"

Viktor closed the distance between them, coming within inches of her. Her pulse raced yet she refused to move, standing her ground. He leaned to whisper in her ear. "I can assure you that once I taste you, drink from you, you will learn to enjoy it as much as I do."

She locked her eyes on his, her fingertips brushed his chest. "You can't have mine, vampire."

"Someday." Viktor's cock rushed with blood as his eyes fell to her full lips.

"You can't have my blood," she repeated, her voice soft. A hint of a teasing smile bloomed on her face. "But you can eat my eggs."

Viktor restrained his urge to kiss her as she sheepishly averted her gaze. Waverly slowly backed away and slid into a chair. He glanced to the food, his own heart pounding. What was it about this mortal woman that enticed him like no other? He should just walk away from the table, leave her to eat.

"Please. Sit. It's good for you," she promised.

Her pleading smile warmed him, and he soon found himself complying to a human's demands. He watched with fascination as she released a grateful breath and set her fork into her eggs. As she slid it into her mouth, she glanced to his plate and then to him.

Viktor had made a choice the day he woke as vampire to lay aside all human ways. His brutal sire insisted on it. Whatever he loved his sire would kill. And humans were so very weak. Like butterflies, the beautiful creatures flew for but a season before succumbing to the inevitable death that would take them from this realm.

Now this lovely human had cooked. For him. He couldn't remember the last time someone had done something kind without expecting anything in return.

Viktor reached for the fork. His gaze set on hers as he scooped up the eggs and slid them between his lips. The sweet, buttery bite coated his tongue, his senses coming alive. Memories from long ago flooded his senses.

"You like it?" she asked.

"Yes," he admitted, his voice soft. Waverly's persuasive, quick-witted nature drew him to her. Lying was useless. "It's delicious."

A broad smile broke across her face. "I have a secret."

"You do, do you?

"I don't like to eat alone," she admitted. "I do it but don't love it."

"You have a boyfriend?" he asked.

She gave a coy smile. "No boyfriend."

"You eat alone often?"

"I work a lot. So yeah, I eat alone."

"Perhaps we'll have to change that in the future," Viktor suggested.

Waverly smiled and quickly changed the topic of discussion. "I've got to get back to California. I have to give a statement. My watch died before I had a chance to respond to the detective. Do you happen to have an extra USB cord you could lend me?"

"But of course. I've already spoken to your boss. I called him after you fell asleep."

"You did? Is he okay?" she asked.

"He's quite unharmed, I assure you. As are all the guests. But I agree with you. I think it would be prudent for us to return. I'd like to learn more about the investigation."

"Of course."

"Dr. LaFleur."

"Waverly. Some of my friends call me Lee."

Viktor smiled. "Am I a friend?"

"You ate my eggs. So yes, I suppose we are on our way as long as you promise not to eat me."

"As I said. When I bite you, you will beg me to do it. Never before." Viktor knew full well it would test him to wait. With the taste of her blood still fresh on his lips, the craving for both her soul and flesh intensified with each minute in her presence.

"I, uh…" she stuttered, not quite finding her words.

Viktor's own heart beat faster, his cock jerked with arousal at the thought of making love to her. He'd break every single one of his own rules to keep her. *Friends?* He'd tell himself it meant nothing, but he'd eaten her food. No, they'd be much more than friends. And he suspected he'd enjoy every second of it.

CHAPTER FOUR

*W*averly nervously tugged at her sleeve as the limo approached the tarmac. She glanced to Viktor then stared out the window trying to wrap her head around the events that had transpired the previous evening at the museum.

Viktor Christianson. The debonair vampire had impressed her with his astute knowledge of Impressionism. From the water lilies to the poppies, he'd described the flowers in the paintings as if he'd walked the gardens in Giverny and breathed the same air as Monet. Within an hour, she'd found it nearly impossible to resist his charismatic personality, soon losing herself within his arms during the waltz.

Waverly recalled being shot and rubbed her thigh, astounded her skin had healed. She'd heard the rumors of the gifts vampires possessed, but she'd purposely kept her nose to her paintings, her body in the waves, refusing to fall into the paranormal crowds.

Viktor was everything and nothing she'd ever expected in a vampire. His lethal nature had been utterly terrifying, yet both times he'd put himself at risk to save her life. His flirtatious, charming wit shattered all her preconceptions.

When he'd whispered to her, his lips teasing her neck, he'd awakened startling desire. A double-edged sword, both fear and arousal speared through her, revealing an unsettling truth she'd heard about vampires, their ability to seduce humans. Resisting temptation would challenge her. Every second in his presence would make it more difficult to sever the connection. She needed to say goodbye as soon as they landed, make it clear she couldn't date a vampire.

But her curiosity persisted. Why did the vampire concern himself with her? Did he know something about her friend he hadn't told her? Could he really help her find Teagan?

As the limo pulled onto the tarmac, she realized they'd entered a private airport and weren't taking a commercial flight. She stole a glance at Viktor who leaned his head on the back of the tanned leather seats. The handsome fellow next to him, who the vampire affectionately called 'wolf', grinned as she caught his gaze.

"You all right?" he asked, toying with a bottle of water.

"Yes, thank you." She gave a hesitant smile.

"I'm Rafe by the way. Dad didn't introduce us properly." He cupped his hand around his mouth, pretending to whisper just to her. "He doesn't like to tell everyone about me. Might be the wolf thing. I dunno."

"I'm Waverly." *He has a son?* Her expression remained pleasant but flat, attempting to conceal her surprise.

"Can you see the resemblance?" Rafe joked.

"Well," Waverly smiled broadly, noting his relaxed demeanor and clothing. In contrast, Viktor wore well-fitted, black jeans, an Italian silk shirt with a leather jacket. The stylish outfit was accessorized with a pair of white and silver Versace sneakers and aviator sunglasses. "I suppose you both have nice smiles."

"You hear that, Vik? I have a nice smile. You might not know this, but Viktor is a little more boujee than me. Some might say, extra."

"Fuck off, Rafe," Viktor shot back and turned to Waverly. "Everything I do is extra. It's just how I roll."

She laughed, her eyes widening as she took in the sight of the private jet. Uniformed flight crew stood waiting for them.

"Nice little plane. Food's pretty good too." Rafe looked to Viktor who'd opened his eyes, shooting him a look of irritation. "Don't worry. I promise he won't be cooking."

"It was toast. It burns easily," Viktor commented. "Bread and whatnot."

"Yeah, I could still smell it when I got back from the gym. You do know that if you wanted to impress her, you could've called the Ritz, Four Seasons…a half dozen fancy breakfast places in Miami."

"I was attempting to take care of my human friend." Viktor smiled at Waverly. "Besides, her eggs were delicious."

Waverly melted inside as his smile washed over her. "Thank you."

"Wait. Hold up there. You ate? Like actual food?"

Viktor grinned at Waverly, refusing to indulge the wolf.

"All right, then? That's how it's gonna be? You're smooth, I'll give you that, but next time order out." Rafe reached for the door. "Chicks shouldn't have to cook their own food on a first date."

"It wasn't a date," Waverly blurted out, her cheeks flushing pink with embarrassment. "It was breakfast."

"Dude, I can teach you to cook."

"It's the thought that counts," Viktor replied, unfazed by Rafe. He reached for a silver, glittery gift bag and extended it to her. "Put them on. It's sunny."

Waverly reached inside, removed the case and gently

opened it. A rush of anticipation washed over her as she tugged the silk bag off the sunglasses. *CHANEL.*

"I can't accept these." She slid them into the case and snapped it shut.

"Don't be silly. Of course, you can."

"They're too expensive. No, I'm sorry, here." She held out the box to him.

Viktor locked his eyes on hers and spoke, never once looking away. "Rafe. Get in the jet. Give us a minute."

A warm breeze blew into the limo as the driver opened the door.

"You got it, Boss." Rafe made short work of shuffling over the seat, quickly exiting, leaving them alone.

Waverly's pulse raced as Viktor slid next to her. He reached for the case, slowly opening it, unfolding the glasses. Under his intense gaze, her heart pounded as he closed the distance. Her eyes drifted to his lips, mere inches from hers.

"They are a gift. Best not to have the sun in those beautiful eyes of yours."

"I..." Desire burned hot through her body, her tight peaks strained against her blouse and warmth flooded between her legs. She lost herself in his eyes, and swore she saw flecks of fire dancing in them. As he leaned toward her, she released a sigh.

"It's a gift, mo chroí," he whispered, his lips mere inches from hers.

Waverly closed her eyes, anticipating his kiss, but as he slid the sunglasses onto her face, she blinked them open to find him staring at her. A rush of disappointment washed over her, followed by confusion. *What am I doing? What spell am I under? I almost kissed him. Oh my God. This is crazy.*

"You're beautiful," he told her and then quickly exited the limo.

Waverly reached for his hand, and stepped onto the

tarmac, the blistering Miami sun instantly warming her. With a gentle arm he guided her to the steps and ushered her onto the plane.

As she stepped into the plush cabin, she accepted a glass of champagne from the flight attendant. She slipped into the cushioned leather seat and set her drink onto the table in front of her, fastening her seat belt. As the plane door shut and the plane rolled down the runway, she stared out the window, overwhelmed by the experience.

Her mind raced as the wheels lifted off the ground. This vampire, this force of nature, tempted her like no other man. No matter what she'd told herself, in that moment, she knew her life would never be the same again.

WAVERLY ANXIOUSLY BIT HER LIP, staring out into the blue sky. She released a sigh of relief as the jet leveled off and finally reached its cruising speed.

"Do you enjoy traveling?" Viktor asked.

"Love to travel. Flying, not so much. It's a necessary evil." Waverly looked around the lavish interior. "Although I've never flown on a plane like this one before."

"May I freshen your drink, mademoiselle?" The flight attendant who seemingly appeared out of nowhere handed Waverly another flute of bubbly.

"Um...sure." She accepted, reluctant to appear rude.

Viktor and Rafe, who both sat facing her from their individual captain's chairs also accepted fresh glasses.

Waverly smiled at the handsome young wolf. His unruly, curly brown hair spilled over his shoulders. With board shorts, a hoodie and flip flops, he rocked a casual vibe, fitting for California.

Her gaze drifted to Viktor who held his glass into the

air. As if he'd walked off the pages of GQ, the white shirt fitted him like a glove, accentuating his tanned skin. The hint of his woodsy cologne teased her nose and she restrained herself from asking what kind he wore. *No girl, no.*

As he removed his sunglasses, he pinned her with a heated gaze. Warmth coursed through her body, and she crossed her legs, willing it to go away. *What is this man doing to me? How is a vampire so damned tanned?*

"A proper toast?" he suggested.

"A toast, um, yes," she managed.

"To our wonderful new friendship. May we only thirst for each other." Viktor didn't wait for a response as he brought the glass to his smiling lips.

Waverly laughed and sipped, the bubbles teasing her tongue. *Where am I? On a private jet drinking champagne with a vampire and a werewolf, because this happens every day. Yep.*

"What's going through that beautiful mind of yours?" Viktor asked.

"It's just that…well, I'm not exactly used to this." Waverly looked around the cabin, noting a small chuckle from Rafe.

"My pilots are the very best. No need to worry about anything up here."

"You'd think I'd be used to it by now." At the sight of dark clouds in the distance, Waverly took a gulp of her champagne. "Is that a storm?"

"The pilot will fly around them. Would you like something to eat?" Viktor asked.

As if on cue, the perky brunette flight attendant appeared. "Would you like lunch, mademoiselle? We have croissant sandwiches, charcuterie, homemade pastries, chocolates."

"A sandwich would be lovely." Waverly recalled their conversation about food and wondered if he'd drank blood yet today.

Rafe pulled out a pair of headphones from his backpack. "Noise cancelling. I'm gonna get in a nap."

Viktor smiled, silent as the flight attendant set out a china platter topped with petite sandwiches. She unfolded a napkin, draping it over Waverly's lap and set a bottle of Perrier onto the side table.

Waverly reached for a croissant and attempted to bite down as gracefully as she could. Tiny pieces of bread flaked everywhere. A delightful, flavorful bite of turkey and spiced mayo danced over her tongue. "Mmm...this is delicious."

"Good," Viktor responded.

Waverly's eyes narrowed in on his strong fingers as he tipped his glass and sipped.

"How is it you don't eat food but drink champagne?"

Viktor gave a secretive smile. "Long story."

"Long flight. What gives? Is it a requirement for vampires to look debonair and drink expensive wines?"

"I enjoy champagne every now and then," Viktor commented blithely. "In truth, it's linked to a memory, a brief encounter with an Englishman. While it was the monks who are often credited with the creation of champagne, he was the one who really discovered it."

"A monk?"

"Oui. Dom Pérignon. He was a Benedictine monk. But it was my lad, Christopher Merrett who discovered the bubbly one fine eve. And what a lovely eve it was."

His story reminded Waverly that he wasn't just another human. He'd been walking the earth for many years. He spoke as if he'd known so many who lived long ago, because he'd experienced it himself.

"Please don't take this the wrong way. But exactly how old are you?" She gave him a tight smile as if bracing for bad news.

"I'm as old as the night and day." Viktor gave a small

laugh. "Over a thousand years I've walked this big, blue, space rock."

"Thousand?" A knot formed in her throat.

"Yes, pet. Don't look so shocked."

"There's no way that's possible. Look at you. You're so young. So fit. So..." *Handsome. Ripped. Ridiculously fucking sexy.* Her eyes drifted to his chest and snapped back up to meet his gaze. "Well, I just meant you don't look—"

"Immortal? I've seen lifetimes of joy. And of death." Viktor sighed. "But all you need to know at this moment is that I find you quite fascinating. Intriguing, indeed."

"I'm not that exciting." Waverly smiled, warmth in her expression. She wished she could tell him she wasn't interested in him, but she'd be lying. This dangerous vampire attracted her like no other man...but he wasn't just a man. With a deep cleansing breath, she willed away the feelings that curled in her chest. *No dating vampires.*

"Why are you doing this? Any of this? Taking care of me. Following me," she pressed.

"You really want the truth?" He raised an eyebrow at her.

"Yes, but you shouldn't get involved anymore. I have this feeling something very bad is going to happen. Something worse is going to happen." Waverly contemplated revealing her visions but decided otherwise. While some people might consider her ability a gift, she thought it a curse.

"After you left, I talked to the maître d', and he kindly offered me your information."

"Did he?"

"Perhaps he had a little persuasion." He grinned. "The reality is that ladies who go to blood clubs are there to be bitten. You clearly weren't interested. Regardless of why you were there, I don't like bullies. I suppose the second I decided to intervene, to kill that vampire...you're my responsibility now."

"But I'm not. This is my responsibility, not yours. It's not fair to ask you to put yourself in any more danger for me. It's my fault. I should have never gone looking for her there. I'd heard those places are dangerous. But Teagan—"

"He would have killed you. Can't have that now, can we?"

"You said you saw the apartment?"

"Yeah, I did. Was Teagan into drugs?"

"No, never. I mean I guess I don't know for sure. But she said she'd been drinking blood. I tried to tell her...well, I guess in the end it was other humans who got her into trouble.

"She wasn't always so unstable." Waverly recalled the crazy spiral her friend had descended into, a life of conspiracy theories and little restrictions. "When she moved to Miami, I was all for it. She was going to save money, do street art shows. She'd wanted to have her own gallery. Then out of the blue she started a store. It had occult items. Sage, crystals, books, things like that. But she couldn't make it work financially. After that, she seemed to get lost in life. Some nights, she'd leave me crazy messages, call me...she sounded high as a kite but insisted it was her just her 'awakening.' Who knows really?" Waverly shook her head, wearing a disappointed smile. "I know it all sounds crazy. She was always sort of a free spirit. When she said she'd met this guy and drank blood, I didn't want to believe it. I wasn't entirely sure if she was hanging out with some kind of role play group...seriously, it's kinda crazy to think there's a group of humans doing this kind of thing."

"We're going to find this group." Viktor's expression grew serious. "I need to tell you though. When I went to her apartment looking for you, something else had been there."

"Something? Something like what?"

"I suppose there will never be a better time for me to tell you this."

"What?"

"I don't know exactly what yet but it's something dark. The kind of evil that's not from this realm."

"No...please. Don't say it." *No really, please don't say it.* She took a swig of her champagne, finishing the glass. *I've got to know.* "Okay. Say it. Just lay it on me."

"Demon."

"No, no, no. I've changed my mind. Take it back." She covered her eyes with her fingers, shaking her head.

Viktor laughed. "My dear, lovely human. I'm afraid it doesn't work that way."

"But I was in her apartment. I didn't stay but I was there. Oh my God. Do I need an exorcism or something?"

"No, but between Teagan's human friends, her drinking blood and her involvement with vampires, she could have brought evil to where she lived."

"Here's the thing. I think I've kind of explained this, but I think it bears repeating that I am not like Teagan. The only reason I'm involved is because of her. Going to the blood club was a mistake."

"Indeed. But what's done is done. It's going to be okay. I promise."

The plane unexpectedly rolled with a bump. Waverly clutched the seat as the flight attendant frantically gathered the glasses and plates. "I'm afraid we're going into a bit of a storm. The pilot will fly around it, but we'd like you to put your seatbelts on."

"I hate flying." Waverly released a yelp as the plane dipped once again, her stomach flipped in response.

"May I?" Viktor asked, gesturing to the empty seat next to her.

Her face flushed at the thought of having him close to her. "Yes. Of course."

Waverly's heart pounded in her chest as Viktor slid next

to her and reached across her waist, tugging on her seatbelt, making sure it was secure. Between the storm and Viktor, she wasn't sure she'd survive the flight.

"I told you I'd keep you safe," he assured her. "And I always keep my promises."

"I...thank you..." Waverly's thoughts spun, her senses on alert as he slid his palm down her thigh and reached for her hand.

"I've got you," he said, his voice calm.

Within seconds of their palms joining, the vision slammed into her. Viktor, clad in thick scaled armor, with an axe in his hand, ran through a smoky battlefield. Far from the clean-cut, debonair, well-dressed man beside her, this Viking wore a long beard, his hair twisted up in braids. Dirty and bloodied, he fought, striking down his enemies with an axe. A deafening whinny sounded, and he spun around, readied to attack. An ominous figure on horseback rushed upon him. Viktor raised his weapon in preparation, but the cunning rider outmatched him. Like a knife cutting butter, the rider drove his sword through Viktor's armor, slashing open his abdomen. White hot pain stabbed through his body as Viktor crumpled to the ground, his entrails bulging from his gut.

As the vision played in Waverly's mind, she clutched her stomach, watching the man writhe on the ground, slowly succumbing to his brutal death. She sensed the moment he relented, his soul accepting his fate. He stared to the sky, the stench of smoke and blood in the air. Death is coming.

"Waverly, come now, love," Viktor consoled her as her head swam with confusion. As if she were stuck in soft taffy, she struggled to release herself from the compelling vision. *Viktor isn't dead. He's immortal.*

As the vision dissipated, her vision focused onto Viktor's mesmerizing blue eyes staring down at her. "I'm sorry."

"The turbulence will be over soon. Are you feeling okay?"

"It's just the champagne." The lie sat in her stomach like a rock.

"This happened to you at the museum the other night?"

"Yes." Exhaustion threaded through her. "I...I promise to tell you what's going on later."

"Come." With the press of a button, Viktor reclined the seats, and wrapped an arm around her.

Waverly melted into his embrace and leaned onto his chest. She had so many questions about the vision but simply chose silence. Peace enveloped her and in that very moment, she knew she had lost the fight to resist the vampire.

WAVERLY STEPPED out of the limo and breathed in the fresh salt air. With her head still spinning she attempted to regain her balance. She glanced to Viktor who gave her a knowing smile. In the bright sun, he appeared the Viking she'd seen in her vision, yet logic told her otherwise.

It had been years since a vision had caused her to black out. Normally they'd pass, forgotten within hours, but not this one. No, something about this vampire ignited her abilities, and she was quickly losing control.

Waverly's body went on alert as he exited behind her, acutely aware of his every move. The warmth of his hand on her lower back heated her body and she resisted the urge to lean backwards, to feel his touch once again.

"My place is right up here." Waverly quickly stepped ahead of him, heading toward her apartment.

"You sure you don't want to talk about what happened on the plane?" he pressed.

"I'm good. Is Rafe going to be all right?" Waverly avoided

answering his question and set off up the path toward her building.

"He's visiting with Jake and his pack. We'll meet up with him later."

"This way. Third floor," she directed. Her stomach curled in anxiety along with a slice of embarrassment. She'd fallen asleep on his chest. It should have been uncomfortable to wake up in his arms. Quite the contrary, she'd taken her time, her body on fire with arousal.

She couldn't understand what was happening to her. *No dating vampires.* It was a rule that had served her well...until now. She couldn't afford to catch feelings, not when there was no possibility of being with him.

The sudden warmth of his palm against her shoulder sent tingles throughout her body, shaking her from her thoughts.

"You all right, pet?" he asked with a smile.

"Yes, I..." She exhaled a ragged breath. *What is he doing to me?* "It's just...I remembered that I was supposed to help out at the marine rescue this afternoon. I'm a volunteer."

"Marine rescue?"

"Yes. Sea mammals. Pinnipeds." She typed her security code into the security gate, and it buzzed, slowly sliding open.

"Pinnipeds," he repeated with an amused lilt in his voice.

"Yes. Sometimes the pups end up on beaches, but we rescue adults too. Malnutrition. Injuries. We nurse them back to health. Rehab and release. Whenever we can, anyway."

"Interesting. A surfing art curator who takes care of seals."

"Mostly sealions. But yes. One who is now friends with a vampire."

"It's sufficient for now," he casually commented.

"What's that supposed to mean?" She knew damn well what he meant. She inwardly cursed, regretting the question.

"Considering you said you'd never date a vampire. Friends is acceptable. Although I think we know it's much more than that."

Waverly swallowed her words, refusing to agree with him. She'd deny it to the grave and she prayed it wouldn't get that far. "We just met. I'm generous in admitting we're friends. Maybe I should remind you that I have no recollection how I got to Miami. With the time being what it was, I don't think I took a plane, but I don't know how else I could have gotten there. Care to explain?"

"I will tell you in due time. But regardless, I can assure you that we will be more than friends," Viktor mused.

"How could you possibly know that? We just met." As she reached the door, she spun to confront him. Not realizing how close behind her he was, her palms brushed his chest. His energy danced on her fingertips. "I just don't think—"

Viktor smiled at her. "Perhaps we've known each other before. Or perhaps it's destiny."

"No, that can't be." Waverly's heart pounded as he leaned in towards her. Her gaze fell to his lips, her body on fire anticipating his kiss. But as she closed her eyes, she felt the warmth of his breath upon her ear.

"I can hear your heart race, pet. You know the truth." He reached his arm around her waist. "We will be more than friends. Rules or no rules. I'm quite certain you're thinking what I'm thinking."

The air rushed from her lungs as she heard the doorknob click open. The warmth of his body brushed hers and she fluttered her eyes open to see him swing open the door and walk into her condo.

"Sweet baby Jesus," she whispered under her breath, willing her body under control.

"Please allow me to go first. Wouldn't want to run into anything woo-woo, now, would we?" Viktor walked through the entrance and looked to a set of glass sliding doors. "Nice view."

As she stepped into her condo, she wrinkled her nose as the stench hit her. "Oh my gosh. I'm sorry. I must have forgotten the trash." She made a beeline into the kitchen and flipped open the lid of the bin. "There's nothing in here. What's that smell?"

"That, my darling, is the stench of a demon," Viktor explained as he slid open the door.

"A demon? In my home? Oh, hell no. This isn't happening." Waverly frantically tapped at her watch. "It must be the pipes or something. I'll text my landlord."

"I don't sense anything here right now. Whatever or whoever was here is gone."

"Are you sure it's gone?"

"Demon." Viktor shrugged.

"Stop saying that word. No, it's not that. My neighbor, Janet, is always cooking fish. That must be what it is. She needs to stop leaving it unwrapped."

"It's a demon," he insisted.

"Oh my God. Please stop saying that word." She looked to the small plastic statue of Mary she kept over her door and made the sign of the cross.

"You can say the word. It's conjuring them that's the problem. Well, I suppose some humans think that is how it works but I can assure you it isn't."

"How could you possibly know? I mean really. You're a vampire." Waverly frantically tapped the watch face again. "She's not answering my text."

"I know quite a bit about Hell, I'm afraid." He shrugged with a nonchalant air.

"I'm sure you have carnal thoughts. But it's not like you've been there or anything."

A corner of his mouth tugged upward, and he raised an eyebrow. "I travel for business. Not every destination is for pleasure."

"Hell? A destination?" The air rushed from Waverly's lungs, her pulse racing. *No, no, no.*

"Work is work. Actually, the last time I was there it was for a friend but…"

"That's crazy. Demons? Hell? Just no. I can't even." She flung open the refrigerator door and reached for her favorite strawberry mango kombucha. She hesitated and contemplated a shot of tequila but decided on the healthier option.

"Something was in your friend's apartment in Miami. And now that something or maybe even a different something has been here. But as I look around, your place seems undisturbed. Or at least on first glance. You tell me. Is anything amiss?" Viktor reached for a scented candle and sniffed it. He smiled. "Nice. Peppermint."

Waverly hurriedly unscrewed the bottle top and took a large gulp. The bubbles rushed down her throat and she coughed. "I can sage. I know I have it around here somewhere." She opened a drawer and began rummaging through it. "Where the heck did I put it?"

"Sage?"

"This is SoCal. Everyone sages. I sage pretty much every week. Do a little yoga. I figured it couldn't hurt. Although it didn't keep a demon out of my house, did it? Ugh. I can't find it."

"You're not safe here. You shouldn't stay here," he suggested.

"I can't leave my house. The new exhibit is supposed to open to the public next week." Waverly took another drink and released a long audible breath. Her limbs felt like lead as the reality set in that she was no longer safe, that a demon had been in her home.

"You can and you will. Look around. Do you see anything out of place? We need a clue as to why demons are snooping around here. You wouldn't happen to have security cameras?"

"I've been looking at getting one, but I don't have one yet. It's pretty safe here though. Look, maybe whatever was here realized that I am not the one it's looking for. I don't know anything about that woo-woo stuff."

"You have sage," he countered, a chuckle following. "Maybe you're a witch. A witch who won't date a vampire."

"Ha ha. Funny guy. I'm a perfectly whatever…I'm human. I'm certainly not a witch. And sage doesn't count as being woo-woo. Everyone in California buys sage. It, uh, it feels good to release whatever negative vibes I'm feeling."

"I hate to tell you, but sage isn't going to help you with this demon problem."

Waverly opened a storage cabinet and stared inside, searching. "I liked the way it looked. It was in this pretty pearly shell. I think it might be in the bathroom. I put it on a shelf." Waverly turned around, expecting to make a beeline to the bathroom but instead found a hard chest blocking her path. A deep breath filled her lungs as she attempted to calm down.

"It's going to be all right, Waverly. I promise I will be at your side. I'll keep you safe. Sage, however, won't remove this demon from your life. It's following you. Which means it needs you for some reason. From the looks of your friend's apartment, I'm thinking it's looking for something."

"Why would a demon want me? So my friend got mixed up with some bad people. I have nothing to do with any of that. I was just her friend. Seriously. I swear I'm just this normal person. I'm boring. I work all the time."

"I hardly find you boring."

Waverly smiled at him, her cheeks flushing. "Thank you, but I assure you I am. Why is this happening? This makes no sense."

"One thing my years on earth have taught me is that reasons are not always ours to know. Shall we check the bedroom?" Viktor shot her a cheeky smile.

"Why do you need to go in my bedroom?" Waverly asked, attempting to tamp down the dirty thoughts spinning through her head. *Stop. What if he can read your mind. Think about fruit. Oranges. Strawberries. Peaches. Bananas. Hmm... Bananas. Whipped cream with my banana. Stop.*

Viktor smiled at her and raised his eyebrows. "Well?"

"Don't read my thoughts," Waverly blurted out as she turned and strode toward her bedroom. "It's this way."

"I would never dream of it."

Waverly peered into her bedroom; her nerves steeled as if a giant, green, horned creature was waiting for her. A breath of relief escaped her lips as she realized her room was exactly how she left it. A pile of shoes heaped in front of her closet. The only speck of color on her virgin white comforter was the crimson cashmere chemise she'd decided not to wear.

"It's fine. My bedroom looks okay." Waverly took a single step inside, still unsure if something diabolical was hiding in her closet.

"It was here." Viktor entered the room and sniffed the air. "Everything's very neat. But the blood—"

"Blood?" Waverly croaked. "What blood?"

"Perhaps you should go in the kitchen," Viktor told her, his demeanor serious.

"No. You just said there was blood. Whose blood?" Panic seized Waverly as the vampire approached her bed. As his face tensed in concentration, his eyes locked on hers.

"More like a what. Sorry pet, but I'm afraid I need to rearrange your furniture."

"My furniture? What are you talking about?" Waverly's eyes widened as Viktor shoved her bed aside, its wheels screeching across the hardwood floor until a pool of blood came into view. "Oh my God. What the hell is that?"

"You need to go in the hallway," Viktor insisted.

"No. Whatever this is, it affects me. This is my bedroom and…" The air sucked from her lungs as she caught sight of the decapitated goat's head, a pentagram smeared in its blood. The color drained from her face. "What is that?"

"It's a goat. Sacrificial, generally."

"Why is this happening to me?" She reached for the door-jamb, steadying her wobbly knees.

"Let's get your things and get out of here."

"Is it a message? Why leave that there for me?" She shook her head. "Who did this?"

Viktor reached for his cell phone and snapped a picture. "Something about this isn't right."

"Ya think? There's blood all over the floor. And that poor animal…where's the rest of it? Is this," she hesitated to speak the word, "Satanic?"

"I'm not sure. Something about this looks like humans did it." He glanced to the floor. "The goat head? It's been dead for over a week. The cut is clean. My guess is it came from a butcher."

"What?"

"I can't be certain, but this mess. This symbol looks familiar. I don't believe this is totally correct. I took a picture because I have a friend who might know."

"But you said a demon was here."

"There was a demon. But this might be the work of a very ordinary human. This blood here." He pointed to the ground. "This isn't from a goat."

"How do you know that? Tell me you didn't taste it." She bit her lip, nausea rising in her throat.

"Taste it? Ew, no. I'm a vampire not a heathen."

"How do you know it's not from the goat?" she pressed.

"At risk of pointing out the obvious. I'm a vampire."

"Ha. Ha."

"Vampire 101. Lesson number one. I have the ability to differentiate blood types by taste but more importantly by smell."

"You can tell the difference between a human's blood or an animal?"

"Yes."

"My blood?" Her mind wandered to the memories of his lips brushing her skin.

"Absolutely," he responded, his voice low.

Under Viktor's heated stare, Waverly averted her gaze and wrapped her arms around herself.

"Humans have very distinct scents from animals and from each other. While I don't drink animal blood, there have been times when I'd scrounge for anything." Viktor appeared to lose his thoughts and changed the subject. "Is anything else amiss? Any other rooms?"

"Um, not that I can see. But given there's blood and body parts under my bed, I'm thinking that's about enough."

"I'll send a cleaner later. Right now, you should pack a few things you want to bring with you."

"Pack?" Waverly rubbed between her eyes, attempting to release the stifling tension.

"I'm sorry. But your place isn't safe. And even if it were cleaned up, are you going to want to stay when someone has defiled your bedroom? No. You'll come with me, and we'll find your friend and most importantly, find the bad guy."

"You're not wrong though. Someone did this." She glanced around the room in frustration. "I really liked this apartment too. Do you know how hard it is to find a place near the beach?"

"Location, location, location," Viktor quipped.

"Okay. I'll go with you," she acquiesced with a nod. She could stay at a friend's house or a hotel, but she didn't want to put anyone else at risk. "I don't really have a choice right now. At least not for tonight." Waverly raked her fingers through her hair, nervously twisting her hair into a bun. "We have to go back to the museum and talk to the police. What am I going to say?"

"I'm going to call PCAP, tell them about the demon, the blood. They'll come check out your condo. Make sure there's nothing else we're missing. Maybe they can pick up some prints. I'll also text Jake and let him know what happened so he can follow up with them after we leave to go to New Orleans."

"New Orleans?" Waverly asked, wearing a shocked expression. "Why are we going there?"

"I've got a contact there who might be able to help. Whoever did this might come looking for you again."

"Okay, but I have to get back to work. The exhibit is opening. What am I supposed to do?" Waverly's stomach churned. She knew Viktor was right. Whoever got into her place had made it look easy and they'd be back.

"It's going to be all right." Viktor closed the distance between them.

Waverly nodded. She glanced to the pool of blood and her lips tightened. Emotion brewed inside her, and she fought the tears that welled in her eyes.

Viktor wrapped his arms around her, and Waverly melted into his protective embrace. She clung to him, allowing her energy to flow. She opened her mind as his warmth surrounded her. In that moment she wished they could escape, pretend none of this had happened, that this ancient vampire she'd met was merely an art philanthropist who she found entertaining and ridiculously handsome. But the voice in the back of her head wouldn't allow her to indulge in fantasy. The sight of the blood-splattered floor out of the corner of her eye slapped her with reality. This was no fantasy, it was horror.

As WAVERLY ENTERED the museum's lobby, she recalled the previous night, the sound of gunfire, the blood. She walked to the column that she hid behind and pressed her palm to the cool stone. As if she were living a surreal nightmare, she'd been shot in this very spot, yet not a speck of blood remained. All the catering furniture had been put away, leaving the open space nearly ready for visitors. Save for a mill of officers remaining in the building and workers replacing broken glass, all was perfectly normal.

This is messed up, she thought to herself. Instinct told her nothing would be the same. Whatever had come for Teagan had now come for her. She'd packed her things, left her home, her sanctuary. Her second home, her work, her museum had been defiled.

This is still my life, she told herself as she glanced to the chic signs that announced the arrival of the new Impressionism exhibit. *Her exhibit.* It reminded her of her accomplishments.

The rhythmic tapping of her boots on the marble floor was drowned out by the sounds of voices quarreling. The argument grew louder as she approached the rotunda. Two uniformed police officers stood silent while a woman dressed in a tan pantsuit lectured her boss.

"Dr. Williams, this is a police investigation. This is a crime scene. We need time to collect evidence. And even after this is all cleaned up, we may need to come back if the detectives have questions or if they need to look at the space again. This is how investigations work."

"With all due respect, the shooter is dead. You know how he died. He slipped and broke his neck. Everyone saw it. Crime solved. I, on the other hand, have a responsibility to the public to give them access to one of the world's most spectacular exhibits, to live and breathe Impressionism. As they say, the show must go on."

"Well, I'm afraid that may work for some things but in this universe, where I'm running the show, I need more time. I'm sure you can refer patrons to Balboa Park for one more day. The fine city of San Diego would like to thank you for your understanding."

"This is ridiculous. Our donors, our staff, they stayed late last night. They answered your questions. You took names and addresses. What more could you possibly be looking for?"

"As I said, there are nuances when collecting evidence. We need to be thorough. While it appears the shooter broke his neck, it seems unlikely he simply fell."

"Does it really matter how he died? I don't mean to appear insensitive, but who really cares? He's a criminal. The bigger question is why the museum must suffer further loss by keeping us closed? Everything has been cleaned up. You've got the body. Deal with it at the station." Dr. William's cheeks flushed red with anger as he huffed and dragged his palm over his head.

"He's got a point. Although so does the detective," Viktor interjected as he confidently crossed the room and addressed the police.

Waverly gave her boss a sympathetic smile, aware that every day the museum remained closed, they'd lose money.

"My name's Viktor Christianson. We spoke earlier on the phone. Please pardon our late arrival."

"Nice of you to finally join us. I'm Detective Trent," the officer told Viktor. "You do realize that time is of the essence in these matters."

"As I explained last night, Dr. LaFleur and I left prior to the shooting to attend a late-night, exclusive showing at my home in Miami. Dr. Williams. You do remember us telling you we'd bid out early?"

A look of confusion washed over Waverly's face as her boss nodded in agreement. "Yes, I do recall Mr. Christianson saying something about another painting you'd wanted her to see."

Waverly stood dumbfounded at their explanation, knowing that she'd been shot. Viktor turned to her and winked as he brought his fingers to his lips.

"Is this true, Dr. LaFleur?" the detective asked her. "You expect me to believe you went all the way across the country last evening to see a painting?"

"Well, yes. Mr. Christianson had donated a Monet and he'd offered access to another rare painting." Waverly glared at Viktor, annoyed and confused as to why he'd lie. "We took his private plane."

"And you're certain you weren't injured in any way?" the detective pressed.

"Does she look like she's been shot? I mean come on. She's rockin' those Louboutins. Looks like she stepped off a runway."

"Do you find this amusing, Mr. Christianson?" The detective asked.

"I'm always serious about fashion. I don't know about you, but I love fringe. Sexy and sporty all at once." He smiled, his eyes lit with amusement.

Waverly glanced down to the ridiculously expensive

boots he'd bought for her. While impressed with the way the low-heeled suede shoes supported her feet like she was walking on a cloud in heaven, she still had a hard time accepting the extravagant gift.

"I want to run through this again." The detective glared at Viktor, not amused with his attitude.

"If you'll excuse me, I'm going to put a call in to the mayor. You may not be in a hurry to open this museum, but I am!" Dr. Williams turned on his heels, angrily stomping out of the rotunda.

"Your boss seems tense," the detective commented as she tapped at her phone.

"Perhaps he should take a yoga class," Viktor suggested with a wide smirk. "Get his chakras aligned and all that good stuff."

"I do yoga. You got a problem with yoga?" Waverly challenged. Her confusion warped into anger.

"Hardly. Hot yoga is my jam. Hotter than hell." He laughed, giving her a knowing smile.

Waverly feigned a smile, attempting to hide her displeasure. The sound of the detective clearing her throat drew her attention and she caught the look of annoyance on her face as she glared at both her and Viktor.

"I'm sorry. Truly," Waverly apologized.

"Let's go over it one more time. Were you aware of any threats against the museum?" The detective asked.

"No."

"Did you notice anyone unusual? It's my understanding that you gave Mr. Christianson a tour?"

"Yes, I did. He'd donated a painting. We met in the exhibit. And then my boss had asked me to show him around the museum."

"Did you know the shooter?"

"Absolutely not," Waverly protested. "What would make you think that?"

"You're sure of that?" The detective held up her phone with an image of a white male subject, dressed all in black. With his eyes wide open, his death stare haunted her.

"Yes, I'm sure," she shot back without taming the shock in her voice and diverted her gaze from the picture.

"All right then." The detective proceeded to flip through the edges of the notebook paper she had in a plastic sleeve. "Perhaps you'd like to explain why the shooter had this on his body. Is this you?"

"Who took this?" The blood drained from her face as Waverly reached for the photo. *Miami.* "Where did you get this?"

"I was hoping you could explain why this shooter, who is still unidentified by the way, was carrying a picture of you."

"I..." Waverly looked to Viktor who nodded at her in support. "I was recently in Miami."

"Why does the shooter have this picture of you?" the detective pressed.

"I don't know. I don't even know who the shooter is."

"What were you doing in Miami?"

"I was there to see a friend. She's an old college friend who, uh, she went missing a week ago. I've already reported it to the Miami police."

"What were you doing in this picture?"

"An anonymous donor had texted me about a painting. And before you ask, I don't know how they got my number. Maybe the office admin gave it to them. Or maybe they got it online. I don't know. It's not really that unusual these days to get someone's mobile number. But somehow they knew I was in the area."

"How could they possibly know that?"

"I don't know. Social media, maybe? I made a few posts

while I was out. Nothing special or identifying. Just palm trees. The beach. I guess they could maybe tell where I was staying in South Beach by looking at them. I don't know."

"And?" The detective pressed for more information.

"And what?" Waverly's body temperature rose as the detective interrogated her.

"Who was the person you met?"

"I don't know. Like I said. It was a courier. I signed the paperwork he'd handed me acknowledging I was going to take custody of a painting."

"And you didn't ask about the owner or anything?"

"It's not necessarily the norm but it happens. People don't want me to know who owns it. I sign off for the property from the intermediary and take temporary possession. Sometimes an offer is made. Sometimes not, depending on if there's already existing documentation from a reputable source. When I arrived back in San Diego, the painting was already at the museum. Right now, I don't even know if it's real."

"Do you have it now?"

"Yes. I'm in the process of evaluating it." Waverly shook her head, losing her patience. "Look. Anyone can find me on social media. There are lots of sickos out there. What happened in Miami is no different than any other time. But I don't have any idea why the shooter had a picture of me. Or how he got the picture. How would I possibly know that?"

"I'd like to see the painting if you don't mind." The detective slid the papers back into the sleeve.

"Of course." Waverly reached for the elevator buttons. "My office is upstairs."

"Detective. If you'd indulge me for a minute. Could you tell me if there was anything else unusual about the shooter?" Viktor asked, his voice smooth and direct.

Waverly's eyes widened in astonishment as the detective smiled at him. *What the hell?*

"We've already established that he's a white male in his twenties. No ID on him. He had several knives on his person as well as the assault weapon."

"Any unusual marks? Tattoos? Scars?"

"He had a tattoo of a goat. Multiple scars on his body. Pock marks."

"A goat? Like the white, fluffy kind?" Viktor inquired, his voice sickeningly sweet.

"No. More like the scary kind. It had long horns. Like some kind of a devil. It's possible he was in a gang, but we haven't completed our investigation yet."

"Interesting." Viktor turned to Waverly and raised an eyebrow. "Where was it on his body?"

The detective released an audible sigh and pursed her lips. "I probably shouldn't be telling you."

"I promise I won't tell a soul." Viktor smiled at her.

"It was inside his cheek."

Waverly scrunched her nose in disgust. "Oh my God. That's gotta hurt."

"Yeah. Well. It's not the first unusual place a perp has decided to put ink. You have no idea."

"Detective," Viktor continued. "I have some friends, of the occult persuasion if you will, and they probably should know about this. PCAP. I'm sure you know about them. They handle unusual circumstances."

"I don't believe in that paranormal shit. Crimes are crimes," she spat out.

The elevator opened and Waverly looked to the detective. "After you."

As they stepped inside, Waverly heard an unfamiliar male voice call out to them.

"Excuse me, ma'am. We've got something down here we want you to look at." A uniformed officer stood waiting.

"I'll be up in ten minutes," the detective said, her tone flat as she exited the elevator.

"We'll be in my office. Take a right through the watercolors and then another right," Waverly told her. "I'm at the end of the hallway. Big red doors."

She turned to Viktor, her eyes locked on his, her body tense with anger, waiting until the doors fully closed to speak. "What the hell was that?"

"I was right," he replied. "Those boots look amazing."

"Viktor, tell me what is going on?" Waverly demanded.

"We're going up to your office." A loud ding sounded. "And we're here. After you. Please."

Waverly didn't think twice as she strode out of the elevator and through the exhibit, the tapping of her heels echoing throughout the marble floored hallways. She didn't look back, her rage teetering on an explosion.

"I want the truth, Viktor. No more bullshit. Do you hear me?" Waverly turned toward her office and set her face and fingers to the security scan. The door slid open, and she made a beeline for her desk. "Why does she think we left before the shooter shot me? Why does my boss think we left for that matter? I was shot. You know it and I know it." His smartass smile only fueled her anger. "I want to know how I got to Miami. Like in the snap of the fingers."

"Well," he shrugged with a nonchalant air. "It's not my fingers, per se."

"What is that supposed to mean?" Waverly sunk down into her comfortable office chair and sighed in exhaustion.

"It means that yes, I told them all we'd left. And I did it at the exact moment we left," he explained.

"So, you just told a room full of people that we'd left. And by some miracle, they just repeat what you told them? Despite knowing differently."

"Yes, I suppose so. That is kind of how it works. Most of the time. And mostly with humans."

"What works?" Waverly immediately regretted asking, already knowing she wouldn't like the answer.

"I'm vampire, pet. Not just old. Ancient. My gifts have developed over the years. It's a simple command to draw the energy, to warp perception. It was the easiest option at the time. There was confusion. Heightened emotions. Which meant there was lots of energy in the room. So yes, I simply told them we already left. Not everyone saw you get shot anyway. It was relatively easy."

"What? Are you serious?" She laughed, her mind struggling to accept the unbelievable.

"This skill I have is true to an ancient. Very few of us have it. It's kind of like fashion sense. You either have it or you don't."

Waverly glared at him in both disbelief and annoyance. She silently counted to ten, her stress reaching epic, mind-blowing levels.

"I hate this situation. And I'm starting to really dislike vampires."

"Lying doesn't become you, pet."

"Lying? Hmm…are you ready to tell me how I got to Miami?"

"Well, you know. It's a bit more complicated than making suggestions to humans, but let's say it's also a gift."

"I see." Waverly rubbed her forehead in an attempt to calm her mind.

"While I'd love to show you, perhaps we should take a look at that painting you were given before the detective gets here. What information do you have from the person who contacted you?"

"I don't really have any. I have a text number that may connect to an actual person but at this rate, my guess is it's a burner. I've texted it several times because I was trying to get more information, but no one is responding. The painting is over there. I showed it to you last night. The angels. I told you about the irregularity I found." She shoved to her feet and made her way over to the painting. With a flick of an overhead switch, blue light splashed over the canvas. "This here. It's purple. You can see how this was overtreated at one time with varnish. It must be cleaned before we can really see how it looks. Honestly, I've only done minimal research so far. I've kind of had my hands full with the exhibit, making sure the event went well." She released an audible sigh. "Ugh. At least we raised money. What a cluster."

"You'll meet your goals," he assured her. "For now, let's focus on the painting. Gut feelings. What do you think about this spot here?"

"I don't know yet. It's possible this extra paint is just a varnish buildup. Dirt. Old paintings come in in all kinds of conditions. Something about this though." She inspected the canvas. "I just have this hunch it's something else. Like maybe an object or a botched repair. Which again, I have no idea why anything would be in there. Why would someone do that?"

"Do you believe this is real?" he asked.

"Plautilla Nelli's work is rare. It would be an incredible discovery. She didn't sign her work. Well, there's one. The Last Supper. Took years to restore it. It was simply hanging in a monastery somewhere when it was found. It's supposedly the only painting of hers in existence."

"Humans," Viktor mused. "They assume to know only what they see."

"I can't argue with that. But it's entirely possible this is her work. The story I was told is that it had been passed down through the generations as a religious item but since there was no signature, the artist's name had been lost. But who knows? This could be a con of some sort. I'd like to verify with the Church."

"Do you mind if I take a closer look at it?"

"Sure. Why not?" Waverly studied Viktor as he leaned in and inspected the art piece.

"I feel like I've seen this painting before."

"That's impossible," she asserted.

"Many of the nun's pieces ended up in the homes of wealthy families. I haven't always lived in the States. I do enjoy a fine Italian meal." Viktor smiled at her.

Waverly stared at the handsome vampire, attempting to come to terms with the reality. Despite his youthful appearance, his striking good looks, the man before her had walked through centuries of time.

"Something wrong?" he asked.

"Sorry, it's just...I mean you look so, so..." *Sexy. Hot as fuck.* She bit her lip, settling on a more appropriate word. "Amazing."

"As do you," he countered.

"But I'm human. And I'm aging. I wonder what it must have been like to live during the Renaissance. To sit at a wealthy family's dinner table. Drink their wine. Enjoy their art."

"It's a quite useful memory when you've met a beautiful curator who needs your assistance." He shot her a smile and then looked to the painting, continuing to study it.

Waverly found herself captivated. She wanted to hate him, to live her life happily without ever having known Viktor Christianson. But she doubted that even after a day, this man would be out of her life. As much as she loathed his lethal nature, the violence she'd witnessed, Viktor spoke to her heart, her passion, her art. While she still couldn't explain the connection, the roots of attraction had already grown deep.

"Regardless of whether this painting is real or not, someone finds it valuable, and they were willing to shoot you for it," Viktor told her. "Have you done an x-ray?"

"No. I didn't get a chance to run one yet." Frustrated, she snapped the rubber band off her wrist, ran her fingers through her hair and pulled it into a ponytail. "God, I just want to get out of here right now. What do you think is taking the detective so long?"

The faint ding of the elevator sounded. "Speak of the devil."

"Don't say that word. Nope." Waverly held up a dismissive finger at him. She crossed the room and opened the door. As she stepped halfway into the hallway, she heard footsteps. She peeked around the corner and spied the detective.

"We're right down here." She waved with a forced smile.

A low growl resounded in the showroom and Waverly's body went tense with fear. Her heart pounded in her chest at the sight of the disheveled detective, her eyes glowing red.

"What the..." She lost her words as a low demonic laugh erupted from the possessed creature.

Waverly ran back into her office, and slammed the door shut. She leaned against it, attempting to form words.

"What's wrong?" Viktor crossed the room to meet her.

"D...d...demon," she managed, her heart pounding.

"Get what you need now," he ordered. "Does your door automatically lock?"

"Yes. It's locked." She nodded.

"Have you got a bag of some sort in here? I need you to gather anything you need," he ordered.

"What?"

"Just do it. I'll get the painting."

"How are we supposed to get out of here?" As Waverly

reached for her backpack, a loud bang sounded, shaking the room. She screamed and quickly began stuffing supplies inside the bag. "It's going to get in here."

"We've got to take this," Viktor carefully removed the painting from its workspace.

"But that thing is out there. There's no way out." Another loud thump sounded, and Waverly scurried behind Viktor. Splinters flew into the room as it pounded its fist through the wooden door, claws reaching for the door handle.

"Give me the key," it growled.

"Key?" Waverly's heart pounded against her ribs, sweat beading on her forehead. She looked to the apex of the ceiling, eyeing the small, rectangular, skylight windows. *I'm never going to fit through there.* She reached for her cell phone and began tapping at the glass. "I've got to call the police."

"The detective *is* the police. I'm afraid we're going to have to flash out of here. No worries, pet. Do you have your things?"

"What? I just told you we can't get out of this room. I need to find a weapon."

"I'm afraid we don't have time to deal with this demon right now. I need to get you and this painting to a safe place." Viktor wrapped his arm around her, his eyes locked on hers. He gripped the painting in his other hand. "This may make you a bit dizzy. See you in New Orleans."

"New Orleans?" Panic swept through Waverly as it set in there was no feasible escape route.

"About those special things I can do. Please forgive me if I say just relax. I promise it will be worth it."

"What? How are we getting to New—"

Waverly squealed as his energy slammed into her. Lost in space and time, her mind flashed with visions as she was sucked into another century. The vampire wore leather and fur, he stood watching a roaring fire. An attractive woman crossed the room and dropped her clothes, baring herself, offering her neck. As he kissed her shoulder, a possessive streak stabbed through Waverly.

Before she had a chance to process her feelings or what she'd seen, the vision shifted. She struggled to breathe as Viktor came into view. On his knees, he cowered as a taskmaster beat him with a whip. A male she didn't recognize, tied to a stake, lapped at his wounds. Her heart broke for him, yet her energy simply swirled in the ethos, she was helpless to stop it. As the flagrum snapped, her heart caught in her chest. The scent of blood swirled in the air, making her nauseous. She froze as Viktor raised his head, his eyes looking to her.

As her feet thumped onto the ground, she immediately snapped into reality. Waverly released a mournful cry, the memories fresh in her mind. Her sadness quickly dissipated as Viktor came into view.

"Are you okay? Sorry, but I had to get us out of there. No time to fuss with demons. Or possessed humans."

"Viktor," she whispered, her eyes brimming with tears. He'd seen her in her vision. No one in her life had insight to her gift, her curse. Both fascinated and terrified, she reached for him, her palm brushing his cheek, her fingers tingling.

"Are you all right, pet? I'm sorry I had to do that without proper warning." He released her hand.

She glanced at his lips as her body hummed with his energy. "Viktor. You saw me."

CHAPTER FIVE

*L*ike a dream, Viktor sensed her in his mind. He hadn't intentionally shown her specific memories, but rather let it play as a reel. Although Viktor no longer suffered the agony of the floggings, the memory lingered. "I'm not sure what you're talking about."

"That man, he was beating you." She shook her head. "I saw you. You saw me."

Waverly pulled out of his embrace, shaken, as she took in her surroundings. Lights twinkled in the distance through a wall of glass. Her eyes adjusted to the darkness, drawn to a lone flickering candle on the fireplace mantle. "Where am I?"

"Home."

"This is your house? It's dark outside. Why is it dark outside?" Panic flashed in her eyes.

"Because it's night," Viktor responded without pause.

"No. It was daytime when we were in the museum. Wait," she defensively held up her hands, confused, "what just happened?"

"We're in Louisiana. It's night here. Time difference and whatnot."

"Louisiana?" Her voice grew louder at the realization that he'd defied physics, somehow transporting them across the country. "No. No, we were just in California."

"I'm vampire, Waverly."

"Is this some kind of trick?"

"It's no trick. It's simply a skill. One I've mastered. For your first ride, you appear to have traveled well." He gave her a warm smile. "Technically it's your second. But this time you were awake."

"You mean you can just disappear and reappear? Take someone with you?"

"Precisely."

"This! This is how I got to Miami?" she exclaimed.

"Yes."

"Oh my God. My vision…I saw you. I saw you there," she repeated, her voice weary.

"I think you should rest. Humans, wolves. They react differently when I flash them." He gestured to the sofa and flicked a switch on the wall, igniting the fireplace.

Waverly walked to a large, crushed velvet sofa and sat, staring blindly at the fire.

"How long have you had visions?" Viktor asked as he took a seat in an overstuffed chair.

"I don't know. Since I was younger," she confessed. "They started when I was ten. I really can't remember."

"Why didn't you tell me you were…sensitive?"

"Because I'm not."

"But you said you saw me just now," he pressed.

Waverly curled her feet under her, relaxing deeper into the large sofa. "I don't know what's happening. The visions. I had them when I was younger. But I've trained my mind to control it. I can touch anyone, anywhere, and nothing. Until you."

Viktor grew solemn. "What are you?"

"What do you mean, what am I?"

"Your scent," Viktor smiled. "It's discretely human."

Waverly wrinkled her nose at his description. "That's because I *am* human."

"A medium?" he guessed.

"I don't talk to dead people," she insisted.

"Do you want to?"

"No. Absolutely not. Are you kidding me right now?"

"A witch?"

"I'm human. Just a plain ole human woman. I know, it's probably not too exciting but it is what it is. The visions?" She blew out a breath. "When I was a kid I saw things, things that would happen. But then, you know, it scares you. You force it away. But you...you broke me. I've been seeing things ever since the night...when you touched me at the club. And tonight, just now, I saw you. And I don't know how I knew it but when you looked at me, you saw me too. Please tell me that was real."

"It's real. I felt you in my mind. It's not as if I can normally read other people's thoughts. But I do have an innate energy. I can often use it. When we flashed here, I can't explain how, I could just feel you. So I sent you pictures. It's all just energy."

"But how is this happening?"

"It's my belief that paths cross for a reason." Viktor extended his hand to her. She glanced at it and slowly reached for him. He blocked her from his mind but allowed his energy to flow to her. "Can you feel this?"

"I...yes. I'm not seeing anything though."

"That feeling right there...it's the magick."

"I don't have magick," she insisted.

"We all do. Every person has magick. Even humans. Life itself is magical, is it not?" he mused.

"Yes, but there's nothing magical about me. It's true I used to have visions, sometimes. I was like a jacked-up psychic hotline. But it's been shut down and out of business. These days? I'm just another human."

"You are so much more, love. You're the very soul of life. Like any other creature, you control the universe. But humans…" *They're fragile.* Long ago he'd learned the painful lesson. He'd forced himself to see them only as food, else suffer the infinite grief of losing them. "What makes humans special is the very essence of their soul. But life here on Earth is fleeting. Once it's gone, it's gone."

"I'm not fragile, but I don't think there's any magick. Seriously, I'm just a human."

Viktor took a deep breath, reminding himself that Waverly, too, would die. "You have magick in you, Waverly. Perhaps far more than you even realize yourself. But it's there."

"Maybe," she reluctantly agreed. "But it's not going to help me find Teagan. Or find whoever did that to my apartment. Why would someone want to shoot me?"

"I have someone who might be able to help us. Here in New Orleans."

"Tonight?" Waverly unsuccessfully fought a yawn.

"Tomorrow." Viktor backed away from Waverly, her delicious scent calling to him. "You must be hungry."

"I guess. Where did you say we were again?"

"Slidell, Louisiana. Like you, I've always fancied living near the water. Close enough to New Orleans but away from the noise of the city."

"You don't like cities?" She gave a small smile. "The French Quarter seems like it would suit you."

"Depends on the city. I do have a condo in the Quarter. But I prefer the seclusion of the lake right now. It's secure. Isolated."

"What happened at the museum? The detective. She'd changed. I mean physically...she was a monster."

"My guess is full possession. So, we've got that going for us."

"How's that?"

"Demons that have managed to break free of Hell are more dangerous than weaker ones who need humans. Whatever was going on with the poor detective...well, she's going to need an intervention."

"An exorcism? Is that a real thing?"

"Yes, and that would be a good place to start," Viktor agreed.

"I can't believe that happened to her. Do you think we should call the police? I mean we just skipped out."

"No. I'm going to put in a text to PCAP. It's time to put an end to this nonsense." He pulled out his cell phone and began pecking at the glass.

"What's PCAP?"

"Think of it as a woo-woo FBI. If it's paranormal, they handle it. Humans can't handle the shit that goes down in our world. Bullets don't kill supernaturals." He shrugged. "Unless it's silver or wooden. But regular bullets are merely a nuisance."

"I know there are humans like Teagan that want to get bitten, make a choice to go to blood clubs, but I swear I don't do that. I'm not sure why it's important for me to keep telling you. But I've never been bitten." Waverly's fingers trailed down her neck.

"As I said, you just needed to meet the right vampire."

"Maybe," she hedged, the corner of her mouth tugging upward.

"Ah, progress!" Viktor declared in victory, his voice light-hearted. "It's good you're finally coming to acceptance. I'm irresistible."

"You're impossible." Waverly flashed a flirty smile but quickly averted her gaze and fiddled with her hair.

Viktor smiled at the human on his sofa, his chest tight with emotion. Despite the recent unfortunate events, Waverly proved resilient, perhaps unfazed to an extent, that he'd dematerialized them to his home. Beautiful and determined, she challenged his own rule not to date them. *Fuck them? Yes. Friends? No. Girlfriend? Absolutely not. Love? Hell to the no.*

Yet here she was. Sitting in his home, no less. And he couldn't bring himself to let her go.

Her delicious scent grew stronger. His attraction to the beautiful human was too far gone; he struggled to control the thirst. The feelings creeping in threw him off kilter, an unfamiliar craving only she could sate. Hunger gnawed at his gut. If she'd been any other donor, he'd have bitten her by now. *But she isn't a donor.*

"I've got to go." Viktor took a deep breath, attempting to rein in his appetite.

"What? Where are you going?" she asked, her voice laced in disappointment as she pressed to her feet and walked toward him.

"I've got to feed." Viktor settled on the truth.

"You're going back to one of those blood clubs?" Her expression fell flat.

"I have a regular donor here in the city. She's…" Viktor inwardly cursed, not expecting to have this conversation with her. Regrettably this was who he was. He couldn't expect her to fully understand. "There are professionals. It's simply business."

"She's a woman? Will you have sex with her?" Waverly bit her lip. "I'm sorry, it's none of my business."

"I'm vampire. This is a part of my existence." Viktor scrubbed his fingers through his perfectly coiffed hair.

"Donors are donors. Some are male. Some are female. It's of no consequence to me. Human blood is blood. Sometimes I throw in a witch or wolf for variety. And no, I don't always have sex."

"I'm sorry. It's none of my business. I shouldn't have asked." She averted her gaze.

"Waverly." His fingers brushed her cheek, magick danced through his palm. Desire burned as she lifted her gaze to meet his.

"It's okay," she whispered, her hand brushing his chest.

Heat sizzled between them as Viktor gave in to his true craving. His mouth crushed upon hers, tasting, seeking the beautiful human that had divinely entered his life. Her energy threaded through him as if he'd become one with her, his soul demanding more. As her body molded to his, hunger spiked. He tore his mouth from hers, moving to her neck.

She moaned as his lips brushed her ear. Losing control, his fangs dropped, nearly nicking her neck. *Do it. Bite her,* temptation whispered.

"Viktor," she breathed, her body writhing against his rock-hard erection.

His fangs hovered above her delicate skin, her pulse beckoning him to taste her. As her delicious scent enticed him, his erection pressed tight to her hip. Their magnetic energy intertwined, urging him to bite her.

Viktor retracted his fangs and reluctantly pulled away from her. "I should go."

"What? I shouldn't have—" Waverly panted, steadying herself.

"I'm sorry," Viktor apologized. Though drawn to her, he didn't move to touch her.

"No, it's fine." She blinked, averting her gaze, attempting to conceal the rejection. "It shouldn't have happened."

"I'll bring you back something to eat," he responded

without disputing her. Perhaps she was right. His utter lack of self-control was driving him mad. Pure lust for a human that didn't like vampires had been one of the single most asinine things he'd engaged in in his lifetime. "Are you okay?"

"I said I'm fine," she bit out, turning toward the windows.

"Don't go anywhere. The house is protected by wards, but I can't help you should you decide to leave." Viktor knew full well she couldn't escape the gates or the magick. "My property is safe from everything."

"Everything? You mean like what we just ran from in the museum?"

"Yes. The possessed. Demons. Witches." *Fucking hell.* Who knew what the hell else might be after her? "I'll be back in an hour. Don't leave."

Viktor and Waverly exchanged a heated stare, the room still thick with frustration and desire. It took every ounce of self-discipline to leave, but if he stayed one minute longer, both his fangs and his cock would be deep inside the gorgeous Dr. LaFleur.

"Hello, brother." Viktor glanced up at Quintus and sipped his blood, not quite satisfied.

"So, you just left her?" His brother gave him an amused smile and shook his head.

"Yep. I had no choice," Viktor replied with a tone of regret. Nothing would sate him but Waverly.

"And the wolf? Your son." His brother laughed.

"He's with Jake. It's only been a day. He'll be fine for a while. I'll get him soon. I just need a minute."

"You sure that's a good idea?"

"He shows good control. He's got to get back with pack. The full moon is upon us."

"What does Hunter think of this?"

"He agrees. Rafe needs time away from his own pack. He's no longer pure wolf. This is better for him. He can get lost in California. Go surfing."

"You're serious?" Quintus laughed.

"The wolf will find his way back to pack or he won't." Viktor circled his finger around the rim of the glass.

"You think he'll go rogue?" Quintus raised a curious eyebrow at him.

"Perhaps." Rafe had already insinuated as much. Viktor swallowed his guilt with another gulp of blood. "Finding brotherhood within the pack will be difficult. He's no longer like them."

"But he is a wolf. He shifts," Quintus explained.

"He's far superior to a simple wolf. He's a miracle. A gift from the Goddess if you will." Viktor looked to Quintus, who stood behind the bar, and laughed. "Or a curse. Whichever, no matter. What matters is that he is vampire. He carries the blood of an ancient in his veins. He will grow stronger, faster than any other wolf."

"He'll best any Alpha, but without an established pack, he'd be forced to fight. It could be a disaster."

"He won't fight. Not yet anyway."

"How do you mean?"

"It means he knows how to fight as wolf. But not as vampire. Regardless, he's going to need a mentor of the lupine nature. Someone who can keep him in line. Help him while he gets adjusted."

"You should go to Yellowstone. Go stay with Hunter," Quintus suggested.

"Do you seriously think I plan on running all over Wyoming? In the forest? During winter?" He gestured to his red, crocodile leather loafers. "Steffano Ricci. I've already ruined enough pairs of shoes lately. I've spent a fortune."

"Jesus fucking Christ, you're something else." Quintus shook his head and laughed.

"Just stop already. You know it's not happening." Viktor held up a dismissive hand. "Does running through mud in the forest with a bunch of dogs sound like something I'd be interested in? No fucking way. I'm going back to Miami."

"He's going to need guidance," Quintus told him.

"I think I've got just the person to help me. Hunter's mate has a brother who's rogue. Julian. The wolf is decent. I'll simply make it happen."

"Have you discussed this with him?"

"No, but I will. Eventually." Viktor sipped his blood. "I've got bigger issues at the moment."

"The art dealer?"

"She's the head curator at one of the finest art museums in southern California. She's smart. Funny." Viktor's thoughts drifted to Waverly and he smiled, the scent of her still fresh in his mind.

"Attractive?" Quintus asked with a knowing grin.

"She's a surfer. You should see her ride the waves."

"Athletic, is she? I'm guessing a wave isn't the only thing you'd like to see her ride."

"She made me eggs," he confessed with a smile, ignoring Quintus.

"Eggs?" Quintus slapped the granite counter and laughed. "You ate human food? For real?"

Viktor gave a small chuckle and glanced to Quintus. "Yeah, yeah I did."

"This human. You've tasted her?"

"I have, but only to seal a wound." Viktor smiled, recalling the taste of his lovely human. "She's delicious."

"But you haven't bitten her?"

"No." He wouldn't ask her. He'd told her she'd beg for it, and he meant it.

"May I suggest you fuck her and then leave her be," Quintus advised. "PCAP is involved. They don't need you."

Viktor glared at his brother. "*She* needs me. That's all that matters."

"She will be fine," he replied.

"A bloody sacrifice was left in her home. I hardly think that's safe."

"Let me see. You care for the human, yet you have not bitten her or bedded her?" he mused, his voice smug. "And you ate her food." Quintus shook his head with a tight smile. "This is trouble."

"Well, I attempted to cook for her, but it didn't go very well."

"Hold up. You cooked? You? Viktor Christianson?" Quintus laughed.

"It's the effort that counts."

"Where is my brother? You must be an imposter," he joked. "Ah, Viktor, my oldest, favorite brother, I'm beginning to have suspicions about this human...she could be tied to you."

"Don't be ridiculous," Viktor chided, secretly suspecting the same.

"You ate eggs." Quintus shook his head with a smile and poured a cognac. "No wonder you sent your donor running. This is all making sense now."

"Can we stop focusing on me? I need your help," Viktor told him, attempting to change the subject.

"Oh, I suspect you're going to get all the help you need from the human."

"Be serious, brother. I'm perpetually single and enjoying every minute of it. Listen. I've got a painting. I've seen a similar piece once, a long time ago, but if I could only have someone else take a look at it for me. Someone who knows art. Someone who knows about the doings of the church."

"No." Quintus tapped at the face of his cell phone, not looking up at him.

"Greyson dabbled around the church for a time. If you could just reach out."

"I'm not doing it."

"He was no stranger to the nuns," Viktor continued.

"They protected him."

"This painting. I suspect it's an original Plautilla Nelli. I'd like to have him look at it."

"The woman is a curator, right? Let her look at it."

"She is, but—"

"Then why do you need Greyson? You know he's still angry with you." Quintus laughed.

Viktor tilted his head, recalling the incident. "It wasn't my fault."

"You were drunk. Drunk as a skunk," Quintus alleged.

"Young Edward was a right chap. I did him a favor," Viktor claimed.

"By letting him know his fiancée was doing more than praying with Greyson?"

"She was on her knees." A smile formed on Viktor's lips. "The way I see it she was most certainly worshipping something."

"I believe he's still angry," Quintus informed him.

"He should be grateful. We both know that no matter how infatuated he was with the lass, they couldn't bond. She didn't belong to him except to sate his thirst and his dick. I did what any brother should do. I did him a favor by nipping problems in the bud. One day he'll meet the one woman for him, but we all know it wasn't her."

"I agree, but he doesn't see it that way."

"I need his help, so he'd better get over it." Lady Chadwick was better off without Edward or Greyson. Baxter would have killed her the second he discovered his brother fancied her. Their brutal master had killed everyone they'd ever cared about, taking pleasure in torturing every one of the children he sired.

Viktor stood and set the glass on the table. "I need this favor, Quint. Contact him and tell him to meet me at my place."

Quintus released an audible sigh, shaking his head. "I will try. But I can't promise you anything."

"Where is he, anyway?"

"Last I heard he was restoring a castle in Romania."

"Well then, he should need a break from his project. I'm sure he's got plenty of time to pop over for a chat."

"Grudges die hard." Quintus eyed the empty glass. "Do you need another donor?"

"No, this blood will do," Viktor insisted, still craving the one human he could not have.

"It's been some time since I've taken a donor myself...now that I'm bonded it's not necessary."

"Well, I'm not bonded. And it has worked well my entire immortal life and I don't intend on changing."

"How do you know this human isn't yours?" Quintus asked, with a playful curiosity.

"I don't want to talk about it," Viktor replied.

"The hunger will grow. There will be no other who can satisfy you. This is how it works. The Goddess—"

"Don't bring her into it. The Goddess knows what I like just fine. I don't do relationships. Especially not with humans. It's pointless."

"You didn't do food either, but apparently you've eaten eggs." Quintus smiled knowingly.

"It's complicated." Viktor went silent and rubbed his hands together, recalling her energy. "*She's* complicated."

"This is going to be entertaining to watch."

Viktor grumbled as he strode across the room and stared

into a large round metal mirror that hung in Quintus' study. He smoothed back his hair, attempting to appear nonchalant. "I'm going to help Dr. LaFleur stop whoever is threatening her. I'm not sure what they want with this painting, but I'm going to find out and put an end to the nonsense. I don't care if humans are responsible or not."

"Humans?"

"Yes, I believe some are involved. Paranormals too. Someone left a parting gift in her apartment. A ritual of some sort. You know how it goes, it's all fun and games until you conjure a demon you can't control. I've caught the scent both in Miami and San Diego."

"Humans should be easy to track down."

"The demons could cause issues," Viktor countered. "One of her human friends is missing. And we've got this painting to deal with. At the museum, a detective was asking questions one minute and beating down an office door the next. Possessed." He sighed. "It's all a bit of a mystery at the moment. But I'm sure that painting has something to do with it."

"You may need help. Perhaps Kellen has information."

"The fae?" Viktor gave a curt laugh. "As if. He's in Hell kissing Satan's ass, just sitting there like a sticky charred marshmallow."

"The high priestess? Samantha," he specified.

"At some point, but right now, I think it's best to talk to someone who knows demons."

"Who then?" Quintus asked.

"A demon who owes me." Viktor checked his appearance one last time before turning back to his brother. "A demon who loves to socialize, who has his pulse on both demons and humans, Hell and Earth."

"Thorn," they both said in unison.

"You know it." Viktor nodded at Quintus, knowing what

he had to do. Sometimes you had to lay down in the mud to get the dirty details.

~

VIKTOR APPEARED in his kitchen and set down the takeout he'd bought for Waverly. He listened for her but heard nothing but silence. *I shouldn't have left her so long.* He inhaled, detecting her delicious scent. Although it still lingered in the air, she'd been gone from the room for hours.

Drawn to a flickering light outside, he moved to look out the floor-to-ceiling window that lined the back of his home. At the sight of her outside in the yard, his pulse sped. Wearing his red satin robe, she walked barefoot along the patio toward the pool. *What is she doing outside? In my robe?* The temptation from earlier in the evening haunted him, the taste of her lips still burning fresh on his.

Viktor stood in the darkness watching her through the window as she reached for a switch on the table and fired up the lights around the jacuzzi. A circle of fire roared to life in the center of the table, reggae music sounding into the night. Viktor's heart pounded as she turned to the lake, and slowly removed the robe. Slow as molasses, the crimson fabric fell from her shoulders and revealed her tanned skin. Her blonde hair spilled down her back, teasing her full bottom. She draped the robe onto a chair and faced the home once again. Bared to him, she stood nude and stared up to the second floor, smiling as if she knew he could see her.

Viktor took a step back, laser focused on Waverly. *She sees me?* It was impossible, yet his instincts warned him that she sensed his presence. His excitement spiked. She knew he watched yet exposed herself, her vulnerability. As she dipped a foot into the hot tub and descended into the water, he sensed her energy.

Resisting temptation had never been his strong suit. As Viktor dematerialized and his feet hit the ground, he wore a sensual smile.

"Are you stalking me?" she asked, her voice calm and even.

Like the predator he was, Viktor strode around the edge of the pool with the air of confidence he always wore. Through the billowing steam, Waverly came into view, her eyes closed, the bubbles teasing over her breasts.

"Tell me, how does a human see me, feel me?" he asked.

"I'm not sure what you think I do." She flashed open her eyes, pinning him with a stare.

"I've never met a human like you," he confessed.

"Humans have instincts too. Like the humans you saw tonight?" She quickly concealed the jealousy that shone in her eyes.

"I wasn't *with* humans tonight. It's not what you think."

"But you fed?" She averted her gaze. "Did you go to one of those clubs? Like Miami?"

"No." Viktor shook his head with a smile, amused by her jealousy. If she only knew that she was the only person on his mind. She was quickly turning into a delicious obsession.

"You had blood? You bit someone?"

"Indeed, I had blood. But my donor, who happened to be male, procured the blood for me." Viktor removed his suit jacket, folded it and set it on the chaise longue. "I've brought you food. You must be starving."

"I'm okay. I, uh, poked around in your kitchen. I found a few things in your freezer."

"Ah, yes. I'd forgotten about the dreadful meals Rafe insisted on."

"It's macaroni and cheese. It wasn't bad." She shrugged.

"I have proper food for you upstairs. I can go get it. I just wanted to—" See you. Touch you. Taste you. "Make sure you were okay. I know today was rough."

"I'm better." She sighed. "I'm sorry for asking about the blood. It's none of my business. You must eat too. It's not like I'm giving you my blood, so..." For the first time, she hinted at a smile. "You have a beautiful home. I saw the pool and I couldn't resist. Borrowed your robe. Hope you don't mind?"

"Of course not." Viktor sat on a cushioned ottoman. "The house works for me. I love the water. New Orleans. I'm close to town but not in the city."

"I got the impression that you liked Miami."

"It's a different city."

"What do you mean?"

"Houses are like pairs of shoes," Viktor removed his leather shoes and set them aside. "Different ones for different situations. New Orleans is a beautiful city, but I prefer the lake most nights."

"But of course you do," she laughed. "Well, Mr. Christianson, it's a beautiful home. I especially like this hot tub."

"It's beautiful because you're in it. Dr. LaFleur, do you mind if I join you?" Viktor's mind spun as the words left his mouth. *What the actual fuck? I'm a vampire. I don't ask in my own home. Yet I just did.* This human had turned his world upside down.

"Sure. Why not?" She sighed with a small laugh. "It's been a hell of a week. My friend is missing. I almost got killed. Someone put a dead animal in my apartment. A demon attacked us in my office. And I split into a million atoms, was put back together and now I'm sitting in a hot tub. And a handsome vampire is joining me. Could be worse."

Viktor made quick work of removing his clothes. As he turned, he caught her stealing a glimpse of his half-hard cock, which hung heavy between his legs.

"Ah but we're just friends," he said as he eased into the hot water.

She locked her eyes onto his.

"What happened earlier…we shouldn't have." Her cheeks flushed. She dipped further into the water almost as if she wanted to shrink from the conversation.

"But we did." Viktor's leg brushed against hers.

Waverly froze, her heated gaze settling on the vampire. "I shouldn't get involved with you."

"But you are." His arousal spiked. Although tempted to move toward her, to kiss her, he resisted.

"You're dangerous," she challenged.

"I am." There was no denying the obvious.

"I don't understand what's happening to me," she confessed, inching closer to him. "What's happening between us. I don't date vampires."

"I don't date anyone." Viktor closed the distance between them, his hands falling to her bared hips. "But I find myself reconsidering."

"We shouldn't do this." Her fingers brushed his chest.

"We definitely shouldn't." Viktor's lips hovered within inches of hers.

"I can't explain this…how I feel," she breathed, sliding her hands up his chest. "What are we doing?"

"This." Viktor released his inhibitions, his lips crushing hers.

"Viktor," she moaned.

More than lust, emotion swirled inside him as he kissed her. Her honeyed lips brushed his, and Viktor took her in his arms, lifting her onto his lap.

He tore his mouth from hers, peppering kisses down her neck. She cried out as he took a nipple between his lips, sucking and flicking his tongue over its tip. She took his cock into her hands and gave him a firm stroke. His dick hardened and he resisted slamming inside her, reveling in the slow delicious torture.

"Please, I need you in me now," she cried.

"Waverly—" His fingers traveled down her stomach and he slid a finger into her slick pussy.

"Yes," she managed through a ragged breath.

Viktor flicked his thumb over her swollen nub and added another finger inside her tight channel. As he released her taut tip, his mouth captured hers. Relentlessly, he fucked her pussy with his fingers, drowning her with his kiss.

"Please," she begged, shivering with arousal under his touch.

"Do you want me to fuck you, my sweet little pet?"

"Yes, don't stop. I'm so…" Waverly breathed, her body writhing into his hand as he continued to pump his fingers inside her. With a slow torture, he put pressure onto her clitoris, edging her closer to orgasm. She released him, her fingernails digging into his shoulders as she clutched him, tilting into his hand.

"I'm going to have all of you," he warned. Viktor reached around her bottom, his fingers trailed down the crevice of her ass.

"Oh God…I…" Waverly broke apart with a cry, her climax shattering through her as his fingers circled her tight hole.

Water dripped from their bodies as he stood and lifted her out of the hot tub. Within seconds he'd flashed them to his bedroom, laid her back onto his bed and settled between her legs.

"I need you in me," she whispered, her arms wrapped around his neck.

Viktor locked his eyes on hers as he pressed the tip of his cock to her entrance, slowly teasing her. Instinct warned him that once they made love, he'd never be able to let her go, but desire burned hot. He looked deep into her eyes and gave in to the temptation that had haunted him for days.

"You're beautiful," he told her, guiding his cock inside her. As her pussy tightened around him, he stilled, the urge to come inside her already beckoning.

"Fuck." He filled her to the hilt, going slowly, as she adjusted to his thick shaft.

"I...I..." Waverly arched her back and tilted her hips.

Viktor pressed his lips to hers, devouring her with a feverish frenzy, kissing her, tasting. The urge to sink his fangs into her sweet flesh called to him. Though he attempted to restrain his nature, the wild beast in him would have its due.

"On your knees, pet." He removed himself and flipped her on her stomach.

"Oh God," she cried, unaware of the animal that she'd unleashed in him.

As his cock slammed inside her, her pussy contracted around him. With each deep thrust, she cried out, begging him for more.

"Harder, harder, I'm going to..." Waverly clutched the sheets, her head lolling forward.

As he held her hips, she rocked back toward him, his cock deep inside her. His thumb teased her bottom, circling her puckered skin, and she shattered into her climax.

"Yes, yes," she screamed.

Viktor lost control as her pussy quivered around his dick. His fangs dropped, the craving for her blood near impossible to resist. His lips found her shoulder, his tongue swiped over her skin.

Don't bite her. Viktor battled his thirst for the gorgeous woman beneath him. He slammed into her, again and again, turning his head, careful not to nick her skin.

As the waves of her orgasm slammed into her, her pussy

tightened around his shaft, milking him. With a final thrust, Viktor abandoned his restraint, exploding deep inside her. He stiffened in release, giving a loud groan of satisfaction.

Panting for breath, his head spun with the consequences of what he'd done. Never in his life had he restrained his thirst, yet he wouldn't bite without her begging, without her consent. A spark ignited in his humanity, controlling the monster he'd long embraced.

CHAPTER SIX

*W*averly curled onto her side, lost in thought. A nagging warning reminded her Viktor was a lethal predator, but she promptly brushed it away. Everything about making love to Viktor changed what she thought she wanted. She'd deliberately separated her world from the paranormal, had hidden her own abilities. Yet within Viktor's arms, for the first time, she'd experienced acceptance. He stimulated her mind and body, unrelenting, pushing her into a new paradigm.

A kiss to her bare shoulder brought a smile to her lips. Warmth stirred in her chest. *Don't catch feelings. Don't catch feelings. Too damn late.*

"Are you hungry?" His arms still wrapped around her waist, he spooned her from behind.

"Hmm...for what?" she softly laughed.

"This." Without warning, he rolled her onto her back, pinning her arms to the bed. She smiled, raising her dreamy gaze to Viktor's. Her chest caught with anticipation at the sight of the domineering vampire giving her a hungry grin as if he'd devour her.

"You have no idea how much I'd like to have a repeat performance."

"Maybe I'll eat you." Waverly teased, her body still ripe with arousal.

"You're not afraid?" Viktor asked.

"You won't hurt me." *But he could break my heart. I told you not to catch feelings.*

"I'm dangerous."

"Are you trying to scare me away?" *Does he regret making love?*

"Perhaps you were right about vampires?"

"No, I think…" Her breath quickened as his erection hardened between her legs. Waverly tilted her pelvis, his cock brushing against her thigh. "I'm finding you hard to resist."

"You don't know me, pet. What you saw at the club. That's who I really am."

Waverly gasped as his fangs dropped, terror and arousal pulsing through her. She tugged her arm loose and reached for his face, cupping his cheek. Her heart pounded, imagining his fangs slicing into her flesh as her gaze fell to his mouth. Stirred with curiosity, she brushed the pad of her thumb over his lower lip.

"I'm sorry. I should have asked." As she withdrew her hand, her thumb caught on his fang. "Ow."

Before she had a chance to say another word, he'd caught her wrist, his tongue darting over the wound. He sucked her thumb between his lips, setting her body on fire with desire.

"Viktor…" she panted. Visions of him over the centuries flashed through her mind. A child hauling water on his back, shivering in the snow. A Viking warrior. Beaten and bloody on his knees, a slave to a cruel and violent master. A wealthy lord. A prisoner in the fiery pits of Hell. A playboy in the hottest club in Miami, surrounded by beautiful women.

As the vision faded into darkness, he released her. *What is happening to me?* Waverly blinked, her breath ragged as Viktor rolled off the bed onto his feet. Disappointment tore through her.

"Where are you going?" She reached for the sheet, hoping to conceal her shock.

"Be right back." Viktor strode out of the room naked as the day he was born.

Waverly took a deep breath and pulled the sheets up to her neck. *Why do I keep seeing him in my visions? That thing he did with my finger. What was that? Is that what would happen if he bit me?* Warmth pooled between her legs. *No, no, no. Stop it girl. He's gone already. He didn't bite you. You aren't supposed to be with vampires.*

She rolled onto her side and her stomach growled. Waverly laughed inwardly at herself. In just over twenty-four hours she'd been shot at, attacked by a demon, had her apartment desecrated by a bloody ritual, made love to a vampire, and she was as human as ever. Sated by sex but starving.

She sensed Viktor's presence before she saw him. Not hearing even one footstep, she assumed he'd done his vampire thing, reappearing out of thin air. She laughed at the thought of it, refusing to think about the reality of the situation.

The scent of food filled the air and she rolled over, taking in the beautiful sight of him. With the body of a Greek god, tanned and hot as fuck, he strode across the room, exuding confidence and sexual magnetism. From his broad, muscular chest to his ripped abs, his physique outrivaled any of the thousand fitness enthusiasts she'd witnessed working out on the beach in San Diego.

Without a stitch of clothing, he winked at her and placed a large gold tray onto the coffee table. "Come eat."

Viktor reached for an open bottle of red wine and poured

it into a large, royal blue goblet. He set it down and reached for a crystal decanter. As he poured the crimson liquid into the second glass, Waverly assumed it to be blood.

Viktor reached for a throw blanket, spreading it onto the large black sofa, creating the perfect picnic. Waverly tugged a silk sheet from the bed and wrapped it around her body and then slid onto the couch.

"Voilà. Human food." He set a plate in front of her, placed the food onto it and gestured to the table.

"Po Boys?" Her mouth watered at the sight of the delicious sandwiches, brimming with shrimp.

"Yes, cher," he replied in his best Cajun accent. Viktor reached for a second throw blanket and made quick work of wrapping it around his hips. He reached for a goblet, extending it to her. "Come now, eat something. I plan to take care of my lovely human as if she were a rare flower. I shall make love to her, water and feed her."

"A flower?" She laughed as she accepted the glass, examining the unique golden stem that had been molded in the shape of a nude woman. "This is, um, interesting. I've never seen wine glasses like these."

"Yes. It's a set. Adam and Eve and whatnot. Fit to hold the forbidden fruit."

"I thought that was an apple, not grapes."

"Apple. Grape. What's the difference really?"

"Quite a bit," she laughed.

"Do we really know it was an apple? Was anyone there? Only the Goddess knows." He held his glass up to her in a toast. "To the most enchanting human I've ever met."

"I'm sure that can't be true."

"You most certainly are. I've never met anyone like you."

"Well, you're the most intriguing vampire I know." Waverly melted inside, her cheeks flushing. "I think it's safe to say you were right…we're more than friends."

"Lovers," he corrected.

"Lovers," she repeated in a whisper as she brought the rim to her lips, attempting to conceal her blooming feelings. Dark tones of cherry and chocolate danced over her tongue. She moaned in delight. "Merlot?"

"Pinot Noir."

"What are you drinking?" Waverly regretted the question as soon as she asked. *What is wrong with you? The man needs to eat. It doesn't matter, it doesn't matter.*

Viktor smiled. "I'm having blood. Nourishing, I assure you. But I'll share your wine if it's an issue."

"What happens if you don't drink it?" She inwardly cringed realizing she probably shouldn't ask him details, but curiosity won over manners. "I'm sorry. It's—"

"I weaken. Just as you would if you didn't drink water or eat food. The life blood sustains the magick of our species. Some of us can sustain ourselves using wolf blood. It's rare but happens. Same with witches. Luca. He's in my brother's line. He married a witch." Viktor glanced to her sandwich and changed the subject. "You need to eat."

"I'm sorry, yes. I'm starving."

"One's roast beef. One's shrimp. I wasn't sure what you'd like."

"Both are perfect, thank you. This looks amazing." She reached for the shrimp po boy, attempting to eat gracefully. As she brought it to her mouth and bit into it, she moaned, the delightful flavors dancing over her tongue. "Hmm...this is delicious."

"I go to this little place down in the Business district. Rafe likes it." Viktor handed her a black linen napkin, which she accepted.

"How long has Rafe been with you?"

"A few months." Viktor glanced at his glass. "I don't have any other children in my line. It's never been my thing. But the wolf...he'd been injured during a fight. Long story short. He's alive but he's hybrid. And he's my responsibility now."

Waverly nodded without asking any other questions and took another bite of her food. Although she wondered how he was turned, she didn't want to pry any further. After a few awkward minutes of silence, she glanced up to find him staring at her. "I'm sorry I'm stuffing my face." She laughed, embarrassed.

He smiled. "It's fine. Please eat."

"Do you want some? I know you don't usually eat food, but—"

"I'm fine with this." He lifted his glass to her.

Waverly gave a small smile. How long had it been since Viktor had given up on humans, on his own humanity? "I would love it if you ate with me."

She turned toward him, crossing her legs underneath her. She glanced at the po boy then to him. "It's just...well, I don't know if you remember. But eating a meal with someone. Sharing. It's more than just sustenance. It brings people together. It's family. It's intimacy."

Viktor shrugged. "Do you have any idea how long I've lived like this?"

"I've seen you...in my visions," she whispered.

"Tell me, pet. What do you see?" He raised an eyebrow at her.

"I saw everything." Waverly licked her lips, her voice shaking. "It's been such a long time since I've had visions. They were blocked. But with you, it's like they pour into my head. It's as if I'm flipping through a photo album one minute with snippets of audio and video. When it first happened to me, I was really freaked out. But the more it happens with you, the more I'm getting used to it. I can't explain it. It's like I'm seeing you without being there. It makes me feel closer to you."

"And you wanted this? To feel closer?"

"You know I didn't, at first. But now? I've never felt like this. And I don't know what *this* is. I just know that I'm not scared of you. I know I said I'd never see a vampire but—"

"Date a vampire. You said you'd never *date* a vampire." He chuckled.

"I don't know if what we are doing would qualify to be called dating. But what we just did...it was amazing." A broad smile broke across her face. "And it made me feel good. And I want to do it again. But I also want you to—"

"Eat with you?"

"It's stupid. Forget it."

"My lovely Waverly. You're not stupid. What you are is human." He smiled with a nod and reached for her wrist. With his gaze locked on hers, Viktor slowly brought the food to his mouth, bit down and licked his lips. "Tasty, indeed."

Waverly's body heated in arousal. He literally just took a bite of her sandwich, and she was ready to throw him on the sofa. *Why was he so damn sexy?*

Her mind raced as they sat in silence eating. If he could bite a sandwich like that, she wondered what it would be like for him to lick her pussy and eat her. Desire rushed through her at the thought of his fangs sinking into her flesh.

Waverly averted her gaze, not quite certain the powerful vampire couldn't read her thoughts. Never in her life had she considered making love to a vampire, let alone allowing one to bite her. Yet his kiss burned hot on her lips and the idea of him being with another woman for any reason, to feed or fuck her, speared jealousy through her gut.

None of it made sense but in the moments of their intimate encounters, it didn't matter. The craving grew stronger. Prior-held beliefs slipped from her fingers.

She wiped her mouth with the napkin and leaned back on

the sofa. Sated by food but starving for his touch, her body tensed with arousal as he shot her a wicked smile.

"Dessert?" he asked with a grin as wide as the Cheshire cat.

"You're hungry?" She watched with interest as he reached for a paper bag.

A flirty smile broke across her face as the sexier-than-sin vampire held up a white powdered pastry. With the small throw blanket barely hanging onto his hips, he leaned toward her.

"I'm ravenous." His tongue slid over his lips. "Now that you've got me eating food, perhaps I can interest you in my way of life."

"Perhaps," she whispered, her pulse racing at the thought.

Waverly's heart pounded in her chest as Viktor leaned over her, teasing her lips with the sugary treat. Her tongue darted out, stealing a taste of sweetness. He dipped the beignet between her lips so she could bite into the delicious pastry. Waverly moaned with pleasure, slightly shifting underneath him, her body heated with arousal.

"I don't think I've ever met such a beautiful woman." His intense gaze burned through her.

"Viktor, I—'

He silenced her words, his lips pressed to hers. Waverly kissed him back, her palms sliding up his chest until her hands wrapped behind his neck. With her fingers tunneled into his hair, she completely let go, losing herself in his devastating kiss.

"Viktor," she cried as he peppered kisses down her shoulder. The thought of his fangs slicing into her skin, with him deep inside her, flashed in her mind. *Beg him.* It was the only way he'd bite her.

Waverly arched her back as he tore the sheets open exposing her flesh, his mouth traveling over her collarbone and down her chest. His lips brushed over her nipple, and she released a gentle sigh as his tongue swirled around its tip.

She teased her fingers through his hair as he settled between her legs. Her body exposed to him, every nerve in her body was on alert. His warm breath teased her thigh, sending desire threading through her entire body.

His palm brushed over her mound and she tensed, desperately seeking his touch.

"Mo chroí. It's time for my dessert," he growled.

A shiver ran through her as he dragged his tongue over her clit. She clutched the sofa as his thumb stroked through her wet folds.

"Viktor," she cried as he drove a finger deep inside her.

She writhed in pleasure, her breath ragged. He sucked her swollen bead into his mouth, plunging his fingers in and out of her pussy. Waverly wanted so badly to restrain her release but as he curled his finger inside her, teasing her sensitive strip of nerves, she lost control.

Her hips bucked up into his face, her fingers tunneling through his hair. She screamed, seized by a rush of sheer ecstasy. Her body shook in release, gasping for breath as the waves of orgasm rippled through her.

Waverly's mind spun in confusion, her body still tingling from her climax. As Viktor moved upward to kiss her, her pulse raced. She wanted him to take her in every possible way, to devour her body, her blood. The sight of his fangs hidden behind his sexy smile, terrified and excited her all at once. She couldn't deny her dark desire, the yearning to give herself to him.

"Viktor...I want you...please—" she gasped as his erection pressed between her legs. "Bite me...I—"

A stranger's voice boomed from the hallway. Waverly froze in shock, her attention drawn to a large man staring at them from the doorway.

"Get out," Viktor growled, promptly covering her with the sheet.

"She's a fine one. Perhaps you'll share?" The ruggedly handsome vampire looked to Waverly, his fangs still bared. "I'm Greyson."

"No." Waverly defensively clutched the sheets to her chest.

In a flash, Viktor sprang off the sofa, crushing the stranger into the wall. "She's mine."

The man gave a hearty laugh in response. "Jesus Christ, Viktor. What the fuck is your problem? I'm just takin' the piss out of ya."

"Get out." Viktor shoved him toward the door and turned his back, waving him off. "I'll meet you downstairs."

"Lovely meeting you, bird." Greyson nodded to her.

"I'm sorry, love." Viktor stood in front of Waverly, protectively blocking her from the gruff vampire's view.

"You know him?" Her gazed burned with fire, both angry and terrified.

"Yes, yes I do." Viktor glared at Greyson.

The vampire eyed Waverly with curiosity and gave a sardonic laugh. "You brought a human to your home? Interesting."

"Out. Now!" Viktor yelled.

Waverly glanced to the knife that sat next to the food on the table. But as she looked back to the stranger, he'd disappeared. "What is happening?"

"It's all right. That's Greyson." Viktor returned to the sofa and sat next to her.

"Why is he here? In your house? In your bedroom?" she asked, her voice escalating.

Viktor lifted her wrist to his lips and brushed a kiss to the back of her hand. "I'm sorry."

At his touch, her body relaxed. She nodded, overwhelmed

with the calming sensation. She smiled. "How are you doing that?"

"What?" He winked.

"You know."

"Ah, at least some of my tricks seem to work with you." Viktor opened his mouth as if to continue but abruptly switched topics. "Greyson is my brother."

"Your brother? Wait. What is he doing here? Does he live in New Orleans?"

"So many questions, pet. To be honest, it's been years since I've seen him. I wasn't sure he'd come."

"You invited him here?" Her mouth gaped open in shock.

"Yes, I did invite him. I wasn't banking on him showing up but here he is. Pleasant as always." He shook his head. "I needed to see him."

"How did he get in your bedroom?"

"Yeah, that." He gave a tight smile. "I'm sorry."

Waverly flushed with the memory, still hungry for her vampire. His sultry gaze told her he was thinking the same.

He sighed. "As tempting as you are, I'd better get dressed before he grows impatient. He's already pissed at me, and I don't want to keep him waiting long."

"He's upset with you?" she asked.

"Ah, yes. Long story."

"Why did you ask him here?" Her mind swam with questions.

"To help with the painting. He's an expert of sorts. Once upon a time, he knew the nun's family. He most likely can verify its authenticity. Maybe give us insight as to why this thing is after you."

Viktor stood and crossed the room. He swung open the doors to a large black armoire and retrieved a pair of gray sweatpants, dressing as he continued. "He knows about the works that the church commissioned. Spent time at the Vatican as well."

"You don't look alike." The domineering vampire's dark curly hair was a stark contrast to Viktor's sleek blond mane.

"We weren't born to the same human mother, but we were sired by the same master. And we've spent hundreds of years together. We have saved each other more than once."

Waverly gave him a sympathetic smile. She'd seen the visions, the beatings. She couldn't take away his pain, only attempt to understand. *I'm sorry this happened to you.*

"No worries," he replied although she'd spoken no words.

"Sorry, what?" Waverly shot him a look of surprise. *Did he hear me?*

"I've survived all these years. It's going to be all right." Viktor moved toward her, reaching for her hand and pulling her to her feet. "I'll be downstairs. You can join us if you'd like. Don't rush. I have a few things to straighten out with him."

Waverly gave a closed smile as he brushed a kiss to her forehead. With her arms wrapped around him, safely in his embrace, she knew their time was fleeting.

CHAPTER SEVEN

*V*iktor steeled himself as he strode into the kitchen, avoiding the conversation that was hundreds of years overdue. Determined not to take the bait, he'd focus on the current issue at hand.

"Jesus, Vik. Don't you ever eat normal food?" Greyson commented, his back to Viktor as he rummaged through his refrigerator.

"You're a vampire. Blood is normal food," Viktor replied.

"Blah. There's nothing better than homemade Sarmale and Țuică." He slapped his hand on the outside of the appliance.

"We need to talk," Viktor began. His brother would test his last nerve, but he needed his help.

"What's with the lass? She must be a hellion in bed if you've brought her to your home." Greyson looked over his shoulder and shot him a devious smile. "Oh yeah. You got a live one in there."

Viktor took a deep breath, deliberately delaying his response. He tamped down his anger, refusing to allow his brother to draw him into a fight.

"With the way she was moaning, I'm surprised you hadn't bit her already. I'd tap that—"

"Waverly. Dr. Waverly LaFleur is her name. She's an art curator in San Diego." Viktor dragged his fingers through his messed hair.

"So, you're shagging her but not biting her? Interesting." Greyson threw a block of cheese onto the counter and began opening kitchen drawers.

"None of your business. On the counter next to the stove." Viktor sat at the kitchen bar staring at his brother. No worse for wear than he'd seen him years ago, he hadn't aged a minute. Save for the modern clothes he appeared the same as he had the last day they'd spoken.

"Thanks." Greyson withdrew a large chef's knife and waved it in the air.

"I need your help. *We*," Viktor corrected, "need your help."

"Quintus said as much," he grumbled. "All this time has gone by, and you call me when you need me."

"You spent time with the nuns. There's a piece here that appears authentic, but I'd like you to look at it for me. It's been altered."

"Why should I help you?' He shook his head and landed a swift blow to the cheese, cleaving it in half.

"I give you my word that once Waverly is safe, we'll have it out. I know we have our differences. But I need your full attention on this. Someone shot her at the museum. They've left a Satanic shit stain in her apartment. Demons may be involved but there's also a human element driving this. I don't know if it's a coordinated effort or not. This painting. Someone arranged for her to get it without providing ownership documentation. I want to know everything about the piece. Where it came from. Who could have had access to it? Why would they seek out Waverly? Why did they want her to have it?"

Viktor heard her before she walked into the room. His pulse raced at the sight of her standing in the kitchen in his robe. The fabric brushed her feet as she glided toward him.

"Waverly." Viktor smiled as he took her hand, bringing her protectively to his side. "I'd like to introduce you to my brother, Greyson."

"Dragavei. Greyson Dragavei." The imposing vampire extended his hand toward Waverly. "What a pleasure to meet you."

Viktor glared at his brother, cold as ice. As Waverly responded to shake his hand, Greyson captured it, kissing the back of it briefly. Viktor dropped his fangs, and Waverly jumped backward, tugging her hand away.

"Possessive of a human, my dear brother?" Greyson laughed and returned to slicing the cheese. "If I didn't know any better, I'd think you'd bonded."

Viktor retracted his fangs, the words hitting him like a stake in the heart. *Bonded?* In truth it wasn't as if the thought had not crossed his mind. From the second he met her, he'd gone out of his way to help her, to find her, protect her. Making love to her, he'd become obsessed with Dr. LaFleur, the craving to taste her lingering in the back of his mind at all moments. Had Greyson not interrupted, he'd have bitten her.

"Cat got your tongue?" Greyson laughed and shoved a piece of cheese in his mouth. "So, I guess you won't be sharing your human with me?"

"Let's get something straight. You touch her, I'll kill you. We're brothers but I won't tolerate your disrespect," Viktor bit out.

"Settle down. Despite what you did to *me*, I won't ruin your fun." Greyson turned to address Waverly. "Cheese?"

"No thank you," she responded.

"We need your help. The painting is—" Viktor began.

125

"It was given to me to evaluate. Someone first contacted me while I was in Miami," Waverly interjected, her voice calm but strong. "I'd gone there to look for a friend. She'd told me she was involved with a vampire group, and I was worried about her. I went to a blood club to look for her and well, I got into a bit of trouble. Your brother helped me and—"

"You met my brother at a blood club? How romantic." Greyson rolled his eyes, his tone dripping with sarcasm.

"Enough." Viktor pinned him with a glare.

"Before I'd left San Diego," Waverly continued, ignoring Greyson. "Teagan texted me about the club. Told me she was going there. But I'm not like that...I don't want to be bitten." Viktor's eyes met hers as the lie rolled off her tongue.

"Hmm." Greyson shrugged. "I'm not one to judge but you're looking pretty cozy with my bro."

"Stop," Viktor snapped, aware he'd awakened her desire to be bitten.

"Soon after I landed in Miami, an anonymous donor contacted me. I agreed to meet them. Someone handed me the portfolio with the information...but he was merely a courier. I signed off on the paperwork."

"And you didn't find that strange?" he asked.

"Not really. As I've told Viktor, owners sometimes want to remain anonymous. Sometimes the owners of art," she glanced to Viktor, "they don't want people to know their identity."

"So, you go to the club and she's not there?"

"First, I stopped by her apartment. It was empty. Looked trashed."

"It wasn't locked?" he asked.

"Now that I think of it, no, it wasn't. The door was closed but it was unlocked. I thought maybe she'd moved. I went back to my hotel, and then decided to go look for her."

"You didn't tell the police?" Greyson asked.

"Eventually I did, but I imagine many people go missing in Miami. Teagan doesn't have any family, so it's not like anyone is going to press them to look for her."

"True." Greyson nodded.

"When I got back to San Diego, the painting was already at the museum. I really haven't had a chance to process it properly. Sister Plautilla Nelli was mostly known for large pieces, but it's been rumored she also did smaller ones."

"Is the painting still in San Diego?" he asked.

"No. I have it here," she told him.

"I'd gone to San Diego to check on Dr. LaFleur," Viktor explained.

"That's one way of describing what I saw earlier." Greyson laughed.

Viktor continued, ignoring his brother. "I'd gone to an event the museum was holding. A charity event."

"He'd donated a Monet," Waverly told him.

"Quite the flex," Greyson teased.

"I don't have to explain myself to you," Viktor replied, his tone curt. "All you need to know is that I went there to check on Waverly."

"There was a man with a gun. He shot me," Waverly whispered, her voice shaken.

"I took care of it." Viktor and Greyson exchanged a look of understanding. "Then I took Waverly to my place in Miami."

"He healed me," she managed with a deep breath.

"Did he now?" Greyson raised a questioning eyebrow at him with a knowing smile. "I'm sure he enjoyed the taste."

"He doesn't drink from me," she stated flatly, her eyes on Viktor.

She'd called his name, whispering the words. *Bite me.* But he wanted her certain. Surer than anything in her life.

127

Because he suspected she belonged to him. And once he bit her, he'd never be able to give her up. If they bonded, he knew more than anyone of the sacrifice that came with bonding to another. She'd not only need to accept him, his existence as vampire but his thirst, his immortality. And her own.

The sound of his brother laughing broke his contemplation.

"I see how it is," Greyson said.

"You see nothing," Viktor countered.

Greyson gave a long pause, staring at his brother and then switched the subject. "Are the police involved?"

"Yes, they are aware of Teagan's disappearance. Waverly reported her missing to the police, but they likely won't investigate for long. She has no family. No one is pressing to find her."

"I am," Waverly said, determination in her voice. "She had issues. But she didn't deserve what happened to her."

"We need you to look at the painting." Viktor pinned him with a stare.

"First glance, it appears authentic, but I didn't get a chance to complete my evaluation," Waverly said. "I can't be sure."

"The nun created many pieces of art. Had trained others to do so as well. But her artwork is rare. That being said, new pieces of art are discovered all the time. It's not unheard of." Greyson looked to Viktor as he popped a piece of cheese in his mouth, chewing while he spoke. "Where do you keep the wine?"

"White or red?" Viktor attempted to be polite.

"White? Blah. It looks like piss. Tastes like it too. A hearty glass of red will do."

"I'll get it in a minute. There are a few other things you should know." Viktor continued explaining the situation.

"We returned to San Diego and stopped off at Waverly's apartment."

"Someone left a satanic message in my bedroom," she told him.

"I suspect it was done by a human. There was stale human blood on the floor. They'd thrown in a goat head for good measure."

"Hmm." Greyson shrugged; his face grimaced in consternation. "The plot thickens."

"And then we went to meet with the detective at the museum…she said the shooter had a picture of me in his pocket." Waverly fought tears but remained calm.

"Don't cry, lass. We'll get you set right. I promise," Greyson assured her, his tone softening.

Viktor noted his brother's change in demeanor. The gruff vampire had always had a soft spot for humans, much more so than he ever had. Hard as granite on the outside, his brother had a soft jelly center.

"The detective appeared perfectly normal just minutes before. Then she turned like a dog with rabies. My guess is possession," Viktor said.

"An oldie but a goodie." Greyson nodded.

Viktor crossed to the temperature-controlled wine cabinet and selected a bottle. He made short work of opening it and retrieved three glasses. As he poured, he caught sight of Waverly staring at him. She knew he didn't indulge but he'd already broken his own rules. He inwardly laughed. One more broken rule seemed in order.

Viktor handed a glass to Waverly and slid one in front of his brother. They both watched in interest as Viktor reached for his wine.

"You're joining us?" Greyson cracked a wise smile and looked to Waverly. "Perhaps leopards do change their spots?"

"Cheers." Tones of blackcurrant danced over his tongue, and he smiled at Waverly.

"Ah, I get what's going on," Greyson grumbled and nodded to Waverly. "Well, I knew it'd happen someday."

"Not now," Viktor told him.

"I'm going to enjoy this." Greyson winked at Waverly and took a sip of his wine.

"Let's have a look at the painting, then we can go to—" Viktor began.

"Hold the train, brother. I told Quint I'd come help you with a painting. Look at art. I said nothing about going on a scavenger hunt. And what are we looking for? A secret, bumfuck human society that wants to play vampire? Nope, I'm good. And you know what? I sure as shit don't want anything to do with demons."

"You're afraid of a little demon?" Viktor scoffed.

"You know I don't like demons. I don't do stupid shit like you do. Shit like going into Hell. Sticking your neck out for alphas and playing with packs of dogs. No. I'm not you. I don't need or want demons in my life."

Viktor shook his head. "Stop lying. You know damn well you'd do whatever you needed to do to save a friend."

"Not get involved with demons. Nope. That's a firm no." He held up a dismissive finger at him.

"You're a pussy," Viktor scoffed.

"I'm smart. It's called self-preservation." Greyson shook his head. "Nope. No demons."

"It's true that I need your help with the painting, but can you just help me sort this thing out? I'd ask Quintus or Hunter, but they just became bonded with mates. Look at it as teambuilding. Healing the brotherly relationship. You know about art. And wolves."

"I don't know—"

"I'm sure you heard I've got a hybrid. He's a handful and I need help."

"Heard all about it from Quintus. I was quite surprised, given you've no children." Greyson sipped his wine and released a loud exhale. "Ah, fuck. I'm not here to help you with your baby vamp. If you didn't want a child, you shouldn't have sired one."

"It's complicated. It wasn't exactly planned. But what's done is done." Viktor shrugged.

"So, what's the issue? Sounds like you've done better in a few months than our sire did in a lifetime."

"A lifetime of torture," Viktor reminded his brother.

"You know that's right."

"The thing is, well, Rafe may still need guidance. He doesn't wish to return to his pack. And you can see how this may be an issue."

"It can take many years to fully train a vampire. Or so I'm told."

"Baxter didn't train us. He turned us into slaves." Viktor looked to Waverly who sat at the bar. She gave him a sympathetic smile. She'd only seen but a fraction of the abuse.

"Yeah, well, it didn't stop Quint from turning others. He got on with things. But you? Me?" He sighed and looked into his glass. "It was never in the cards."

"I don't regret what I did. In that moment, I couldn't let Rafe die," Viktor explained.

"Guess ole Baxter didn't beat the humanity out of ya after all, did he?"

"Not for lack of trying," Viktor agreed, his voice soft. "But I won't do that to Rafe. He had no choice in his turning. It won't be an easy path, but his life can be good again. He can be whole."

Viktor stole a glance at Waverly and then changed the

subject, unwilling to acknowledge the feelings gripping his chest. He shook them off, focusing on the task at hand.

"I don't normally ask you for anything. It's been years. I just need—"

"I'll help," Greyson gritted out, setting his glass on the counter. "Where's my room?"

"Take the third floor. Tomorrow morning I'll grab Rafe. Flash him back here."

"We should look at the painting now," Waverly insisted.

"It's late." Viktor moved toward her, noting her reddened eyes.

"But I can do this now. If your brother...if Greyson knows about art, I need to know more about it."

"It's one in the morning. You need to get some rest. I promise you we'll start fresh in the morning."

"But—" she began.

"Viktor's right. Humans need to sleep. You'll get sick," Greyson told her.

"I'm not tired." Waverly clenched her face as she attempted to hide a yawn.

"He's right. We've got a lot to do tomorrow," Viktor said.

"You must realize your limitations as human." Greyson glanced at his brother. "Um what I mean is that, uh, you seem like a smart human. You may not know but us vampires must rest too. You know, keep up our strength for all that killing and whatnot."

The color drained from Waverly's cheeks and Viktor frowned at him.

"Did I say killing? What I meant was, well, not killing per se. You know. We've got business. We're businessmen," he corrected. "Entrepreneurs need sleep. Not as much as humans but—"

"So, you're saying you're an art dealer?" A smile softened her face.

"Sure, yeah. That's what I am. How'd ya know? I'm an art dealer, and your boyfriend there has a vast collection."

"He's not my boyfriend," Waverly protested.

"Technically not a girlfriend. A lover, yes." Viktor questioned his own words. A seed of doubt was planted as she denied her feelings. *What the hell is happening here?*

"So that means you're available?" Greyson asked with mischief in his eyes.

"No," Viktor and Waverly both answered at the same time.

"Well, all right." Greyson gave a hearty laugh. He stood and yawned, stretching his arms well above his head. "This vampire here, had a busy night. Came halfway around the world to help my long-lost brother. I think I'll just nip off for a nap and let you two figure out what's what. Tomorrow we'll get to the art. Sounds like we're gonna have a busy day."

"Thank you, Greyson." Viktor told his brother as he strode toward the staircase. "I won't forget this."

"No hanky panky, my chickadees." The vampire spun around and gave a salute. "Ah, young lust."

Viktor turned to Waverly, who set her wine glass in the sink.

"Are you sure Greyson can help us?" she asked.

"Yes of course." *Not really.*

"He seems...different than you."

"That's because he is. He's not like me at all." A flood of memories flashed in his mind, and he promptly shut it down, unwilling to let the past root anger.

"Viktor. About what I said. It's just that I know you probably have other girlfriends. I don't want you to worry about...well, you know. I mean, it's just that I don't want you to think that because we were together this is something serious. You live in Miami, and I live in California. Long distance relationships and all that. I just want you to know I get it." She stared up at him, feigning indifference.

"Mo chroí. I have no other girlfriends." *Only donors, one-night stands and empty sex.* Viktor's stomach sank as he considered his thoughts. She'd admitted she wasn't his girl-friend. She told him she didn't date vampires. The crushing hunger for her blood drove him wild but he wondered if it was simply the chase of the unattainable that drove him. "But perhaps we should go more slowly."

"Um...yeah, sure." She nodded.

Viktor extended his hand to her, his chest full of emotion at the thought of letting her go, "You need to know though, the truth is not just that I don't have girlfriends. I honestly don't have anyone. A few paranormals here and there of course. I may be the life of a party, but I don't have friends. I have acquaintances. Whereas you, on the other hand...you are," he smiled at her as he gently brought her into his embrace, "a friend now. A lover. So, I'm afraid whether you wanted a vampire in your life or not, you're stuck with me."

"I was wrong about that, about vampires," she admitted. "It's just my mom. She, uh, she didn't like what happened with me. I know you think I'm something special but not everyone likes their kids to have visions. It's not particularly cool in mommy circles."

Viktor's heart sank at her admission. "Did someone hurt you?"

"My parents were very strict. Those kinds of things weren't allowed. The devil's work and all."

"What kinds of things?"

"Paranormal things."

"Well, those sorts of things are highly encouraged around here." Viktor smiled. "It's pretty much required."

"I can't seem to control the visions when I'm around you. Actually, everything seems out of control," she admitted.

Viktor sighed as Waverly wrapped her arms around him, resting her cheek upon his chest. "I swear to you. Tomorrow, we'll figure out what's going on with the painting."

"And Teagan?"

"We're going to head back to Miami. Visit the club. We'll check again to see if she's been back," he told her.

"And what about the humans who are doing this?"

"We're gonna find them too. But tonight? You've got to get some rest." Viktor pressed his lips to the top of her head.

His scent lingered on her skin, and it pleased him. *I am so fucked.* There were a thousand reasons why he shouldn't bite her. Once his fangs pierced her skin, he suspected the bond would initiate.

He'd never allowed himself to get this close to a human. Yet here he was. Not only had he brought her to his home, but he'd also introduced her to his brother. Thoughts warred in his mind. Even as he told himself to let her go, he stole one last embrace.

Viktor released her, his gaze meeting hers. "Ready for bed?"

"Yeah." She nodded.

Without asking he flashed them into his bedroom. "I can sleep on the sofa."

"Viktor. Please." She settled onto the bed and looked up to him. "Can you maybe just stay?"

"Mo chroí." Her energy filled the room, surrounding him. Resisting the urge to bite her would drive him mad. "You need sleep."

"Help me." She patted the bed.

Viktor released a deep breath, acquiescing to her wish. As he slid next to her, she rolled to her side, reaching for him. She gave a sleepy moan as he wrapped his arm around her waist. His nose teased her hair; the sweet scent reminded him of purple cranesbill, his favorite summer flower from his childhood home. She seemed all too familiar, yet he'd only just met her.

But he'd force himself to live in the moment, to resist initiating the bond. As he settled his thoughts, Viktor told himself he'd simply take control over his feelings for the beautiful human. Even if he knew it wasn't true, he'd stave off the craving until tomorrow.

VIKTOR MATERIALIZED into the kitchen and glanced to Rafe, who remained in his wolf form. Before dawn, he'd flashed to San Diego to acquire his protégée. He'd briefly texted with both Jake Louvière and Hunter Livingston and explained the situation. The respective Alphas agreed his child needed to remain with him until a formal decision to leave pack came to fruition. He suspected the youngling would turn rogue, but Viktor would never repeat what had been done to him. He may not have wanted a child, but he'd make damn sure he cared for his own. *I am not my sire.*

Viktor's thoughts were interrupted as he caught sight of the kitchen. French pastries on crystal plates and gold catering dishes rested upon the counter. The kitchen table was adorned with fine china on white linens. Roses and day lilies overflowed from an ornate vase. *What the actual fuck?*

Rafe barked and jumped up, his front paws nearly knocking over an entire plate of pastries. He snatched a croissant, loped across the room and settled onto the sofa.

"Bad wolf!" Viktor called to him.

Rafe gave an apologetic whine, wagging his tail and making quick work of devouring the food.

"Jesus. H. Christ," Viktor snapped as Greyson materialized out of nowhere.

"No, not him. It's just me." Greyson waggled his

eyebrows. Dressed in a black t-shirt and jeans, the vampire stroked his beard, while he lounged on the sofa.

"What are you doing?" Viktor looked to the table. "What is all this food?"

"I thought our human would be hungry."

"She's not *our* human. She's *my* human," Viktor growled. The urge to protect her roared from within. He turned away from Greyson's line of vision and forced his emotions under control.

"Ah, but is she?" Greyson mused.

"I'm not up for games," Viktor stated as he avoided answering the question.

"No bonding yet, I take it." His brother laughed. "Let me give you a little lesson. I may not have a revolving door of playmates like you, but I know humans well. And I know enough about their women to keep one happy. Let me let you in on a little secret, brother. Food is one of those very important elements. It's essential. Things can take a turn for the worse if she's not fed."

The wolf, still lying on the sofa, whined in agreement.

"Dammit. I'll admit I struggle with the care and feeding of humans. And until now, I've successfully eluded this dilemma. She got me to eat again last night," Viktor admitted, unsure why he'd shared this information with his brother.

"She's reminding you of who you were. Or perhaps who you could be," he suggested.

"She, uh, she doesn't date vampires," Viktor said, annoyed with the situation.

"Ridiculous! Everyone dates vampires, whether they know it or not."

"Not Waverly." Viktor lifted the lid on one of the catering dishes and peeked inside. "Pancakes?"

"All humans dabble."

"She doesn't." *Until now.* He perused the pastries. "Croissants? I never understood the insistence of humans on eating layered bread."

"That's because you never eat," Greyson said. "It's awesome. Come on, then. Have a pastry."

The gorgeous brown wolf transformed to human, drawing the vampires' attention. "You ate for her again? Like actual food?"

"Yes, he did." Greyson laughed. He stood and crossed the room to the kitchen table. He reached for a pastry and held it in the air.

"I ate a po boy." While delicious, it couldn't compare to the taste of Waverly.

"Damn, you're really into this chick." Rafe lifted the lid to the catering dish, reached for a pair of gold tongs and began to pile pancakes onto a plate. "Nice work, on the breakfast."

"Of all the things you could start with, you went with a po boy?" Greyson asked.

"It was the first thing that popped into my head. It was great."

"Ya see, women will do that to you." Rafe put his plate down onto the table and pulled out a kitchen chair.

"Hold up there, hybrid, I know you wolves enjoy your um, freedom, shall we call it, but you're not in the woods. I'm afraid I'm gonna have to insist on covering up." Greyson picked up a throw blanket and tossed it at his feet.

"Wolves. Such free-living creatures." Viktor looked to Rafe as he wrapped it around his waist with an unapologetic laugh. "May I remind you that you're vampire now. I shouldn't have to tell you how to behave outside the woods. I'm not your Alpha."

"But you're my daddy," Rafe said with a sly smile as he stabbed his fork into the pancake and stuffed it into his mouth.

"He's impossible." Viktor rolled his eyes.

"The humans say the apple doesn't fall far from the tree." Greyson smiled as he took a seat at the table.

"I intentionally saved you, wolf. But believe me, you were more like an accident," Viktor said. "Put in human terms. You're the result of a weak pullout game."

"He's such a caring father." Rafe smirked at Greyson and then to Viktor. "What did I do to deserve you?"

"Believe me, you have a cake walk compared to our sire, so stop complaining." Viktor listened for Waverly. While she walked softly, he detected her footsteps. "Please attempt to act civilized around Waverly. She's not used to all this paranormal stuff."

"This should be interesting," Greyson replied.

"I'm not sayin' nothin'." Rafe shrugged.

"Keep your clothes on," Viktor ordered.

"She might see something she likes." Rafe held a sausage up in the air and took a bite.

"She already has," Viktor shot back.

"Poor sap here doesn't realize he's bonding with her." Greyson laughed. "I suppose it's inevitable."

"She's your mate? Did you claim her?" Rafe asked.

"Claim her?" Greyson laughed. "He hasn't even bit her yet."

"Enough. She's coming. Just, uh, just act normal." Viktor shook his head, aware none of them were capable of such a thing.

"Two vampires and a wolf walked into a bar—" Greyson began.

"Enough. Now play nice." Viktor's chest tightened as she walked into the room. Her long curly blonde hair tumbled over her shoulders, a contrast to the black sweater she wore.

"Morning," Waverly said with a shy smile. She smoothed her hands over her jeans. "Thanks for the clothes."

"You look beautiful as always." Viktor stepped toward her, resisting the urge to take her in his arms.

"You were gone when I woke up." She looked to Rafe who nodded at her, shoving another fork full of pancakes into his mouth.

"Hey," he managed, his speech garbled while he chewed.

"Hello." Greyson stood and bowed slightly, his eyes never leaving the human. "I apologize for the way we met last night. I wasn't aware my brother had found his—"

Viktor shook his head, his lips pursed tight. *Do not say it.*

"His, uh…human. And you are a lovely human."

"Thank you," she said, her voice uncertain. "You are a lovely…um, vampire."

"Please. Eat." Viktor gestured to the kitchen table and looked to Greyson. "Would you like—"

"A café au lait." His brother pointed to the breakfast spread. "Omelet? Pancake? Grits?"

"I could use some caffeine and maybe a pastry." She reached for the carafe. "Who can resist a croissant?"

"Told you." Greyson glanced at Viktor then turned to Waverly. "You're going to need sustenance today. We must look at this painting and find out who's doing this to you."

"We?" she asked.

"Yes," Viktor replied, still unsure if he'd racked up the right dream team. "Rafe is my pupil. This will serve as a training of sorts. My brother will help with the art. Help keep an eye on things."

"Make sure things don't go to Hell." Greyson nodded.

"None of us are going to Hell," Viktor said. Distracted by the food, he studied the plate of pastries, attempting to recall their taste. He reached for a chocolate éclair and sniffed it.

"You touched it. Now, you have to eat it," Rafe insisted.

Viktor sighed and sat next to Waverly. He looked around the table and supposed this was the closest thing to family he'd ever experienced. His child, a wolf hybrid. Two ancient vampires and a human. All from different parts of the world, all coming together for a purpose.

They ate in silence, exchanging an occasional glance as if knowing darkness was coming. Viktor never shied away from a challenge. Finding the owner of the painting would lead them to answers.

He considered the very essence of what brought them together. Food, the epitome of the human existence. It represented everything Baxter had beaten out of him.

Viktor looked to the pastry he held in his hand. The life he'd resisted all these years had been summed up in the éclair. Temptation loomed as Waverly glanced at him, a flirty smile melting his heart.

By denying himself love, food, every single last thing that made him human, Viktor had let Baxter win. But no more. As he bit down into the éclair, savoring the sweet chocolate and cream, he reclaimed his humanity. Baxter would no longer hold rein on him from beyond the grave.

"That can't be possible," Waverly insisted.

"It is indeed," Greyson said with confidence. "I was there after she'd created it. This painting appears real."

"But you couldn't have..." Her words trailed into silence, and she briefly closed her eyes, attempting to regain her composure.

"Old dudes," Rafe commented.

"I prefer ancient." Greyson shot him a look of disdain.

"I prefer newbie vamps keep their fangs up and lips closed." Viktor studied the painting and pointed to the raised area. "Can you remove this spot here?"

"Well, of course, I can just tear it open, but that's probably not a great idea," Greyson said.

"Tear it open? Are you serious? This is a relic. A valuable piece of art." Waverly pressed the tips of her fingers to her forehead. "This cannot be happening."

Viktor ran his finger over the painting. A jagged mound of paint edged a corner of its canvas. "Yeah, it's definitely not paint."

"You shouldn't touch it," Waverly insisted. "There's something in here. I've never seen anything like it."

"It's not just extra paint," Greyson said.

"I just don't understand why someone would do this to this painting." She leaned in closer, examining it with a lens up to her eye. "It could be anything. It wouldn't be the first time someone tried to hide something in a painting, or maybe they tried to fix it, and it clumped. It happens. People don't know how valuable a painting is, so they attempt to repair it. They use glue. Extra paint. Here. The paint is a slightly different hue of blue. It's a very good job. Just a subtle difference, but it's not the same color. If we had time, I could date it exactly."

"Time is something we don't have," Viktor said. "We're protected in my house, but we can't stay holed up here forever."

"I don't have all the proper tools," she explained. "I just wish I'd already done an x-ray. For all we know there could be another layer of paint underneath this one. It's not uncommon. Just a few years ago they discovered another painting under a Picasso."

Rafe approached the painting, sidling up next to Waverly. Viktor watched intently as he sniffed the air. He leaned toward the painting, hovering his nose over its surface.

"I smell blood," he told them.

"What?" Waverly asked, panic in her voice.

"There's no blood on the painting," Greyson insisted.

Viktor leaned toward the painting and sniffed, concentrating. He detected the faint scent of old blood. "He's right. I don't know where it's coming from, but I definitely smell it."

"You should open it up," Rafe urged. "I've got a penknife."

"Open it up?" Waverly's cheeks reddened. "No. No way. You can't just slice into my painting."

"But it's not your painting," Viktor countered.

"Are you sure you want to take a blade to it?" Greyson plowed his fingers through his hair. "I mean that seems a little extreme. I did mention I knew the very nun who painted this. Everything about it looks familiar. Like I said, I'm fairly sure it's an original."

"If it was repaired then someone else already broke it. Y'all might be able to do a better job," Rafe interjected.

"No. Stop. We can't just slice it open. I just can't..." Waverly's words trailed off into silence.

"What other choice do we have? There might be something in here that can help us. I know it's an original." Viktor looked to Greyson. "But this one has already been tampered with. It's like you're fixing it. A restoration, if you will."

"Home edition." Rafe nodded.

"I think we should do it," Greyson conceded.

"What?" Waverly exclaimed. "No."

"While I agree with you that this painting is rare, you must know that the nun painted others. The church owns many. Others are kept in private collections." Greyson gave Waverly a sympathetic look. "It's going to be okay."

"You can do this," Viktor encouraged. "The painting is going to need repair anyway."

"Well technically she's not repairing," Rafe began.

Viktor shot him a silencing stare. Restraining his anger, he continued. "Consider this the beginning of a repair."

"But we don't have permission. This painting. I don't know the owner."

"Exactly. You say that it's an anonymous donor who sent you a painting. But we all know there's something not right about this one. We don't know if they are trying to help with something or implicate you in something, but we have to find out what this bump is. There's something in here the demon in the detective wanted. And we need to find out exactly what it is."

Waverly sighed. "In 2015. There was this painting. Flowers. A kid accidentally put his hand through it. Right there in the exhibit. It happens. So sometimes they do get repaired. Okay, okay, I can do this."

"Yes, there we go, pet. You've got this."

"Did anyone take pictures? I mean, we've got to document this," Greyson suggested.

"On it. Video and pics. Got it all. You know. Just in case. It's one of the first things I did," Waverly told them. "I don't have a straight edge. I'm going to need a knife or something. A razor would work best. Do you have one?"

"Razors are in the case in the bathroom," Viktor told Rafe, noting Waverly's look of surprise. "What? I may be a vampire, but I don't always bite."

"I don't want to know." She held up her hand at him.

"I'm saying there are donors who prefer—"

"Nope. Don't want to know." She gave him a tight closed smile. "I'm good."

"It's not as bad as it sounds," Greyson offered.

"Said I don't want to know." Waverly took a deep breath and carefully accepted the blade from Rafe. "Thank you."

"Do you need more light?" Viktor asked.

"No, just um," she adjusted the desk lamp that hovered over the painting, "there's a lot of natural light from the window."

"I do enjoy a view," Viktor commented with a blithe inflection to his voice.

"You always did enjoy the water," Greyson noted.

"Please. Guys. I need a little quiet." She studied the painting and blew out a breath.

"You've got this." Viktor stood close as she worked on it.

"I'm sorry Sister, but we've got to see what's inside your beautiful work," Waverly apologized as she took the razor to the canvas. She gently worked the blade over the paint. As it began to flake away, she hesitated. "I can't believe I'm doing this."

"Whatever is in there. There's definitely blood involved," Rafe commented.

Waverly began to scrape the paint, careful not to tear the canvas. "I can feel it. It's hard."

She set down the razor and retrieved a small brush she'd brought from the museum. With great care, she gently swept away the flecks of paint and revealed the object.

"It's so small." Waverly set down the brush and used a pair of tweezers as she gently extracted the foreign object. "What is this?"

As she held it under the bright desk light, Viktor quietly studied the inch-long piece of metal. He sniffed, still detecting a hint of human blood.

Waverly exhaled a nervous breath. "What is this thing? Is that writing?"

"Is it gold?" Rafe asked and sniffed. "Blood."

"Looks like brass," Greyson guessed.

"May I?" Waverly nodded as Viktor reached for it and he took it from her hands. With a cotton cloth, he brushed away the specks of dried paint, a shine coming to its surface. As the letters came into view, a tight knot formed in his gut. *B.A.O.*

"No fucking way." Viktor's gaze locked on Greyson's.

"There's no way this can belong to him," his brother told him. "He's dead."

"What? Who are you talking about?" Rafe asked.

"Baxter Anwir Ó Cléirigh." Viktor sighed. Hundreds of years had passed since he'd died, yet the memories, the terror would never be forgotten.

"Bastard's dead." Greyson slammed his hand onto the arm of a chair as he fell back into it and propped his feet on an ottoman.

"This metal. It's a tool." Viktor's blood pumped hard in his veins as his mind churned, realizing its purpose. *What the fuck?*

"Tool?" she asked.

"A lancet," Viktor replied.

"For what?" she pressed.

"For bloodletting." Viktor closed his eyes, attempting to draw energy from the object but he detected a vast sea of nothingness. No life. No emotion. No humanity.

"I know what you're thinking, brother. But the initials are random. It's a coincidence. He's dead," Greyson repeated.

"Jesus Christ. This can't belong to him," Viktor said, not quite convincing himself.

"This is some kind of sick fucking joke. That's what this is." Greyson laughed, the smile not reaching his eyes.

"This lancet. The fleam. It's missing its handle." Viktor rubbed his thumb along its edge. "Where did this come from?"

"We've got to be able to research it," Rafe said. "And if there's one thing I'm good at, it's research."

"Why would someone want me to see this?" Waverly asked.

"I don't know," Viktor admitted, still shaken by the initials. "But this painting has to have been hidden for years.

There is no way this was an accident, that an antique blood-letter was concealed within the painting."

"I know you both thought I could identify its owner but I'm afraid that's going to be difficult. The nun painted many paintings." Greyson rubbed his beard. "I could ask my contacts at the Vatican. Maybe they know who it belonged to."

"Who would own the painting and this tool?" she asked, her voice laced with tension.

"Anyone could have owned the painting. But the tool? Most likely a human." Viktor suspected it belonged to a doctor. "Bloodletting is thousands of years old."

"Dates back to ancient Greeks. While it's generally accepted by medical doctors today that it doesn't cure disease, there are a few places in the world that continue its practice," Greyson offered.

"You're a fountain of knowledge brother," Viktor replied, his voice tense.

"That's what I'm here for. And my charming personality."

"My head hurts, and it's only ten in the morning." Waverly stretched her neck from side to side.

"Rafe. I want you to examine the blade for any other clues to its origin. It looks like brass, but it could be something else."

"What if another vampire owns it?" she asked.

"Humans probably used this for bloodletting, but it could be used for simple torture. Vampires are well versed in torture," Greyson said with a cool smile.

The look of shock registered on Waverly's face, and Viktor quickly corrected his brother in a failed attempt to calm her. "He didn't mean that's going to happen. He meant...well, you know, vampires have to intervene in disagreements from time to time."

"Don't lie to me."

Viktor turned to her, his voice serious. "I will never lie to you."

"What if a vampire engaged in an activity where he didn't want people to know they did it? To blame it on a human?" Rafe suggested.

"It happens." Baxter's evil laugh echoed in his mind. It was one of Viktor's master's favorite tricks. He'd taught them well to leave no trace. No matter where they traveled, victims suffered unspeakable violence. No one would ever identify a puncture wound. If they were to spend more than a week in the location, he'd take pleasure in setting up villagers, watching them be punished by other humans.

"Stop getting him wound up, wolf. Vik, it wasn't him," Greyson told him, shaking him from his thoughts.

"You're right. The blade most likely belongs to a human." Viktor refused to entertain the possibility Baxter lived. *I saw him die, saw Quintus hurl him into the canyon.* He'd never forget the day he gained his freedom.

"Is there anything else on the blade?" Greyson asked.

Viktor studied the lancet and turned it over to inspect it, his gut clenching as he caught sight of the symbol. "This."

"It's similar to the symbol that was in my house," she exclaimed.

"Hold this, please." Viktor handed her the blade and reached for his cell phone, sliding his fingers along its glass, searching for the pictures he'd taken. He set the phone onto the desk so the others could see it. "She's right."

"Someone targeted her." Greyson plowed his fingers through his dark hair.

"Teagan got mixed up with some bad people. Is it Satanic?" she asked.

"It looks to me like some kind of spell maybe," Viktor guessed. "But again. The whole vibe in your apartment screamed human to me."

Rafe approached the desk and glanced at the picture. "Dude. That's some fucked up shit."

"Maybe a fae could help," Greyson speculated. "Or Ilsbeth."

"Hell no," Viktor scoffed.

"A witch?" Waverly asked.

"The High Priestess, herself. Mommy," Rafe declared with a bow. "That's right, Waverly. My pa's a vamp and my ma is a badass witch, who is occasionally helpful but is mostly evil."

"I'd like to believe she's in transition, so to speak. Hell has left her refreshed," Viktor said.

"Refreshed?" Rafe laughed. "Dude. She was in Hell, not Beverly Hills."

"It changes one's perspective. She needed an attitude adjustment. Better than therapy."

Greyson slammed his hand onto the armrest and gave a boisterous laugh. "You're a crazy motherfucker, Vik."

"This is my lineage." Rafe shrugged and smiled at Waverly.

"How does a vampire and a, um, witch make a wolf?" she asked.

"Viktor saved me." He wore a solemn expression.

"It's nothing, really." Viktor turned his attention back to the blade, uninterested in discussing the transformation.

"I almost died," Rafe told her.

"Siring children is a tricky business, dear human." Greyson stood and crossed the room, extending his hand toward his brother. "May I?"

"Of course." Viktor placed the lancet in his palm, careful not to cut him.

"In death, there is a time when the magick of the human is still strong and the soul has not quite left this plane," Greyson said. "We can exchange our blood, a sacrifice if you will, and the Goddess blesses the transformation. But when

149

the magick wanes, and the human crosses over, there's not much that can be done. It becomes too late."

"Vampires can do many things. My brother and I can do more than most. But once death has truly set in, it can be difficult. Our blood alone isn't enough to bring someone back, to rebirth them as vampire," Viktor told her.

"But a high priestess, a really powerful witch. Their blood is rich with magick. And every now and then, when it's combined with the vampire's, it works. And just like that. Mazel tov! It's a boy." Greyson clapped.

Viktor's expression darkened, refocused on the fleam. "It's true that a witch may know the answers we seek. But, the fact of the matter is, both humans and vampires could be involved."

"Never underestimate the evil that humans perpetuate. History has taught us that." Greyson studied the object. "We need someone who understands the symbols. I'd love to see the saucy witch but alas, we didn't end on good terms."

"Tell me you didn't play with the witch." Viktor rolled his eyes.

"I played to win. Rolled the dice and snake eyes."

"You play with fire, you get burnt," Viktor told him.

"A little pain can be delicious." Greyson winked at Waverly. "I've always fancied a bit of the kink."

"My brother is both adventurous and reckless," Viktor told her. "The witch is not to be trifled with."

"She holds answers. She always does."

"She suffered greatly in Hell. It wasn't her first trip. As much as I think she's transformed, I wouldn't bet my life on it. I don't know if she's truly clean."

"Clean?" Waverly asked.

"Clean from the evil," Viktor answered. "In Hell, you lose track of space and time. But the evil, it can stick with you."

"Demons are sneaky fuckers." Greyson blew out a breath. "Ah shite. Well, we've got to see her anyway. She'll know."

"We could go to Samantha," Viktor suggested. "She's also a priestess."

"Ilsbeth has knowledge of the old ways. If something's going down, she's going to know. She always knows," Greyson said.

"Well, up until recently, her brain was scrambled like eggs. A whole different person, in fact. But alas, the bitch is back." Viktor snapped his fingers. "Always lands on her feet. Just like her cat."

"It's why I can't refuse her." Greyson laughed.

"You're asking for trouble, bro. It's been hundreds of years from when you first got with her. She's not who you remember. She rolls with the demons," Viktor warned.

"So, she likes a little adventure every now and then. She lives for the moment. Enjoys a rush. She's one sweet ass daredevil." He chuckled.

"Dude. There's nothin' sweet about her," Rafe told him. "She nearly killed Dimitri. Bitch couldn't keep the big D, so she damn castrated his wolf. That's cold, man."

"She'll have your fangs if you get with her," Viktor warned. "She may be refreshed but she's still dangerous as a rattlesnake."

"It's true. She collects shit. She's got Alpha fur," Rafe told him.

"And she's a witch?" Waverly asked in disbelief.

"She's a smokin' hot witch, is what she is. And that was before Hell," Greyson joked.

"This isn't a good time to play with fire. Besides I've got someone else in mind who owes me a favor," Viktor told them.

"Who?" Waverly asked.

"He's just a guy," Viktor hedged, aware that his brother wouldn't be happy with his suggestion.

"A warlock?" she guessed.

"No, he's got experience with spells though."

"We should see a fae. Kellen," Greyson suggested.

"Nah, I'm good. He's hard work." Viktor didn't want anything to do with Kellen.

"He almost killed Hunter," Rafe told them. He nodded at Waverly. "True story."

"Well, who then?" Greyson pressed.

"I already told Quint. I know a guy. It's not important." Viktor avoided the question a second time.

"Who is it?" Greyson glared at Viktor.

"Just a guy." Viktor glanced down to the lancet and back to his brother, deciding the truth was best. "Look, you know we've both had to do what we've had to do to survive. I've had a few more trips to Hell than you've had. You've got to have allies to survive. He helped me."

"No." Greyson held up a dismissive hand.

"One hand washes another." Viktor shrugged.

"Nope."

"Yes."

"No demons."

"Technically, Thorn is a half demon," Viktor insisted.

"No demons," Greyson replied, staring out the window.

"He just helped Quintus. He's actually quite nice. Brought his A game to the tourney at the club."

"There's something wrong with you. What is a vampire doing at a country club?"

"A bit of golf. Reminds me I need to cancel my lesson."

"This is exactly why we don't talk," Greyson grumbled.

"We're talking now. Don't be so dramatic." Viktor looked to Waverly, who had begun wrapping up the canvas.

"No demons," Greyson repeated.

"You're going to have to trust me. I know you want to see Ilsbeth. And you know what?" Viktor laughed. "I don't care. You're a big boy. Still think it's a mistake, but it's your life. But I've spent way too much time with the witch lately, and I need a little space. Besides, I'm confident Thorn will have information about which humans and supes would be involved with demons. Who out there, besides the fae, are calling on demons?"

"Aw fuck, I hate demons." Greyson shook his head.

"I appreciate your help with the painting. But if you're afraid, or if you just don't want to co—"

"I'm comin'. But if Thorn makes one move to hurt anyone, I'm turning his ass into demon meat," Greyson warned.

"Fair enough."

"Are we going somewhere?" Waverly asked.

"Yes. I may like the guy sometimes, but I'm not stupid. No way I'm asking a demon into my home," Viktor said.

"I want to run this blade by some of my colleagues. I'd like to show pictures of the lancet to them. I won't say how I came by it," Waverly promised.

As Greyson set the fleam down next to the painting, she retrieved her cell phone and snapped several pictures of the bloodletting tool.

"Don't let anyone know where you are," Viktor instructed.

"What about the police? The way we left the museum—" Her expression grew tense.

"I already contacted PCAP. They have the detective in their custody and will deal with the San Diego PD from now on. If they want us to go back for questioning, we'll stall. But for now, they just see this as a stalker tried attacking the curator kind of deal. He's dead. Case closed." Viktor looked to Greyson. "I think we should go back to the blood club in

Miami at some point. But let's meet with Thorn first. I want to know what we're dealing with."

"I'm going to go back through my text messages with Teagan. Maybe there's something I missed." Waverly looked down to the painting. "Is it okay if I leave this here?"

"Yes. It's safe." Viktor turned to her and took her hand in his. "And so are you. I'm not going to let anything happen to you."

"She's about to meet a demon," Greyson called to him.

"Don't listen to him," he told her.

"I can do this." She nodded with a glint of fear in her eyes.

"I know you can. You've already met one of the most terrifying Romanian vampires in existence. Thorn is like a fluffy, little bunny rabbit."

Waverly leaned to the side, catching a glimpse of Greyson, who waved but didn't correct his brother.

"I promise you we will figure out what's going on," Viktor told her, his voice calm and reassuring. "I'm going to find out who's driving the humans to attack you and put an end to it."

"He means put an end to them. So they no longer exist." Greyson looked to Viktor. "You're welcome."

Waverly's mouth gaped open, and she quickly shut it.

"We'll deal with the situation," Viktor corrected.

Greyson stood and crossed the room, continuing to speak. "Humans who conjure demons are no different than demons. They can fuck off and die." He sighed loudly. "Well, folks. This little therapy session has been great and all. But I've gotta go eat. Maybe fuck. Maybe both. Not necessarily in that order. Text me when you hear from the demon. I'll be back."

Viktor exchanged a look with his brother before he disappeared into thin air. Waverly's eyes widened, witnessing his departure. Viktor sensed her anxiety, the sound of her heart beating grew louder.

"Hey." He brought her hand to his lips and brushed a kiss to the back of it. "I arranged to have lunch delivered. Why don't you rest for a while, and I'll come get you when it's here?"

"Would it be okay if I used your laptop?" she asked. "I have my phone, but it'll be easier to do research on a bigger screen."

"Absolutely. It's in the kitchen." Viktor crossed the living room into the kitchen and opened a cabinet door, retrieving the device. "Here."

"Thank you," she said accepting it. "Um, can I just use it? Or is there a password or something?"

Viktor smiled, leaning to whisper in her ear. "Blood-Daddy. All one word. Big D."

"What?" Waverly laughed. Distracted, she fumbled the tablet in her hands, but she quickly regained her grip.

"That's right, woman. Bloooood Daddy!" Viktor brushed a kiss to her cheek and released her with a hearty laugh.

"That's your password? You're messing with me."

"No. No I'm not."

Waverly shot him a look of disbelief. "No way."

"Truly. I went to pick it up and the saleswoman helped me set it. Turns out she's a donor."

"But of course." Waverly rolled her eyes.

"Apparently I'm irresistible or so I've been told by Miss Diana Lord."

"More like incorrigible." She shot him a closed smile.

"I must've been giving off big vamp vibes that day because she just came right out with it. Confessing her guilty pleasure." Viktor smiled.

"Getting bitten?" Waverly asked.

"Well that too, but she apparently had a penchant for giving nicknames to her favorite biters. Declared me Blood Daddy right then and there. Typed it right into my password when she set it up. But don't worry, pet. I never tasted a drop of her blood."

"I'm not believing a word of this."

"Believe it baby." Viktor winked at her and reached for the plate of croissants that sat left over from breakfast. He lifted one to his lips and took a bite.

"I'm not sure what to say."

"You're a lucky woman," he joked.

"Super lucky. So lucky. I'm just not sure what I'm going to do with all this luck." Waverly laughed.

"Stick with me and maybe you'll help me earn my nickname." Viktor smiled as she blushed in response.

"Do you mind if I go sit at the desk in the guest room?"

"Not at all. I have a few things I must do, and you never know when Rafe will be coming back down. Kids. You know how it is."

"I don't have children. But he is adorable. I suppose he's a bit larger than most. Must be difficult to chase after."

"Don't let his cute face fool you. He's a handful."

Their laughter quickly faded into a silent heated gaze. The urge to go to her, to take her in his arms, grew stronger by the second but Viktor restrained himself. Joking about having kids reminded him of the sacrifice she'd have to make if they bonded. It would come at a cost. He'd never father the children she'd want.

His heart tightened as she smiled at him, giving a nod as she collected her things and quickly ascended the staircase. He couldn't bring himself to bite her, to complete the bonding. Viktor lied to himself, logic telling him she'd be better off without him.

The craving for blood haunted him. He wouldn't take hers, though. He'd set off to a blood bar, seek out another human, someone who would never sate his thirst.

CHAPTER EIGHT

*W*averly closed the laptop and rested her head upon her folded arms. She'd sent out several emails to heads of museums across the country. Within the silence in her room, her thoughts raced.

She'd been seconds away from begging Viktor to bite her. If Greyson hadn't interrupted them, she'd have screamed it at the top of her lungs.

Waverly had spent a lifetime happily being human, avoiding her visions and vampires. She considered her mom, how her parents had warned her long ago to steer clear of the paranormal. If they only knew she was currently sleeping in a house with two vampires and a wolf.

Her mind drifted to the shooting, the scene at her apartment, the blood-splattered ritual under her bed. The past two days had been a blur and all of it had begun with Teagan...or so she'd thought. Although a small part of her hoped they'd still find her friend, reason warned her Teagan was dead. But ever since they'd discovered the bloodletting fleam had been deliberately sent to her, whatever was happening had targeted her.

She lifted her weary head as a loud ding sounded from her cell phone. Exhausted she grabbed it, crossed the room and threw herself down in the bed. As she rolled onto her back and tossed the covers over her legs, she glanced at the text. *Adam. Adam Strommell.* "Oh shit."

Her chest tightened with anxiety at the sight of his name. She and Adam had been grad assistants together, friends with benefits until they'd graduated. But as all good things come to an end, he'd taken a job on the East Coast. He'd left California, crossing the country to New York, and neither of them had wanted a long-distance relationship.

Boss sent me your email. How's my fav surfer? Thought you were working on an Impressionism exhibit?

Waverly's stomach dropped. *He's following up on me?*

Hey. Yeah, still working on it. This is a side project.

That sounded professional, she thought. It had been years since they'd spoken.

I may have a lead. There happens to be a fleam handle in our sister museum. Same initials.

Waverly's heart beat like a drum as she tapped on the glass screen.

Are you sure? B.A.O

100%. Log says we've got a fleam handle stashed away. Same initials.

I have to examine it.

Of course. U in Cali?

I'm east coast. She didn't want to give him her exact location.

Can you send me a picture?

It's offsite. In the warehouse. Are you near NY?

Art, and other items not on active display, were often stored within vaults in secret locations. *Shit.* She took a deep breath and began typing.

I may be able to catch a flight. When do you think you can get the piece?

It's going to take a couple of hours to get approval to pull it.

Where's the item?

Brooklyn. I could meet you there. Dinner after? Catch up?

"Nope, can't do that right now," she said out loud to herself.

Sorry no. I'm on a tight deadline.

Drinks?

Sorry. Maybe another time. She lied.

I'll text location and time tomorrow. Gotta run.

Thanks, Adam!

Talk soon.

In the seconds Waverly thought to text Viktor, she realized she didn't have his phone number. The past few days had been a whirlwind. The intense attraction blurred her judgement. Reason cautioned her to stay away from the ancient vampire, but the flames of attraction ignited hotter each time she saw him.

Waverly tossed her phone on the bed, curled into a ball on her side, brushing her fingers to her neck. She closed her eyes, imagining his touch, the slice of his fangs on her flesh. Her core tightened, aroused at the thought of his cock filling her while he took her blood.

A loud knock to the door broke her fantasy. Her eyes flew open at the sound of his voice. *Viktor.*

"Waverly."

"Hey." She sat up as she heard him call to her a second time. "Come in."

"Got some news," he told her as he leaned an arm on the doorjamb.

Waverly's pulse raced at the sight of the debonair vampire. Dressed in a light blue dress suit and white shirt, he looked sexier than ever, and she struggled not to stare at him.

"I have some news too," she managed.

"Thorn has agreed to meet with us. He's having a party later tonight."

"What?"

"You know. A party. A fun get-together where people have cocktails, laugh and engage in casual conversation with strangers."

"I know what a party is," she laughed.

"I know it's a bit unusual, but paranormals do enjoy their parties. It's Friday."

"Friday," she repeated, attempting to massage the stress from her temples. "I'm losing track of the days."

"Ah, I know the feeling."

"I bet you do."

Viktor crossed the room and sat on the bed. "What's your news?"

"The fleam. I have a..." Old lover. Friend. "Colleague. He believes he has the matching handle. It has the same initials. At least that's what it says in the records."

"Sounds promising."

"Yes, well. I'm sure there were other people in this world with the same initials."

"It's odd the handle would be held by a museum without its fleam," he noted.

"The chain of custody will be at the storage facility. We can check it out and see where it came from. Hopefully anyway. It's likely it's dated too. Most items are inspected and catalogued. The owner is designated if there was one."

"Rafe is doing research on the blade to see if there are any notable fleams that may have already been flagged. Humans aren't the only ones who keep records." He patted her thigh. "Hopefully we'll have more info before we get to New York."

Waverly looked to his hand, which burned arousal

through her body. A mere touch made her lose her train of thought. *No, no, no,* she told herself

"Um…did you say New York?" she asked, attempting to hide the surprise. "Yes. We're taking a trip. My brother, Quint, heads up the vampires there so it should be relatively safe. The party, however, is being held in Chappaqua."

"What a coincidence. The handle is in New York as well." She paused. "Actually, the museum is in New York, but the handle is at a secret storage facility in Brooklyn. Adam is going to text me tomorrow with the address and—"

"Adam?" He raised a questioning eyebrow at her.

"Yes. Adam Strommell. He's an old friend from grad school." Waverly released a breath, slowing her heartbeat.

"Old friend?"

"Yes. We studied together in grad school. Then he went to work in New York. And I stayed in San Diego." Waverly carefully considered her words. "I sent a copy and paste email to all the museum curators I know and asked for help, trying to find out more about the fleam. Apparently, his boss passed it on to him. The cataloguing database is quite extensive in any given museum. He got lucky. Got a hit on the initials."

"An old friend finding what you need is serendipitous indeed," he mused.

"He said he'd text the info tomorrow." Waverly stopped mid-thought. "Wait, what time is it? Where are we going?"

"I have a place in the city. We'll flash up, get ready there and take a limo to the party," he explained. "The party doesn't begin until midnight. I'm sorry to interrupt your nap. But I'd like to leave within the hour. I've already asked the maid to have the house ready for our arrival. I know I said I'd order lunch, but I'd like to get up to New York as soon as possible. You and Rafe can eat there. I promise you'll have a bit of time for a nap before the event. I'm having my personal shopper bring over some suitable outfits for you. Perhaps one day we'll have time to see New York together. Go to dinner and the theater. I love Broadway."

Waverly smiled. "Like a date?"

He laughed. "Yes. I suppose so."

"You like Broadway shows?"

"But of course, I do. I'm a vampire, not dead."

"You're full of surprises." Waverly gave him a curious smile. He never ceased to amaze her.

"Just you wait, mo chroí. You're in for an adventure." Viktor stood and leaned toward her and placed a gentle kiss on her forehead. "Once this ugly situation is sorted out, we'll do New York properly."

Waverly's pulse raced as he pulled away from her. Tempted to reach for him, to roll him onto the bed and fuck his brains out, she clutched the blanket as if she was tethering herself to keep from floating off into the sea. Like being lost in a wild storm, her feelings for him had begun to spiral out of her control. *I'm in trouble.*

"Can you be ready soon? I've got to gather Rafe. Make sure he's feeling all right. I shouldn't have left him so long in San Diego."

"Yes. Absolutely." She nodded.

"Perfect." Viktor gave a small smile as he left the room and closed the door behind him.

Waverly sensed the responsibility that weighed heavy on his shoulders. She considered how, while he seemed aloof at times, he'd gone for Rafe, and remained committed to taking care of the young wolf. She wondered if he'd had children when he was human, his paternal nature apparent.

Waverly had never thought to have children. With a busy career and traveling schedule, it wasn't feasible. But it was also true, she'd never fallen in love. As her thoughts began to drift into a fantasy, a life with a family, she shut down the unattainable dreams. Indulging in what ifs wouldn't change the fact that Viktor was vampire.

She lay back on the bed, stealing a few minutes of rest. Within the hour, she'd take on New York City. In a week, she'd gone from surfing and art museums to a world of demons and paranormal parties. She blew out a cleansing breath and prayed for the strength to get through their next jaunt.

"IT LOOKS....UM, SEE THROUGH." Waverly smoothed her hands over the fine lace, floor-length gown. The black satin bra and panties were visible through the transparent fabric.

"Tom Ford, darling. It's stunning," insisted the stylist who Viktor had sent to attend to her. Beverly Stacco. *Personal shopper to the stars.* "You do realize the dress you're wearing costs several thousand dollars? It's the best of the best. Perfecto. You'll be the belle of the ball tonight."

"Wow. Okay. Um, really, I would have been fine with something less expensive. Maybe a dress from Macy's? They've always got a sale going."

"Pfft. Viktor is the epitome of style. You must match." The tall brunette gestured to a vanity set. Dressed in a pair of embellished jeans with a black, ruffled, chiffon blouse, she teetered around the room, her crystal-studded boots tapping about the wooden floor. The diminutive but head-strong woman rummaged through her suitcase and retrieved a tan linen bag. "Now. Come sit at the mirror. Let's try the shoes."

A silver pair of bootie-style, open-toed, dress sandals dangled from Beverly's fingers. Netting, adorned with tiny crystals, stretched over the leather. "These are perfect. Rene Caovilla. Snakeskin. Love them."

Waverly sat down onto the black velvet settee, careful not to tug on the dress. "How long have you worked for Viktor?"

"Since the sixties," she commented, slipping a sandal onto one of her feet.

"The sixties?" Waverly quickly did the math and attempted to conceal her surprise. The woman appeared far younger than her age. *Vampire.* "You must be close...having worked together for such a long time."

"Yes, well. I was turned in the twenties. Met him in Vegas. I've done this and that over the years but somehow ended up styling for him. It's easier when he's actually in the city." She buckled the last sandal and smiled. "They're dope, yeah?"

"They're beautiful. So sparkly. Let's see if I can walk in them," she said with a slight laugh. While Waverly loved a beautiful pair of heels, she spent most of her time in flip flops. She stood, finding the shoes surprisingly comfortable. "They feel really good. Thank you."

"All right then. Go to the mirror and let me check you over," Beverly ordered.

Waverly stared at her reflection. Her long blonde hair had been braided up the sides, wavy locks curling down her back. Blood-red lipstick stained her lips, a hint of blush on her cheekbones.

"You look gorgeous." Beverly clapped her hands together. "Magnifique!"

"Thank you. It sounds stupid, but I'm a little nervous about tonight," Waverly admitted, not sure why she'd shared her emotions with the stranger. "It's just, well, you know, sometimes it helps to feel like you're put together even if you're about to unravel."

"It's going to be okay," Beverly assured her. "You're human but you must have great strength if Viktor is keeping you on. You'll be all right. Trust me. Viktor won't let any of them hurt you. It's just a party. Walk into the room like you own that shit."

"Fake it till you make it?" Waverly nodded.

"Don't show fear. A human as beautiful as you, is going to tempt them. They will be drawn to you like bees to flowers." She shrugged. "But trust me. No one's going to touch you. You're Viktor's flower."

"How can you be sure?"

"I've been to many a party, my dear. And I know paranormals. This party tonight is upscale. People think that money makes them safe. Don't ever mistake wealth for safety. The rich ones are often more dangerous."

"Okay. That's comforting."

"The half demon is throwing the affair but there will be paranormals from all walks of life. Vampires. Wolves. Perhaps even a witch."

"I trust Viktor." Waverly realized in that moment she'd meant what she said. He'd been there for her at every step of her journey. "Thank you for helping me get ready. I'm not sure what I would have done without you."

"It's been my pleasure. You must be pretty special for Viktor to be toting you around." Beverly slung her oversized Louis Vuitton duffle bag over her shoulder. "I'll be seeing you round. Have to go see to Rafe. The boy's a hot mess." She laughed. "Viktor's got a girlfriend and a child. Hell must have really frozen over.

"I'm not his girlfriend," Waverly protested.

"Aw, sugar. You don't need to lie to me. Or yourself."

"But I—"

"You take care tonight, you hear?" Beverly waved as she opened the door. "Speak of the devil."

"My ears were burning," Viktor said as he walked into the room.

"You be good tonight, sir. Take care of this pretty flower."

Waverly's heart pounded in her chest as her gaze locked on his. With trimmed scruff along his chiseled jawline and perfectly coifed hair, Viktor gave off an air of confidence and style. The sophisticated vampire, dressed in a dark blue tuxedo, exuded sex and power.

She blinked, briefly averting her gaze and then looked back up to him, her cheeks flushed. *Waverly, stop staring at him.* Jesus, he made her feel as if she was a teenager seeing her football quarterback crush.

"I, um, I hope this is okay." She held her hands out and slowly spun in a circle. "I call this look, 'naked but dressed'."

"You're stunning." He leaned into her, his lips brushing her ear. "Irresistible."

"Likewise," she managed, her knees weakening. Goose-flesh broke over her skin, heat rushing between her legs.

"Looking this gorgeous, I'm tempted to peel this dress right off you. What's underneath it is much more beautiful."

"I suppose we can't go nude to a party," she teased.

"No. No we can't. While I've indulged in the lifestyle, I find myself too protective of my precious curator to share you with others."

"Hmm…maybe we can leave the party early?" she mused, afraid to imagine the sexcapades he'd engaged in over a thousand years.

"I promise you this is business only. And when we return home, I will have you all to myself." He withdrew, still holding her hands. "Goddess, you're beautiful."

"Beverly worked her magick."

"She's a terrific stylist, but it's you who brings the shine." Viktor's expression flattened, turning serious. "Which reminds me. About tonight. You must stay at my side, understand?"

"Of course." She nodded.

"I mean it. No matter the temptation, don't let them separate us." His tone turned serious.

"Someone's going to try to separate us?" Anxiety curled in her stomach at the thought.

"Thorn. The half demon. He's charming but wily. Cunning. He's the kind of dude I trust until I don't if you know what I mean. The guests will most likely all be paranormal. I'm not worried about the vampires. Quintus will see to their submission. Jax Chandler, the New York Alpha. He'll control the wolves. But you've got other creatures. Witches. Warlocks. Possibly fae. Especially considering Thorn's connections."

"Fae?"

"Yeah." He nodded.

"Are they really that dangerous?"

"Yes. They are one of the few species who can easily enter Hell and come back out again. Easily being the key word. When they're in Hell, they seek out jobs from the netherworld. Blood contracts, possession and whatnot. Think of them as intermediaries between the demons stuck in Hell and the creatures who walk this earth."

"Why do they keep coming here?" Waverly had heard rumors of fae but never met one.

"Because the magick within humans is special. And it's the way of the wicked to seek the most precious gift the Goddess bestows on you. The essence of pure energy. The soul. While it's true humans are fragile, that precious soul is attractive to others who wish to corrupt it, darken it. Ghosts seek the energy they used to have, hoping to change what's been done, to possess humans to use as a vessel. Vampires drink your blood. Wolves mimic some of your traditions. Witches, even. They teach humans their craft, sell them their wares. Even the high priestess was born of humans, that magick helped her to birth a child to a vampire."

"But what do the fae want from us?"

"They've learned their tricks from the very best in Hell. Extortion is what they're best at. They can broker the sale of a soul, or make deals otherwise related to souls. They can even make trades with paranormals. And when things go wrong, which they inevitably do from time to time, they're fairly good at the art of torture, making someone's life like… well, hell in fact."

"Why?"

"They might want a human to do their bidding, to do something only humans would do. Could be mundane tasks or just for money. But for the purposes of this evening, don't ask anyone for any favors. Choose your words carefully. And again, never leave my side."

"Yeah, don't worry about that. I won't." Waverly's stomach clenched into a tight knot. The last time she'd been around vampires and other paranormal creatures, she'd nearly gotten killed.

"We should go downstairs. The limo is waiting." As Viktor reached for the doorknob, he stopped short of opening the door. He reached into his jacket pocket and retrieved a black box, Waverly's heart pounded in her chest. "I forgot something. I picked this out for you. Not Beverly."

Waverly gasped as he opened the box, revealing a graduated diamond necklace displayed upon black velvet. The spectacular, bright stones sparkled under the light.

"Viktor…" She placed her hand across her chest, shocked at the sight of the extravagant piece of jewelry.

"Turn around now, pet," he told her.

Waverly did as she was told and lifted the curls off her back. The weight of the diamonds rested upon her chest as he locked the clasp. She let her hair fall and turned to the mirror, astonished at the gorgeous piece of jewelry, her fingers brushing over the exquisite diamonds.

"This is too much. I shouldn't wear this…it's too expensive. What if something happens to it?"

"There are many diamonds in this world. But this diamond," he brushed his finger along her collarbone, onto her chest, briefly touching the apex of the necklace, a large center diamond. "When I found it long ago, I kept it shielded from the world because I knew others would covet it, attempt to steal it. Over time, I secretly had it shaved, cut in such a way that others would have disagreed with. I enhanced its clarity. Perhaps not as large as it was originally but now it's flawless."

"It's stunning," she whispered, bringing her shaking fingers to touch his. The vision struck her instantly. Viktor stood before her in tattered clothes. As he lifted his head and revealed his unwashed face, she caught a hint of his familiar smile. In his soiled hands, he held a muddy rock. Surrounded by trees, he looked over each shoulder before kneeling and rinsing it through the murky creek water.

Viktor jumped to his feet, inspecting the treasure. With lightning speed, he tore a strip of fabric from his already tattered clothes and wrapped the rock. He again checked over his shoulder and spied a boulder at the base of a tree. Viktor stumbled toward it through the thick brush, fell to his knees and began frantically digging. Within seconds of him burying the rock, voices in the distance shouted his name. He kicked leaves over the fresh dirt and took off into the forest.

Waverly blinked her eyes into focus, her gaze settling on his. He knew. He'd shown her a sliver of his journey. She reached for him and cupped his cheek.

"I saw it. I saw you. You hid it near the boulder," Waverly said, shocked by what she'd seen.

"I retrieved it years later. When I finally got my freedom."

She smiled. "How is this happening?"

"What?" He smiled at her.

"How are you showing me? It's not just a random memory like before. I saw what you wanted me to see."

"I don't know. You're the one with visions. Maybe it's you?" He winked. "You're a clever, talented human. I told you about the magick."

"Are you telling me the truth?" She laughed.

"I will always tell you the truth. This thing that's happening with us..." His voice trailed off as he checked his watch, and then quickly changed the subject. "Ah, the truth is we're going to be late. But I promise you, we're due for a conversation. But it's not one to be rushed."

"All right," she agreed, noting the serious tone in his voice. Waverly rested her hand on his extended arm as he ushered her to the door.

Her attraction to the charismatic vampire had deepened. No matter how much she attempted to rationalize how it had happened, she couldn't shake the strong feelings.

She steeled her nerves and focused on their purpose, attempting to ignore the surreal connection with Viktor. Waverly pictured herself walking into the demon's party like a queen. *Show no fear.*

WAVERLY NERVOUSLY FIDDLED with her fingernail as the limo traversed the hour's drive to Chappaqua, New York. Viktor had warned that although they'd take a car to the party, should the need arise, they might dematerialize back to his penthouse.

Her thoughts raced, imagining a party filled with para-normals from all walks of life. As a human, she suspected she was very much outmatched in strength, but she'd decided to take Beverly's attitude. *Walk in like you own the place.*

The driver turned into the long and winding driveway,

and she peered out the windows, noting a church that edged the property. Pillared candles dripped wax onto headstones, the flicker of their flames illuminating the cemetery.

As the sight of the enormous home came into view, she looked to Viktor. She deliberately reminded herself to breathe, to remain calm.

"You've got this," he told her. "Remember. No favors. Don't so much as ask for directions to the bathroom. It's likely fae are attending and we don't want any issues."

"I heard what happened to Hunter," Rafe said, craning his head to get a better look at the ostentatious mansion. "Fae got him with hellfire."

Waverly's expression dropped. "Hellfire?"

"The fae have the ability to manipulate fire. Use it to enter Hell. Hellfire is poisonous." Viktor gave Greyson a nod and focused back onto Waverly and Rafe. "Listen up everyone. I'm going to say it one more time. No favors. No going off alone. If for some reason we get broken up, buddy system applies. Do not be tempted by the ladies. I'm talking to you, wolf. If you get hungry, tell me or Greyson. Okay, let's go see Thorn."

"I hate demons," Greyson grumbled.

"He knows Hell," Viktor countered, hoping Thorn would give them answers.

"Yeah, fuck him."

"Game faces on. Here we go," Viktor warned.

Waverly's stomach flipped as the car rolled to stop. An attendant in a purple crushed velvet uniform approached the car and opened the door.

"Welcome to Shangri-la," he greeted them.

Wearing a nonchalant expression, Viktor exited the car and turned to Waverly. She accepted his hand as he turned to her, assisting her out of the car.

They walked along the path towards the entrance. With

great dramatic fanfare, two attendants reached for ornate gold handles and swung open a set of enormous brass doors, gesturing for them to enter. As they stepped into the foyer, the sound of pounding bass echoed throughout the open space. Waverly held her chin up, walking with confidence and grace.

"This way." A servant dressed in a red satin pantsuit gestured toward a great arched hallway which led to the festivities.

Waverly did her best to remain calm as she stepped into the extravagant dance hall. As if hung on marionette strings, red pillar candles appeared to dance overhead. Perched above the crowd on a small stage, an orchestra played a classical version of *What I've Done*. Dressed in formal attire, partygoers danced in the center of the ballroom.

"Where are we going?" Waverly whispered, her eyes adjusting to the darkened room. "Is everything okay?"

"All is well," Viktor assured her. "We shall see Thorn when he comes to us."

"Comes to us?" she asked, fighting the anxiety that churned in her stomach.

"Yes, he will find us." Viktor scanned the room and exchanged a knowing look with both his brother and the wolf. "Stay together."

"You know it," Greyson nodded.

"Let's dance," Viktor told her.

"Dance? Yes." Her heart pounded in her chest as Viktor led her out onto the dance floor.

As they walked through a sea of people, Waverly stilled as a tall, lithe woman, dressed in black latex, leaned toward her and sniffed her hair. "Hmm...delicious toy you've brought."

"She's mine." Viktor released a low growl, his fangs dropping. The vampire bared her teeth at him, and slowly disappeared into the crowd.

Stay calm. Stay calm. You can do this. What in the ever-loving fuck?

"Dance with me." Viktor smiled at Waverly as he pulled her into his embrace.

The warmth of his body on hers calmed her soul. The music, eerily rhythmic, grew louder as they danced. As she looked to the others, she caught sight of them staring.

"Look at me," Viktor commanded.

Waverly's eyes locked on his, her pulse racing. With his fangs still visible, he leaned in, and brushed his lips to hers. As if they were the only two people in the room, she kissed him. His tongue swept into her mouth, and her body flared with desire.

As they danced, Waverly lost all sense of time and place. She gasped as his fingers tugged her dress upward and teased her bottom. With a sudden crescendo of violins, the music abruptly ended. He tore his mouth from hers, leaving her breathless, craving his touch.

"Tonight, I will have you," he promised.

"Viktor," she whispered, her voice barely audible.

"Viktor, indeed," a male voice exclaimed from behind her. Startled, she spun around but Viktor held a firm hand around her waist.

"Thorn," he greeted. "Lovely party."

"Your home is stunning," Waverly managed as the mysterious demon came into view.

"You brought a human," Thorn mused. "Interesting choice."

"Can we move to somewhere more private?" Viktor asked.

Thorn laughed. "Why, of course, my old friend. Come. I have just the place for us."

Waverly struggled to compose herself. Flushed and palms damp, she took a cleansing breath, ignoring the stares. Jesus, she'd almost dragged Viktor back to the limo. Her body still on fire from his touch, she hadn't cared who'd seen them, obsessed with his all-consuming kiss.

Viktor's arm dropped from her waist, finding her hand. As he leaned toward her, his lips grazing her ear, she dug her nails into her palm in an attempt to distract herself from the ache between her legs. "We shall finish this later, pet."

This? The desire to taste her ancient vampire would go unsated for now. But indeed, *this*, they would finish.

Aside from the occasional glance to Viktor, Waverly kept her eyes forward as he led her through the crowd. Without showing an iota of fear, she walked beside him. She could feel the eyes on her, hear the whispers in the shadows. None of it would faze her in the moment. She embodied queen energy, drawing on her instinct to survive and the confidence that her vampire would protect her at all costs.

Waverly lifted her dress as they ascended an enormous wooden spiral staircase that led upward to a balcony. Once they reached the second level, she followed Viktor along an illuminated path. Inlaid twinkling red lights danced within the flooring, leading them to a cozy seating area.

"Come sit. We have a bit of time until the show begins," Thorn told them.

Show? What show? Her pulse raced.

You're doing fine, mo chroí. Waverly's eyes widened, shocked she'd heard his voice. *Easy, now.*

"Here we are. I like to think of this as my private viewing area. At this point in the evening, I need a break from the riff raff. I've grown tired of the bland conversation and recycled stories. Please have a seat." Thorn gestured to a set of eight intricately carved wooden chairs, each adorned with black leather cushions. He looked to Waverly. "Don't be shy, dear. Come sit next to me."

No fear. Waverly managed a smile and gracefully sat

down, never taking her eyes off the good-looking half demon. "Thank you."

"Quite a set-up you've got here. Dark but chic," Viktor commented. He nodded to Greyson, who wore a scowl.

His brother grumbled as he took a seat. Rafe slid back into a chair and smirked.

"Greyson doesn't seem impressed." Thorn glared at the cantankerous vampire.

"My brother is adequately interested. He's here, isn't he?" Viktor told him.

"I suppose so, but we all know that he holds a grudge. It is a weakness of humans." He looked to Waverly and back to Greyson. "And vampires."

"Demons don't have a soul, so what do you know about vampires?" Greyson spat out.

"Ah, he speaks." Thorn gave an icy smile.

"My brother may be able to forget that you delivered that *thing* from Hell to Quintus. That Mao lookalike demon or whatever the fuck it was, but not me. That's right. I heard all about it. You're a sick fuck." Greyson's hands tightly gripped the chair arms. "I don't know why Viktor even speaks to you."

"I'm not always responsible for these things," Thorn replied.

"Yeah, well, what about Camille? You took her to Hell, asshole."

Waverly's expression remained nonchalant. Viktor's brother appeared to have a specific, personal issue with the demon. *A woman? A human?*

"Ah yes, I admit I did take her. But in fairness to me, you know I have no choice in these matters. The human made a blood contract. It was her time. It's not as if I had a choice. It happened well before I gained my freedom to walk in this realm. I was in a different head space back then."

"Camille didn't deserve to go to Hell," Greyson said. "She was working to recover her life."

"I'm not in charge of these things. You know there's a hierarchy. There are some things I'll fight for, but not a woman who clearly made a deal with a devil. You know how this works."

"She was a friend," Greyson told him, anger in his voice.

"She belonged to a demon with a higher pay grade than my sexy ass. As I said, not in charge." Thorn pursed his lips, staring at the vampire.

From out of the darkness, a topless woman with pierced nipples, wearing a slate blue taffeta skirt approached. With thick dark hair and striking beauty, she moved in silence as she attended to the guests.

As the server extended a glass to Waverly, she caught sight of her glowing crimson eyes. Though she inwardly trembled, she accepted the drink, wearing an impassive expression. "Thank you."

Waverly looked to Viktor who nodded. *Demon. It's okay. I'm right here.*

"Cheers to reunions." Thorn held his glass to the air and promptly drank without waiting for the others.

Waverly nodded with a dry smile. Although she brought the glass to her mouth, she kept her lips sealed, feigning to drink.

"So, tell me, when are you going to introduce me to this beautiful human? I'm on pins and needles," Thorn said with a snicker.

"This is Dr. LaFleur." Viktor wore a flat demeanor as he introduced her.

"Waverly," she offered.

"A doctor?" he asked with interest.

"A curator," she replied, her voice calm and steady. "Art.

I'm based in San Diego, but I work all over the world on consult. I've been working with Mr. Christianson."

"Consult? Is that what this is?" Thorn laughed. "Viktor, you do surprise me. Brains. Beauty. She's extraordinary. Simply delicious."

Waverly's heart pounded in her chest as his gaze smothered her. She returned his slimy smile with a resting bitch face that wouldn't crack.

"She's under my protection," Viktor stated.

"So, you're saying she doesn't belong to you per se?" Thorn's eyes lit up with excitement.

"She's with me," Viktor insisted.

"But are you bonded?" Thorn inquired, raising a questioning eyebrow at him.

"We appreciate you having us tonight, but this topic is not up for discussion. Waverly is with me and only me. Don't test me." Viktor flashed a cool smile. "I have business to discuss with you."

"Before we begin, I've got a surprise for you both. I was going to wait but I can't stand the anticipation." Thorn clapped his hands. "Consider it a gift, Greyson."

Through a thick cloud of red-tinged smoke, a figure emerged. Waverly steeled her nerves as the striking woman came into view. With long platinum blonde locks and wearing a snow-white, floor-length gown that clung to her body, the otherworldly creature exuded a powerful energy. Drawn to her, Waverly stared, shocked as the woman appeared to glide toward them. *Who is she?*

Viktor exchanged a look with his brother.

"What the hell?" Greyson's jaw dropped in awe at the sight of the guest. "Are you kidding me?"

Thorn laughed out loud and clapped his hands. "I love a surprise."

"Ilsbeth," Viktor acknowledged her, but his tone remained cold.

"Well, fuck." Rafe sighed. "It's Mommy."

Captivated by the ethereal presence, Waverly barely noticed their voices. As the woman approached her, she stood from her chair. Viktor moved to stop Waverly, but she shooed him away. "No, it's fine."

As Waverly accepted Ilsbeth's hand to shake it, the visions slammed into her. Pain. So much pain. The flames of Hell surrounding her as she screamed for mercy. Waverly instinctively jerked her hand away.

"I'm sorry," Waverly whispered.

"What an interesting human," Ilsbeth responded without a blink of an eye, immediately turning to Viktor. "Why are you surprised to see me, vampire? You know I always land on my feet."

"I've learned never to underestimate you," he told her, protectively wrapping his arm around Waverly's waist, pulling her away from the high priestess. "What are you doing here?"

"I was invited, of course." She winked at Greyson but made a beeline for the wolf. "Rafe, darling. Are you feeling well?"

"You're something else, momma witch. Something scary. But still—"

"Teenagers." Ilsbeth shrugged him off and focused on Greyson who stood towering above her. "You are looking well." Her gaze painted over him. "Nice suit."

The great vampire glared at her, heat flickering in his eyes. He stood firm as she placed her palm to his chest.

"Been a long time. Haven't seen you in New Orleans lately." She glanced to Viktor. "Or Hell."

"I've been busy for a few hundred years," Greyson replied.

"We need to catch up soon," she suggested, smiling with her eyes.

"Heard you were taking up with wolves. Betas no less." Greyson stood his ground, staring at her.

"A temporary infatuation, I assure you."

"Infatuation? More like attempted murder," Rafe insisted.

"It was a misunderstanding. We must look to the future if we want to achieve the climax of life. Our greatest desire." A devious smile formed on her lips. Ilsbeth moved past Greyson, taking a seat next to him. "Let the past be the past."

"This is some bullshit here," Rafe grumbled.

"Don't mind Ilsbeth," Viktor told him.

"He's welcome to mind all he wants. He's family." Ilsbeth shot Rafe a side glance. "Just so long as you know your place."

"Know my place? First of all, we're not a family. I needed your blood. And second, I don't need you," Rafe shot back.

"And you, vampire," The witch pinned Viktor with a stare. "Did you think I wouldn't find out about the human?"

"She is none of your concern," Viktor asserted.

"You left Rafe alone in San Diego. He's too young," she chastised.

"He's learned control. He's a grown wolf for fuck's sake." Viktor shook his head. "And by the way, witch. You don't get a say in how he's raised. Your participation was limited to your blood. It's over. You're the one who should mind your business."

Waverly stared at Ilsbeth as they traded barbs. The paranormals had lived lifetimes, and it clearly was not the first time they'd argued. Ilsbeth dripped with jealousy. She treated Viktor as if he were her ex, leaving Waverly with the impression that perhaps there was far more between them. *Did he sleep with her?* Waverly's stomach clenched in anger, but she bit her tongue, remaining silent.

Waverly glanced at Greyson, whose expression revealed

nothing. Yet the slight softening in his eyes as Ilsbeth briefly reached for him and brushed her fingers over his arm spoke volumes. *Did he love her?*

"Enough." Viktor slammed his hand down on the arm of the chair.

Thorn held his goblet up into the air and huffed. "You're killing the vibe, people."

"You can stay, but this is confidential. If I find out either one of you," Viktor pointed, "Thorn. Witch. Like if I ever hear a fucking peep about this meeting, I'm going to hunt you down and drag your asses back to Hell. The only reason either of you are out again is because Hunter came for me." He focused on Ilsbeth. "I've saved your sorry ass so many times over the century, too many times to count." He blew out a breath. "So, this is how it's going to go. I'm going to share with you something that's happening, you're both going to keep it confidential."

Viktor glanced downstairs, his eyes widening. "Mother-fucker. You invited Kellen to this party? He's glowing red like he's fresh out of Hell."

"Well yeah, I mean, I'm half demon so…" Thorn cringed. "Birds of a feather."

"Not a word to him. Not a word to anyone," Viktor lowered his voice. "We have a situation. It may be a small situation or a large situation. Waverly has a friend missing in Miami. She was hanging with some dudes who said they were in some kind of a human blood-drinking brotherhood."

"My friend's name is Teagan," Waverly said.

"On her trip to find Teagan she was contacted by an anonymous donor who sent her a painting," Viktor continued.

"I love art," Ilsbeth said, her expression flat.

"Ooh, so do I." Thorn smiled.

"Viktor donated a painting to our new exhibit," Waverly told her. "A Monet."

"Did he now?" Ilsbeth gave a cool smile, staring at Viktor.

Waverly ignored her and continued. "During the donor preview party, there was a shooting."

"A human shooter. Looking for Waverly," Viktor told them.

"Humans with their silly guns. If they only knew what true power was," Ilsbeth said.

"Long story short. He shot her. I healed her. When we went back to the museum to collect the painting, the detective wanted to see it and then went full-on demon, although I suspect she was possessed. Seemed nice enough before we went to the office." Viktor retrieved his phone and tapped at the screen, holding up an image for them to see. "We took the painting and found something in it. A fleam. But just the tip."

"That's what she said." Thorn's chuckle was met with hard stares. "What? Just offering a bit of levity."

"Bloodletting." Ilsbeth smiled. "Those were the days."

Waverly clenched her jaw, irritated. *What the hell is wrong with these people?* As soon as the thought popped in her head, the answer hit her. *Immortals. Paranormals.*

"This fleam is unique." Viktor's lips tightened in a straight line and briefly glanced at Greyson who nodded. "It has initials on the blade. B.A.O."

Waverly's pulse raced as Ilsbeth's eyes widened. *Fear? Anger?* Whatever it was, it couldn't be good.

"Baxter." Ilsbeth spoke softly.

"I saw him die," Viktor replied.

"But—" she began.

"But nothing," Viktor insisted. "He's dead."

Waverly reached for Viktor and gently rested her hand on his arm. She gave a gentle squeeze.

Thorn and Ilsbeth exchanged a knowing look but remained silent.

"I've got a friend who works for a museum in the city. He thinks he's found the handle," Waverly said.

"May I see the fleam?" Ilsbeth asked.

"No," Viktor replied. "It's in a safe place. I couldn't risk bringing it here. Too many eyes."

"I don't recall any bloodletting fleams that carry magical properties, but as you know, my memory, since Hell...it's not quite what it used to be. That being said, if I hold it in my hands, I may get more information," she explained.

"Since you're here I might as well ask you this." Viktor scrolled the pictures on his phone and selected an image, holding it high so they could view it. "Someone left this in Dr. LaFleur's apartment. Do you recognize this work? The same pattern was also found on the shooter. A tattoo. To me, this looks human in nature, but I'd like to know its origin."

"May I see the picture again?" Ilsbeth asked.

Viktor obliged, holding his phone closer. Waverly's stomach rolled at the sight of the blood, recalling the intrusion into her home.

"Goat heads are used for rituals in many a religion, but this pattern of the blood. It shows a rudimentary knowledge of black magick. Perhaps in an effort to hex her, which would be the best scenario. But if it's being used by humans, worn by humans, they may be attempting to conjure a demon. It depends on the spell. And before you look at me, it doesn't necessarily have to be done by a witch. With the right training and direction, any paranormal or human could carry out a sacrifice. Or a conjuring. What they did appears crude, but it's an attempt at a spell. Have you noticed anything odd?"

"Who? Me?" Waverly gave a nervous laugh. "You're kidding me, right? All of this is odd. No offense."

"None taken." Ilsbeth turned to Viktor. "She's a virgin?"

"I'm sorry, what?" Waverly exclaimed. "Um, no. How is that even relevant?"

"I'm not talking about sex, child. I'm talking about the experience...walking among us."

"I don't frequent blood clubs. Or hang out with vampires. Or witches. Or wolves. But now...Viktor is a friend." *Lover.* She laughed and shook her head. "Look, I don't know either one of you, don't really have anything I can offer to thank you for helping but I have this feeling in my gut, something bad is coming."

"Premonitions?" Thorn asked in delight.

"I have visions," she confessed.

"Don't say another word," Viktor interrupted.

"The way you act with this human, Viktor. So quickly it's happened. How are you not bonded?" Ilsbeth smirked.

"Bonded?" Waverly asked, her voice raised in surprise. *What in the fresh hell is bonding?*

"This is none of your business," Viktor snapped at Ilsbeth.

"Bring me the fleam," Ilsbeth ordered. "Preferably both pieces. We'll meet again in New Orleans."

"I'll check around. See if I can find more about this brotherhood. I may know a few humans in secret societies. Some of which you may be familiar with. Some not." Thorn shrugged.

"You expect me to believe that in this day and age a group of humans could still get together to plot all our deaths and we wouldn't know?" Greyson scoffed.

"Don't ever underestimate the power of humans," Viktor told him, his gaze falling on Waverly.

"Humans are probably known for carrying out some of the greatest atrocities. History has shown us they are capable of evil well beyond what one could conceive of." Waverly straightened her spine, claiming her presence and power in the situation. "Regardless of whether they are human or paranormal, it doesn't matter. We have to find out who this fleam belongs to."

"Of course, darling." Thorn snapped his fingers.

"She's correct," Ilsbeth agreed. "It's important we find out who owned the fleam. If they are playing in the occult, they could be hoping for a much bigger spell. From the looks of it, they're trying to conjure up something."

"You'd know all about that, wouldn't you, Mom?" Rafe sneered.

"Before you judge, junior, there are times we need demon energy to fight," she told him.

"You almost killed Dimitri," Rafe replied.

"We've already discussed this. We all have lapses in judgement. I'm talking about other times, times of long ago. You are young. There are times we make trades in order to fight for our existence. Where we make judgement calls in order to capture power. To win. The human is right."

"We shall reconvene. I'm done now. It's time for the show," Thorn announced.

A handsome man appeared out of the darkness. Barefoot and shirtless, he wore only well-fitted tuxedo pants. He nodded at Thorn and took a seat next to him. The light from above reflected off the sheen of his dark muscled chest.

"Who the hell is this, Thorn?" Viktor asked, anger washing over his expression.

"This is Winsor. Isn't he absolutely handsome?"

Waverly watched in fascination as iridescent scales appeared on his chest and quickly disappeared.

"He's a dragon," Thorn continued. "Quite rare, aren't you darling?"

"I don't care who he is, this knowledge isn't for his ears." Viktor glared at Thorn, his patience worn thin.

"This conversation is over. Get the piece to Ilsbeth. I'll do research and make myself available. It's time for the show. Microphone please." Thorn snapped his fingers.

The topless servant reemerged from the shadows and handed an embellished crystal mic to Thorn. "Ladies and gentlemen, all creatures of the Goddess, and those below, welcome to the playhouse. It's been a pleasure having you all here tonight. Please stand back and enjoy the show."

Panic spiked through Waverly as darkness fell. She couldn't see a soul in the pitch-black room. As Viktor's hand clasped hers, she flinched. His power flowed through her, yet her adrenaline was too far gone to remain calm.

Waverly's attention was drawn to the floor, her pulse racing. The translucent circle below her feet retreated, leaving a clear view down to the first floor. Her stomach flipped and she wiggled back further into her seat, her feet dangling in the air.

"What the..." Her jaw dropped open as the music began to reverberate in the room.

I'm here with you. It's okay. Waverly glanced at Viktor, his face illuminated by the black lights below.

What's happening? Adrenaline pumped through her veins as five creatures walked into the ballroom. With human facial features and scaled bodies, they began to dance.

Hell boy shit and hot girl summer. Viktor gave a small smile.

She shot him a stern look. *How can you joke at a time like this?*

If I don't attempt to see humor in this shitty situation, I'm likely to kill Thorn or Ilsbeth. Maybe both.

As the creatures danced, their bodies ignited on fire. The music slowed, and the sea of dancers fell to crumpled heaps on the floor. A kaleidoscope of colors flashed throughout the smoky arena. A scaled creature emerged, growing nearly seven feet high, baring its fangs. Flames danced over its body, and it gave a mighty roar as wings materialized from its back.

The potent scent of sulphur spilled into the air, and Waverly choked back a cough. As the wild beast took flight, she dug her fingers into Viktor's arm. The whoosh of its billowing wings echoed in her ears. The pounding beat grew louder as the creature flew faster and faster, circling the sea of undulating bodies below. As the crescendo peaked, the dragon ascended straight through the exposed floor, blasting waves of smoke.

Waverly screamed in terror as it swiveled its head towards her and roared. Flames shot from its mouth, licking the bottom of her shoes.

"Enough!" Viktor yelled.

Before Waverly had a chance to move, he'd swept her up in his arms. Through the smoke, she caught a glimpse of Greyson who reached for Rafe and nodded. She curled her face against Viktor's chest, coughing the burning sulfur from her lungs.

"The show is over," she heard him say as they dematerialized from the mansion.

CHAPTER NINE

"Can you hear me?" Viktor asked, still cradling Waverly in his arms. "You're okay. It's safe."

She released a deep breath, sensing the floor beneath her feet. She coughed and the smoke dissipated from her lungs. Viktor's energy flowed through her, guiding a calming sensation through her body.

"Is it gone?" she asked in panic. Her heart pounded in her chest. She blinked her eyes, taking in the sight of the living room, the cityscape sparkling through the wall of windows.

"You're safe now," he repeated. "We're at my place."

"Where's Greyson?" She swiveled her head around, searching for him. "Where's Rafe? Are they okay?"

"They'll be fine. They'll probably go to Quintus' blood club and blow off some steam. Greyson may be sweet on the High Priestess, but he hates demons. He only went tonight because I asked him."

"That monster with the fire. What was that thing?"

"Seems as though Thorn has become friends with a herd of dragons."

"His boyfriend. He was a dragon. His eyes—"

187

"Yeah. Dragon eyes flicker. It's creepy. Some of them wear contact lenses to remain discreet among humans. But these guys were letting it all hang loose."

"That dragon scared the shit out of me. I can't believe what I saw tonight."

"Thorn's an asshole for allowing them to throw fire inside the house like that, but I would never have let them hurt you." He gave a tight smile. "They're usually only aggressive when they are protecting something. I'm sorry about tonight."

"I've never been around so many paranormals. Those dragons. I mean, come on, they were flying. No one would ever believe it." Waverly's head spun, trying to comprehend what she'd experienced. "Do you think Thorn and Ilsbeth will really be able to tell us more about the fleam? It didn't seem like you trusted them."

"I don't trust either of them. But I'm confident I can see the truth from a lie. It's a talent of mine." He winked at her.

"Did you sleep with her?" Waverly regretted the words as soon as they left her lips. She inwardly cringed at the seed of jealousy that had been planted.

"Ilsbeth?" he laughed.

She nodded but didn't say a word, afraid she'd say something else stupid.

"No way. Now don't get me wrong, she's always been attractive, but she's like Lily of the Valley. Beautiful. Fragrant. But deadly as fuck."

"Greyson seems smitten," she observed.

"He's a fool." Viktor shook his head. "They had a thing once. She must be good in bed, because my brother's ancient and still pining over the witch's kitty."

"He loves her?" she asked.

"Aw, hell no. He doesn't even know her anymore. But I do. I've seen her in Hell, and I know how she got there. Rafe is not too far off with what he says about her. She's a piece of work. But," he held up a finger, "she did help me out in Hell. Fed me. And she helped me with Rafe. And it's not the first time over the years. So yeah, she's what you'd call a paradox."

"It's hard to believe she's Rafe's mother."

"Yeah, it is. But Rafe was too far gone. I needed help. I had to make a quick decision."

"Why did you really do it?"

"I don't know. I was helping a friend, and you know, I just thought I could save him right there. But I miscalculated, so I had to bounce. Try something else. I brought Ilsbeth over to my island, and she gave him her blood too. Now he's hybrid. It's not the best situation but it is what it is."

"Why don't you have others? Other children."

"I didn't want that responsibility. My master…Baxter. He was just the very worst. And I didn't want to chance being like him. And it turns out I'm not. Ilsbeth had a point that I probably shouldn't have left him that long in San Diego. But then again, I'm also right about Rafe being an adult. If there were any issues, Jake would've handled it. She's just being a bitch."

"He seems quite fond of you." Waverly looked around the dimly lit living room, through the windows to the city. "It's beautiful here. I don't think I've ever been up this high in an apartment."

"It's a little chilly this time of year," Viktor said.

"Do you spend a lot of time in New York?"

"I spend most of my time in Miami, but I have other homes around the world. New Orleans. LA. London. Amsterdam. Paris. Milan. Fiji."

Viktor retrieved his cell phone and tapped at the glass. Within seconds, the room illuminated with soft lighting. He slid his finger across the screen and a gas fireplace ignited, ambient reggae music began to play. "I'm in the process of buying a property in Croatia."

"Who are you, Viktor Christianson?" she laughed. They'd literally just gone from a fire-breathing flying dragon show to relaxing in luxury, and he didn't miss a beat.

"I'm an ancient vampire with a penchant for living my best life. This includes travel and experiences and fun."

"And sex?" she asked with a flirtatious inflection in her voice. Her cheeks flushed with warmth.

"Perhaps," He shot her a sexy smile but didn't answer her.

"Have you ever been in love?" Her stomach tightened as she asked the question, but curiosity got the best of her.

"I may have thought I was in love a few times as a boy. I didn't have that luxury as an adult." Viktor stared off into the night, his expression solemn.

Waverly sensed his change in demeanor, his pain washing over her. But unlike other times, the vision didn't come.

"You saw some of my past. I don't know why I wanted to show it to you. To be honest, I didn't really know if you'd be able to see it. There are no other humans I've ever done this with. But I suppose there's just something about you. And how I feel when I'm with you…this thing with us. If there is a thing. I'm not good at this, Dr. LaFleur." He gave a small laugh.

Waverly's heart melted at his words.

"When I died, I hadn't learned love. When I was, what you would call 'reborn', my sire made it clear there was not ever going to be love in my life."

Waverly's mind wandered to the initials on the fleam. *B.A.O. Baxter.*

"My sire was the worst of all humans and paranormal. It was like every evil thing in him thrived. I've thought about it. Like maybe he was possessed when he was turned. But however he got that way, he was like the devil himself. One sadistic son of a bitch."

"How do you know he's really dead?" she asked.

"Let's not go too far down this path. He's dead because I saw him die. Quint killed him. I was there. We all were."

"We?"

"Waverly. *We* are among the oldest creatures that still walk the earth. We are the earliest of our kind. We are the children of Baxter Anwir Ó Cléirigh. And we're not all good guys."

"It's going to be okay," Waverly said out loud to calm her mind, the full spectrum of emotions stabbing through her. She craved this vampire with her body and mind. But he was over a thousand years old, and she was only thirty-three. He'd lived lifetimes, lived in a different world. There were a million reasons to take a break from her newest obsession. But as she gazed at him, her heart crushed with emotion.

"This thing between us...for vampires, when we are drawn to someone, and the Goddess presents our person... it's just one of those things...it's bonding." Viktor took Waverly by her hands.

"You're telling me that you've gone over a thousand years and haven't found that person?" Waverly smiled as he brushed the back of his hand to her cheek.

"Yes, that's exactly how it works." Viktor took her in his arms, and slowly danced with her.

A shiver ran through her body as he leaned in, his lips brushing over her neck.

"If I bite you, the bond will begin. You must consider the consequences, mo chroí."

"I—" She ached between her legs.

"If you taste of me, our bond will be complete. I should probably walk away," he rested his forehead against hers, "but I can't."

191

Waverly closed her eyes, attempting to process his words. *Bonded.* With a vampire. It didn't make sense, yet no man had ever made her feel the way Viktor did. She'd never met anyone like him and knew for certain she never would.

"I've spent my life learning about art. Working hard but having fun too. It's been a great life so far. But it's been lonely. I've dated a few guys, but nothing serious. Whatever we are supposed to feel to let us know we've found our person, I haven't felt it...until now," Waverly confessed as they continued to slow dance. "It's like with you...even though I wasn't expecting it, or wanting it, it's been incredible. Imagine going your whole life with people telling you your visions weren't real, so you bury them only to have them awakened by someone who accepts you, who can reach through to your soul. I don't know what bonding means, but the way I'm feeling...I just can't walk away, either. Last night. If it weren't for Greyson...I wanted you." *To bite me.*

"I can't give you children," Viktor told her, his gaze meeting hers.

"It's...it's okay." *Children.* Waverly hadn't given it a thought. Her career had been all-consuming, and she never once gave thought to raising a family. "If I change my mind we can adopt."

"Once we bond. It cannot be undone. Attempting to break a bond can be devastating."

"And if we don't bond at all? If we just walk away from each other? Then what?" A pit formed in her stomach. She was too far gone.

"I can't let you go," he confessed. "It would be really difficult. I want you in my life."

"I guess that settles it." Relief washed over her.

"Settles what?" He gave a small smile.

"I'm saying yes."

"Yes?" he asked.

"Yes, I'll be your girlfriend." The complication of what would happen in the future was too much for her to contemplate. "I'm not going to pretend to fully understand bonding. Honestly, I don't think there's a way for me to understand just yet. So, I'm going to go with 'you're my boyfriend'."

Viktor laughed. "Leave it to a human to simplify vampiric magick. You will be immortal if we bond."

"I can't think about that just yet." Waverly couldn't quite picture herself drinking blood.

"It's kind of an important detail to overlook."

"But I won't be turned into a vampire? I'll still be human?"

"Well, yes. But to complete this bond, and the desire to do so will increase...you'll be immortal with me. The people around you will come and go over the years. Your life will change as you know it. I won't bond with you without your consent."

Waverly's heart pounded in her chest as he released her. She took a step back and slowly reached for her zipper, loosening the dress from her body. She peeled it away, snapped off her bra and draped the fabric over her breasts.

"I want this. Us." With a sexy smile, still in her heels, she released the dress, revealing her bared body to him.

Still fully dressed, Viktor reached for her and pulled her close, brushing a kiss to her lips. "I crave you."

Waverly's body flared with arousal as Viktor hooked his finger around her panties, loosening them over her hips. He brushed his fingers downward over her mound as he sent them to the ground.

"Waverly," he groaned, his lips crushed onto hers.

As he kissed her, Waverly sighed. Her body ached for him, needing him inside her. His hand found her breast, pinching her sensitive nipple.

"I think I like you like this." He tore his mouth from hers, running his palm down the small of her back.

She opened her mouth to speak but lost her words as his fingers brushed over her hip and cupped her mound. Waverly sighed as his fingers teased through her slick folds and flicked over her clit.

"Hmm...wet for me." Viktor nipped at her shoulder but didn't release his fangs. 'I want to fuck you. Everywhere."

Waverly sighed as he drove a thick finger up into her pussy. "Oh God. Please."

"Like this?" Viktor stroked his fingers in and out of her, his thumb circling her clit.

"Oh God. Please...yes," she cried, her body ripe for release.

"You're so fucking wet, pet. Come for me. Come for me now," he demanded.

Waverly shattered into his hand, clutching at his shoulders as he fucked her pussy, her orgasm slamming into her.

Panting, she lifted her head, her gaze meeting his. He brought his hand to his mouth and licked his fingers.

Waverly reached for him and removed his jacket. She yelped as Viktor, without warning, lifted her up and slung her over his shoulder. "Come, pet."

She laughed as he delivered a firm swat to her bottom. He ran his palm up the back of her thighs, stroking her ass.

Within seconds, he set her onto the edge of the sofa. Her heart pounded as she looked up to him. She ran her palms up his thighs, watching in anticipation as he unbuckled his belt and freed his cock. She reached for him, but he promptly stopped her.

"Open your mouth," he ordered, wearing a devious smile.

Bared to him, wearing only her heels, she spread open her knees and leaned back on her palms. She smiled as he moved closer and guided his dick to her mouth.

"That's a good girl." He slid the tip over her bottom lip. "Open for me."

Waverly complied as he pressed his cock into her mouth, receiving him. "Hmm…"

She smiled, sucking his shaft hard as he slowly fucked her. She reached for his balls and teased them with her fingers. Ravenous, she swallowed him, reveling in his moans of pleasure.

"Fuck, oh yeah." he gritted out, plunging in and out of her. "You're going to make me want to come right now, but not like this…ah, ah, ah, stop."

He withdrew his dick and cupped her cheek, her lips glistening.

She gave a satisfied smile and lay back onto the sofa, her pussy wide open to him. Her body lit with arousal as he kicked off his trousers and stroked his cock, readying to fuck her.

Viktor closed the distance and tugged her legs upward, settling between her knees. Still holding her hips up to him, he tapped his cock on her mound.

Waverly sucked a breath as his tip brushed over her clit. Her pussy ached in anticipation.

"Please…I…" She lost her words as the crown of his cock pressed at her entrance.

She cried out in pleasure as he slammed inside her, her pussy contracting around him. With her feet hiked into the air, he pumped in and out of her.

Her back arched as his fingers stroked over her clit. She panted for breath, her body on fire, edging closer and closer.

She looked up to Viktor, his hungry gaze set on hers. She gasped as his fangs dropped in an ominous warning. In that moment, she needed him to fill her, to take every part of her. *Do it.*

Viktor laughed and withdrew his cock, leaving her breathless. "Little pet, perhaps you need to learn a lesson in submission."

"No, no, no…I need you to fuck me," she begged, her chest heaving for breath. Her fingers moved to her pussy, and he scolded her.

"Ah…no, no, no. That's my pussy," he growled with an erotic smile as he tapped his fingers to her mound.

The anticipation of not knowing what he'd do next amped her arousal. Her pussy ached and she pleaded for him to make love to her. "Please…I need you inside me."

Viktor bent over her and caged her with his arms. Her heart raced as his fangs grew closer, his thick cock brushing through her folds. Waverly ran her fingers down his muscular chest and over his ripped abdomen. His lips crushed onto hers, and she reached for his cock. As his mouth moved to her breast, she moaned with pleasure.

"Mine," he growled, sucking her nipple between his lips.

"Oh God, yes. Please," she begged, his cock teasing her swollen nub.

Her breath rushed from her lungs as he rolled her onto her stomach. A firm slap to her ass brought a sweet pain she'd never experienced.

"And this…this is mine," he growled.

"Viktor…" Waverly lost her words as he plunged his cock deep inside her pussy. She gasped as his thumb circled over her puckered flesh. "I've never…I don't know…I—"

"My sweet little pet…yes."

She stilled as the tip of his thumb slid into her ass. "Oh, God."

"Breathe for me, that's it. See how you were made for me," he told her. She moaned in pleasure as he inched his finger inside her. "I'm going to fuck you here too, mo chroí."

Waverly clutched at the cushions as he fucked her, his intoxicating touch overwhelming her body. He increased his pace, slamming into her pussy. She writhed beneath him, accepting each firm thrust.

She gasped as he withdrew his finger from her bottom and reached around to her breasts. Bringing her up onto her knees, he continued to pound his cock up into her.

"Viktor," she cried.

"Do you want this? Do you? Say it," he demanded, feverishly making love to her. "Beg for it, pet. Say it now."

"Please, oh God, please." She glanced back to Viktor, his sharp teeth visible in the dim light. She may not have understood the urgency, the pure agony until that moment, but she craved his bite and the erotic pleasure only he could give her.

"Say it." With his one hand on her breast, and his other teasing her clit, he opened his mouth, his fangs hovering over her neck.

"Do it," she breathed, her pussy aching for release. "Please Viktor, bite me. I want this. I want you. Only you. Please, yes."

"You belong to me, mo chroí. Do you understand?"

"Yes, yes," she panted. "Please."

"Always," he whispered, his breath on her neck.

"Oh God," she cried out as he thrust deep inside her, filling her pussy, his fangs slicing into her flesh. The sting of the pain shattered into bliss. Waverly shuddered in his arms; her body rocked in climax as he drove himself inside her.

As her blood flowed into his mouth, and her body seized with a glorious ecstasy she'd never experienced, she knew the truth of her destiny. Her life would never be the same. She'd been claimed by Viktor Christianson. *My vampire.*

WAVERLY STARED at her reflection in the mirror and brushed her fingers over her neck. The skin had healed, yet a faint scar remained. His mark. *Bonded.* Or at least partially. Aside from being delightfully sore, she didn't feel any different, look any different.

Waverly brought her hand to her abdomen and reflected. No children, he'd warned her. She'd never given a thought to getting pregnant. Yet she couldn't help but wonder if her biological clock hadn't started ticking. Perhaps she hadn't been in love with the right man...but now she'd found him.

Still very much within the human realm, fully understanding the paranormal eluded her, the only thing she knew for certain was that her infatuation with the vampire bordered on obsession. Logic had warned her against falling hard. But caught in an avalanche, she fell helplessly, praying her heart would stay in one piece.

Waverly wrapped a scarf around her neck and donned a soft leather jacket, still wondering what else in her life would change. Though she'd been born human, she'd begun to let down her guard, open her mind to the universe, and she wondered if her spiral into the paranormal had been meant to be. Denying her visions protected her within the human realm, but instinct told her that embracing them could protect her from whatever evil would come her way.

AFTER NEARLY AN HOUR in the limo, Waverly had grown anxious. No matter what pep talk she'd given herself, the reality was that Teagan was still missing and her own life was in danger.

"I've done a little digging on this Adam Strommell," Rafe offered, breaking her contemplation.

"Why were you looking him up? I told you he's a colleague."

"Because even though you went to grad school together,"

he gave her a sly smile, "there's always a chance he's undercover."

"Undercover as what? He was a student just like me," Waverly said in confusion.

"Sometimes vampires take over other people's lives. They find someone who's died years ago. Then they start again with a new persona. Or a modified version," Viktor answered. "Any supernatural can do it."

"Are you saying you think Adam is a vampire?" Waverly pressed her fingers to the bridge of her nose. "There's no way."

"He's not a vampire. That's the research Rafe did," Greyson replied.

"He could be something else," Rafe suggested.

"He *is* something else. He's human." Waverly tightened her lips, her anxiety building with each minute. "He doesn't know you all are coming. When he texted earlier with the address, I just said I'd be here. Please be cool."

"Cool as a cucumber." Viktor smiled at her.

"No blood. No fighting." Waverly looked to each of them, attempting not to laugh. It wasn't funny but at the same time, the level of crazy in her life drove her to find humor in the moment.

"Why do humans always think we're the problem?" Viktor laughed.

"Um, you've already shown your, uh, lack of anger management," she pointed out.

"Greyson gave a hearty laugh. "My brother was always quick with his sword."

"It's as true now as it was five hundred years ago. I have no time for idiocy. Or lies," Viktor mused.

"Life is complicated." Greyson fiddled with the buckle of his black leather jacket.

"But it doesn't have to be. It can be delightfully

predictable, and pleasingly full of adventure, luxury. Pleasure." Viktor flashed Waverly a knowing smile.

Waverly's cheeks flushed as she attempted not to recall the details of their love making. *Don't think about sex. Picasso. Rembrandt. Degas.* Her body flushed with heat, and she tugged at her scarf, accidentally exposing the scar on her neck.

She exchanged a brief glance with Greyson, and quickly covered it up.

"Nice scarf," he commented, smirking at his brother.

"Don't start." Viktor shut him down.

"Viktor is my boyfriend. What's it to you?" Waverly blurted out, her cheeks on fire with embarrassment.

"Your boyfriend. This is the best." Greyson laughed.

"It's true. I officially have a girlfriend. Pretty cool, right?" Viktor waggled his eyebrows.

"My brother has lost his mind," Greyson said with a glance to Rafe.

"Dude. It's not surprising. I mean come on. It's the oldest story in the book. Guy goes to a bar to get blood. Girl almost gets killed. Big Daddy vamp puts the hammer down on the bad guy and chases the girl across the country. Happens all the time." Rafe looked up from his cell phone at Greyson. "Besides, have you seen how he looks at her? It's over, bro."

"Think you're smart, wolf?" Greyson shot back at him.

"Um, I know it," Rafe answered and resumed scrolling through his phone.

"Well, let me teach you a new trick." Greyson paused and turned to Waverly and Viktor who sat across from them. "Have you fully bonded?"

Viktor glared at his brother. "Not that you would know anything about bonding, but we're taking care of business. That's all you need to know."

"Yeah, okay," Greyson replied.

"Can we please focus on what we are about to do?"

Waverly changed the subject, embarrassed by the conversation. She wasn't ready to share her relationship with the world. "The storage facility is near the bridge. There's a series of secret underground tunnels and the warehouse is fronted by Seville Industry. It's listed as an importing company. It's shared by several museums in the upper northeast."

Waverly stared out into the darkness as they traveled over the bridge. "Please let me deal with Adam when we get there. I haven't seen him for years. He asked me to go to dinner and I said no."

"Sounds like you've got some competition," Greyson teased.

"There is no competition," Viktor responded.

"Here we go." Waverly sucked a breath in an attempt to bury her anxiety.

They pulled up to the gate and watched in silence while the driver gave him their names. Waverly's stomach did a small flip as the guard waved them into the yard. A black SVU with its lights on sat parked directly across from a large garage door.

"Okay, I've got this," Waverly said as the driver opened the back door. A bright light shone inside the cabin. Thrumming with eagerness, she quickly gave a wave to Adam, who also exited his car.

Though his once raven hair was now striped with grey, he appeared exactly how she'd remembered him. But the excitement she'd once felt for the dashing grad student had faded.

"Hey beautiful!" he called to her.

"Hey there." As she extended her hand to him, he reached for her, pulling her into a hug. Her body recoiled at his touch.

The vision slammed into her. A wall of darkness, screams echoed through flashing lights. Before she had a chance to process it, a strong hand clamped around her waist, tugging her from his arms.

As if someone had pulled her from drowning in the deep sea, she gasped for air. Specks of light danced in her eyes, and she blinked repeatedly, attempting to regain focus.

"Waverly. Are you okay?" Viktor asked.

"Yes, yes, I'm fine," she insisted. "Sorry."

"Hey, what's going on here? Let her go," Adam demanded.

"Stand down," Greyson growled, putting himself between them.

"Waverly gets lightheaded from time to time," Viktor lied. "We're headed out soon, so if we could make way and get things done."

"Sorry, yes, he's right," she managed, regaining her balance. *What the fuck just happened?* "You see, um, I've had this ear infection. It has me a bit off balance. I've been taking antibiotics, but you know how it is. Takes a few days to kick in."

"Who are all these people?" Adam asked, his voice terse.

"I'm terribly sorry," Waverly apologized. "Adam. This is Viktor. He's, um, he's the owner of an original piece of art that was donated to my museum. A Monet. You see, he's been helping me with another donation that recently came in. He knows about the fleam. This is his brother Greyson and his, um, his nephew. They're in town. We, uh, we've had a few stops."

"I don't know—" Adam began.

"Is it okay if they come with us? Inside the vault?" she asked, her tone sweet as honey. "I promise they won't disturb anything."

An unconvincing half smile on Adam's otherwise expressionless face told her he wasn't happy that she hadn't arrived alone.

"I suppose so," he begrudgingly agreed. "You'll have to

register with the guards before you enter. I've arranged to transfer the item to your possession."

"I'm glad it's not on exhibition," she offered with a cheerful smile.

"It's virtually unused due to the nature of its condition. Doesn't make an especially huge impression without the actual fleam." Adam walked toward the entrance, glaring at Viktor who protectively stood next to Waverly. "I need a minute."

"Of course." While Adam tapped at the biometric keypad and slid his palm over the sensor, Waverly looked to Viktor. *Be Nice.*

I'm always nice. What'd you see?

Nothing, Waverly lied.

You're earning yourself a spanking, pet.

Is that a threat or a promise? She winked at him.

Later, my kinky little minx.

I didn't see much but a black wall. He's hiding something though. I know it.

Viktor nodded in understanding.

"This way." Adam waved them through the entrance and proceeded down a long hallway.

As they followed him, going deeper into the tunnel, Waverly took note of the security cameras lining its bland white walls. Her stomach tightened into a knot. Although Adam appeared to take care of every detail, allowing them into the facility, instinct warned her something was off.

Adam slowed as he came to a large stainless-steel door. He pressed his palm to the security reader and a loud beep reverberated throughout the hallway.

Waverly nervously tapped her thigh and gave a brief look to Viktor as the door slid open. He nodded, cool and on alert.

"It's back here," Adam pointed. "Check out the paintings. So many don't get floor time."

Waverly followed him inside the sterile area, her stomach tight with anxiety.

"I've never been in such an interesting storage facility," she commented, running her finger over the edge of one of the racks. She tugged at the edge, sliding it out an inch. "Andrew Wyeth."

"Yeah, we just got a few on loan. They're slated to go up next week."

"Nice." Waverly gave a side glance to Viktor as Adam continued to walk into the tunnel.

"What's the deal with the storage?" Rafe asked.

"Most museums don't have room for all their artifacts on site. We have a little bit of onsite storage in San Diego, but like this one, we also have a few secret offsite facilities. It's pretty common. I've never seen one like this, though, one that's using actual underground tunnels, but then again, every museum is different."

"I have the fleam handle right here. It's unorthodox to make the transfer like this but luckily for you, you have friends in high places." He flashed Waverly a smile.

Waverly's senses went on alert, as he held a small box up in the air. She bit her lip as he set it onto an artifact table and lifted the lid. Adam donned a pair of white gloves and reached inside the container. She held her breath as he retrieved the dark acacia handle.

"Go on. Put on some gloves." He looked to a container on a side table. "Over there."

Waverly did as she was told and reached for the object. She didn't usually read objects, but as he placed it into her gloved hands, the wooden item tingled.

"Wow. I can't thank you enough for this. By any chance, was there a matching case catalogued with the fleam?" she asked, concealing the uncomfortable sensation that crept up her arms.

"I have a call into a museum in Philadelphia. They may have the matching case. I left a message with a friend of mine. As soon as I find out, I'll let you know." He stared at Waverly as she inspected it. "I have to admit. This was kind of anticlimactic. Is there something specific you were expecting?"

"Does it have initials?" Greyson inquired, his voice brusque.

"I believe it does," Adam replied. "There's not much with the paperwork. Looks like it came to the museum through an anonymous donor who claims to have gotten it at a yard sale."

Waverly slowly rotated it under the light. Her heart pounded in her chest as she located the letters. *B.A.O.* "Viktor. Right here."

"Very good." Viktor's expression remained unflappable, feigning indifference. "Is there anything else? We have to catch that flight."

"Adam, do you have the papers?" she asked as she carefully placed the fleam back into the box. "We need to show chain of ownership."

"Yes, there are some original sale papers in there," He pointed to an envelope in the container. "But it's all documented in detail online. It should all transfer once you approve your acceptance. If you wouldn't mind...I already sent it to you."

"Of course." Waverly pulled out her cell phone, accessing her museum's secure system and quickly reviewed the documentation. "There. Approved." She sighed. "I don't know how to thank you for this, Adam. I thought it was a longshot when I posted."

He shrugged and checked his phone. "Glad to be of help. Hopefully you can find the matching case. You know how it is with antiques though."

"Yeah." She nodded.

"About those initials. B.A.O. Wonder if it was a physician? Strange the fleam and handle got separated." He pinned her with a stare.

"Sure is. It's not really my area of expertise," she hedged. "I'll reach out to the museum in Philadelphia. If you could give me the name of the curator, you contacted I'll—"

"Where'd the fleam come from? And why would the art museum want something like this?" Adam asked. "You never did say."

"Yeah, no, I didn't. Well, I mean, it's confidential and all. You know, it's just one of those things."

"Sure is." He nodded with a smile that didn't match the cold expression in his eyes.

"And these friends of yours?" Adam looked to Viktor, Greyson and Rafe then smiled at Waverly. "They are friends from San Diego? Coming to New York?"

"A girl can never feel too safe in the city," she replied.

"So, uh, are you sure you don't have time for dinner? It's only eight o'clock. I know a great place in the village."

"I'm so sorry but I've got to catch a flight. We're leaving soon. Taking a private jet. Thankfully." Waverly gave a nervous laugh and carefully put the lid on the box while continuing to speak. "It's a long flight. I'm going to have some serious jet lag, right?"

"How about a drink?" Adam closed the distance between them. "We can catch up."

Waverly heard a loud growl and snapped her head around to Viktor who gave her a cool smile.

"I, uh, I'm sorry. We've got to go," she told him

"Just one drink. I haven't seen you in years," he told her, edging closer.

"Dude. She just said it's negative. Let it rest," Viktor told him. "We've got to go."

"Waverly. Who are these guys?" Anger flashed in his eyes.

"I'm someone who doesn't like a lot of questions," Greyson said, crossing his arms over his chest.

"Adam, I really appreciate you helping me tonight, but I can't meet up this trip. I promise we'll go for coffee next time. The truth is that Viktor's my boyfriend. He's helping me and was nice enough to accompany me tonight. We've really got to get going." Waverly picked up the box and handed it to Rafe, who stood ready to help.

As she turned back to Adam, he'd disappeared. Waverly yelped as the lights went out, leaving them in darkness. "Adam! What's happening?"

Viktor rushed to her side. "We need to get out of here."

"Wait. Where's Adam? Something's wrong," she insisted. Within seconds, a thick smoke choked her lungs. Disoriented, her head began to spin.

She clutched at Viktor's arm as he unexpectedly fell to the floor. "Viktor! Greyson, help me! Rafe. Please. Something's wrong with Viktor. I can't see. What's happening?"

"Waverly!" she heard Adam call to her through the din.

"I'm over here. I need help." Choking, she pulled her neck scarf over her mouth. "What's going on?"

Waverly screamed as a pair of unfamiliar arms cinched her waist, lifting her up into the air. "Put me down! Let me go!"

"It's okay," Adam told her. Light peeked into the darkness as a sliding door opened.

Dizzy, she fought the nausea, kicking as he dragged her through the doorway and into the tunnel. Waverly wrenched out of his grip, falling onto the cold floor. The rough cement scraped her palms, a stinging pain slicing through her hands.

As blinding lights flashed and illuminated the room, she squinted, shielding her eyes with her bloodied hands. As

Adam came into view, her stomach dropped. Her heart raced in panic. "What did you do? Where's Viktor?"

"I didn't do anything," he claimed as he calmly brushed the powder off his hands.

"What's going on? Where are they?" She protectively pulled her legs under her, to steady her balance and clear her head.

"I had to get you away from them. I know what they are," he told her, wearing an icy smile.

"What?" A wave of nausea hit her, initiating a coughing fit.

"It'll pass," he said, turning his back to her. "It's a synthetic colloidal silver spray."

"What?" She shook her head in confusion.

"It's part of the high-tech security system we have here. Operates by an app on my watch. We installed it because of security concerns. Humans aren't the only ones who want to steal art."

"Why?" Waverly's legs wobbled as she struggled to stand. She reached for the wall, steadying herself.

"You don't think I know vampires? You know full well it breaks protocol to bring others into the facility. My life was at risk," he claimed.

"But you said it was okay. This was a special circum-stance." Waverly glared at him as she managed to steady herself on her feet. "They're my friends. You can't keep me from them."

"I can. And I did. I'm having security remove them and take them to another location."

"Are you crazy?" Waverly studied Adam. He'd removed his jacket, revealing a tattoo on his forearm. *Horns.*

"I'll call PCAP. Have them arrested in the morning. You and I will be long gone by the time they are released."

"Do you know who you're messing with?" Anger surged through Waverly, realizing he'd planned to kidnap her.

"I don't know who Viktor Christianson is but—"

"I didn't tell you his last name." Her heart pounded in her chest, her mind swirling with confusion and conspiracy.

"You don't think I can do my research? I already heard about the big donor at your exhibition."

"You're following what I'm doing?"

"I know about Teagan. We've kept in contact through the years."

"Teagan? Do you know where she is?" she asked, her voice growing louder.

Adam smiled and tapped at his watch. "I think you should stay here until the vampires are gone. We can have that dinner we discussed."

"I don't think so." Waverly scanned the area for an exit, noting a secondary door at the end of the tunnel. Empty paint buckets were stacked in a corner, paint brushes piled onto a drop cloth.

"There was a time we were close." he smiled. "The fleam was the perfect opportunity for us to connect again. It's a blessing you found it in the painting."

"I didn't say where I got it." Waverly's pulse raced. "You can't keep me here."

"I'm not doing anything of the sort. You're perfectly safe. You saw the guards outside."

"I want to leave. Let me out of here right now," she demanded.

"I'm afraid you'll need my fingerprint for that. Please just give me a second. I've got a text." Adam tapped at the face of his watch.

Waverly looked around the room, which appeared to be under repair. She took a slow deliberate step backwards, and quietly brushed her hand over the edges of the stone wall.

With the tips of her fingers, she tugged at a loose brick, praying it wouldn't make noise.

Waverly froze as she heard a woman's voice call Adam's name from beyond the second door. His head snapped up in attention, his gaze landing on hers.

"I'll be right back," he told her.

"Where are you going?" She swallowed a hard lump in her throat, gaining a secure grip on her rudimentary weapon.

"Don't go anywhere. We're going to have that drink," Adam turned and walked toward the door.

Waverly took a deep breath and tightened her fingers around the brick. *Fuck you,* she thought as she rushed toward him and smashed the stone against the back of his skull. His body crumpled to the floor with a thud, a trickle of blood dripping onto the floor.

"I'm not going anywhere with you," she breathed, enraged he'd planned to kidnap her. The woman's voice from the hallway grew louder, and Waverly looked to the sliding door that they'd used to enter. Nearly ten feet away, she'd have to move him over to the security scanner.

"You can do this. You can do this," she repeated to herself as she reached under his arms and began to drag him across the floor.

A surge of adrenaline shot through her as she hauled him toward the door and draped his limp body against the wall. As she reached for his arm he moaned and she released him, afraid he'd come at her.

"What are you doing, Waverly?" he groaned, beginning to come round.

Just do it. You've got to get out of here. Heart pumping, she summoned the courage she never thought she'd possessed. She grabbed his wrist, yanked his arm upward and flattened his palm to the reader.

As she released him, he attempted to grab her. Without

hesitation she kicked him in the jaw and tore out of the door into the smoky room.

Her heart caught in her chest as she entered the secure storage facility and realized Viktor and the others were missing. She ran down the tunnel, finding her way out, briefly looking back to the security cameras. As she approached the exit, she noticed the guard was missing, the foyer lights flickering overhead.

Broken glass crackled underneath her boots as she stepped through the metal detector. With stealth and deliberate steps, she made her way into the darkened lobby. The doorway came into view, a splatter of light from the parking lot spilling onto the floor.

A low growl sounded in the darkness, and she froze, her focus homing in on its source. Her heart raced as the great beast came into view, a huge brown wolf stalking toward her. *No, no, no.*

"Easy there." She held her hand out to it and slowly stepped closer to the doorway. Out of the corner of her eye she spied their limo. Relief shot through her at the sight of its lights shining. *Someone's in it.*

The wolf growled again at her.

"I've got to go now. Be a good little doggie." *One. Two. Three.* Waverly took off running toward the limo.

Her lungs burned as she sprinted past the wolf. A dark shadow whizzed past her, but she kept running. From out of nowhere, a security guard across the parking lot called to her and began chasing her. As the car came into reach, she frantically tugged at a doorhandle, but it refused to budge. She peeked over her shoulder, catching sight of the great beast as it attacked the guard. It latched onto him, its teeth tearing at his throat, blood gushing onto the pavement.

She rounded the car, her mind churning with confusion. *Where is Viktor?* The wolf howled, rushing toward her. As it leapt into the air, she curled against the car, bracing for impact.

"We've got to get out of here. Get in the car," she heard Rafe's voice call to her.

"It's locked," she managed, shocked to see him standing in front of her, nude.

"Waverly, let's go," he yelled as he swung open the driver's door.

She released a bloodcurdling scream as she looked down to the ground at a dead body sprawled on the pavement. Blood oozed from his mouth, his eyes wide open in horror. "The driver. He's de—"

"Get. In!" Rafe's order shook her, and she tumbled into the car, shimmying over into the passenger seat.

"No, we can't leave," she told him as he slid the car into gear. "We can't leave them."

"Viktor's in the back. Greyson too." Rafe slammed his foot on the gas.

"What? How?" Waverly reached for the dash, bracing herself as the limo surged forward, squealing out of the parking lot and onto the street.

"Whatever was in the powder had silver in it," Rafe told her. "It's poison. Luckily, I was able to get out, shift and heal."

"Adam said it was some kind of security system designed to keep supernaturals out. Open the privacy window. Let me back. I've got to get it off them."

Rafe tapped at the dashboard touch screen. As the partition retracted, Waverly slid through the window into the back of the limo.

"My cell phone is somewhere in the car," he yelled back to her. "I need you to find it and throw it up to me so I can send the pilots a text. Gotta lift off as soon as we hit the tarmac."

"Viktor!" Waverly fumbled in the dark for several seconds until Rafe flicked on the lights. "Oh God!"

"They're going to be all right," Rafe called back to her. "Get their clothes off and toss them out the window. Don't forget their phones."

Tears filled her eyes as Waverly reached for Viktor. She brushed the sticky grey powder off his face and pressed her lips to his. "I'm so sorry, baby."

"You'll have time later. Get it off him," Rafe instructed.

"Yes, yes." She wiped the tears from her face with the back of her hand and focused on her task, removing their clothes.

"Oh God," she exclaimed, realizing the dust had settled all over her jacket. Waverly stripped down to her underwear and continued to brush small particles from Viktor's hair.

"I can't get all of it off. They need to shower." Panic stabbed through her. "Why aren't they waking up? What's happening to them?"

"It's going to be okay."

"Why are they like this, but you're fine? You're vampire too."

"I don't know. I've got mixed blood so maybe it didn't affect me as much. I shifted. The shit stung like a mother-fucker. They tried capturing me but I'm fast as fuck now."

"Humans?" she asked.

"Vampires. A couple of humans took out the limo driver. I don't know who else might have been there."

"Where's the fleam? The handle?" she asked.

"Everything's back there."

"How far to the airport?"

"We're almost there," he promised. "It's right up here. It's a private airstrip."

"Why isn't he waking up?" Waverly cradled Viktor's head onto her chest, stroking his face. "Please wake up."

"Okay here we go," Rafe warned.

Relief washed over Waverly as they pulled into the airport, the guard waving them onto the tarmac. As the car rolled to a stop, she reached for the door handle and shoved the door open. Attendants rushed the car, reaching for both Viktor and Greyson.

"I've got the box," Rafe told her.

Waverly collected the phones and stepped out onto the tarmac in her bra and panties. The roar of engines sounded around her, a cold breeze blowing across her skin.

"Come. Let's get you inside." Rafe appeared next to her and guided her up the stairs.

"Where's Viktor?" she asked, panic in her voice.

"They've taken him to the master bedroom. You'll have to feed him and then get him into the shower. I don't know the strength of the powder, but it was enough to knock them out. I'll meet you in a couple of hours up front. I want to make sure Greyson feeds all right."

Waverly fought tears as they made their way down a small hallway, deeper into the plane. As they approached the doorway, her stomach dropped at the sight of Viktor lying unconscious on the bed. A young flight attendant knelt before him and extended her arm.

"No! Get away from him. He's mine," Waverly yelled. Jealousy flared, but she was far beyond taming it, and cordial words eluded her. "Get out."

"I'm sorry, ma'am. Let me know if you need anything." The woman scurried out of the room.

"Feed him. He'll be okay," Rafe commented as he closed the door.

"Thank you," she managed, tears in her eyes.

Waverly curled against Viktor's body, hot tears streaming down her face. Guilt threaded through her, knowing Adam had done this to him.

She pressed her wrist to his mouth and whispered in his ear. "Please. Viktor. Can you hear me? It's going to be okay.

But you've gotta feed. The silver…it's done something to you. Please just—"

Waverly yelped as his eyes flew open and he grasped her wrist. Feral, his teeth sliced into her flesh. Helpless to move, waves of pain and pleasure threading through her body, she prayed she'd survive.

CHAPTER TEN

lood flowed down his throat, Waverly's essence healing him, liberating him from the poison. Her soul engulfed him, yet the monster inside struggled to restrain itself. *Control the beast.*

"Viktor," he heard her call.

Let her go. He fought the craving as guilt stabbed through him.

"Viktor? Can you hear me? Please be okay."

He fought his unsated thirst. As the fog dissipated, he called for her. *Waverly.*

"Yes, baby. I hear you."

The warmth of her skin surrounded him, waking him, calling him back from his feral nature. His teeth retracted, releasing her.

"Ah," she cried as he flipped her onto her back and his lips brushed over hers.

"Dr. LaFleur," he whispered, his erection pressed between her legs.

"Thank God you're okay." She brought her hands to his cheeks, her eyes widened in relief.

"I'm forever in your service." Viktor's body raged with desire for the incredible woman underneath him. He stole a brief kiss, resisting the urge to tear off her panties and fuck her senseless.

"We're even then," she panted, her chest heaving for breath. "We should, um, we need to get this stuff off you. I need to clean both of us off."

"Shower," he suggested.

"There's a shower on here?"

"Yes." He nodded.

"Let's get you in the shower then. This stuff is poisonous."

"Have I died and gone to heaven?"

"I, uh," her lips grazed his, "I'm already wet."

"You're killin' me," Viktor laughed.

"No dying on my watch. I'm serious." Waverly pressed her palms to his chest, pushing at him. "You need to get this stuff off you."

Viktor rolled onto his back and watched her hop off the bed. Fresh anger twisted through him, as he recalled the attack at the storage facility, her attempted kidnapping. "Nasty little security system. He didn't hurt you, did he?"

"I'm fine," she called out from the bathroom.

"How did you get away from him?"

"I lift weights." A splash of water sounded as she turned on the spigot. "We can talk about it later. Let's get you clean."

"I'm sorry. I should have known it was a trap." Viktor seethed with anger. He'd known long ago that industries had planned to install AgSX. The colloidal silver compound had become a menace, weaponized to 'manage' vampires in recent years.

"There's no way we could have known he'd do that. But I need to tell you," She poked her head out of the bathroom, continuing to talk, "I don't know the extent of it, but I think he sent me the fleam. He knew too much about the painting.

I think there might be others. Someone is working with him. I heard a woman's voice. But at least we have the handle—"

"We have what he intended us to have." Viktor shucked off his boxers and stood.

"Water's ready. We've got to get you clean. Are you coming?" Waverly appeared like an angel in the doorway, concealing her nudity with a towel. She turned on her heels and dropped it behind her.

"I most certainly will be." Though moments earlier he'd been injured, the surge of Waverly's blood and the sight of his sexy woman turned his cock as hard as concrete.

As he entered the bathroom, Waverly stood in the shower, leaning backwards into the stream. She smoothed her hands over her hair, water dripping from her body.

"I'm sorry I couldn't help you. I should have been there," he told her as he stepped inside the shower.

"You were poisoned. Besides, you're here now." She shot him a sexy smile, beads of dewy moisture on her face and eyelashes, her body glistening under the soft lighting.

Viktor wrapped his hands around her waist and tugged her to him, the hot spray stinging his skin. Her pert nipples brushed up against his chest, his cock grazing between her thighs. He brought a hand around the back of her neck and tilted her head, inspecting the faint marks on her skin. "You're mine now."

"I am," she admitted in a whisper.

He leaned in to kiss her, brushing his tongue against hers. A soft, demanding kiss, tasting the only woman he'd ever craved.

Take her, lust told him, but Viktor would savor her like a fine wine. His chest tightened, an inexplicable feeling that he couldn't describe. Soon they'd be bonded, forever together.

For over a thousand years, there had been no one. *Love.* Baxter had taught him he wasn't worth someone's love. He had been starved of emotion. For many years after Baxter died, Viktor wondered if his sire had been right. But in the last few days, his life had changed.

He tore his lips from hers and leaned his forehead against hers. "I don't deserve you."

"Yes, yes you do. Don't ever think you don't," she told him, conviction in her words.

Viktor smiled and briefly closed his eyes, his heart full. He couldn't say the unfamiliar word that danced on the tip of his tongue. *Love.*

Avoiding the uncomfortable emotion, he reached for the bottle of shampoo and squeezed it into his hand. "Turn around."

"Are you sure we should do this in the plane? What if there's turbulence?"

"I'll flash us back home. Now turn around or you will most definitely get that spanking," he warned.

Waverly did as she was told, taking care to brush her bottom over his cock. Viktor smiled, working the lather into her hair, and brushing the soap down over her skin. He pressed his cock through her slick legs, running his soapy hands up over her breasts.

Waverly released a sigh, bracing her arms against the wall. "Oh."

"You have no idea the things I want to do with you." Viktor palmed her breasts, teasing her nipples.

Ravenous, he spun her around and captured her lips in a desperate, urgent kiss. He lifted her up by the waist. With her back pressed against the shower wall and her legs wrapped around him, he thrust up into her wet pussy.

"Fuuu—" Her tight core spasmed around him, nearly making him come. His fangs dropped, and his mouth moved to her shoulder.

"Fuck me," she screamed, undulating, grinding her clit against him.

With a swift thrust, he plunged inside her harder. Pumping in and out of her, Viktor lost control.

"Ah, baby, please," she begged him, breathless. "Yes, yes, fuck me…that's it."

The shower wall shook as he plowed into her, harder and harder. With each thrust of his hips, she gasped in ragged breaths, her fingernails digging into his shoulders.

Rough and raw, he fucked her, brutally claiming his woman. No one would have her but him.

As he deepened the kiss, his desire to complete the bond escalated. Within their bond, she'd have immortality, be safe. Yet a voice in the back of his head warned him it was still too early.

Waverly screamed, her body shaking as she came hard. Viktor lost control, slamming into her.

"Do it," she pleaded.

Without another word, he bit down into the soft flesh in her shoulder, her sweet blood coating his tongue. In a final frenzy, he fucked her hard, with wild abandon. Her pussy convulsed around his cock, milking him as he came hard. With a final short thrust, he drove himself up into her, exploding in release.

"Goddess," he breathed, still holding her, his forearm up against the shower. "I…I…" *Love you.*

The reality of the situation slammed into Viktor. He'd fallen in love with a human, slowly embracing all the things he'd either missed or forgotten. His life would never be the same.

∾

VIKTOR SAT BACK in the leather chair and twirled the fleam in his fingers, ruminating, thinking about Waverly. In all his years, he'd never felt so out of control. More than wild fucking, their trust grew, the bond strengthened, their energies intertwining. Bordering on obsession, he couldn't rest until they'd fully bonded. On the tip of his tongue, he'd almost lost control and told her he loved her.

Viktor ran his fingertip over the initials etched on the fleam and considered that Baxter would have killed Waverly long ago. The cold metal reminded him of the inhumane lessons his sire taught him, the flaying of his skin, each burning lash on his back still fresh in his mind after all these years.

Baxter deliberately starved his children, leaving them weak but functional to do his bidding. He treated them as work horses. From hard labor to murder, there was no task off limits. Refusing, breaking master's rules would bring death. Falling in love was forbidden. Baxter killed humans like crushing ants under his shoe.

No attachments to humans. No attachment to anything. Viktor learned quickly that punishment came swift and hard, and to shut down his emotions. Humans were nothing more than food.

Several hundred years had passed before Viktor learned to keep his shields up, to prevent Baxter from reading his mind. It wasn't until his death that Viktor truly found freedom.

Viktor glanced to Waverly, his heart full of emotion. Even though Baxter had died centuries ago, he still lived rent-free in his head, warning him not to love a human. Pain would certainly follow.

Waverly's laughter broke his contemplation. She was sharing a meal with Rafe who recounted about his battle, how he'd been turned, dropping and retracting his fangs for emphasis. Rafe roared with laughter and raised his glass to her. As Waverly stole a glance at Viktor, he returned her infectious smile.

Viktor looked to Greyson who lay on the sofa pretending to watch football on the flat screen. Although Greyson had been tortured more than most of Baxter's children, the burly vampire remained soft towards humans. His brother looked up to him in understanding.

"I know what you're thinking. It's not him," Greyson commented as he adjusted a pillow under his head. "Quintus killed him. We all saw it."

"Did we? Because if my memory serves me, we saw Quintus throw him in the canyon," Viktor countered.

"The body was recovered," Greyson argued his point.

"It was a body. We don't know it was his." Viktor scrubbed his fingers over the scruff on his chin.

"It scented as his."

"He was nothing but mangled flesh and bones." Viktor blew out a breath, summoning reason. "I know you're right. It's just this situation…I can't believe we're even having this conversation. And humans. This Adam. We've got to get more info on this 'brotherhood'."

"Adam did this on purpose," Waverly interjected. "He knew about the painting. I think he sent it to me. And someone else was there. A woman. I didn't see her but there was something about her that he seemed scared of. I could see it in his eyes. He stopped everything to go to her. Like maybe she's his boss."

"He knew we were vampires, but there's something more," Viktor said.

"You've got a vibe going on, dude. Quintessential vampire." Greyson laughed.

"Well, number one, I'm not quintessential. I'm extraordinary. And number two, he acted annoyed when he saw us. But wasn't surprised," Viktor asserted.

"I agree," Waverly said. "He also knew about Teagan."

"Interesting." Viktor steepled his fingers, his lips drawn tight. "Teagan goes missing. We've got this brotherhood of humans. They might be conjuring demons."

"Or trying. I don't know. It wouldn't be easy for a human to conjure a specific demon on their own, but they could give a generic one a go," Greyson said, keeping an eye on the game.

"It's not easy but it's doable. Nowadays it's not like someone has to go searching far. There're witches out there who practice dark magick, and they're not all anonymous. They've got human clients."

"I just have a feeling that this could be something bigger. The people at that facility trusted Adam, helped him do that to us. He wasn't worried about being caught. The woman must have heard the commotion. I was screaming at him to let me go and no one came." Waverly shrugged.

"To be fair, it could be argued he was threatened," Rafe suggested.

"It could be argued we intimidated him but that's a far road from attacking him. He's a weak man. One who's going to regret the day he ever met me," Viktor promised.

"He wanted me." Waverly's voice lowered to a whisper. "I have a feeling whatever this is it's dark. And Teagan—"

"Tell me again how you know Adam." Viktor's gut stabbed with an unusual sensation of jealousy, a foreign emotion.

"Not much to tell. Adam and I were grad students together. He loved art. I loved art. We spent a lot of time together. It wasn't serious. He left to go to New York for a job. Teagan and I were roommates. So yeah. They knew each other, but they weren't good friends. That I knew of anyway. But back there," she paused in thought and took a sip of her water, "he knew something about her. He knew she was missing."

"He could've read it online," Rafe suggested.

"I mean, maybe, but I'm telling you the police didn't even bat an eye when I told them I couldn't find her. So many people go missing every year. They have bigger fish to fry than worrying about someone with no family or friends. They didn't even want to hear about it because she'd been to the blood clubs."

"Did you tell them about the needles?"

"I can't remember. I don't know. Maybe. But thinking back on it. Maybe they were using needles for their blood… to drink. I hate this," Waverly said, her tone defeated.

"Now we've got to see Ilsbeth again." Viktor shook his head. "Fuck, am I ever going to get away from that witch?"

"There's always a silver lining," Greyson laughed.

"No. No silver lining." Viktor waved him off. "I told you from the beginning that I want nothing to do with that witch. You know better."

"Nothing like having a psychotic high priestess for a mom." Wearing a broad smile on his face, Rafe looked to Waverly and pointed his fingers up into the air. "Rad!"

"I can't imagine," she replied, coughing back laughter.

"There is nothing funny about your mother," Viktor stated. "She's as serious as a heart attack. Deadlier."

"She looked fine as fuck last night though. That dress," Greyson commented. "Hmm."

"Why do you guys get involved with witches anyway?" Waverly asked Viktor.

"It's complicated. Sometimes you've got to play with the devil you know to fly with the angels. We all need a little extra magick now and then." He shrugged. "Average spells aren't needed by vampires. But if you need help with a demon? A witch can help you. There's always a price to pay though. Except for Samantha Macquarie. But she's married to a vampire."

"What about humans, a guy like Adam? Why are they getting involved with this?" Waverly asked.

Viktor looked to his brother who had far more experience within the human world. Greyson swung his feet onto the floor and sat up, looking at Waverly. "Our existence on this earth was born of humans. They are fragile. Usually easy to kill, if necessary. Rarely a threat. I'm not worried about him."

"Rarely being the key word." Viktor sighed, continuing to fiddle with the fleam. "Now that we know Adam's involved, we'll be better prepared to deal with his antics."

Greyson reached over to a bowl of potato chips and selected one, holding it up in the air, gesturing with it as he spoke. "Humans want for things. Goods. Money. Power. And when they get a taste of power, the thirst for more never stops. It's like a drug. Many a leader would sell their soul to Satan himself to get more, to keep the power."

"And they do." Viktor held the fleam up, light glinting off its blade. "And this Adam is surely up to something. This woman he was with. Was there anything special about her?"

"I don't know. I didn't see her. But she had to have heard me. I was screaming for him to let me go." Waverly took another sip of her water, pausing in thought. "I think she had an accent. French, I think. I can't be sure."

Viktor and his brother exchanged a concerned look. "It's not her."

Greyson shrugged. "There's a lot of French women out there. Thousands."

"What is it?" Waverly asked.

Viktor shook his head and pinched his fingers to the bridge of his nose. "Nothing. It's nothing."

"Whoever the woman is, she may or may not be French," Greyson said. "That's all we know. That and this Adam dude has a hard-on for your girlfriend and may be involved with this underground vampire wannabe brotherhood."

"Why would he give Waverly the handle to the fleam if it was really some kind of clue? Why go to all that trouble?" Rafe asked. "It doesn't make sense."

"I don't know," Waverly said. "If he was involved with the brotherhood, why the blood in my apartment? And what about the detective?"

"Maybe there are a couple of players," Viktor suggested. "Maybe they were working together, and something went wrong."

"While we're going down the conspiracy rabbit hole," she gave a small laugh, "let's talk about Teagan. I have a feeling Adam may have hurt her. Maybe they kept in touch? Or maybe they both became part of this brotherhood, got reconnected? Maybe he wanted me to get the fleam because, as Rafe said, I think he has a thing for me. I don't know why it was important for me to be there in Miami though. Like, if she thought Adam was going to hurt me, why bring me to Miami? I don't know. How would they know I'd be there that night?"

"Maybe the guy who was hassling you in the club was part of it? But it failed." Viktor plowed his fingers through his hair, frustrated. "This brotherhood, whatever it is, it could be a fragmented organization, if it's organized at all. Who knows?"

"I couldn't find much online," Rafe said. "But I was able to find a few threads in college forums about drinking blood. They believe they'll eventually be paired with a sire. By the way they talked about it, it almost sounded like the leader was vampire."

"Jesus Christ." Viktor's phone buzzed and he tapped at the screen. "We're landing in five minutes. Keep working on the research, Rafe. Check with Kade and Quintus. See if you can find anything else. After visiting the witch, I'm thinking it's time we take a more aggressive approach and go back to the blood club."

"I'm thinking we should find Adam and make things uncomfortable for him," Greyson said with a smile. "Find out where he lives. Have a chat."

"Maybe we should bring Adam here?" Viktor suggested with a sly smile.

"Throw him a little party?" Greyson suggested.

"I do love a good party. And I've got the perfect shoes to match," Viktor said.

Silence filled the cabin as the wheels touched down on the tarmac. Viktor dared not speak his suspicions, arguing with himself about the facts he knew to be true. *Baxter is dead. You witnessed his death.*

Yet this situation reeked of the diabolical bastard or of that ilk. As he locked his gaze on Greyson and exchanged a look of understanding, they both knew there were others who were every bit as sadistic as Baxter.

"Why couldn't we meet at Ilsbeth's?" Greyson grumbled as they stood in front of the antebellum mansion. "Could this place be more pretentious?"

"It's boujee, baby," Rafe stated.

"It's neutral territory. That means it's protected from things looking to harm us," Viktor explained.

"Where the hell are we?" Rafe asked.

"St. Tammany Parish. Folsom." Viktor tapped at the face of his phone, checking his messages. "Looks like Quint and Kade are already here."

"Do I smell cows?" Waverly asked.

"Horses. This club is run by Tori Shinning. She's a vampire. Former socialite. She has a stable full of horses and every luxury you can imagine. It's a distance from New Orleans. This little shindig is invite-only. Professional donors are brought in from all parts of the world to mingle with guests." Viktor unzipped his black leather coat and smiled at Waverly. "It's upscale."

"Does upscale mean it's going to be safer?" Waverly asked.

"No," Viktor, Rafe and Greyson all responded at once.

"I'm not really dressed for this." Waverly looked to her jeans.

"Don't worry about how you're dressed. No one will say a word."

"Are you sure Adam won't be here?" she asked.

"He won't be here. Even if he's working with a vampire, he'd have to fly to get down here. There're only a handful of us that have the ability to dematerialize."

"But this sitch may be a little, you know, unstable. You never really know. So, stay on your toes. And you," Greyson said, staring at Rafe. "Don't mess around."

"Dude. I'm cool." He shot him a look.

"Everyone ready?" Viktor asked. The wolf and his brother gave a silent nod. "All right then. It's showtime."

As they followed the path toward the mansion, Viktor took Waverly's hand in his. He sensed her pulse race as they passed though the pillars on the porch and entered the epic Acadian styled ranch. The large oak front door appeared to open by itself, welcoming them into the club.

It's going to be all right, Viktor told her telepathically. He closed the distance and put his arm around her waist, and she nodded in understanding.

A diminutive woman in a fitted pink tuxedo and matching fairy wings fluttered into the foyer and greeted them. "Viktor, darling. How delightful to have you at our establishment."

"Thank you for having us, tonight." Viktor smiled at her, all the while scanning the room. "Love the wings."

"Kade Issacson speaks highly of you. I'm honored to have you to the ranch," she told him. "Please come inside. Your brother and Kade are already in the garden enjoying the show. This way."

They followed their host through the home to a great room. Strings of white lights hung across the cathedral ceiling. Five-foot pillar candles illuminated the stark space. Brightly colored modern art contrasted with its otherwise clean, white, modern architectural design.

A man dressed in a black satin suit played Bach on a white grand piano, while a nude woman lay splayed naked on its lid. She moaned loudly as several vampires fed from her while a woman with blue hair feasted between her legs.

Viktor looked down to Waverly as her fingers gripped him. *It's okay. We're going outside.*

Did you see that? Her eyes widened as the donor screamed. *Oh my God, are they killing her?*

Unlikely. Though it sounds like they're sending her to heaven. Almost there, pet.

As they exited through a set of opulent French doors, a rush of damp air hit them. The scent of fresh grass and manure hung heavy in the air.

Their host, vampire Tori, turned and gestured to an ostentatious pool area. Guests watched neon turquoise mermaids frolic in the water through a glass wall in its side. The topless performers slapped their iridescent tails on the surface before diving to the clear glass theater below, waving and blowing kisses.

"Lovely, aren't they? The teams switch out each hour and are available as donors," Tori explained.

"Sushi." Viktor laughed. *Joking.*

"Darling! You're a cad," Tori gushed, placing her hand on his arm. "I've heard rumors about you. Those fangs have seen a lot of holes."

Viktor joined her in laughter with a smile that didn't reach his eyes. The hostess expected attention, adoration of her sex-driven blood party.

"You're a sick pup, Vik," Rafe commented.

"Of course, it's an honor to have the notorious Greyson as well." Tori flashed him a flirtatious smile. "I've heard your bite is delicious. And that beard...hmm...I could ride that all night."

"I'd be honored to show you my fangs." He reached for her hand and pressed his lips to the back of it.

She laughed wildly, snatching her hand back. "Oh darlin', you're a rough one. Your biceps," she gave a squeeze to his arms, "are straining to be released from that shirt. Perhaps you should do us all a favor and take it off. You can go play with the mermaids."

"Sweetheart, I always appreciate fine tail, but we've got business tonight. Don't wanna get my new kicks wet." Greyson played with a toothpick he'd been chewing at for nearly thirty minutes. He nodded to his brother.

"Well then, do as you wish. I'm planning on having the banker or the lawyer for dinner tonight. Maybe both. There's a smorgasbord to choose from. Please feel free to have whatever you'd like. I'll have a server bring you a menu."

"Impeccable taste, I'm sure." Viktor stroked her ego, attempting to wrap up the conversation. He caught sight of

Kade who gave a wave. "Ah there, our party awaits. I'm afraid I must go. Tick tock."

"Another time, perhaps?" She dropped her fangs and fluttered her wings, batting her eyelashes at him.

"Of course," he answered, aware he'd never be with another woman again. The only one in his heart was the determined human at his side. He glanced to her and smiled.

"Have fun, darlings!" Tori called as they headed down the path.

"Mermaids?" Waverly whispered.

"I don't think these ones are real," he guessed.

"Are you saying that mermaids exist?"

"Many creatures exist. Some well beyond our imagination," he mused.

"The Goddess is a sneaky bitch," Greyson told Waverly. "Just when you think you've got it all figured out, she'll throw you a curveball. Heard Léopold Devereoux is paired up with a naiad."

"Here we are," Viktor said as they approached a well-landscaped courtyard.

Pink wrought iron chairs arranged in a half-circle faced the pool, so guests could view the swimmers through a thick glass wall. A large three-tiered fountain bubbled behind them. Throughout the garden, life-sized metallic gargoyles loomed over the guests.

"Brother, good to see you again," Viktor greeted Quintus. "That woman of yours looks good on you." He turned to Kade. "Thank you for graciously arranging this meeting in neutral territory."

Viktor glared at Thorn and Ilsbeth, declining to greet them, and simply nodded in response to their presence. He gestured to a seat, waiting for Waverly to sit first.

"Viktor. How long are you going to act like this?" Wearing a skintight crimson satin ballgown, Ilsbeth sat like a queen, her hands folded in her lap. The shiny fabric clung to her like a second skin. Her long, platinum hair tumbled over her shoulders, a choker of blood-red rubies sparkled around her creamy, pale neck.

"One thing I love about you, Ilsbeth. You've got style," Greyson told her with an ingenious smile. "I mean look at that dress. Red is the new black."

"He's not wrong," Rafe commented with a shrug.

"Your mom gives zero fucks what other people are doing," Greyson commented.

"Your father is still angry with me," Ilsbeth stated, her mouth drawn tight.

"Everyone is mad at you. Give it a rest," Rafe shot back at her.

"Do you have the handle?" Ilsbeth asked.

"Yes. Although nothing appears unusual about it," Viktor told her.

"May I see it?"

"Is there a way to block the mermaids?" Greyson asked.

"I believe they've signed NDAs," Thorn said. "Tori sees to the details."

"I've got it." Rafe reached over to the table and held up a small black remote. With the press of a button, an aluminum curtain slid over the glass, blocking their view. "Who's the child now?"

Greyson laughed.

Viktor reached into his pocket, retrieving an object bound within a black silk handkerchief. He unwrapped it and held the blade in the air.

"We suspect a paranormal is involved with this human brotherhood. Giving them inside information about vampires," Viktor said, referring to Adam. "Helping them drink blood. It's not unheard of. These groups of humans. Posers if you will."

"Some of them could have fake fangs of course, but it's more likely they're using fleams, bloodletting rings or other tools," Greyson added.

"When we acquired the fleam handle, this human, Adam. He mentioned Waverly's friend," Viktor said. "He may know where she's at."

"But Teagan never mentioned Adam. I guess it's possible they've remained in touch. But the way he said it...it was almost as if he knew I was at that club looking for her," Waverly told them.

"The human, Adam. He works for a museum, but we believe he is the one who sent Waverly the fleam. He gassed us with silver. Tried to kidnap Waverly. We got away," Viktor sighed. "But there were others helping him. And Waverly said he responded to a woman's voice. It's possible she's a boss. Could be vampire. We don't know."

"What did she look like?" Thorn asked.

"I didn't see her," Waverly replied. "When she called him from outside the room, he acted nervous. But she had to have heard me scream and she didn't do anything."

"Why do we think she's paranormal then?" Thorn pressed.

"Instinct," Viktor said. "All hell was breaking loose."

Waverly shook her head. "Everything was chaos. But Adam knew Viktor was a vampire. And the odd part is that he didn't seem to care about the fleam. It was like it was all just some sham to get me to come to New York. I don't know if it was his plan to kidnap me. He didn't tie up but there was no way out of the room. The woman who called for him had a French accent."

"So, this." Viktor ran his finger over the wooden handle noting the gold inlay. "The handle. This wood is Acacia."

"Shittim," Greyson agreed.

"Acacia has been around for thousands of years," Viktor said.

"It was used to make the ark of the covenant," Kade told them.

"May I?" Ilsbeth held out her hand. Viktor stood and leaned toward her. With care, he placed it into Ilsbeth's hands.

"The blade is old as well," Ilsbeth said as she examined it. "Like the covenant, they used gold."

"It's unholy," Thorn stated flatly.

"Would you like to hold it?" the High Priestess offered.

"Nope. I'm good." Thorn crossed his arms and shook his head. "That thing there. I don't know where it came from, but I can feel the bad juju from over here."

"Demonic energy?" Viktor asked, surprised he hadn't detected any energy one way or another from the object.

"I'm getting more of a directly from Satan, do not pass go kind of vibe. Someone made a deal with the devil himself. Maybe a blood contract. Literal soul-binding black magick shit."

"Are you saying the devil's energy is on the bloodletter?" Viktor asked.

"I'm saying the energy coming from that belongs to its owner. That person. That monster. He or she made a deal with Satan. Sold their soul. But the true evil is not from Hell. It's from the Hell within." Thorn removed his glasses and rubbed them against his pants and reset the frames on his face. "Hell lives in the hearts of those who walk on earth. Immorality. Sadism. Torture. Serial killers."

Baxter. Viktor and Quintus exchanged a knowing look.

"He's dead," Greyson told him.

"I killed him. But—" Quintus began.

"But nothing. We've gone hundreds of years with no trace of him," Viktor insisted.

"I'm just saying. Mao was dead too. Then she wasn't," Quintus said.

"No." Viktor held up a hand. "Mao was different. Anyone can attempt necromancy. But coming fresh out of Hell, I know for a fact he's in there and he's not getting out."

"How do you really know? Demons aren't to be trusted. Whatever allies you've made could be lying," Thorn challenged him.

"I can't wrap my head around what you're saying." Viktor stared at Ilsbeth as she examined the fleam. There was no way he was about to believe that the monster who'd tortured him still walked the earth. "Let's just say I'm about to indulge your crazy theory. Someone would have to help him get out of Hell. And let's just say he got out, that diabolical piece of shit wouldn't spend time fucking around. He'd be here right now."

Thorn glanced at the bloodletter. "All I can tell you is that there are no absolutes…no matter what you think."

"Quint. Have you heard anything about this brotherhood?" Viktor changed the subject.

"There's always rumbling about humans playing as vampires. But nothing serious. Most secret societies are no more harmful than a knitting group."

"Even wooden needles can take out a vampire," Viktor countered.

"Here in New Orleans, we've got more groups than I care to have. And of course, there are the humans who embrace vampire culture, indulge in drinking each other's blood. But it is the very nature of our city to celebrate the unique. The unusual. Paranormals and humans alike." Kade looked to Ilsbeth. "What do you sense from this situation?"

The high priestess fell into a contemplative silence, humming as she stroked the handle. She raised her head, her gaze landing on Viktor.

"This fleam was brought to you by someone who knows you care for this woman." She glanced at Waverly. "Brotherhood or no, the human who sent you this is being directed by another. Likely a paranormal creature who knew your sire. I know you don't want to hear this, Viktor."

"Don't say it. I don't want to—" Viktor's lips pressed tight together.

"Mom and Dad are about to have another fight." Rafe whispered to Waverly.

"I believe this fleam belonged to Baxter or someone who knows of Baxter," she stated flatly.

"There are other vampires who knew Baxter," Quintus stated.

"Who in the hell would play this kind of game?" Viktor reflected upon the words he'd spoken. Nothing would have pleased Baxter more than a brief game of cat and mouse before killing them all. A master of manipulation, he knew every button to push, saving his worst torture for the finale.

"The mess they left for Waverly in her apartment sent a message to her. It was sent to scare her. She was shot, yet she's here. Harmed, but not dead...simply tortured a bit. And this fleam. It leaves you wondering. Is he lurking?" Ilsbeth took a deep breath and straightened her back. "Someone knows. Someone who knows the same agony he put you through. Someone who knew Baxter is helping the humans."

"Just tell them, already. You know if it's a witch helping them, they could be working to get Baxter out of hell," Thorn theorized. "But breaking a blood contract is serious business. It would not be easy to get him out. Let's face it. Your sire had his chance at Earth. He made choices that are eternal in nature. Once the devil got his soul, he's not just going to spring him. Once you're in Hell, paying the terms of the contract...it's eternal. That's how it works."

"What is this hole?" Ilsbeth asked.

"What hole?" Viktor responded. He reached for the fleam and inspected it.

"Do you see it? It's on the tip. It's barely visible."

Viktor homed in on the miniscule pin prick within the inlaid gold.

"Maybe it's like a door lock," Waverly suggested. "You know. Like the ones you'd have at home on bedroom doors."

She was greeted with silence.

"I'm talking about a modern home. For humans. I know a locked door is probably nothing for supernaturals such as yourselves, but us regular old humans have doorknobs with holes in them. You need a small pin to depress the lock."

Ilsbeth made quick work of removing a stud earring and gave it to Viktor. "Here. See if this works."

Viktor took a deep breath, ruminating about his sire. There was no way the sick bastard could have survived the fall. No way he escaped Hell.

"Viktor." Ilsbeth's voice shook his contemplation, and he refocused.

Without answering the witch, he slid the end of the earring against the gold. As the pin slipped into the hole, an audible click sounded. His heart pounded in his chest as a minute section of the gold inlay popped open, revealing a secret compartment.

He tilted the metal towards the light so he could better see inside it. His stomach dropped as he read the numbers. *22:11* "The fuck not."

"What is it?" Waverly asked.

Viktor lifted his gaze, his expression flat. He swore that monster wouldn't ever hurt him again. "Two, two. Eleven."

"Mother fucker," Greyson grumbled.

"Fuck him," Quintus said.

"What is it? What does it mean?" Waverly asked Viktor.

"Revelations," he stated, his tone cold. "One of Baxter's favorite quotes. The sick fuck."

"Let the evildoer still do evil, and the filthy still be filthy, and the righteous still do right, and the holy still be holy," Greyson recalled.

"Told ya." Thorn gave a smug smile. "Big Satan energy right there. The owner knows the deal. Yo boy made a deal."

"Maybe this belonged to him. I don't know." Viktor held up the fleam. "But it doesn't mean he's out of Hell or raised from the dead. It's nothing more than a prop."

"I suggest you keep it in a safe place," Ilsbeth warned. "I could hold it for you."

"No fucking way." Viktor shook his head.

"So now what?" Waverly asked. "We just wait around for Adam? I think I should call him. Confront him."

"We'll smoke the fucker out all right, but we need to catch the bigger fish," Viktor replied, anger coursing through him. "Whoever is orchestrating this grand chess game wants my attention. And now they've got it. I think it's time to go back to the blood club in Miami. The same one Teagan told you to go to. It was all planned. They wanted you there."

"Maybe Teagan went back to the club," Waverly suggested.

"She's probably dead," Thorn offered. "I could look for her in Hell."

"Perhaps someone saw an opportunity that night in Miami. The guy I killed. I didn't bother to find out who he was. And when I saw you…" Viktor recalled the first time he'd laid eyes on her, the immediate interest she'd stirred within him. "I don't normally get involved. Someone could have seen us. Read something into my reaction."

"But can we all agree Baxter's dead?" Quintus said, standing. "I killed him. Viktor said he was in Hell. Thorn just said he's in Hell."

"Well," Thorn held up a dismissive finger, "what I said is that I *think* he's in Hell. I can't be one hundred percent sure about these things. I don't have those kind of clearances. But in general, I'd agree. Like ninety-nine percent. Someone who makes a blood contract with Satan isn't just going to walk away. That soul is gonna be locked up tight. It's eternal damnation at its finest."

"If anyone would try to get out of Hell, it'd be Baxter." Viktor wrapped the fleam in the cloth and stuffed it into his pocket. Frustration boiled inside him. "We know what he was capable of when he walked this realm. He spent centuries turning humans, torturing us. The things we saw... those days are over now."

Viktor ruminated in the silence, anger burning in his gut. He blew out a breath and pinned both Quintus and Greyson with a serious stare. "Whoever is playing this game doesn't realize we, too, know evil. We learned from the grandmaster. While it's true we may have chosen other paths, his lessons are branded in our souls. The violence. The darkness. It's like a stain you can't quite get out, what we were taught, it never really goes away. Whoever this is is about to learn a hard lesson of their own."

VIKTOR HELD WAVERLY tight as they materialized in front of the blood club. He nodded to Greyson, who gave a low chuckle as he released Rafe. With his hands on his knees, Rafe bent over, heaving for breath.

"You okay, pet?" Viktor asked her, his lips pressed to her hair.

"Yeah," she responded.

"Goddammit, that's a trip," Rafe laughed.

"He's wet behind the ears." Greyson gave him a pat on the back.

"Fuck off, old man," Rafe shot back. "I could run circles around you."

"The pup has spirit," Greyson laughed.

"He's vampire now," Viktor reminded his brother.

"I'll always be more wolf, Dad," Rafe asserted.

"Stop calling me that." Viktor gave Waverly one last squeeze before releasing her. Warmth tugged at his heart as she smiled at him. Fuck, he hated dragging her into this sleezy blood club.

A cold breeze blew across his skin and Viktor stilled, on alert. Something was watching. Out there waiting for him. Evil, as cold as a dead heart.

"Do you feel it?" Viktor asked.

Waverly and Rafe shook their head no.

"Something is here, all right." Greyson stepped in front of Rafe and cased the building.

"What are we looking for?" Waverly asked, her voice strained.

"I don't know just yet. But there's something here. It's cold." Viktor held out his hand. "Do you feel it?"

Waverly closed her eyes and extended her hand. "Yes." Her eyes flew open. "That's so weird."

"Fucking bad vibes is what it is," Greyson told him.

Viktor stared at the club, taking in the sight of the run-down building. Flecks of lime green paint peeled from the crumbling brick exterior. A large neon sign hung above its entrance, its hot pink letters flickering. *Beijo de Satanás*

"Beijo de Satanás?" Greyson crossed his arms over his chest. "Satan's Kiss."

"Well, that's a fucking hell of a name," Rafe commented.

"Perhaps we should take it at face value," Greyson suggested.

"It's a sign from the Goddess. It means stay the fuck out," Rafe joked.

"We've got to go in," Waverly said, her voice strong. "We've got to end this. One way or another, Adam will come for me again. The more we know, the better we can fight."

Viktor smiled down at her, impressed with her determination. While most humans didn't quite understand the level of risk, she'd seen first-hand what monsters lie within, yet she wanted to fight harder, smarter.

"Keep her covered." Viktor nodded to Greyson. "Anything could go down. We get in, we get out."

VIKTOR SHOVED the bar door open, keeping Waverly at his side. The scent of blood and sex mixed with the stench of stale cigar smoke lingered in the air. Viktor brushed past the host podium, noting the absence of the maître d'. He ignored the hum of whispers and headed to a clearing at the bar.

Viktor approached the bartender, who wore a smug grin. The passage of time showed on his weathered face; once-fresh tattoos faded on his wrinkled skin.

"Where's the maître d'?" Viktor pinned him with a glare.

The bartender dried a glass with a dirty rag and turned his back to him. "He's dead."

"Don't give me that shit. Where is he?" Viktor demanded, slamming a fist onto the bar.

The room fell silent as the bartender set down the glass and turned to him. Viktor swiveled his head to address the nosy patrons. "Mind your business."

"There's plenty of humans here for the plucking." The barkeep's gaze painted over Waverly. "Though looks like you already have one. Are you bringin' her to us? I'd like a go at her."

"She's mine," Viktor growled, stepping in front of her and blocking his view. "You have five seconds to tell me where he is, or I'm going to rip out your throat."

"I told ya he's dead," he grumbled.

"Stop fucking around. Tell me where he is. Someone has to be running this place."

"Boss man's downstairs. In the playpen. Had a few bleeders he needed to take care of. You know how it is. Someone took things a little too far."

"What do you do with the bodies?" Viktor sensed Waverly's fear but continued to press for answers.

"We got a tunnel."

"A tunnel?"

"Yeah. You know. For pickup. We keep on the up and up. PCAP is called for perps. But the bodies gotta go. We send em' down a tunnel for pickup. Can't be bringing them through the lobby. Bad for business."

"This is Miami. There are no basements." Viktor tightened his fist. He hated liars.

"Yeah, well. We got one. Building on the other side technically owns it." A cockroach scampered across the bar and the bartender smashed it with his hand. He smiled at Waverly and licked the entrails off his palm, a leg still twitching on his tongue. "We're respectable."

"This building's a shithole." Viktor glared at him, unfazed by his antics.

"It's in the new building behind us. Tore down the old property a year ago." He shrugged.

"Who owns this place?" Viktor asked.

"The Missus." The bartender picked a wet glass out of the sink and began to dry it.

Viktor had never made it his business to know the bar's owner. When it had first appeared on the scene over a year ago, he'd never treated it as more than it was, fast food. On the rare occasions he'd frequented the blood club, he'd come and gone like the wind.

"Is she here?" he asked.

"Nope. She leaves it for Ivar."

"Where's the basement?" Viktor's jaw ticked in anger, his patience wearing thin.

"I ain't gotta tell you anything." He eyed Waverly and licked his lips. "But I'll help you out if you let me have a go at your bitch. Hmm…her pussy smells fresh."

In a flash, Viktor's hand smacked across the bartender's face, knocking him to the ground. Blood splashed onto the glasses he'd just washed.

"Where's this Ivar?" Viktor growled.

"Behind the purple curtain." The bartender coughed and spat blood onto the floor. "Follow the no trespassing signs."

"Sit tight, and I might let you live," Viktor told him.

"Piss off," the bartender muttered.

"Best keep your mouth shut." Greyson glared at him as he pulled out a stool.

"Do me a favor and monitor things up here while we go have a chat with Ivar. Keep an eye on him." Viktor glanced over his shoulder toward the back of the bar.

"You can't go back there. Ivar doesn't—" The bartender attempted to speak.

"Shut the fuck up or you'll be in the tunnel next," Greyson warned.

Viktor took Waverly's hand in his and headed toward the back of the club. Not a soul dared to look up as he passed through the crowd. Toward the back of the room, a sign on the wall warned off trespassers. A dark purple curtain hung in the doorway. Viktor brushed it aside and entered a small vestibule that led to a staircase.

He stared down the stairway. A single lightbulb swung from a wire above. The unfinished concrete appeared cracked and crumbling. He glanced down to his feet, anger surging at the sight of his boots. "Every time I get a new pair of shoes. Well fuck."

"Are you sure we should go down there?" Waverly asked, her voice a low whisper.

"We'll be but a minute." Viktor's words sounded far more confident than what lay in his thoughts. Going down into the basement of a potential lowlife was never a good idea, but questioning Ivar was long overdue.

"Oh my God," Waverly exclaimed as she snatched her hand away from the wall.

"What is it?" he asked.

"This place." Waverly's voice shook as she spoke. "I can feel something through the wall. Something terrible is happening." She briefly touched it again. "Someone's down there. More than one person. I can't explain what I'm feeling. I can't see anything specific, but it doesn't feel okay. I don't know if we should go down."

"It's going to be all right. He won't get you," Viktor promised and looked to Rafe. "You're ready to shift?"

"You know it," the wolf nodded.

As they descended, the light flickered, heavy metal music growing louder with each step.

"What is that sound?" Waverly asked.

"Lorna Shore. Death Coffin," Rafe replied with a fist pump.

"Cliché." Every damn wannabe used the music to conceal screams. It worked most times to keep the humans at bay, but still struck Viktor as amateurish.

I can barely think. Waverly looked to Viktor without speaking and covered her ears.

It's okay. Stay close. When they reached the landing, Viktor poked his head into the basement, quickly scanning the empty space. A string of black lights hung from the ceiling.

The walls appeared to move in the dimly lit room. An upside down cross hung upon the single black wooden door.

Waverly released a muffled scream as a roach crawled over her foot. She kicked at it, and it flew into the air towards her head. "Jesus Christ. I hate bugs."

Viktor swatted it out of the air, sending it slamming into the floor. "Are you okay?"

"What's in here?" she gasped. A low hum grew louder as she took a step towards Viktor. "Something's in here with us."

Well before Waverly's eyes had a chance to adjust to the darkness, Viktor saw them. Hundreds of cockroaches swarmed on the wall.

Then he heard the heartbeats. *Humans.*

"I need you both to get ready to flash." Viktor suspected that whatever lay beyond the door was far worse than bugs.

"I hear them." Rafe nodded in understanding

"We've got to get through the door, and we'll deal with whatever is on the other side." Viktor reached for Waverly's hand. "I'm going to need you to close your eyes until we get on the other side of the door."

"What?" Waverly asked, panic in her voice.

"I need you to trust me. There's something in…" Before he had a chance to finish his sentence, a single cockroach flew into the air, setting off a mass flight of hundreds of cockroaches. Waverly screamed in terror as the swarm attacked them.

In a split decision, Viktor laid his other hand on Rafe and dematerialized, despite being unsure of his destination. The stench of urine rushed him as they appeared inside an enormous basement area. His stomach clenched as he caught sight of dozens of dog cages, filled with men and women. Dirty needles and IV bags were strewn all over the floor.

"Oh God," Waverly cried at the sight. She attempted to

run to a cage to open it, but Viktor caught her by the wrist, stopping her. He yelled to Rafe. "Call PCAP. Now."

"Let me go. They need help," she told him, attempting to wrench her arm from his grip.

Rafe retrieved his phone and tapped at the glass. "Done."

"Ivar!" Viktor yelled. He looked to Waverly. "Don't move. I need you to stay here with Rafe. It's too dangerous. I promise you I'll help them. Understand?"

Shaken, Waverly nodded, tears streaming down her face.

"I smell you, little pig." Viktor kicked an empty beer bottle, sniffing the air.

"What's happening?" Waverly's eyes widened as she caught sight of a wall of knives, whips and restraints. Tools of all shapes and sizes sat atop a rectangular table. A reticular saw rested upon a drain on the floor. A stainless-steel bed with leather straps sat on the blood-stained floor.

"It's going to be okay," Rafe told her, taking her hand. "Let Vik handle this."

Viktor stole a glance at Waverly. Furious, a fresh rush of anger stabbed through him. "Ivar!"

A singular rapid heartbeat stood out among the barely living humans. Viktor stalked through the rows. Like a laser beam on its target, the ancient vampire detected its source. He reached for the cage door and tore it off, tossing it clear across the room. The quivering vampire inside rolled onto his back holding up his hands defensively.

"Come here!" Viktor reached for him, grabbing him by his throat and dragging him out of the container. "What is this place?"

"It's none of your business. She...she will not be ha...ha... happy," he stuttered, scrambling back towards the wall.

"Who is she?" Viktor reached for him and held him off the floor by the back of his neck.

"The Missus. She owns th...thi...this place. You have to

get ou...ou...out." Ivar kicked his feet in an attempt to break loose of Viktor's grip.

"What are you doing with all these humans?" Viktor growled, sickened by the stench. *Torture. Bloodletting.* "PCAP is going to be here any second. And when they see what you've done, they're going to kill you...if you're lucky. Because if I do it, I'm going to break every finger in your hand and rip out your tongue. Now answer me. What is her name? What are you doing with the humans?"

Viktor tossed Ivar onto the cold concrete floor, looming over him.

"They're just blood bags. No one will miss them. Why do you care?"

"Because they're human beings." Viktor grabbed Ivar again and flung him across the room. He flashed to his side and stomped his boot onto the vampire's throat. "You've got one minute. PCAP is coming for you soon. Will you be alive or dead?"

"They're food. Nothing more," Ivar managed, blood dripping from his mouth.

Viktor pulled out his phone and swiped to a picture of Adam he'd copied off the museum website. He shoved the screen toward his face. "Do you know him?"

"I'm not telling you—"

Viktor landed a kick to his jaw, sending a blood-soaked tooth skipping across the floor. "Do you know him?"

"Yeah." Ivar coughed and spat bloody sputum onto the floor.

"What's his name?"

"I don't know. The Mis...Missus is coming."

Rage tore through Viktor. He strode over to the blood-soaked table. Using the cuff of his jacket, he selected a silver knife. Careful not to burn himself on the toxic metal, Viktor returned to Ivar and held the blade to the vampire's forehead. It sizzled as Viktor held it to his skin, the stench of burnt flesh filling the room.

Viktor lifted the knife and released a feral growl. "What the fuck are you doing with these humans? Where is the owner? What's her name?"

Ivar began to laugh, a deep maniacal laughter that echoed amongst the moaning humans who'd begun to wake.

The sound of gunfire echoed from above. *PCAP.*

Ivar stumbled to his feet, blood streaming down his face. His laughter grew louder.

"What the fuck?" Viktor looked to Waverly and Rafe as the floor beneath his feet began to shake.

"We've got to save these people," Waverly cried, her face swollen with tears.

"Dude, what the fuck is happening?" Rafe asked.

A pounding thud rumbled throughout the room. Flecks of concrete stung their face as a wall crumbled before them. A silhouette stepped out of the shadows as debris sprayed throughout the room.

"Missus! Missus!" Ivar screamed as he ran toward her and cowered at her feet.

Wearing a tight candy apple red jumpsuit, the feminine figure stood silent. Her jet-black hair had been tied into a high ponytail. With her face covered with a mask that revealed only a set of dark eyes, she glared at Viktor. Then in a flash, they disappeared.

"Goddammit!" Viktor yelled as they escaped.

The voices from above grew louder, and he flashed to Waverly and Rafe, taking them into his arms. As he demate-rialized, he realized what they were up against was far worse than a human brotherhood.

~

VIKTOR SAT in the great chair, staring at Waverly who slept in the bed. They'd come full circle. Once again, she'd been traumatized, and once again, it was his fault. He wasn't deserving of her love. Death had followed him his whole life and tonight had been no different. He'd released his beast, showing her his true nature…she'd never love a monster.

Viktor sensed his brother before he'd said a word. "I shouldn't have taken her there tonight."

"Where would we have left her? Nowhere, that's where." Greyson leaned on the doorjamb but didn't enter the bedroom. "She's in shock. She'll be fine."

"Will she though? This is our world, not hers." Viktor's heart bled knowing he'd endangered her, aware she'd always face danger as long as she was with him. "And now—"

"This is her world now. You've already begun your bonding. You love her. I see it in your eyes."

Viktor sighed, refusing to discuss his feelings with his brother. "The person who came for Ivar. She was able to dematerialize. I couldn't see her face. But I could sense her. I could sense the evil."

"So, she has a few tricks. It's doesn't mean she's like us."

"It doesn't mean she's not. All of this. It's tied to him. Don't tell me it's not because it is. This is all some sick game."

"There are a lot of sick fucks in this world, Vik. It could be tied to any ancient out there. There are other bloodlines."

"But what if…" Viktor hesitated to share his thoughts, questioning his own sanity. "You didn't see what was down there, what they'd been doing to those humans."

"I know what you're thinking, but he's not alive," Greyson assured him.

"But what if it is one of our siblings? Someone out there who was sired by Baxter. That motherfucker made others."

"It doesn't matter who it is. We'll take her out. PCAP will be looking for her too."

"Pfft." Viktor gave a dry laugh. "They won't find her. No. She'll come to me."

The brothers sat in silence, ruminating, questioning everything they'd known to be true. Baxter had turned more vampires over the centuries than Viktor had socks. While most died an early death, he'd never been sure how many or who else was out there.

Torture. Death. Just a few of Baxter's favorite things.

CHAPTER ELEVEN

*W*averly stirred, her mind churning with emotion upon her first waking thought. Clouded memories of the night lingered, and she struggled to shake the disgust and sadness that hung over her. She recalled Viktor flashing them to the safety of his home. Shaken, she'd needed time alone. She'd curled into a ball in the hot shower, scrubbing her skin, hoping to wash away the death.

Lying in bed, with a blanket still wrapped tightly around her, Waverly fluttered open her eyes. *Viktor.* Across the room from her, he reclined in a black leather chair with his feet propped on its ottoman. Though he wore a white fluffy cotton robe and pure white satin pajama pants, he was no angel.

She'd seen his monster. Enraged, he'd beaten the vampire and crushed his throat. *Lethal. Protector. Immortal.*

Waverly took a deep breath and glanced to her own fingers that still fisted the sheets. Although her skin was clean as virgin snow, she knew her soul had been forever tainted by the horror she'd witnessed. It was as if she'd inhaled the evil, taken it inside her body and now couldn't release it.

The scent of lavender teased her nose and she glanced over to the nightstand. A gold rectangular diffuser sent a steady stream of vapor swirling upward. Overhead, silver metallic bubble lights illuminated the bedroom. Black furniture contrasted with three white walls. A fourth wall made of black brick housed an A-framed gas fireplace.

"How are you feeling?" he asked, his voice soft.

"You slept on the chair?" Startled, she refocused on Viktor.

"I'm fine. How are you feeling?" her vampire repeated.

"I guess I'm all right," she lied.

"Last night—"

"I'm not okay," she whispered, considering how she'd reacted to what happened the night before. *Distant. Broken.* "The people in the cages...did they save anyone?"

"I spoke with a detective from PCAP, and he said about seven of them were alive. All humans. They're being attended to in the hospital." Viktor scrubbed his fingers through his hair with a sigh. "I'm sorry. It was bad."

Relief flooded through her at the news that some survived. But there'd been at least fifty kennels...she suspected so many more had died. "Who would do something like this? I don't understand it. I've never seen anything like it."

"Unfortunately, there is much suffering in this world. I'm just sorry you had to see it. I shouldn't have taken you there."

Waverly shoved up to sit. "No, this isn't your fault."

"Yeah, it is. I shouldn't have brought you to that club. Whatever is happening...we'll find out who is behind all this."

"Last night...I was terrified. Shocked. But I can't live the rest of my life being afraid."

"The truth is that this horrible kind of stuff has been going on since the beginning of time. Murder. Stealing. Torture. I've been around many years. Looked evil right in the eye. And the only thing I can tell you is that good will win eventually. But you've got to fight. Turning a blind eye to it is like letting it win."

Waverly sighed in contemplation. What had happened last night was just the beginning. She feared they'd only peeled back one layer of the onion and would discover more.

"Who was that woman?" she asked.

"I don't know. I've never met her before. She's an older vampire, though. I know that much."

"How can you tell?"

"That disappearing trick I do?" He gave a tight smile.

"Yeah." She nodded.

"That's not something just any vampire can do. It takes several hundred years to build up the generational power to dematerialize. I'd guess she's at least five hundred years old. I know it sounds crazy but when she looked at me...it was almost like I recognized her. There was something about her eyes. They were familiar..." Viktor shook his head. "But I don't know who she is. I do know that Ivar knew Adam. And Adam has been to that blood club."

"Adam? I don't get it. Why is he doing this?"

"I need to ask you something. I need to know what exactly went down between you guys. I know you said you worked with him at one point but did anything else happen? Anything I should know?"

Waverly took a deep breath, detecting jealousy in his tone. *No lying.* "It wasn't really anything. We both worked as grad assistants. And you know, things just happened. We had a fling. Nothing more really. He left for the East Coast after graduation, and I stayed in California. I never really thought that much of it. I haven't had any contact with him at all."

"And Teagan? How does Adam know her?" Viktor asked.

"I told you. We were roommates. Lived in the same apartment complex in Pacific Beach. A lot of college kids lived there. Typical California kind of set up. Pool in the middle. Parties. But honestly, I was usually either working or studying."

"I don't like the idea of you dating anyone else. Is that terribly human of me?" He laughed.

"I don't like the idea of you dating anyone either. And yes, it's a horribly human trait. But one I'm afraid I don't mind you having." Waverly smiled at Viktor.

"I won't share you with anyone, mo chroí," he told her, his tone serious. "If we bond—"

"I don't share well either," she interjected. "So I suppose you're stuck with me."

Waverly's heart pounded in her chest as he rose and stalked toward her. No matter the beast inside him, Viktor exuded the kind of sex and confidence she found irresistible. She wanted this man with her, around her, in her…forever.

She craved his touch, his kiss, his bite.

He gave her a sexy smile as he reached for a robe lying at the edge of the bed. As she swung her feet onto the ground to sit, he draped it over her shoulders. She tunneled her arms through its sleeves and stood, facing him. Her heart melted as he carefully wrapped it closed and tied it. His energy thrummed through her, his palms running over her shoulders, then taking her hands in his.

"I have a surprise for you. Something I've never shown anyone. Are you ready?" Viktor asked, a mischievous glint in his eyes.

"I'd go anywhere with you." Waverly's pulse raced at her own words. She hadn't meant to commit but there was no way she'd give him up.

"You're going to love this."

AS THEY MATERIALIZED into the majestic ballroom, Waverly's eyes widened in surprise. She took a step onto the cool, white, marble floor, her attention drawn to its walls that had been hand-painted with decorative murals, crown molding adorning its borders. She glanced to a Steinway grand piano that sat in the center of the room. Gold inlay within the intricately carved rosewood sparkled underneath the light.

"What is this place?" she whispered, looking upward to an epic, domed glass ceiling. With a crystal-clear night, the stars appeared so bright she thought she could touch them. Green and bluish lights danced across the sky.

"This is my private gallery. I've never brought anyone here but you." Viktor gestured to the seating area. "I come here when I need to think."

"Where are we?" Waverly asked, her instinct warning her he'd taken her far from Miami.

"Iceland." Viktor smiled and walked to the golden antique table and chairs that had been meticulously set for dining for two. He reached to retrieve a bottle of champagne from an ice bucket and poured the bubbly into glasses.

A rush of adrenaline shot through her as she took in the sight of the magnificent room. *Viktor Christianson.* At every step, the charismatic vampire surprised her. Hours ago, she'd been surrounded by death, and she now stood within the walls of a palace.

"Is this a castle?" she asked in awe.

"Technically no, but it's my sanctuary. My home." Viktor handed her a flute of champagne.

"You were born here?"

"No. I was born in Ireland. I'm a Celt. I was brought over to Iceland with a group of monks."

"You're a monk?" she asked, attempting to conceal her shock.

"Who? Me? Hell no. But I did spend time with them as a boy. You see, I was orphaned. I don't have much memory of my parents. They both died when I was a boy. My aunt sent me off to be raised by the monks. Which really meant I was a servant. I sometimes think about how different my life would have been had she kept me, but she was unmarried and but a peasant girl herself. She could hardly afford to feed another mouth. Times were difficult back then." Viktor shrugged. "After nearly a year with the monks, we were attacked. The Vikings invaded and took me. I was raised to fight, which I did...until I died. And that's all she wrote."

"I'm sorry." Waverly placed her hand on his arm.

"No reason to be sorry. Every year on this big blue space ball has been a lesson. And I'm very happy to say this year has been the best year yet, because," he smiled, his eyes on hers, and held up his glass, "I met you. To my beautiful art curator."

Waverly's face heated as she brought the rim to her lips, the bubbles dancing over her tongue. "I'm glad we met too."

"Aaaand..." Viktor gestured to the table, "...we can celebrate with some food. But first, I've got a surprise for you."

"Another surprise?" She laughed, confused as to how he could have arranged for food in his home in Iceland, let alone planned something else.

"What I'm about to show you. I want you to know that you're the only person who's ever seen this. Are you ready?"

Viktor smiled as he reached for a concealed button on the wall and pressed it.

Waverly's jaw dropped open as the walls slid down into the floor, revealing the rare paintings, hung on an identical wall behind the façade.

"What is this?" Her voice hushed to a whisper, her pulse racing. "This can't be." Frozen, she looked to the artwork and back to Viktor. "May I?"

"Of course." He gestured to the wall.

Waverly's heart sped in excitement as she approached the paintings. A singular spotlight shone on each individual piece. She studied the familiar artwork and placed her hand over her mouth in astonishment.

"What? How did you get this? It can't be. This piece was destroyed in a fire." Confusion threaded through her as she inspected the painting. "Ghirlandaio. Virgin and Child in Glory with Saints John the Evangelist, Francis, Jerome, and John the Baptist."

"The one and only. I knew you'd like it," he told her.

"But it was reported as destroyed in the Flakturm Friedrichshain fire," Waverly replied. "I can't believe this."

"One of the greatest losses of art," he agreed. "Good thing it's still here."

"But how?" She studied the piece, her mind racing. The realization hit her, and she turned to Viktor. "You were there."

"I don't know who started the fire but yes. I was in the vicinity when I saw the fire. As you can imagine, vampires, like humans, don't do well with fire so I'm afraid I could only pop in and out. The fire was so intense that I literally was only there for a few seconds. I reached out and touched a painting and this is what I brought home with me."

"Why doesn't anyone know about this?" she asked him, wearing an expression of awe.

"The world has many secrets, pet. Whether it be a painting collecting dust in someone's attic, or a piece that's been stolen. Or even ones that are reportedly destroyed… there are great treasures that will never be seen by all."

"But it's exquisite. It should be shared," she protested.

"Perhaps, but I'm afraid it's not possible. There are vested interests who would love to see it stolen or destroyed. This one piece must be protected. Fret not, the Vatican is aware of its location."

"I'm sorry, what? Did you just say the Vatican?"

"It shouldn't shock you. The hand of God has been instrumental in the safekeeping of texts and art for centuries. *Secrets.*" Viktor brought his hand upward, holding a finger to his smiling lips.

"This is…" Waverly scanned the room, taking in the sight of nearly fifty pieces of artwork, "it's incredible."

"I only collect it," he explained.

Waverly pointed to an empty showcase. "The Monet?"

"Oui," Viktor grinned. "It will do well for the world to see that particular painting. It reminds people that just because you don't know something exists, it doesn't mean it's not real."

"I can't believe this is happening. I mean, I know there are private collections but these paintings…I don't ever want to leave this room." Waverly beamed.

"I do have my vices. I enjoy collecting the most beautiful, treasured pieces." He gestured to the paintings. "Baxter would never allow me to have anything that brought me joy…no matter what it was. Like the monks I once lived with, love, a family, all those were out of my reach. And they've stayed out of my reach for centuries. Until now."

"Viktor…" Waverly's words failed her.

"I have something else to show you." Viktor nodded his head toward the side table. "Over here."

"I can't believe this is real," she managed as she followed Viktor back to the seating area.

"This piece must be kept sealed to account for humidity and whatnot. Come sit." Viktor reached for a copper box, careful as he opened its lid.

Waverly slid onto the sofa next to him, her eyes wide as saucers as the item came into view. "Is that? There is no way. They were all destroyed."

"Since we're not in the library, it's best we leave it concealed behind the glass. Do you recognize it?" he asked.

"I Modi?" Waverly gasped, her heart pounding against her ribs.

Viktor nodded.

"The Sixteen Pleasures. Marcantonio Raimondi. No, this isn't impossible. The church had all copies of it destroyed," she told him.

"This one includes the writings by Pietro Aretino. Good thing I was there to flash away a copy when the Pope sent out his order. Had to keep it hidden for years. The Vatican doesn't know about this one."

"I can't believe I'm seeing this. Any of this." A broad smile broke across her face. Heat flushed her cheeks. "Erotic, isn't it? I can't imagine what it would have been like to see this when it first came out."

"Positively scandalous." He grinned.

Viktor pointed to an image of a couple engaged in sex. "I think we should start with this position. We can work our way through the book. What do you say, pet?"

"You're a naughty vampire." Waverly shot him a sensual smile, her body thrumming with energy. The ache between her legs throbbed, and she was tempted to jump the vampire right there.

"You have no idea," Viktor confirmed.

Waverly took a sip of her champagne in an attempt to cool down her libido. "Delicious."

"Yes, you are." Viktor brought the rim of his glass to his lips.

"Viktor...this is so special." Her smile faded; her expression heated. "You're special. I'm honored you'd share this with me. When we first met, I shouldn't have judged you." Waverly's fingers curled around her glass, emotion tightening in her chest. "When all this is over. Because I believe it will be. I don't know if it's possible, but I want this...us."

"I want us too. But you need to understand," Viktor turned to her, his expression serious, "there are things about being with a vampire."

"I know, but—"

"No. Hear me out. You've only spent a few days with me. The bonding. Once it's done, we'll be together. Eternally. You will remain human, but you won't age."

"That sounds pretty nice to me."

"Ah, yes. But think of this. Because you won't age, you won't die. But everyone around you will. You will be forced to choose where to put your energy. Who deserves that loss you're going to feel when they die? Because if you allow yourself to feel, that's what's going to happen. And the alternative is choosing the path I was forced upon...to never feel, to not care for humans."

"Viktor." Waverly reached for him; the vision slammed into her instantly. The whip cracked; his flesh sliced open with each lash. Viktor on his knees, in agony, refused to cry out.

"It was beaten out of me every chance Baxter could. No humans. No feeling. No relationships. But the thing is, it takes years to do this to someone. Humans are meant to be with each other, to care for others, so to take away that very thing, it's very difficult but once it happens, the monster is created."

"You're not a monster," she told him as she reached to cup his cheek.

"Once Baxter was dead it became an excuse not to feel. Quintus? He moved on. I, on the other hand, preferred to be insulated from the pain. I never formed relationships other than the casual acquaintance. I had no children until Rafe. And that happened by accident."

"But you did it for a friend," she challenged. "You seem close to Rafe."

"I suppose he's grown on me. Everything happened so quickly. Now the wolf is forever in my care." Viktor shrugged. "And I don't know I'll be able to give him what he needs. Wolves are different than vampires. Vampires can be solitary creatures. Not wolves though. They live in packs. They have children. Families. That's not something I have."

"But I..." Waverly brought his palm to her cheek. "I could be your family. You don't have to be alone."

"You need to understand what it will be like. I won't sugarcoat it." Guilt dripped from him like thick molasses.

"I want this." She kissed his palm and closed her eyes, leaning into his hand. "I want you. Us."

"Mo chroí." Viktor wrapped his arms around her and brought her into his embrace. "You must be sure of these things. We have time."

"This is my choice." While she understood his reasons, his hesitation stung. "I choose you."

"You are the only one I've ever cared about. I will always choose you. But I must consider the consequences. Protect you."

Waverly relaxed into his embrace and closed her eyes, reveling in his warmth and power. No matter what she'd told herself about not catching feelings, she was so far gone. She'd never given a thought to getting married let alone bonded for eternity, but within his arms, she knew for certain she could spend the rest of her life with him.

Waverly's eyes fluttered open, spying the piano. Inspired, she pulled out of his arms and gave Viktor a flirtatious smile as she set her glass onto the table. "Come."

She slipped onto the piano bench and brushed the pads of her fingers over the cool smooth ivories. "May I?"

"Of course." Viktor nodded.

"It's been years, but I used to play." Happiness filled her soul as the notes sounded. She smiled, playing *Stay with Me*.

Viktor slid next to Waverly, his leg brushing hers. He lent a third hand, adding a harmony as they finished the song.

The room went silent save for her heart pounding in her chest like a drum. His gentle finger brushed over her chin, turning her head. He leaned into her, his lips feathering over hers.

"You're perfect," he whispered, his mouth capturing hers in a devastating kiss.

Waverly moaned, her tongue sweeping against his, probing, desperate for him. She lit with desire, tasting her vampire. His strong lips commanded hers, his fingers tunneled into her hair as he kissed her.

"Viktor," she breathed, her heart beating fast as Viktor lifted her by her waist and settled her onto his lap.

"Mo chroí." Viktor made love to her mouth, his tongue dancing with hers.

Waverly sighed as his hard cock brushed against her thigh. She pulled his robe open, and reached between his legs, taking his firm shaft in her hand. She moaned as she stroked his hardened dick, sliding her thumb over its wet slit.

"Fuck," Viktor gritted out as he tore open her robe and lifted her upward, her bottom brushing over the piano keys.

Waverly brought her hands to her breasts and tugged at

her nipples. With her eyes on Viktor's, she sighed as he pressed open her knees, exposing her pussy.

"Touch yourself," he ordered.

Through a heated gaze, her fingers traveled from her breast over her stomach and past her belly button. He groaned as she licked her lips, her hand delving between her legs.

"Like this?" she moaned, the tips of her fingers brushing over her clit.

"Fuck your pussy. Let me see you," he ordered, taking his cock into his hand.

"Ah—" Waverly drove a single finger inside her core, her thumb caressing her glistening bead.

"You're so fucking sexy," Viktor told her as he stroked his swollen shaft and leaned between her legs.

Like a wild wolf, his feral eyes looked up to her. Ravenous, he brought his lips to her pussy, sucking her fingers and clit into his mouth.

"Ah...yes," Waverly breathed as his tongue brushed over her clitoris. Relentless, he flicked at her quivering nub, his lips sucking her pussy.

As he slid two fingers inside her, Waverly's hands slammed onto the keys. "Oh God."

Waverly sucked a desperate breath, arousal threaded throughout every cell in her body. She writhed her pussy against his mouth, his tongue ruthlessly lapping at her clit.

As she looked to Viktor, he raised his gaze, his face glistened with her essence. Her heart pounded as she caught sight of his fangs. His fingers plunged inside her, teasing her toward her orgasm, the tip of his tongue flicking over her flesh.

"Please...yes." Bordering on obsession, she allowed the dark fantasy to consume her. Waverly would beg. She would plead. Anything for Viktor's bite. *Complete the bond.*

"Bite me, bite me," she repeated, breathless with desire. "Please, do it...do it...ah!"

Waverly screamed in ecstasy as Viktor struck, his fangs slicing through the creamy flesh of her inner thigh. She convulsed in orgasm, her fingers clutching at his shoulders.

Without warning he flashed her over to the sofa, bending her over its arm. She panted for breath, still reeling from her climax. With her butt perched upward and her head on the sofa cushion, cool air grazed over her pussy as he spread her thighs open.

"What are you doing?" Her body tingled with his power, her own climax still threading throughout her body.

"I promised I'd have every part of you." He grinned.

"Complete the bond," she whispered. Still unsure of the consequences, a feral instinct drove her desire.

"Patience. We will have eternity," he told her.

"Please," she begged, an ache of arousal throbbing.

"This." Viktor's palm brushed over her calf and moved to her thigh, finally cupping her bottom.

Waverly gasped as he spread her cheeks open with his strong hands, his fingers teasing through her wet folds. "Vik—"

"This too. I want all of you, mo chroí." He landed a swift slap to her bottom and rubbed the reddened cheek.

Waverly's heart pounded in her chest as the cool gel dripped over her ass, his finger circling her puckered skin.

"But first, we shall play,"

"I don't know..." Waverly lost her words as his finger pressed into her ass. The pressure built as he inched inside her. His other hand brushed through her pussy and over her swollen bead, teasing her orgasm to the surface.

Without warning he withdrew, and she released an audible sigh in protest. As she looked back to Viktor, her pulse raced. With a wicked smile, he dangled a golden bulbous toy attached to a long leather tail within her sight.

Though he spoke no words, she knew what he planned. The fear of exploring her dark fantasies surfaced, yet her body craved him. She trusted her vampire to bring her to the highest level of ecstasy. There was no part of her that would not accept him.

Every cell in her body went on alert as he trailed the soft leather over her cheek, brushing it over her neck, down between her shoulder blades to her lower back and bottom.

Waverly sucked a breath as the cool object teased open her anus, its tip pressing into her. "Ah...I..."

"Relax, my pet. I will always bring you pleasure," he assured her, his voice raspy and dark.

Waverly sucked a breath as the plug stretched her. His fingers teased her pussy as he gently slid the plug inside her ass.

"What a beautiful little tail," he said, giving it a tug.

"Oh God, please," she begged, her core tightening in anticipation, the sensation leaving her full and aroused. "I need—"

"Slow," Viktor whispered, bringing his cock to her entrance.

"I need you to..." she pleaded, her body on fire with desire, "fuck me."

Viktor groaned in pleasure as he eased himself inside her, filling her to the hilt. "That's it...ah yeah."

"Oh my God," Waverly breathed, her body full. She reached her arms forward, clutching the sofa. Overwhelmed with the sensation, she writhed back on him, her clitoris aching for release.

"Ah, fuck. You feel so tight. Your pussy..." Viktor grunted, withdrawing and plunging back into her several times. "Fuck."

Waverly sighed, her body protesting as he withdrew. She squealed as Viktor lifted her up into the air and gently placed her onto the sofa on her back. He settled between her legs and buried himself deep inside her.

"You are everything," he told her as he pumped in and out of her tight channel.

Viktor's mouth crushed onto hers, and Waverly kissed him back with an urgent fervor. Their bodies moved as one. Viktor slowed his pace, grazing his pelvis against hers.

With her bottom full and her pussy filled with his cock, her swollen clit pulsated with pleasure. She lifted her hips to his and rocked against him, meeting each slow thrust. She gasped as he cupped her bottom and tugged on the leather cords.

Viktor's lips moved to her collarbone, his tongue tasting her skin. His fangs nicked her flesh, sweet pain and pleasure threading through her.

"I...I...com..." She lost her words, her climax teetering on the edge.

Viktor slammed into her, pumping harder and harder. She screamed with pleasure as his fangs sliced deep into her neck. As he tugged the plug from her ass and gave a final thrust, Waverly screamed into his shoulder, her own teeth nipping at his skin.

Viktor rolled her to the side, his ravenous eyes set on hers. He gave a loud groan, his seed exploding deep inside her. Waverly's body shook in release, stiffening as the waves of pleasure rushed over her. She cried his name in ecstasy, her orgasm seizing her.

Waverly panted, attempting to catch her breath. Her heart pounded in her chest as the realization hit her. She'd almost broken his flesh. She swore she could hear his pulse calling to her in her mind. The craving for his lifeblood that lingered beneath the surface of his skin, driving her to bond with him, her hunger would go unsated.

As Viktor brushed a kiss to her head, she relaxed into his embrace, exhaustion washing over her.

"I love you," she whispered as she drifted off to sleep. God, she loved this man. Bonding or not, she'd never let him go. *My vampire.*

I LOVE YOU, Waverly had whispered to him. She'd fallen hard for a man who was everything she'd avoided her whole life. It didn't matter that he was vampire. It was as if she'd found a perfect half to make her whole, something that filled holes in her life she'd never known were there.

His bite was the most erotic sensation she'd ever experienced in her life. But he hadn't solidified their bond. And she knew why. Humans are born, grow up, get married, have babies, raise them and let them go for their offspring to repeat it all. Entire lives are wrapped up in families. She'd never imagined watching all her friends grow old while she stayed young, losing people she loved.

Yet it was the single love of her life she'd miss out on if she didn't choose Viktor. And the truth was her heart had already chosen him. More than his bite, he appreciated art and made her laugh, cared about her choices in this life-changing decision. Waverly pictured a future of lifetimes exploring the world and knew he was the one.

But the darkness of the paranormal wasn't a reality she'd known before Viktor. Teagan had indulged in the occult, embraced the excitement and mystery, knowing the risk that came with the lifestyle. And although Waverly had stayed friends with her, she never discussed her interests in the paranormal.

For so long, Waverly had suppressed her own powers, never disclosing her visions to others. Besides her own parents, Viktor had been the only person she'd ever trusted enough to share her gift, to explore it. Not only did he accept her abilities, but he also shared memories with her, embracing them. Within the safety of her vampire's presence, her powers had already begun to expand and grow.

A kiss to her forehead brought a smile to her lips, shaking her from her renumerating thoughts.

"Sleep," he told her, easing out of the bed.

"Hmm, just a little." Waverly smiled as she watched him walk to the bathroom, admiring the hard planks of his lean, muscular body. A perfect ass, she laughed silently, thinking of how she'd like to return the favor he'd done to her.

The spray of the shower sounded, and she curled the covers up to her chin. In her line of vision, the fleam sat wrapped on the nightstand. A reminder that the dream of making love with Viktor had been spawned by a nightmare that remained.

Waverly rolled onto her back and stared up at the ceiling. Despite her spinning thoughts, she needed to rest before they strategized. But her mind still raced with thoughts of Adam. Why would Adam still be interested in her after all these years? What had he been planning to do if he'd succeeded in kidnapping her? Had he done the same to Teagan? Did he murder her?

Restless, Waverly shoved up onto one elbow and reached across the bed for the fleam. She adjusted on her pillow so she could look at it. As she unraveled the cloth, she thought of Thorn and his reluctance to touch the object. Unholy, he'd called it. A blood contract with the devil.

"Dear God, please protect me from anything that can hurt me. I reject Satan and all he represents." Waverly may have been lapsed, but still believed in God, that both good and evil existed in this world.

As it came into view, she couldn't help thinking how unassuming it was. Adam had devised an elaborate scheme, sending the painting to her, knowing she'd investigate and track down the other piece. And like a lamb to slaughter, she'd given herself to him on a platter.

"Fuck him," she said to herself, carefully running her finger over the smooth wood handle. She wondered how many humans had been supposedly 'healed' by bloodletting despite there being no scientific basis for it.

B.A.O. No matter how many times Viktor protested, whether there was a rational explanation or not, this object was tied to him.

Waverly considered what she experienced in the blood club. Her visions had morphed, from seeing when she touched Viktor to seeing when touching objects. Determined to try to glean more information about the fleam's owner, Waverly closed her eyes and placed her fingers on both its handle and blade. She took a deep breath, attempting to sense its energy, its story in time.

Like a tidal wave crashing against the rocks, the vision slammed into her. Viktor lay unconscious on the ground, his bruised and bloodied body motionless in the dirt. A dark figure hovered above him, but she couldn't make out the details in the darkness. As a fire raged beyond him, flames licking high into the air, the silhouette of a goat's head appeared in the blaze. The robed figure stood, reaching its clawed fingers up into the air.

Waverly's heart raced as the diabolical creature grew taller. *Please don't. Please don't.* The stench of rotten eggs hung heavy in the air. Flames ignited from the ground as it turned and looked directly at her, its blazing crimson eyes burning into her soul.

Waverly released a gut-wrenching scream as it rushed toward her. As if she were running through wet sand, she struggled to get away. It closed the distance stretching its arms outward, cackling as it came within feet of her body. Deafening maniacal laughter sounded in her ears as it scraped its talons down her back. Her skin burned like fire, pain stabbing through her entire body.

She blinked and was transported to another realm. Flames all around her, she realized she'd been tied to a stone pillar. Terrified she yanked on the leather restraints but couldn't break free. "Let me go!"

"Is this what you wanted to see?" it growled, mere inches from her face, its foul breath choking her.

"Let me go! Let me go! Let me—" Waverly repeated, struggling to breathe. Her eyes snapped open, desperately sucking air, tears streaming down her face.

"You're okay. I'm here," Viktor assured her.

Waverly's stomach rolled with nausea as she looked down to her bloodied hands. With tears in her eyes, her back burned in pain. Viktor took her hands in his and wiped her palms, cleaning her.

"What happened?" She sucked back a sob, looking to Viktor for answers.

"You were having a nightmare. The fleam. You cut your hand." He brought her palm to his mouth, sealing the tiny cut in her skin. "It's okay. You're all better now."

"Where is it?" Terror laced her voice, her chest tight in panic.

"It's on the nightstand. I wrapped it back up. What were you doing?"

"I was just…I don't know. I just wanted to touch it. I don't normally have visions when I touch things. Just people. But when we were in the club. I could see them. I thought if I could just touch the fleam…maybe I'd feel something."

"What did you see?"

"You." She held her palm to his cheek. "This thing. It did something to you."

"Thing?"

"I don't know what it was. It looked like a goat. It had horns but looked like a man. I couldn't see it very well." Tears brimmed in her eyes. Confusion swept over her.

"Mo chroí." Viktor pulled her into his embrace.

"It had claws. I couldn't get away. I tried to run but I couldn't. It got me. Oh my God, it touched me." She pulled from his arms and turned away, showing him her back. "Do you see anything? It was so real."

"See what? I…" Viktor's words trailed away as he caught sight of the reddened marks on her shoulder.

"What is it?" she asked, her heart racing.

"It's going to be okay." He hesitated. "I can heal you but—"

"Oh my God." Waverly jumped out of the bed, and ran to the bathroom, inspecting herself in the mirror. "That's impossible."

"It's going to be okay," he repeated, his voice calm. "You may have manifested this somehow."

"I can't believe this is happening." Waverly stood naked, trembling, staring at the marks. Horror overwhelmed her as reality set in…a demon had touched her. *Evil.*

Viktor came up behind her with a blanket and wrapped it around her shoulders, taking her into his embrace. Petrified, she looked up to him, her emotions raw.

"That thing was here." She glanced to the bed and the bloodstained sheets. "It's going to come back."

"No. You're safe. We're safe. No one even knows about this house. I have wards set on it. As long as you stay inside, you'll be fine. It's the fleam that did this."

"I didn't do this to myself," she yelled, tears streaming down her face.

"Hey, hey," Viktor reached for her hands, "Look at me." He patiently waited until she calmed, meeting his gaze. "Whatever your gift is. Your visions. You said you kept this under wraps your whole life. What if it's starting to change? What if it's getting stronger?"

She nodded, having suspected as much. Yet she still couldn't control the visions.

"You said before it was only touch," Viktor continued. "Human to human. Then it got stronger, you sensed something by touching an object. The wall at the club. Now this."

"But how is this happening?" she asked. "How did *it* touch me? I didn't even leave the house. It's like I'm hallucinating."

"But you did leave. Maybe it's a form of astral projection. In this world there are many realms. Heaven. Hell. And many other places. Wherever you went when you touched this… the energy tied to that fleam is, well, it's not exactly great. You heard Thorn. And believe me, he knows Hell. There's something evil about it. And that evil belongs to someone. Or something. In that realm, it was able to touch you."

"Oh God." Waverly slumped in defeat, her forehead rested on his chest.

"The good news is that you got out. And you got out on your own. And if you ever end up there again, you will deal with it."

"I don't want this. I'm scared." She'd tried to be brave, to hold up next to shifters and vampires, but the truth was she was human. *Vulnerable. Weak.*

"We're going to figure this out. We're going to get rid of this Godforsaken fleam that was sent to us. And I'm going to find Ivar, Adam and our mystery vampire. You've got to trust me. This ends now."

"Please don't lie to me," she pleaded.

"I swear to the Goddess. By the end of the day, this will be done. Just give me a little more time. I'm working with

Quintus to track down the vampire from the bar. And then I'm going to kill her."

Waverly held tight to Viktor. She slowed her breath until their hearts beat in rhythm, absorbing his peaceful energy. Although grateful for the respite, instinct warned her that the creature in her vision would come for her. It wanted to make Viktor suffer, to see him humiliated and on his knees again. And even though she was human, she'd give her own life to protect him.

CHAPTER TWELVE

*V*iktor sat in front of the fireplace, its volcanic rock masonry reaching up toward the cathedral ceiling. With his feet propped up on an ottoman, he leaned back into his brown leather chair. Viktor cupped his glass, but didn't drink, his eyes closed as his mind raced.

For hundreds of years, he'd lived free of his sire's tyranny, thankful the bastard had been sent to Hell. No longer a slave to his sadistic hellish existence, Viktor worked hard, prospered, immersing himself in all the luxuries and pleasures the world had to offer. Despite the success, there was no recovering all that was lost; Baxter had stolen his humanity... until now. Viktor prayed Baxter was suffering in Hell, but it wouldn't even be a fraction of the agony he'd inflicted on him.

Viktor's thoughts drifted to Waverly, the one who reminded him that the ability to love someone, the very essence of being human, still existed within his soul. *I love you.* In a sleepy whisper, she'd said the words to him that no one had ever spoken. Love had been an elusive, precious treasure that he'd long resigned himself to never owning. Yet his heart, the burning in his soul for her, told him that, indeed, he'd found the one, and he loved his incredible human woman.

Nevertheless, Viktor hadn't completed the bond. He'd never do to her what had been done to him, to steal her choice, to deprive her of growing old, experiencing life with her friends and family. Whether he simply completed the bond to give her eternal life, or further turned her, it would inflict pain she'd never comprehend, an acceptance of continual loss over time. Being forever young, while watching others around you die, was a living hell for some vampires. Although the instinct to bond would grow stronger within him, the craving tearing at his heart, he'd resolved to give her as much time as she needed.

He considered how they'd met at the bar, how it at first appeared a serendipitous event designed by the Goddess to bring them together. But was it fate or an orchestrated plan? Viktor had shown weakness the night he'd met Waverly. Saving her was a mere indulgence at the time, but going after her to San Diego, taking interest in a human tilted the scales, making her a more than casual interest.

When Waverly had touched the fleam, something powerful, something evil had reached through the realm and attacked her. With her abilities strengthened, he wondered what else she could see, possibly conjure. With the scratch still fresh on her skin, Viktor raged with vengeance, determined to exact retribution.

The sound of the wolf's footsteps jarred his contemplation and Viktor sighed. Rafe had been endangered as well. The weight of responsibility rested heavily on his mind.

Viktor had contacted Greyson and given them their location in Iceland. His brother flashed himself and the wolf to his home.

"You all right, Vik?" Rafe asked as he walked into the room.

"Yep." Viktor kept his eyes closed. "Brennivín's on the bar."

"Uh, what? I don't think I've ever had this stuff." Rafe glanced at the bottle.

"Well today's your lucky day," Viktor's eyes remained closed, both his expression and tone detached. "Welcome to the land of ice and fire."

"When in Rome," Rafe joked.

"You're not."

Rafe sniffed the open bottle, shrugged and then poured the liquor. "Is Waverly okay?"

"Nope. She isn't." Viktor opened his eyes and stared at the fire. "This is all my fault."

"Can't blame her. That was some kind of scene back there at the bar. What the actual fuck was that thing? She was one scary bitch." Rafe shook his head.

"I dunno." Viktor concealed his thoughts, waiting on his brother to tell them what happened with the fleam and Waverly's vision.

"Dude. Is Baxter alive?" Rafe asked point blank.

"No," Viktor responded without hesitation. "He's in Hell. And that's where he's going to stay."

Greyson materialized next to Rafe, who jumped back almost spilling his drink. "What the hell, bro? That's not funny."

"Yeah, it is." Greyson laughed.

"No, it isn't. It's old. Just like you." Rafe chuckled and pointed to the bar. "Grab some."

"How's Waverly?" Greyson asked, going to the bar.

"She's shaken up," Viktor replied not taking his gaze off the flames. "And Rafe here was just asking about Baxter again."

"Bro. We've got to stop going down this road. He's dead." Greyson shook his head as he poured a glass.

"Someone knows him though. That vampire back there in the bar. She knows that son of a bitch," Viktor speculated, "and she's a monster just like him."

His brother took a sip and grimaced, releasing a loud breath. "Like fire! Argh."

"She's playing us." Viktor raised his glass to the flickering lights of the fire and took a sip. "A puppet master."

"She's playing way too well for an amateur. Perhaps she's gettin' a little help?" Greyson walked to the sofa and sat. With his knees spread open, he leaned toward the fire. "Who would do this?"

"I don't know yet but I'm gonna find them and kill them." Viktor paused in thought. "The last time I went to Hell, Baxter was still there. I don't know. Maybe the fucker really is making a play to get out."

"Devil's not going to simply release him from a blood contract."

"Maybe he's doing favors for Fae. Who the fuck knows? He could be down there sucking Satan's cock for all we know."

"Yeah, not an image I want stuck in my head." Greyson grimaced in disgust.

"I'll tell you one thing. That goddamn fleam belongs to Baxter. I feel it in my bones. I don't know where it came from. But it's his. He's a motherfucking demon piece of shit." Viktor didn't want to use or hear his name again as a fresh rush of anger twisted through him, as he recalled the scratches. "It did something to Waverly."

"What?" Rafe asked, concern in his voice.

Viktor sighed and turned to them. "It, uh, it did something. It's her powers. She's got these visions. She never used them until recently, but they're changing. I don't know why.

Maybe something about our bonding kicked things off? Who knows?"

"What's happening?" Greyson pressed.

"When I first met her, it started right away. But it only happened when she touched me. But now, it's expanded to objects. When we were in the club, she had a vision when she touched the wall. I got the impression it was more of a feeling. I don't know. But she knew there were people down there." Viktor's stomach turned, as he relived what had happened. "So uh, while I was in the shower, she said she'd wanted to try seeing something with the fleam."

"I'm guessing it wasn't good," Rafe said.

"No. It wasn't." Viktor blew out an audible breath. "It fucking scratched her. Left marks. I don't know how. Maybe it was a kind of dream realm where it could touch her. She said it was a goat-like creature. A demon or something. I don't know."

"It touched her from a freaking vision?" Rafe asked.

"Fucking hell." Greyson sighed.

"Yeah. My guess is that something about her ability brought her there. It was a message." Viktor looked to Greyson and Rafe. "It's coming for her. But it's also coming for me."

"We should go to New Orleans and ask the High Priestess if she can help," Rafe suggested.

"Ilsbeth?" Greyson smiled.

"No. The actual High Priestess. Samantha. I've heard she's cool. Let her run the location thing. Scribe. Use that fleam."

"My protégée is on to something. Once we have the location, we'll launch an attack. Take out Adam, Ivar and the vampire."

"What's their end game, though? Why go through all this?" Rafe asked.

"With Baxter there was no end game. Torture was the

only game. Sadistic, brutal cruelty," Greyson said. "This vampire. This woman. She's been taught by him. Or maybe she's just a fan. There's some sick fucks out there."

"It could even be someone we know." Viktor stretched his neck from side to side, recalling the familiar voice. He turned to the fire, his thoughts racing, wrath shooting through his veins. "Doesn't much matter. I don't care about her reasons. I'm going to kill her."

Greyson moved toward the fireplace. "We need to protect Waverly. Who else knows about this place?"

"Literally no one." Viktor pressed his palm to the cold pumice that had been forged from Mount Hekla. "This is my private sanctuary. No one has ever been here but me…until now."

"You've got staff, though?" he challenged.

"Yeah, but they've been with me for years. They're only allowed to enter when I say they can. This place is pretty isolated. It's not like most people will be able to get here without being noticed."

"You've got wards set up?" Greyson asked.

"Of course, but you know how that goes sometimes." A seed of concern was planted in his mind, concerned Waverly might inadvertently divulge their location. "Also, I've hidden the fleam. I don't want Waverly or anyone else to touch it again. Too risky after what just happened."

"Where is it?" Greyson asked.

"It's here in the house. In a pandora's box," Viktor told him.

"*The* pandora's box?" Rafe asked.

"Indeed. I have one of them," Viktor replied. "Seven exist."

Rafe looked to Greyson who nodded in confirmation. "He's right."

"Waverly's coming." Viktor stated flatly. He heard the wooden floor creak, her footsteps grew louder. "Don't freak her out. Don't ask about the scratches. No demon talk. This is bad enough."

"Is she still mortal?" Greyson whispered.

"She's mortal," Viktor confirmed.

"You must bond," he insisted. "She's too vulnerable."

"Don't you think I know that, brother?" Viktor kept his voice low. His jaw tensed, annoyance teasing every nerve of his body. "It's her choice to make. She hasn't had enough time. She needs to decide if she can handle seeing loved ones die. If she's up for this life we live. It's not fair for me to do this to her. I can't constantly expose her to it. These won't be the only monsters who cross our path. You and I both know it."

"You can't deny your own bond. You won't ever be happy."

"I've got to protect her first. If he's…" Viktor began but stopped himself from speculating on the impossible. He pumped his fingers into a fist. "No, no, some psychopath is out there, playing his games. Playing all of us. And this is all happening because of me."

"It's not your fault." Viktor heard Waverly's voice travel from the hallway.

Despite the dark topic of conversation, the sight of her brought a smile to his face. Dressed in an off-the-shoulder red cashmere sweater, blue jeans and tan suede snow boots, she looked as if she were ready to hit the slopes. She wore a loose side braid, her golden locks resting on her shoulder.

"How do you feel?" he asked, going to her.

"Can't sleep." She shrugged and put a hand into her front pocket.

"Can I make you some tea? Are you hungry?" Viktor asked.

"Do you know how satisfying it is to see my brother

waiting on his girlfriend?" Greyson laughed. "He's properly smitten."

"As am I." Waverly's cheeks flushed pink.

Viktor turned to his brother, with his back to Waverly, raising his eyebrows, a stern look on his face. "What the fuck?" he mouthed and promptly turned to face her again. "Ignore him."

"When are we going to New Orleans?" she asked.

"I want you to rest up before we go. Once we find out the location, we're going to find them." *Kill them.* "If they have Teagan, we'll get her out. I'll have you stay with Quintus. It's too dangerous."

"What? No. I'm going with you. This involves me as much as it does you. And I meant it. This is not your fault. The truth is we don't know why all this is happening. We don't have all the pieces. You said it yourself, Baxter is dead. And even if he was standing here right now, it's not your fault. I hate him for what he did to all of you."

"Let me make you some Chamomile tea. If you look out the back windows there, you can see the northern lights. Then off to bed," Viktor told her and brushed a kiss to her forehead.

"Are you trying to distract me?" she asked with a small smile.

"Maybe." Viktor walked to the kitchen and set to work, filling the kettle. Out of the corner of his eye, he watched Waverly stare up in fascination at the sky.

"It's beautiful," she said. "Do you mind if I get some fresh air?"

Viktor glanced to Rafe, and back to Waverly. "Of course. Just stay on the deck there. Don't go further."

"I'd like to see it too." Rafe jumped to his feet and approached the door.

"I hate to state the obvious but it's freezing outside.

You're not wearing a coat. You could freeze to death," Greyson called to them. "Viktor, do you see what your human is doing? She's mortal."

"I promise I'll be fine. We'll just be a minute," she assured him.

"Look at you making tea like a good husband," Greyson joked.

"That's a human sort." *Married?* Viktor set the cup onto the counter, hearing Waverly's laughter. She pointed to the sky, watching the spectacular display. Rafe glanced back to him for but a second, and in that moment, the word popped into his head. *Love. Family.* He'd gone all his lifetime walking the earth alone, and in a matter of days, he'd begun to bond with another, a beautiful human…who made him eggs.

"You okay?" Greyson asked.

"She's special, isn't she? I guess I never thought this could happen. You know how it's been. Humans were always good for food and a fuck. But with all their human habits, watching them die…I just couldn't do it. I couldn't be like you and Quint. And now there she is. She's my person."

"Bond her," Greyson told him. "Protect her."

"She's pretty awesome, isn't she?" Viktor nodded, still shocked he'd fallen for her, had rediscovered his humanity.

A high pitch whistle sounded, the tea kettle spewing steam into the air, breaking his contemplation. As Viktor reached to grab its handle, his heart seized. The vampire appeared next to Waverly, and she wrapped her arm around her neck. Rafe ripped his shirt off readying to attack, and shifted.

"Don't come any closer or I'll kill her," the vampire warned, glaring at him from the deck. "Don't flash to me, Viktor. Don't even try it. I see you."

As the creature called his name, his mind flashed to a time long ago. *Théa.* While he'd stopped Baxter from raping her,

Viktor had been unsuccessful in preventing his sire from turning her. That very night he'd been beaten, been sent away, while the cat played with its toy. Later that year, Quintus had killed Baxter but not before she'd been indoctrinated into the ways of vampire.

"Sister," Viktor called as he slowly stalked toward her. He proceeded with caution, choosing to heed her warning. Although he could attempt to dematerialize, it would only take a split second for her to kill Waverly.

Rafe growled, readying to strike.

"Brothers." She laughed, her arm tight around her prey. "Call off the wolf. I'll kill her, I swear it."

"Get off me," Waverly gritted out, struggling to break free.

"Théa," Viktor yelled as he looked to Rafe. *Stand down.* "The human belongs to me. Release her. You won't win against me. You'll die."

"Are you really going to take the gamble?" she asked, the slight French accent growing thicker as she spoke. "You're not allowed to have a human. You'll be punished."

"Baxter is dead. He's been dead for years, and you've got the audacity to take my human? To show your face in my house? Walk away now and I'll grant you an honorable death." He'd slit her throat and never think of it again. Anger burned in his stomach as he heard Waverly struggling to breathe. He bared his fangs. "I'm going to kill you."

"Father is rising." A sickening, evil smile bloomed on her face.

"I've been to Hell and back. He's dead. I know he's there. He's not coming back. Not ever."

"Hell isn't impermeable. You will suffer for your crimes." She sniffed at Waverly's hair. "This human does not belong to you. It's impossible."

"Let her go," Greyson urged.

"Brother. Join me and our master will spare you," she promised.

"Let me go, bitch," Waverly spat, kicking her to no avail.

"She's a spirted one. All the more fun to kill." Théa licked Waverly's cheek and grabbed at her breast. "Hmm...tasty. Perhaps I'll turn her instead. Fuck her. I could use a slave. She'll be forced to do anything I want. Even to kill you."

"What do you want?" Viktor surged with anger but attempted to keep the discussion going until he got closer. He walked with great trepidation. She could flash Waverly anywhere, and there would be nothing but their blood tie for him to try to find her.

"Many sins are owed to Satan. Father is more than willing to earn his way, to do favors to pay his blood debt. And then Father will take his place again in this realm. He will walk on Earth again. We will teach humans their place in this world. We will do as we wish without interference from others," Théa told him, wearing a cold expression. "Until then I do his bidding."

"There's nothing for him here," Viktor told her, inching closer. He glanced to Rafe. Holding his hand outward, he waved him away. *Stand back.*

"You don't know what I know," she challenged him. "He's already aware of what happens on this realm. He knows about you. He takes special interest in you."

"No more than the others," Viktor lied, knowing he'd given up his humanity.

"You were the favorite. His star." Théa laughed. "The golden child."

Waverly's eyes widened in shock. "Let me go."

"Don't listen to her," Viktor yelled.

"Oui, oui, ma chérie. It's true. This vampire is every bit the monster Baxter is. His prize student. Tell her. Tell her what you've done."

"Let her go, Théa." Viktor watched as Waverly's eyes went blank, processing the vampire's lies.

"He was Daddy's favorite. He sold his soul." Théa tightened her grip around Waverly's neck. "And because you've become his favorite, well I'm afraid you must die. But oh no, no." The vampire stuck out her tongue and dragged it over Waverly's cheek.

"Get off," Waverly struggled but could not break free.

"Torture will serve him well. You, and her." Théa gave an icy smile. "He is coming. And there's nothing you can do to change it."

"Let her go. Take me instead," Viktor begged. With no options, he'd have to risk it all and flash to her. "Let's talk this out. I'll go with you…just leave Waverly."

"The next twenty-four hours will be delicious. Come watch her death. I will drink your tears." Théa pressed her lips to Waverly's temple. "See you tomorrow night, brother. We'll meet where Satan lives."

"No!" Viktor yelled, flashing to them.

As he appeared where Théa had just stood, he released a guttural scream. Viktor fell to his knees and banged his fists on the ground, the air burning from his lungs. "Waverly!"

Théa had taken her.

CHAPTER THIRTEEN

"I've got to get her back," Viktor avowed. Guilt punched a hole in his gut.

"I can't believe it's Théa. I thought Kellen staked her." Quintus placed a large bowl of food onto the long, wooden kitchen table and stared at his brother. "You should eat. It'll make you feel better. Come sit down."

"Don't have to ask me twice." Rafe, already sitting at the kitchen table, reached for the ladle and spooned spaghetti and meatballs onto his plate.

"She could have taken her anywhere. I've tried sensing her. Calling to her. And I've got nothing. This is my fault. None of this would have happened had I not chased after her." Viktor leaned his forearm onto the fireplace mantle. "I should have completed the bond. She would have more protection."

"You can't keep beating yourself up," Greyson said.

"Théa would be stronger than her anyway. She's older, and bonding wouldn't make her invincible. There's no super-power. It only allows her immortality in that she won't age," Quintus told him.

"It doesn't matter." Viktor stared blankly at the stone, regretting ever bringing her into his diabolical world. "I didn't do it. Fuck."

"She won't be able to have pups," Rafe commented and rolled the spaghetti with his fork. "When that's taken from you...well, it's better if it's a choice. Vik was right to do what he did."

"*You* may still be able to have pups. We don't know that yet," Viktor said without looking at him. Like Baxter had done to him, he'd done to Rafe. If he'd been human, having children would have been impossible, but his magick as wolf could influence his fate.

"Can't have pups without a mate. I'm single as a pringle. But who knows what will happen? Given my circumstances, I'm not even sure I'll have one. But this isn't about me. I'm just seeing why you didn't rush things with her. I get it. This isn't your fault."

"This has always been about me. From the minute I walked into that blood bar. Someone saw me, saw something in the way I looked at her."

"How could Adam have planned all this?" Quintus asked.

"I don't know. Théa must have given him the fleam. It's the ultimate mind fuck."

"Baxter may be dead and in Hell but he's very much alive in Théa," Viktor reflected, embarrassed to admit the truth. "I could see it in her eyes. Fuck. It's not like I don't get it. For years, he was alive in me. But that's not who I am." Viktor turned to them. "I can't believe she's trying to get that moth-erfucker out of Hell. What if there's more of his spawn working with her?"

"We will get Waverly," Greyson assured him.

"It would take a lot to get him out and even then. Dead is dead. Even when conjurings are involved or necromancy, even at its best, it just doesn't work well," Quintus told him.

"But she knew I'd meet Waverly, that she was my soul-mate. None of us knew that. That shit only comes from two places, Heaven or Hell, and we know it wasn't the former. It would take a lot of favors in Hell to get sight to know the future. To predict where I'd go. To know she'd be the one."

"Baxter always did have a way of bringing all the right parties together. Like some psycho ringmaster. He's got humans who drink blood, worshiping vampires. Vampires who hate humans, trying to break their sire out of Hell." Greyson spooned food onto his plate.

"That's a tall order," Rafe observed. "I still don't under-stand why she's got humans working with her. How badass can she be if she needs Adam?"

"Who the hell knows? It's not often humans have a go at vampires like they did back at the storage facility."

"And vampires," Rafe added. "Adam had a few of those too. They were younger vampires. Not too hard to take out but still."

"What about the fleam?" Greyson asked

"She knows we'll bring it back to her…to him. Maybe it's got value in Hell. Even if it has no value, it lured us into the game. It took Waverly into a different realm, gave them our location." Viktor shook his head, his eyes intense. "Look what she's done. From the beginning she's caused confusion. Chaos. Fear. This game is his."

"I'm never gonna ever say he's alive, but it's kind of hard not to think of him when you look at that bloodletter. It's his fucking initials," Greyson said.

"Théa's taken the only person I've ever…" Loved. "It's all about fear, humiliation, pain. Even if he's in Hell he knows this. And Théa knows it. She's felt it to the core of her exis-tence. We all have."

The room fell silent. The fear that Baxter generated had

once fueled his days. Hundreds of years ago, he'd stopped looking over his shoulder, and he'd buried the fear so deep he'd forgotten the emotion. But since Théa had now kidnapped the only woman he'd ever loved, the darkness had returned, the terror of losing her churning in his gut like a ticking time bomb.

"We need to find her. Now." Viktor told them, determined. "Waverly saw a demon when she touched that fleam. We must kill Théa before she has a chance to bring it to this realm. We have to stop all of it."

"Okay let's talk about where they are. What did Théa say again about the location?" Quintus asked him.

"She said to meet her where Satan lives." Viktor walked to the table and took a seat, looking at the food. *Waverly.* Everything reminded him of her.

"That sounds so familiar," Quintus replied.

"Revelation 2:12-17" Greyson held a piece of bread up in the air, staring at Viktor.

"Pergamum," Viktor replied, his eyes lit with excitement.

"Turkey?" Rafe asked.

Quintus nodded. "Though he hated the Goddess, he studied all religions. Hence Revelation 2:12-17."

"Bastard loved a riddle." Viktor recalled the Bible verse from long ago. "'And to the angel of the church in Pergamum...The one who has the sharp, two-edged sword...I know your works, and where you dwell, where Satan's throne is.'"

"And you hold fast my name, and did not deny my faith even in the days of Antipas, my witness, my faithful one, who was killed among you, where Satan dwells,'" Greyson finished the verse.

"She will go to where the veil is the thinnest. She won't kill Waverly yet because she wants me to suffer. This is about watching her inflict the most pain on me. To show him I'm not his favorite." Viktor's face flattened, regret threading through him.

"You did what you did to survive. We all did," Quintus told him.

"I'm not that person anymore. That empty soul he created. Waverly changed that. She's given me back my life. Reminded me of the man I can be. The man I never was."

"Remember that Viktor," Quintus told him. "Because you don't know what she may have done to Waverly by the time you get there. No matter what, don't lose control. It's what she wants."

"Keep it together," Greyson seconded. "Show no weakness."

"Where are we going?" Rafe asked.

"Pergamon Altar. The Altar of Zeus. The throne of Satan. Most of the actual structure is now in Berlin but the land that holds the energy...where the veil is thin, we go to Perga-mum. Where Satan lives." Viktor's anger simmered. His beast would have justice. "Théa wants a fight? She wants death? Tonight, I'm bringing it to her, and it will be her last day in this realm. She's right about one thing. She's going to see Baxter again, all right. Because I'm sending her straight to Hell."

IN THE DISTANCE a lightning bolt struck the Aegean Sea. Several seconds passed before thunder rumbled in the distance. From the valley, Viktor took a deep breath and looked up to the ancient ruins. Wearing Kevlar, guns and other weapons, Quintus, Rafe and Greyson stood ready behind him.

"Are you sure she'll come here?" Rafe asked. "Looks pretty quiet up there."

"I guarantee she'll be there." Viktor knelt and took the earth into his fingers, sensing the sting of evil in its energy.

"I searched online and got recent specs. There's hardly anything there now," Rafe told him. "Couple of trees. A few steps."

"I'm telling you, she's there. Don't underestimate her. She's vampire so knows all the ways we die. If she managed to tunnel a line to Hell, she'll have more surprises. But we'll have one of our own." Viktor smiled as their old friend appeared. *Sebastian Loubeteux.*

"Brothers." The tall, handsome vampire materialized next to Viktor and hugged him.

"Yo, brother." Quintus extended his hand and brought him into a hug. "Glad you made it."

Greyson crossed his arms and shook his head, staring at Sebastian. "You seriously brought him into this?"

"All hands on deck," Quintus commented.

"I see you're still as delightful as ever, Greyson." Sebastian smirked. Dressed in black jeans and a black sweatshirt, the vampire gave off a casual vibe. Yet as he removed his sunglasses, he revealed his intense expression. "We've all got a stake in this if this sitch gets screwed."

"Thank you for blessing us with your presence, Hollywood," Greyson said, his tone dripping in sarcasm.

Sebastian folded his sunglasses. "I have a right to be here. As do others. You're my brothers. If Théa...if she's doing this—"

"She *is* doing this," Viktor told him. "And she's going to die. If she's hurt Waverly...it doesn't matter, she's dead anyway. Look, Bastion. I appreciate your help with this but if it gets too hard...if you can't watch, then maybe Quint shouldn't have told you. You can still go."

"No, man. This is my life that's at risk too. Fuck all if they're trying to bring that psycho back."

"Whatever we do tonight, I have this bad feeling that this is just the beginning. Who knows who else is out there with a hard on for the fucker?" Greyson crossed his arms over his chest.

"One step at a time, brother." Viktor looked to Sebastian and unclipped his holster belt. He rarely carried a gun, but tonight he'd use all the weapons at his disposal. "She'll use silver. As will we."

"What about the witch? The half demon?" Sebastian asked.

"I made a judgement call. Thorn wants nothing to do with this mess. And Ilsbeth is taking another shot at getting her shit straight. She can't risk…no, *I* can't risk the responsibility of her getting sucked back into Hell." Viktor looked to Rafe. Regardless of his feelings about the witch, his child might need her. "The four of us are enough to take her out. She might be able to dematerialize, but our energy will slow her down. Gonna suck it from the air, baby."

"Rafe?" Viktor turned to the wolf, that barked in response. "Don't take any risks. This is your first battle since you've turned. I know you're comfortable as wolf but you're vampire now. Remember that. If you want more power, flip to vamp and tear out their necks, drink the blood."

"Goddess, I fuckin hate this shit. None of you mother-fuckers better die," Greyson warned. "Let's make this quick. I've got a late-night date. She's all about a fuck and a fang."

"You'll keep that date," Viktor promised. "Now let's go kill Théa and get Waverly."

VIKTOR MATERIALIZED upon the edge of the ruins. On alert, he scanned the area. As if they'd flashed to a different realm, flames shot up from the cracked scorched earth. In the distance, upon a slab of ruins, Théa waited for him.

He looked to Greyson, speaking to him telepathically. *Do you sense the humans?*

Greyson nodded. *I smell them. Must be at least forty or fifty. Bitch must have flashed them all in.*

Viktor sniffed the acrid air, her faint sweet scent called to him. *Waverly. She's here. Up there.* A wall of fire separated them but no matter how hard Théa attempted to keep him from his love, she'd fail.

You okay Bastion? Greyson exchanged a look with Viktor.

Yeah. It's just been a long time. That's definitely her. Sebastian stared into the distance.

Don't get in my way, Bastion. You can distract her, but Théa is mine to kill. Okay, folks. Let's get it. Viktor gave a nod to Greyson and flashed.

"DON'T EVEN THINK about it, dear brother," Théa warned as Viktor materialized near the ruins.

Viktor steeled the white-hot rage that seized him as he caught sight of Waverly. She lay motionless on the ground, blood splattered over her nearly nude body. Her dull eyes stared into the darkness, her face drenched in blood.

"Don't touch her," Viktor yelled.

Wearing a black hooded robe, Théa lifted her gaze and shot him an icy smile. "You're outnumbered. We are blessed by Father."

"Let her go. She has nothing to do with this." Viktor bared his fangs.

Naked, Adam stood over Waverly with a sword to her throat. He spat onto her stomach and stroked his dick.

"What the fuck are you doing? Get away from her!"

Viktor demanded. He took a slow deliberate step toward them.

"Ah, ah, ah…" Théa whistled, and Adam responded, stabbing the tip of the blade into Waverly's neck. Blood trickled down her grey-hued skin.

"Leave her alone or—" Viktor began.

"This is all in your honor, dear brother." Her eyes lit with a whitish glow, emotion draining from her face. Hooded, with guns slung across their shoulders, her human soldiers emerged from the shadows.

"Brother Viktor, look at what I've accomplished. These humans. They work for me now. They are committed to the way of the vampire. They worship us. *This* is the natural order of things. They exist for our kind."

"So what? This is your army?" Viktor looked to the humans and laughed as he continued to move toward her. "A bunch of broke ass vessels? I can take them all out myself."

"I have done this all for Father. Tortured you. Taunted you. And this human." Her diabolical smile wavered as she took a step toward Viktor. "It's been fated. I've waited patiently for years for her to grow, to set up this delightful game. Did you not enjoy it? Yes, yes, brother. I knew all about her. It was foreseen by Father."

Théa gave a maniacal laugh and turned back to Waverly. She knelt beside her body, stroking her hair. "This human. So very fragile." She brushed her hand across Waverly's neck, dabbing the blood to her fingertips and slipping them between her lips. "She's delicious. Father will like her. But first Adam will fuck her. He'll fuck her in front of you and our brother until she's so very close to dying. He'll make her scream, beg for mercy. And she'll think it's coming but it won't be. Just like father, Greyson always enjoyed the kink. Does it make you hard, brother?"

"Get the fuck away from her, Théa. You may think you

have it all figured out with your sick games, but you're done. This is it. It's the end of the road," Viktor told her.

"Just one little nick and oh, so sorry, she may not survive. Father didn't teach us well how to care for them. Especially you. No, no, no...you were always his shining star." She laughed and tilted her head. "He was so certain you'd never fall in love. But I saw you that night in the bar. I saw how you looked at her. The prophesy wasn't wrong. I'm afraid now you're going to have to take your lashes like a good boy. Submit to me. Submit to father. Maybe I'll let her live," Théa turned to Waverly and dropped her fangs. "Or not."

"Just let her go and we can sort this between us." Viktor gauged the distance to be about ten feet away. He could run or flash, but it'd be likely Théa would strike her first. "I'll do anything. You can have the fleam."

"But of course you will." Théa pressed to her feet. "I've always liked you on your knees but then again you never did choose me. No matter how much I threw myself at you, you ignored me."

"Did you hear me? I said I'll give you the fleam."

She laughed. "The fleam? It means nothing. It was a tool. Another riddle for you. Another reminder of Father."

"Leave Waverly alone. Remember. I saved you from him once," Viktor told her.

"You think you saved me?" she screamed, her eyes glowing white and spit flying from her mouth.

"I know I saved you that day. He would have killed you—"

"And you call this living? Did he tell you how many times he beat me? How many times he fucked me until I bled from every hole? Did he? To do it over and over and bring me back each time until one time he took it just a little too far and decided to turn me." She spat onto the ground and her saliva bubbled on the dirt like acid. "You know nothing about me, brother. But you're about to find out. Take off your clothes! On your knees now. Do it or I'll kill her."

"We're bonded. She won't die," Viktor told her, inching closer.

"Liar." She laughed.

Waverly released a gut-wrenching scream as Adam stabbed the sword clear through her arm.

"On your knees. Now! Take off your shirt," she ordered.

Rage tore through Viktor but he remained calm, focusing on Waverly. *I'm going to get you out of here. Do you hear me?* His question was returned with silence. He slowly removed his Kevlar and placed it on the ground, his fangs bared.

Waverly's eyes flashed to his. Though her torso remained motionless, her fingers wiggled. *They drugged me. Help.*

I'll be there in a flash, pet.

"Move it, Viktor, or she loses an eye," Théa demanded. Adam hovered the tip of the sword over Waverly's head.

"Take it easy, now. I'm doing what you want," Viktor lied as he stepped forward and moved to unbutton his shirt. Out of the corner of his eye he caught sight of Sebastian and gave him a nod. *Now.*

"Théa darling." Sebastian stepped out of the shadows. "What's all this business about, love?"

"What? No." Théa's voice fell to a whisper. "What are you doing here?"

"Well, you see, it turns out my brothers and I are quite happy with the way things are. Living our best lives and all that. So, I was quite surprised when I heard you've been messing around in Hell." Sebastian held up his palms defensively, slowly moving toward her. "I want to talk about it. Stop all this nonsense."

"This doesn't concern you. You shouldn't be here," she told him.

"Yes, but can you guess what would happen to me if Baxter walked again?"

Théa's mouth opened, her eyes flickering with understanding.

"That's right, lovey. This," he held his arms out wide, "would be dead. So, you see, I can't have you digging up that bastard piece of shit."

"He'll never hurt you," she insisted.

"Now you know better than to lie to me. Do you enjoy being a bad girl?" he asked with a flirtatious lilt in his voice.

"He listens to me. He speaks to me," she whispered. "The beast wants to rise. The goat will come forth to set him free. It's the first step."

"You and I both know he'll never let us be together. You know it's true."

"You left me! You left me for that cunt! The human!" she screamed. "You left me with him!"

Viktor smiled as the final straw broke. Sebastian had shattered her heart into a million pieces all those years ago, and she still held the torch. Viktor gave a knowing look to Quintus and Rafe who still lingered in the shadows. *Three. Two. One.*

Viktor flashed to Waverly. As he laid his hands on her body, Adam sliced the sword through the air, missing them as they flashed away.

They reappeared beneath a tree nearly a hundred feet away from the melee. Viktor pressed his lips to hers, holding her in his arms.

"Waverly. I'm so sorry," he told her. "Jesus, what has she done to you?"

"You have to stop her," she breathed.

He rested her body onto the grass. Within seconds he'd removed his shirt and draped it over her. "Are you okay? Your neck is bleeding."

"You have to stop her," she repeated.

Viktor leaned over her and lapped his tongue over her wound to stop the flow of blood. He brushed her hair away from her eyes, looking down to her.

"I'm so sorry. I'll never let her hurt you again. Here," Viktor removed a gun from his ankle holster and unlocked the safety. "Do you know how to use this?"

"Yes, yes. I go shooting every month." Waverly took the gun into her hands and held it to her chest.

"Stay here. Anyone comes near you, shoot them. I promise this won't take but a minute." Viktor stared into her eyes, his soul swirling with emotions. *No regrets.* "I love you."

"I love you too," she breathed. Tears brimmed in her eyes, a small smile on her lips. Now go kill that bitch."

Viktor pressed his lips to her forehead and flashed away to Théa. Chaos erupted, smoke and ash in the air. Screams and gunshots echoed in the night as Quintus flashed from human to human. In the distance he caught a glimpse of Rafe, as wolf, tearing into the throat of a man wielding a gun.

Sebastian held Théa by the shoulders as she slashed a silver knife toward him. "Let me go! He's coming."

The ground beneath their feet began to shake, the earth cracking and erupting. The tips of horns punctured the earth. *Demon.*

Viktor flashed to Sebastian and Théa. "May I have this dance?"

"He comes! He comes!" Théa screamed.

"Sorry, lovey. But I promised my brother a go," Sebastian told her.

As Viktor flashed in between them, clasping his hands onto her shoulders, Sebastian released her.

"No!" she screamed. "He comes! He comes!"

"This is over," Viktor told her.

"There are more of us," she spat at him "This was my test! This was my test!"

"Well, then, you failed."

"Father is here!" She raised the silver knife to strike him.

"No, he isn't. He's in Hell and that's exactly where you're going." Viktor dropped his fangs and tore into Théa's throat, ripping her trachea in half. With his claws extended he ripped her muscles and ligaments, tearing her head clear off her spine.

Viktor held it up by her hair and stared down the horned demon whose eyes bored a hole in him. With the earth cleaved open, the fire licked up into the air.

"Now it's time for you and this bitch to go join Baxter in Hell. Give him a little message for me...he's never getting out." Viktor tossed the head at the demon, and it burst into flames. The ground shook as it sucked it back under the earth. "Fuck you, you sadistic son of a bitch. You're going to rot forever."

Quintus and Greyson flashed to his side, the wolf running to join them. Darkness fell as the flames retreated into the ground, the stench of silver and sulphur hung heavy in the air.

"Where's Sebastian?" Quintus asked.

"I don't know. Flashed I guess," Greyson answered. "Every human and vampire has been neutralized."

"Did you get Adam? Where's Ivar? I've got to go get Waverly. She's—" Viktor began when he heard her call to him.

Viktor!

Gunshots sounded in the night as he disappeared.

CHAPTER FOURTEEN

*W*averly's hands trembled, her grip still tight on the gun. She stared at Adam and Ivar lying dead at her feet, blood pooling onto the ground. Her mind and body went numb. For the first time in her life, she'd killed someone. She looked to her shaking hands. *What have I become?*

Only hours earlier, she'd been abducted, stripped and humiliated. From the cold interior of a dog cage, she'd witnessed Théa and Ivar murdering humans. As they slashed their throats, warm blood splashed onto her face through the wired barrier.

Although Théa threatened Waverly with the same fate, they'd kept her alive, planning on using her as bait for Viktor. Starved and dehydrated, she'd begged for water. When they'd finally brought her a drink, she'd gulped it. Within seconds, she'd realized she'd been drugged and immediately lost consciousness.

Terror seized her as she'd woken in a new location, restrained and lying on the ground. With Adam looming above her and drugs still flowing through her veins, she struggled to move.

After Viktor flashed her to safety, her body began to tingle with awareness, but her legs still weren't stable enough to allow her to stand. Although he'd left her in the darkness, Viktor had given her the gun. *Kill Théa.* There was no other choice but to kill the diabolical vampire.

Waverly clutched the gun to her chest. In the distance she'd heard the screams, Viktor and Théa arguing. She startled as she heard Viktor's scream, his rage tearing through her as if it were her own. In the silence that soon descended upon the night, the sound of a branch snapping set her on alert. She'd curled her finger around the trigger and readied her aim.

Adam came into view first, his sword held high into the air. She knew he'd kill her on the spot. He'd threatened her more than once. Ivar appeared behind him. With his fangs bared, dripping with saliva and blood, he'd also promised he'd kill her.

"Look who is here," Adam had growled. "Whore of a vampire. Spread your legs wide for him, didn't you?"

"Little cunt is going to die. But I need a taste first. I ain't drinking a dead slut's blood." The sadistic vampire hissed at her.

Waverly didn't engage in discussions. She waited patiently as they descended upon her. With no hesitation, looking straight into their eyes, she pulled the trigger, emptying the cartridge.

"Waverly!" she heard Viktor call as he ran to her.

As he reached her, her body went limp with exhaustion. Her fingers fell open, dropping the gun onto the ground. Her vision blurred, a swirling black tunnel closed in as Viktor took her in his arms. As darkness blanketed over her, she heard her name on his lips. *Waverly.*

∾

As the wave crested, Waverly paddled hard, the ice-cold water splashing her face. Distracted, she lost her balance as she jumped to stand onto the board. Tossed into the churning sea, she fought to swim upward. She sucked a hard breath as she breached the surface. As she swam toward her board, her mind continued to race.

The day after Viktor killed Théa was the last time she'd seen him. He'd flashed her to safety, set her up in the Ritz Carlton and told her he'd return in thirty-one days. Thirty-one days to decide if she'd choose to remain mortal or to bond eternally with a vampire. He'd insisted she needed enough time to decide on her own, time without him.

In the moment, she hadn't argued. Numb and exhausted, she'd slept for three days, waking ravenous and disillusioned. Though loved burned in her heart and soul, she'd nearly died and had killed with her own hands. Théa confirmed every reason she'd ever had for avoiding vampires.

Yet Adam and Teagan, both human, had also chosen evil, to embrace demonic energy to suit their lives. Adam had immersed himself in the occult, drinking the blood of humans, and had been singled out by Théa, to help her inflict pain upon them. Adam had been ready and willing, engaging in the wicked, doing her bidding.

Waverly would never get to know the truth about Teagan, the extent of her innocence. Whether she'd been willing or had been manipulated, Teagan had successfully lured Waverly to Miami. Unfortunately for Teagan, she'd breathed her last breath the day Waverly had touched down in Miami. No longer needing her services, Théa had proudly confessed that she'd ordered Ivar to torture and kill her.

Like clouds clearing from a storm, the truth had become apparent. No single kind of paranormal or human who walked the earth did so without sin. For a millennium, evil had been perpetuated, often in the name of virtue.

Even though Baxter had sought to hurt Viktor, to eternally torture him to the point he'd forever lose his humanity, he'd failed. And though the virus of evil still spread among humans and paranormals, both could choose light. And on rare occasions, they'd go above and beyond, protecting the world by fighting the demons that lingered in the underworld.

I love you. The first time she'd spoken the words to Viktor, the decision to bond with him had been made. In her heart, in her mind, she'd fallen in love with an incredible man, who just happened to also be a vampire. And every single second since he'd been gone, she yearned to taste his kiss on her lips, to hear his heart beating as he held her in his arms.

As she reached her board, another wave rolled toward her, forcing her focus to the sea. Waverly instinctively dove into it, breached the water on the other side, and exhaled a deep breath. As the sun dipped into the horizon, she gazed at the skyline.

A set rolled toward her, and she caught sight of a surfer paddling toward the beach to catch the swell. He popped up on his board and began shredding the wave. As he turned his head and winked at her, her heart caught in her chest. *Viktor.*

Waverly took off paddling toward him but within seconds, another wave rolled in, and she'd lost sight of him. Frantically, her arms propelled her through the sea. As the surf once again calmed, she stopped and scanned the ocean. "What the hell?"

Confusion washed over her. Was what she saw real? Were her visions morphing into hallucinations? "Dear God, what is happening?"

"Hello, pet," a familiar sexy voice said from behind her.

Waverly whipped her head around to see Viktor swimming toward her. He rested his hand on her board and turned to her, wearing a mischievous smile.

"Viktor! Oh God!" She pressed her cold lips to his, her heart pounding in her chest. "What are you doing here? Is everything all right? It's not thirty-one days."

"So, it appears I'm not the most patient man in the world," he laughed. "Patience was never my forte."

"You didn't need to leave. I mean one day would have been fine. A few hours. I didn't even need that. Sorry, I'm rambling," she laughed. "What I'm trying to say is that I don't need time. I didn't need one day. I just…" Her lips trembled, her eyes brimming with tears, emotion bursting in her chest. "I know what I want. I want you in my life. Forever."

"Waverly—"

"I know you were trying to protect me but I'm stronger than I ever was. There's only one thing I need…I need you."

Still clinging to the surfboard, Viktor wrapped an arm around her waist, drawing her to him. "I love you so much, Waverly. I want you in my life." His lips brushed to hers. "Today. Every day. Forever."

"I love you too," she whispered, her heart pounding like a drum in her chest.

As his lips captured hers, Waverly released her board and wrapped her arms around his neck. *I love you.* He'd said the words she'd felt for so long. His energy threaded through her, and she poured her love into his devastating kiss.

"I've got a surprise," Viktor whispered against her lips.

"Another surprise? Because this is the best. There is nothing better." Waverly smiled.

"Ah, mo chroí. You're going to love it," Viktor promised as he dematerialized them out of the ocean.

$\sim$

"WHAT ARE YOU DOING?" Waverly glanced to her surfboard as they appeared, and inwardly laughed that he'd managed to bring it with them. *Is there anything this man can't do?* "Where are we?"

"Do you like it?" Viktor gave her a mysterious smile.

Towering above Waverly, wearing a devilish expression and looking sexy as fuck, he made quick work of removing his wetsuit and wrapped a towel around his hips. She reached behind her back for her lanyard.

"Allow me." He walked around her and tugged on her zipper, efficiently removing her wetsuit.

Waverly instantly broke out in goose flesh, the cool, late afternoon breeze sweeping over her skin. She smiled as he wrapped an oversized sun-warmed towel around her.

"Where are we?" she asked, taking in her surroundings.

"La Jolla."

"La Jolla? Whose house is this? Oh my gosh." Waverly's jaw dropped open as she took in the incredible view from the top of the cliff. The sun kissed the horizon, and the sky lit with a kaleidoscope of colors. "It's beautiful."

"It's a killer view, isn't it?"

"It's amazing. I love the water." Waverly draped her hands over his as Viktor came up behind her and circled his arms around her waist "Every single day when I go down to the beach, I'm just awestruck. I love it."

"I've always loved the water, too. It's why I love Miami. I've got my yacht and can take it out whenever I want. Beaches are like sugar. I love the culture, the food. Art. Nightclubs."

"Miami is beautiful." Waverly's stomach tightened at the thought of moving.

"Yes, it is. But I've grown fond of the West Coast. You see, there is one thing that isn't in Miami."

Waverly smiled. "Is that right?"

KYM GROSSO

"Yes. It's been quite hard living without you in my life. Do you have any idea how long we've been separated?" he asked.

"Um, thirteen days?" she replied without hesitation.

"Thirteen long fucking days. And you know what I did during that time? I'll tell you what I did." Viktor brushed his lips to the back of her head. "I thought about you. Every single hour, minute and second. I also thought about what I've been doing my whole life. Travel. Parties. Enjoying the finer things."

"Doesn't sound so bad."

"But I did it alone. I never loved. I never felt love. I didn't allow myself to ever think about the family I once had. I didn't have a family."

Waverly turned in his arms to face him, gazing into his eyes, her palms on his chest. "You *are* my family."

"I don't want to live this life without you. I know it's selfish of me to ask you to give up your mortal life. But I want everything neither one of us has ever had. I want to travel the world with you. I want lazy Sunday afternoons watching movies. I want to spend my life with the woman I love. I want to eat your eggs." He smiled. "But after what happened to me, I could never do that to you. Bonding forever, staying with me eternally...it had to be your choice."

Waverly reached to cup his cheek and he kissed her palm. "I choose this...our bond. I choose you."

"You're sure of this?"

"I'm sure. Surer than I've ever been in my life."

"Really sure?"

"One hundred percent sure," she told him.

Viktor's smile widened; his eyes lit in excitement. He released her and held up his finger. "One minute!"

"Hey. Where are you going?" Waverly laughed as he ran into the house, holding his towel closed with one hand.

Within seconds he returned, and *La Vie En Rose* began

306

playing through the audio system. Twinkling lights lit up the pool area, and she noticed vases filled with bouquets of white lilies interspersed with candles that had seemingly lit themselves.

"Wait. I want to get this right," he told her as he sprinkled a red rose petal heart around where she stood. "I'm afraid I've missed the actual sunset, but we will have many more together if you allow me. I wanted to do this in France, but I actually think this is quite perfect."

"Viktor? What are you—" Butterflies danced in her stomach as he dropped to one knee.

"Mo chroí. Dr. LaFleur. My human existence...hell, my entire existence period has been empty, meaningless until you walked into my life." He laughed. "Or perhaps I walked into yours. No matter how you got there, that day, I still chose of my own free will to go to that bar in Miami. And you were there. It was destined we'd meet."

"Yes." She nodded.

"You asked where we are, and we are home. Our home."

"What?" Waverly released a nervous laugh. "You bought this house for us?"

"Yes, I bought this house."

"It's beautiful. It's amazing. Oh my God. I can't believe you bought a house here."

"It's going to be great. Surfing suits me, don't you think?" A broad smile formed on his face.

"Yes, yes it does." Waverly laughed, her arousal spiking at just the thought of him shredding up that wave. "I suppose I could help you get out of your wetsuit from now on."

"The thing is...I could live anywhere but then you wouldn't be with me. I want to be with my heart. My love. My wife." Viktor opened his hand and revealed a black velvet box.

She covered her mouth with her hands, tears welling in

her eyes. Waverly's heart pounded in her chest as she looked down into his loving eyes. Clever and witty, her vampire had once again taken her by surprise.

"Will you marry me, Dr. LaFleur?" Viktor asked as he opened the box.

"Yes, yes, yes," she repeated as she dropped to her knees.

"This is all very human," he joked, accidentally reaching for her right hand, then successfully taking her left hand in his. She trembled as he slid the stunning emerald-cut diamond ring onto her finger. "I love you, Waverly."

She cupped his cheek and pressed her lips to his. "I love you, baby. I'm so glad you came back...came home."

Viktor's mouth crushed onto Waverly's, his tongue sweeping against hers. She melted in his embrace, receiving his devastating kiss, her heart full of love.

"Viktor," she breathed. "Your house—"

"Our house." He continued to kiss her.

"Our house...oh God," she sighed as his lips traveled to her neck, her body tingling with arousal. "Bedroom...there's a bedroom?"

"Many bedrooms. Excellent idea." Viktor's fangs dropped as he flashed them away.

LOST IN HIS KISS, Waverly stripped off his towel and reached for his cock. He groaned as she tightened her grip and stroked him.

"Ah. Jesus, woman. We haven't made love in a few weeks. What are you trying to do to me?" Viktor tore off her towel, his lips peppering kisses over her shoulder.

"Make love to me. All night. Forever." Waverly squealed as he lifted her into the air, and they rolled onto the bed. His mouth smashed onto hers, tasting, seeking.

"God, I've missed you," he told her.

Waverly moaned as his hand reached between her legs, his thumb grazing over her clit. As he drove a thick finger inside her pussy, she flooded with arousal. She writhed against his hand, arching her back and tilting her hips as he fucked her.

"Please...the bond." The urge to bite him escalated, the feral instinct driving her to taste him.

"First, come for me, pet." Viktor plunged another finger inside her, teasing her sensitive strip. "I'm going to fuck you so hard. Consume every inch of your body. And this pussy... my pussy—"

"Ahh...yes, please, I—"

"Is mine. Nice and wet for me. That's it."

"Viktor," she managed with a ragged breath. Her body reeled toward orgasm, every cell in her body on fire with arousal. "Please...please..."

Viktor's lips moved to her breast, his tongue lapping over her taut nipple. Waverly cried for him as he sucked her sensitive tip into his mouth, the pinch of pain in contest with the pleasure. As his fingers plunged into her, faster and faster, his thumb strumming over her clitoris, she lost control.

"I'm coming...oh, yes, please, do it...do it." Waverly craved his bite, the bond. Her body shook with release, his lips still teasing her nipple.

As his fangs pierced her breast, she cried out with ecstasy. "Oh fuck, yes, yes!"

The waves of orgasm rolled through her, leaving her shuddering with pleasure. She sighed as he withdrew his fangs and his hand, leaving her with a sense of loss.

"You want this?" he asked her.

Her body lit with excitement, the tip of his dick slipping through her folds, pressing into her entrance. "Yes...yes."

She panted for breath, looking up to him as he sliced his

own flesh with his fingernail. Blood trickled down his shoulder. His heated gaze bored through her soul.

"Be my wife. My forever."

"Always." Waverly's mouth moved to his flesh, her tongue brushing over his potent blood.

She sucked at the wound, drinking his powerful essence, allowing the bond of her vampire to seal them together for eternity. She screamed with pleasure as his cock slammed inside her pussy and his power threaded through her body.

Viktor fisted her hair and Waverly gasped, as he tilted her head backwards. His lips crushed onto hers. Ravenous, she kissed him back with desperate passion.

He tore his lips from hers, reached under her knees and lifted her legs into the air. With her feet hiked onto his chest and his eyes locked on hers, he drove his thick shaft inside her. Every cell in her body quivered as he plunged in and out of her. His blood swirled inside her, the magical energy flickering though her mind and body.

"I love you," Viktor grunted as he thrust inside her pussy.

"I love you too...ah," she cried. She fisted the sheets, bracing for each hard stroke, her body ripe with pleasure.

Viktor released her legs and dipped his head to her breast. Waverly's body crept toward release. She lifted her hips, meeting each deep thrust, his pelvis grazing over her swollen nub.

"I want all of you," Viktor growled.

Waverly cried out, her orgasm slamming into her. Her body shook with unbridled pleasure as he made love to her.

"Oh God, yes. Please. Viktor, Viktor," she repeated, her mind and body one with his.

"Oh no, little pet. I meant all of you," he told her with a devious smile. "Tonight."

"No, no, no...I need..." She lost her words as he withdrew his cock.

"Patience," he laughed as he flipped her over on her stomach, pulling her bottom upward. "I wouldn't want you to think I went back on my promises."

"Please," Waverly begged. She arched her back, seeking relief from the throbbing between her legs. "I need you inside me. Oh, yes...please."

"Let me see you now." Viktor rubbed his palms over her rounded cheeks and slid his dick deep inside her slick pussy.

"Ah yes," she cried as he filled her once again, her fingers curled into the pillow. With each slow thrust, she braced herself and gave a small grunt.

Waverly sucked a breath as cool gel dripped over her bottom. She knew what he'd planned. *All of her.* Anticipation twisted through her, her pussy tightening around his shaft as he circled his thumb around her puckered skin. As he dipped his finger into her ass, she moaned, the delicious dark sensation of the taboo spiking her desire.

"Easy, pet," he warned, withdrawing from her warmth and pressing the broad crown of his dick to her tight hole.

Waverly breathed into the pillow, stilling as he slid inside her. Inch by delectable inch, he filled her with his cock.

"This...all of you. Goddess you're so fucking tight," he grunted.

"Please, oh God," she panted. "I...I...ah..."

So full, with her body on fire, she teetered on the edge of release. As his fingers circled around her clit, she cried out for him. "Viktor...I can't...I'm coming."

"You feel so goddamned perfect." He thrust deep into her ass, flicking his fingers over her swollen bead. "I love you so much."

"Fuck me. Fuck me harder," she grunted out, overwhelmed in sensation. From her pussy to her ass, her heart full of emotion, she'd never in her life been so alive.

Still inside her, Viktor rolled them onto their sides. With

his fingers on her pussy, he fucked her ass. His lips kissed her shoulder as he thrust slow and deep, so she felt every inch of him.

"Please...bite me," she begged, breathless.

As Viktor's fangs sliced into her neck, Waverly screamed in ecstasy, a rapture of sheer pleasure seizing her.

"That's it, pet. I love watching you come." With a final hard thrust, Viktor grunted, exploding inside her. He retracted his fangs, lapping over her skin. "Goddess I love you."

As Waverly's body slowly recovered from her mind-blowing orgasm, she barely noticed the warm cloth as he cleaned her. Within seconds, he'd tucked her safely against his chest, the downy comforter pulled over them.

"I love you, Viktor. Always." Waverly snuggled into his embrace, her heart still pounding.

Everything she'd ever feared was all she'd ever need. Her one love. Her vampire. *Viktor.*

VIKTOR PRESSED his lips to her hair, his body and senses still tingling with pleasure. *Waverly LaFleur.* She'd come into his life by fate and now bonded with him by choice.

There was a time he never thought he could be happier, more complete. But his beautiful curator had given him the gift of his humanity, opening his eyes and heart to a future that he'd never imagined.

Love. Perhaps the most precious, yet elusive possession he'd ever experience on the planet had taken him by storm.

Mo chroí.

EPILOGUE

"*T*ell me again why you need me?" Julian took a swig of his beer and reached for the bowl of pretzels.

"Rafe. The wolf. Viktor called you," Greyson reminded him.

"Yeah, I know he did. I didn't agree," Julian told him, staring straight ahead.

"Rafe's a wolf. You're a wolf. You know how this works. Do your part now. He's going to be here soon." Greyson tapped on the bar.

"Yeah, not my problem. I'm not pack."

"Rafe belongs to Hunter. You know…Willa's mate. Your sister. That should mean something." Greyson looked past Julian, checking out a couple of women playing pool.

"Yeah, I'm not in his pack either. I love my sister but it's none of my business. I'm rogue. I'm not my father. That life isn't for me." Greyson looked up at the flat screen TV, watching the hockey game.

"Look, I hear you got daddy issues. Don't we all, but you've gotta help the kid. He's uh, he's had a rough go of it."

"Yeah, so have I. I'm telling you that I'm not your guy. Find someone else," Julian insisted.

"I wasn't planning on going there, but it sounds like my brother did you a solid. Rescued your ass from Hell. You owe him."

"I wasn't in Hell. I was somewhere…but I don't know where. It doesn't matter. What matters is that I've got my own problems."

"Wherever you were, I heard Vik got you out. So, I'm gonna need you to do this. I know whatever happened to you must've been bad, there's got to be something good left in you."

"This isn't a good idea," Julian warned.

"Maybe you're right." Greyson stared at him "But you're a helluva lot better than Ilsbeth. Because you know the kid might have a little of that old black magick in him too."

"Just because I've got some in me…just because I'm rogue, that doesn't mean I'm the best guy for the job."

"You're the guy. Viktor trusts you. Hunter trusts you."

Julian released an audible sigh and set his focus on Greyson. His palm came down hard onto the edge of the bar, loud enough to draw the attention of a few patrons. "Fuck, I can't believe I'm saying this."

"You'll do it?"

"Yeah, yeah. I don't want to do it, but I'll do it."

"Good deal." Greyson smiled and signaled the bartender. "Two tequilas please."

"On one condition." Julian turned to him. "You stay. Be available. I'm not dealing with vamp shit."

"You know I'm in the middle of a renovation. Castle in Romania. Cool shit. I don't have time to stay here in Idaho." He looked around, laughed and popped a pretzel into his mouth, continuing to talk as he chewed it. "My days in dive bars are over, my friend."

"We've got some killer golf courses." Julian raised an eyebrow at Greyson.

"Goddammit, now."

The corner of Julian's mouth ticked upward. "I'm friends with a guy."

"A guy, huh?"

"He plays professional. Has the best tips around."

"You don't fuckin' say." Greyson picked up a shot glass and handed it to Julian. He toasted with his other hand. "I'll give you a few weeks, then I'm out. The wolf's not my problem, but I don't want anything bad happening to him."

"I can't promise that. I can only give him a taste of being rogue. He may still choose pack."

"We just gotta train him and keep him alive. My brother seems to have faith in you. Must be that sister of yours."

"Yeah, Willa's got a way of doing that to people." Julian gave a closed smile.

"It's settled then. Rafe will be here soon. Drink up, wolf!" Greyson brought the shot glass to his lips and slammed it down, the caustic liquor burning his throat.

As Julian brought the glass to his lips, a stranger burst through the doors.

"Fucking hell, bro," Rafe cursed at Greyson as he stumbled into the bar. "Like you couldn't have given me a ride. You just flash off without me? Seriously. Not cool." He looked to Julian and then back to Greyson.

The ancient vampire released a boisterous laugh. "Wolf. Meet your new best friend. This is Julian Lobos."

THE BLACK WOLF took off running through the woods. Harder, faster, his adrenaline pumped through his veins.

What the hell was he thinking, taking on a hybrid wolf? It

wasn't as if he was an expert in hybrids or vampires. Julian had left his own pack, gone into hiding. An Alpha without a pack, he chose to remain independent of others. And it wasn't a lifestyle he could possibly recommend to others.

Rogue. It was a lonely last resort for those who, for whatever reason, would never fit in. No pack. Few friends. Run alone. Survive alone.

His royal family legacy haunted him, keeping him from the life he'd always wanted. A prince of werewolves, he'd known the darkness would come for him. But life within the wilderness suited him, protected him…until it didn't.

Thunder sounded in the distance, a flash of lightning illuminating the mountain. A few drops morphed into a deluge, the sheets of rain soaking his coat. Carefully he edged along the cliff, running fast back to his home. Leaves and branches crushed beneath his paws, the thunder chasing him, growing louder. The cracking of a tree trunk sounded, and he dashed around it as it fell crashing onto the ground.

Though the storm escalated, both stronger and closer, he didn't fear the elements. One with the forest, he made his way down the last mile toward his home.

Julian froze as an unfamiliar voice cried out from the canyon. *What the hell is someone doing out in this weather?* He edged the cliff, barking into the cavernous space. A flash flood would come soon, washing loose debris and anything in its path down the mountain.

A garbled cry became nothing more than a barely audible whimper. A rumble from above grew louder, the rushing water beginning to flow down the cavern. Through the darkness and sheets of blowing rain, its source came into view. The crumpled body lay on the rocks, its face not visible from the cliff.

This is not my fuckin' day. In a split decision, Julian tore down into the canyon. As he reached the body, the water had already started to flow in a steady stream. Within seconds a tsunami would gush through, destroying everything in its path.

He shifted to his human form and knelt beside it. As he brushed aside the wet hair, her face came into view. The stranger drifted in and out of consciousness.

"Help," she whispered, her hand clasping his.

"What the hell happened?"

Julian's stomach dropped as he looked at her torn party dress, her breast exposed. Instinct told him she'd been brought to the woods. It wouldn't be the first time someone had been abducted. He scooped her up into his arms, noting her bruised and bloodied limbs.

As he turned to run up the cliff, the wall of water hit him. He clutched onto a boulder, attempting to shield her from the flood. Within seconds, they'd wash down the mountain. Gunshots rang out from above, setting Julian on alert. Someone was after his lost bird. What they didn't know was that the wolf never gave back his prey, what belonged to him.

A shot ricocheted off the bolder, nearly striking his head. With no good options, Julian made the decision. Holding tight to the stranger, he released his grip on the rock. A whoosh of water and debris rolled over him, and he prayed to the Goddess they'd come out alive.

ROMANCE BY KYM GROSSO

The Immortals of New Orleans

Kade's Dark Embrace (Immortals of New Orleans, Book 1)
Luca's Magic Embrace (Immortals of New Orleans, Book 2)
Tristan's Lyceum Wolves (Immortals of New Orleans, Book 3)
Logan's Acadian Wolves (Immortals of New Orleans, Book 4)
Léopold's Wicked Embrace (Immortals of New Orleans, Book 5)
Dimitri (Immortals of New Orleans, Book 6)
Lost Embrace (Immortals of New Orleans, Book 6.5)
Jax (Immortals of New Orleans, Book 7)
Jake (Immortals of New Orleans, Book 8)
Quintus (Immortals of New Orleans, Book 9)
Hunter (Immortals of New Orleans, Book 10)
Viktor (Immortals of New Orleans, Book 11)
Julian (Immortals of New Orleans, Book 12) *Coming soon…next in series*

Club Altura Romance

ROMANCE BY KYM GROSSO

Carnal Risk (A Club Altura Romance Novel, Book 1)
Wicked Rush (A Club Altura Romance Novel, Book 2)
Crushed (A Club Altura Romance Novel, Book 3) *Coming soon…next in series*
Solstice Burn (A Club Altura Romance Novella, Prequel)
Hard Asset (A Club Altura Romance Novelette)

ABOUT THE AUTHOR

Kym Grosso is the New York Times and USA Today bestselling author of the paranormal romance series, *The Immortals of New Orleans*, and the contemporary romantic suspense series, *Club Altura*.

In addition to romance novels, Kym has written and published several articles about autism, and is passionate about autism advocacy. She is also a contributing essay author in *Chicken Soup for the Soul: Raising Kids on the Spectrum*. In 2012, Kym published her first novel and today, is a full-time romance author.

Sign up for Kym's Newsletter to get Updates & Information about New Releases:

https://www.subscribepage.com/kymgrossomailinglist

Kym's Website: http://www.KymGrosso.com

Printed in Great Britain
by Amazon

33132709R00185